Oracle

by

Susan J. Boulton

Copyright © 2015 Susan Boulton

Published by Tickety Boo Press –www.ticketyboopress.co.uk

Edited by Teresa Edgerton – www.teresaedgertoneditor.com

Copy-edited by Sam Primeau – www.primoediting.com

Cover Art by Gary Compton

Book Design by Big River Press Ltd

Acknowledgements

To all the members of the Sffworld and Sff Chronicles writing forums, and the old Del-Rey writing group for their help and advice during Oracle's first days. To my many friends and family members for their encouragement. To Mr Gary Compton for having belief in me. To Teresa Edgerton for pushing me to make the story better. To Sam Primeau for giving Oracle a final posh.

A big heartfelt thank you.

Finally, to the late Deborah J Miller, author and friend, who encouraged me, and believed in Oracle from the first rough draft.

CHAPTER ONE

She had crossed Timeholm's southern border when the heat wave began. Now, as it reached its peak, the voices in her head had become frantic, screaming at her to hurry.

A storm was coming. Oracle could see it in the small dust eddies, which danced in the dried-out ruts cut deep into the clay road. She could hear it whispering in the heavy heads of wheat swaying in the fields. It was a storm of gun flashes and bright swords, broken promises and murder.

***

Oracle squeezed down between two large wagons and joined a ragged line waiting to use the drinking fountains. When her turn came, her hands shook with anticipation. She placed one of the small brass cups under the stream of water and lifted it to her lips.

"Sails in the water. Bubbles and rope. Storm and flood." The words forced their way out of her mouth between gulps of water. Her small respite was over. The cup fell from her hand. It swung on its chain against the stone and rang like a chapel bell. The noise disturbed a haze of flies hovering round the horses at a nearby trough. The insects buzzed their annoyance and flew between the people waiting to use the fountain.

"Flies. Summer flies. Winter flies. Bloated on bodies. Train. Trick. Pick. Bones. Hack and slash. Good man. Goddess' sacrifice. Turn the world on its head." The words were not shouted, yet they cut at the back of Oracle's throat as if screamed with all her strength. She was being watched, the voices told her, by a priest of the Inner Ring. He would stop her saying the words to those who needed to hear. He wanted them for himself. All the hints of possible futures, dire prophecies and majestic fates must be his, so that he could order the world according to his vision.

The main entrance to the railway station was on her right-hand side. Images flickered through her mind, ragged and overlapping. Fragments of what might be merged with what was. The voices began to shout. She clapped her hands over her ears and ran, not up the steps to the station, but towards the small alley on its eastern side.

1

The sounds of the square began to fade. She slowed her pace and tried to catch her breath. The voices in her head screamed at her to keep moving. Oracle glanced back over her shoulder: four men followed.

Dizzy from exhaustion, she stumbled forward. On the station side of the alley ran a six-foot high brick wall, topped with glass fragments. On the other was a wooden fence, its interlocking boards shrunken by the summer heat. Through the thin gaps Oracle caught glimpses of railway wagons in a marshalling yard. She began beating the fence with her clenched fists, heedless of the pain as the skin on her knuckles split open.

"Wait! Stop! We mean you no harm — you must trust us." It was the priest.

Oracle stopped her attack on the fence and looked back. Her pursuers had come to a halt. The priest was standing there, his right arm extended sideways, holding back his three companions. He was short and stocky, with a neatly trimmed beard and hair at odds with the rough workman-like clothes he wore.

Words formed in her mouth, unwanted, sour as crab apples. "No trust. Twist and turn. Run Oracle, run. Find Pugh. Trick, track, wire and thunder."

The priest stepped closer. She backed away and renewed her attack on the fence. Oracle threw herself at the barrier. It gave way under her weight. She toppled through onto the churned soil of a small stock pen, instinctively bringing up her hands to protect her face. She heard the priest shout, and the sound of feet smashing wood.

For a moment she lay there, pinned to the ground by the weight of what the visions were demanding of her. "*No, up! Up! Go!*" It was not the voices of possible futures, but the small fragment of who she used to be.

Oracle struggled onto all fours and crawled forward. A hand closed round her left ankle. She kicked out with her right foot. The man bellowed. His fingers lost their hold. Oracle scrambled to her feet, and as she did, one of the voices in her head gained control of her vocal cords. "Captain Pugh. Find him. Flames and fire. Death in the dark. Hack, slash, swords in the air. Message on a wire. Sails on the water."

The three men with the priest stopped moving:

marionettes with their strings cut.

"Mathew!" the priest shouted to the young man standing nearest to Oracle.

"Carter, I don't think we should ..." Mathew looked from Oracle to the priest, then back again. A frown creased his brow.

"We mean it no harm. The Glimpser is confused." The priest walked forward.

Oracle looked from one man's face to another. Slowly, she inched backwards to the open gate of the stock yard, which stood on the left of a half-full horse trough. A small shunting engine began to push the wagons in front of it down the track behind her. *"Run. Get on the wagons,"* the voices in her head screamed as one. The priest lunged and grabbed her left arm. Instinctively, Oracle lashed out, hitting him hard on the left side of his face. Off balance, the priest stumbled sideways. The rear of his thighs caught on the edge of the horse trough, and he plunged backwards into the lime-scummed water.

His grip on Oracle's arm tightened.

"Bite him." It was not her companion voices which spoke; again, it was what was left of the woman she had been. She bent forward, her teeth bared like a small terrier in striking distance of a rat. Oracle felt the skin on the back of his hand break, and a rush of salt-tainted blood filled her mouth. The priest yelped. He let go of her and plunged deeper into the horse trough.

Free, Oracle ran. The wagons slowed as they neared a set of points. She could hear the neigh of horses from inside the last wagon. The fear in the animals' cries matched that of the voices in her head. She stumbled. Her right hand reached out to break her fall, and her fingers brushed rust-covered metal. It was the step of a metal ladder running up the side of the wagon. She grabbed it. The shunting engine blew its whistle in acknowledgement of the points being changed. The wagons increased their speed. Oracle was dragged off her feet. The toes of her wooden clogs churned the limestone ballast by the side of the track. Her body weight dragged on her arms, wrenching at her shoulder sockets. She screamed in pain and wanted to let go, but the words in her head wouldn't let her.

The wagons shuddered over the points. Oracle's body slammed against the metal ladder.

"Get your feet up."

Her hold was slipping.

"Do it! Don't let them win." The voices swirling through her mind echoed the words of the woman she had once been.

"On train, trick-track. North, click, click. Message on the wire starts it all soon. Goddess' sacrifice. Toby dog. Bear the consequences." Each word was punctuated by a spasm of pain in her elbow and shoulder joints. Slowly, she forced her hands to inch up the rusted metal and managed to put first her left foot, then her right, onto the lower rung of the ladder. She leant against the side of the wagon, and tried to regain her breath. The visions of the future tore through her mind. They were a storm cloud getting darker and deeper with each passing second. Places and people lost in the blackness. Oracle was totally closed off to the outside world. She was a frail tool driven beyond its strength, yet she was required to do more. Slowly, she climbed to the roof of the wagon. She looked forward, then back: her pursuers were gone.

The wagons were being pushed towards a green-painted carriage which marked the rear of a train standing in the station. Oracle began to run, stumbling along the roof. At the end, she jumped over the gap to the next wagon. She ran again, jumping from one wagon to the next, then she misjudged and fell. Driven to extremes by the howling voices in her head, she caught the edge of the wagon as she dropped. The downward pull of her body weight wrenched at her already strained shoulder joints. Oracle squealed in pain.

Sobbing with fear, Oracle tried to pull herself up. She failed, slamming into the end of the wagon. She heaved upwards again, caught her nose on the edge of the roof and split the skin. With one final effort, she managed to hitch her right leg up onto the roof and dragged herself onto the top. She lay there, shuddering. The train came to a stop. She could hear the men connecting the chains between the buffers. Their shouts to uncouple the shunting engine at the rear merged with the words and visions exploding in her mind.

She drew a deep lungful of air and began to crawl forward. "Pugh, find, hide. Red robe, never say the words for him, twist them. Hack slash, crash smash. Death in the dark, soon. Mountain and home. Turn the world on its head." The voices drove Oracle down the ladder, across the gap and into the carriage. She wrapped both arms round herself. With her head

4

down, she moved forward at a shambling run. She dismissed the shouts of the senior conductor behind her. All Oracle was concerned about was that she was near to her destination.

CHAPTER TWO

Pugh Avinguard had hoped that the clouds forming on the eastern horizon last evening were a sign that the heatwave was in its death throes. Unfortunately, it had not been the case; today was hotter than its predecessors. His left hand strayed up to the row of brass buttons on the front of his green uniform jacket. He reluctantly resisted the temptation. His top button remained fastened. He was on duty, and had to set an example for the men under his command.

"Captain." The non-commissioned officer saluted his superior.

"Yes, Sergeant."

"The station manager wishes to make a complaint."

"About?"

"Our activities disrupting his trains' schedule."

"Have him put it in writing. In triplicate, Sergeant."

"Yes, sir." Sergeant Mason grinned.

"Are all our preparations complete?"

"The private cars for Lord Calvinward's party have been searched, and I have placed the first watch in position, but—"

Pugh interrupted. "Rota done? I want the men replaced every second watch." He had a full half-company under his command, all career militia. All experts in spotting a cushy number and taking advantage of it.

Politics: they were the reason he and his men were here. That damn bill currently before the High Forum had quickly polarised the opinions of all classes. Eggs and rotten fruit thrown at the carriage of the Speaker of the High Forum were, Pugh supposed, par for the course. A trio of bullets embedding themselves in the coachwork were not. The event was followed by a number of luridly written threats to various High Forum members. This prompted the government to act in typical fashion: they passed the problem over to others, in this case to the general-in-chief of the country's small, standing militia.

"Aye, sir. Done and dusted. Just got to finish loading his lordship's horses. The grooms are having a few problems."

"Problems, Sergeant?"

"Nothing I can't handle, sir. With your permission, I will get back." Mason saluted.

"Carry on." Pugh returned the sergeant's salute and watched Mason push his way down through the crowds mounting the steps that led up to the railway station. The steps were flanked on each side by a trio of wide rose marble columns, which supported a façade made of an ornate carving depicting scenes of commerce overseen by the Goddess. When Pugh had first seen it yesterday in the pink-tinged light of dusk, the Goddess had looked anything but benign. Today it was a carved likeness of a well-formed woman sitting above a black-faced clock, surrounded by bales of cotton, steam engines and smoking chimneys. Yet the memory of the expression still made Pugh uneasy, for reasons he could not quite understand.

The clock above him began to strike four. It was time he got his charges on board. Pugh entered the main concourse and winced at the thunderous noise, which echoed round the huge, vaulted ceiling of glass and steel. It was a chapel to the new god of industrial progress, far more lavish than any that had been built in the last thousand years to the Goddess. The concourse narrowed at its far end; travellers funnelled into queues before iron barriers that marked the entrance to the platforms.

Pugh moved through the crowds towards the doors of the Station Hotel. As he placed his hand on the handle of the door, his reflection twisted in the large glass pane. For a moment, in his mirror image, he saw a stranger: a man with deep-set, dark grey eyes surrounded with lines that belied his age of thirty-two; a career officer encased in green and grey, with seemingly no other thoughts than those of his duty.

He shrugged away the feeling and opened the door. The raucous noise was replaced by the soft swish of ceiling fans, whispered conversations and footsteps muffled by thick carpets. Pugh's eyes struggled for a moment to adjust to the change in light. His stomach began to churn in apprehension. This so-called easy assignment could quickly turn to anything but. He found himself assessing each person passing through the foyer as a potential enemy.

On the right of the door, the hotel's concierge was supervising the arrangement of a large amount of luggage onto a porter's trolley. Lady Elizabeth Hotspur would not be continuing with the rest of Lord Joshua Calvinward's party to Gateskeep, but would be journeying on to the Hotspur summer estate in the mountains.

"There you are, Pugh. I am glad I have seen you before I leave. I was about to light a small candle to the Goddess." Elizabeth's hand right waved in the direction of a recess set to the left of the door. Set in the niche was a small bronze statue of the Goddess. A number of candles were already burning on the tiered candle racks below the statue: candles lit for safe journey; the protection of loved ones; health, wealth and happiness. Prayers said, and offerings given, for lots of different reasons in hundreds of different chapels, public and private shrines. Religious obligations were an ingrained part of everyday life in Timeholm. To what degree, like many things in the country, depended on your place in society.

"For me?" Pugh turned to face Elizabeth. She had been goddess-mother to Pugh's late wife, Claire. Over the years he had known her, they had progressed from a mutual dislike to respect — but he doubted he had, or would ever, feature in Elizabeth's prayers.

Without answering, she opened her reticule and removed a thin candle made up of seven layers of coloured wax. She held the wick against one of the already-lit candles and placed it on the top rack. The light created a reflection of the candle colours on the bronze statue. Elizabeth waved her right hand over the top of the flame and watched for any change made to the reflection. None occurred. If anything, the colours brightened. It was considered a sign of upheaval.

It was a trick of the light, but Pugh saw the effect it had on Elizabeth. Her stance changed. It was if she was struggling with her thoughts. She bowed her head once in reverence. Pugh had always thought it strange that, for someone with no illusions about the world she lived in, Elizabeth had a deep and somewhat outdated religious streak.

"Pugh." Elizabeth stopped and glanced round. "I have heard, from a reliable source, that an old player in the game is active hereabouts. And they are — how can I say this — 'up to their old tricks.'"

Pugh's mouth tightened. Was the Inner Ring taking an interest in the party he was escorting? Damnation. The religious order might have convinced the public at large that their days of politicking were over; that they left all such matters to the chapel's senior ministers who sat in the High Forum. However, no right-minded politician believed it, nor did Pugh. A leopard did not change its spots.

"It could explain many things happening of late," she said. "It could have a bearing on why Constance is dangling her daughter in front of Calvinward. It would be considered an ideal match in many circles. I swear Constance is acting for those who want to reel Calvinward back into the bosom of the Stategentry party."

"I think you do the lady a disservice. Besides, I can't see Calvinward toeing the Stategentry party line no matter who his future wife might be. And he is currently relishing his role of being the leading voice of the opposition. Your husband has had something to do with that, has he not?"

Elizabeth ignored Pugh's barb. "I see you, like others, have succumbed to the artful innocence of Constance's blue eyes."

Pugh tried to ignore the small twinge of annoyance at Elizabeth's remark concerning his interest in Constance. Was he so transparent?

Elizabeth's eyes crinkled at the corners in amusement. "That's enough of politics, my dear Pugh. Remember, I am just a woman, and you are making my delicate mind hurt. Besides, it is time I left. I have a train to catch." Her expression changed, and the seriousness there dispelled any annoyance he felt with her. He took hold of Elizabeth's hand and kissed it.

She smiled in acknowledgement and left his side, pausing for a moment to re-arrange the long, fine veil on her unfashionably large wide-brimmed hat. The hotel concierge held the door open for her, and she and her maid vanished into the crowds.

***

Pugh turned and threaded his way through the hotel patrons to a wide staircase. He walked up to the first floor, continued down the corridor and came to a halt by the door of a private parlour, guarded by three of his men.

The corporal saluted and opened the door. Pugh returned the salute, fixed a smile on his face and entered. The private parlour was well furnished with a number of overstuffed wing-backed chairs and elegant two-seat upholstered benches. The two tables were littered with the remains of afternoon tea and the morning papers.

Lord Joshua Calvinward stood by the large, cold fireplace.

From the top of his well-groomed, light brown hair to the soles of his shiny black boots, Calvinward matched the public perception of a gentleman politician. He was talking to Lady Emily Manling, who was sitting with her back towards Pugh. From the tilt of the young woman's head, Pugh gathered she was having difficulty keeping an interest in Calvinward's conversation.

Lady Constance was having no such problems. She was an intelligent as well as beautiful woman, and she had been by her late husband's side at the heart of the political world for eighteen years.

"My wife get away satisfactorily?" Sir Clive Hotspur asked, between puffs of his pipe.

"Yes, Sir Clive."

"Is it time for us to board, or is there another delay?" Calvinward said.

"Sergeant Mason was having a few problems in the marshalling yard. They should be cleared by now. The express is due to leave at half past the hour."

"With the horses?"

"They were having difficulty settling. It could be the heat or unfamiliarity with the horseboxes."

Emily turned and looked at him. "Oh, the poor darlings." Her white-cotton gloved hands fluttered like two small birds to her mouth.

"Do not fret, my dear," Calvinward said, as if addressing a small child.

The girl did not seem to be Calvinward's type. Then again, Emily had beauty and status. More importantly, the girl had no original thoughts of her own. She was the perfect accessory for the arm of a fast-rising politician. Pugh curled his lip. Could Calvinward be so calculating? Of course he could. Marriage was a means of cementing political alliances and money. Pugh's own had not been; his time with Claire had been far too short.

His sour expression was noticed. "Something wrong, Captain?" Lady Constance said. She rose, flicking out the fullness of her dress with a twitch of her slender fingers.

"No, Milady, it's the heat."

"It is again so hot?"

"Hotter, I believe, Milady. But you shall not be in it for long. It is just a short walk across the platform."

"Indeed," said Calvinward. "Are you looking forward to this,

Emily?"

"Oh, yes, indeed so. Nearly three days on a train. So much to see."

"And so little to do," Hotspur remarked, dryly.

CHAPTER THREE

The concrete platform reflected the heat, making the air above it shimmer. Plumes of smoke and steam drifted from the train through the horde of passengers. Pugh could feel beads of sweat forming on his forehead, but resisted the temptation to rub his brow.

Emily had a frown on her face. Her fingers fumbled with the catch on her parasol. Pugh could guess her thoughts. It was only a few steps. Was it worth putting the parasol up? Her frown deepened. She glanced at her mother, then at Calvinward. Was she incapable of making even this small decision?

"Something wrong, Emily?" Calvinward asked.

"Err, no, it's the heat."

"Yes, it is abominable. But it will get better as we go north." Calvinward looked down towards the rear of the train, then forward to the engine. It was more than a casual interest. One of the things Pugh had learned about Calvinward was that he was interested in everything. It reminded Pugh of his former father-in-law. Sir Henry Fitzguard was a politician by profession and an experimental scientist by inclination. Since the sad event of his daughter's loss, Sir Henry had shunned the former, and pursued the latter locked away in his country estate. Pugh frowned. Was that where Elizabeth was bound? Had she been sent to sound out Sir Henry on the matter of that cursed Forum bill? On behalf of her husband or Calvinward? Blast this so-called easy duty — it was giving him too much time to think.

Sir Clive was the last of Calvinward's party to board. Pugh followed.

"How can you be sure it will get cooler as we go north?" Emily said.

"I know," Joshua replied, almost indifferently.

"You don't know everything, sir," Lady Constance gently teased. "Is that not so, Captain?" She paused, waiting for his answer. If he did not know better, Pugh could have sworn that Constance had a small wager with Elizabeth over the last few days, as to how many times she could get him to say the same words.

"I am just a soldier, Milady," Pugh gave the obviously desired reply.

"And a handsome one at that," Lady Constance said.

Lady Emily giggled. "Oh, Mother, you are a one. Is she not a one, Joshua?"

"Yes, she is a one." The inflection in Calvinward's voice hinted that he meant something more than Constance's flirting.

The carriage shuddered, making the glasses on the sideboard at the end of the lounge rattle. The carriage was opulent to the point of being obscene. The walls were lined with rosewood wall panels, inlaid with fanciful pictures of flowers and fruit. It was furnished with fine chairs and tables, thick carpets and curtains of silk damask. An ivory-tipped ceiling fan slowly turned overhead. Its blades reflected on the glass shades of the oil lamps hanging from the gently curved roof.

Emily reached up and removed her small, round, yellow hat and placed it on one of the chairs by the window. She patted the mass of curls at the base of her neck and stood watching the crowds on the platform. A large number of the people were moving towards the rear of the train and the third-class carriages. Each one had coloured labels tied to their outer clothing and their personal bundles. Bond contract workers.

"Poor things. My father privately spoke of his distaste for bond contracts. He often used the words, 'legalised slavery.' He worked with the sect of the Inner Ring, you know, to alleviate the poverty with the current upheavals."

It was plain to Pugh that the girl had adored her late father. She obviously believed he had been a paragon.

"Stuff! What on earth, Constance, have you been teaching the girl?" Hotspur said, and began to inspect the labelled decanters on the sideboard. He laid down his pipe, picked up a shot glass, took hold of the whisky decanter and poured himself a measure.

"Lofty ideals, my dear," Calvinward said, "but, as you said, your father only expressed them privately. There is not, and never has been, any slavery in Timeholm. We are currently in a period of great change, my dear, yet we must not forget the institutions that made our country what it is. The same institutions that are the power behind these great advances we are currently making."

Pugh found it difficult to hide a snort of amusement. Calvinward had spoken in the manner he would at a political rally, uttering platitudes that could be interpreted in a number of ways. Yet there was a sparkle in the man's eyes. It was not one of amusement. A warning perhaps. Directed at whom? Hotspur? No, the man was firmly in the camp of those opposed to the bill and made no secret of it.

"Gentlemen, would you excuse us, the heat..." Constance said. She moved towards her daughter. Her expression gave no hint that she was aware of anything untoward, but Pugh doubted she had missed the look in Calvinward's eyes. "It would be best if Emily and I retire for a while. Then we will be bright and engaging company for you over dinner."

"Of course. Ladies." Calvinward gave them both a slight bow.

***

After the women had left, Calvinward took one of the periodicals off a table and began to flick through the pages. One of the articles caught his interest. He sat in a chair and began to read. Sir Clive Hotspur was pouring himself another drink, as well as one for Calvinward. The carriage shuddered again and jolted forward. A sharp blast of a whistle penetrated from outside.

Calvinward lowered his paper. "We are off."

Pugh wondered if he should answer such an obvious statement. Was Calvinward looking to engage him in conversation? He was rescued from having to answer by a sharp tap on the door. It was Sergeant Mason.

"Sir." Mason's stance and expression were tense.

"If you will excuse me," Pugh said.

Hotspur merely waved his hand in dismissal, but Calvinward asked, "A problem, Captain?"

"Duty, Milord."

"I see." Calvinward returned his attention to the periodical, but Pugh knew he had seen the tension in Mason's demeanour.

Pugh joined his subordinate in the passage. "Well?"

"I have been informed we have a stowaway of a sort."

"A stowaway?"

"Yes, a junior conductor spotted it, and got hold of his superior. They were going to stop the train and throw it off, but Corporal Jones realised what it was. Besides, it is asking for you. Not exactly asking, but gabbling your name."

Pugh felt a cold shiver between his shoulder blades. It.

14

There was only one type of person Mason would refer to as an it: a Glimpser. Pugh began to feel physically sick. It had been seven years. It had to be another poor wretch. Another innocent who had had their mind ripped away and been left tortured by the insanity that had rushed in to replace it.

Pugh led Sergeant Mason into the first-class dining carriage and saw a small knot of figures standing at the far end. Corporal Jones turned at the sound of footsteps. Here there were cupboards on either side stacked with plates and other wares. One of the doors was open and the contents lay broken on the floor.

"We should stop the train," the senior conductor said.

"Wouldn't it just try and get on again?" Corporal Jones said. "Most likely kill itself doing so. Don't fancy answering a judge for its death."

"You sure it is one?" said the young man who blocked Pugh's view.

"If you move...," Pugh said, his voice brittle with suppressed emotion.

The junior conductor looked round. He opened his mouth to retort to Pugh's sharp request, but the look Pugh gave him made him blush and stutter. The junior conductor quickly moved forward and stood by his superior.

The carriage swayed. The train picked up speed. Pugh steadied himself by grasping the edge of the seat. The Glimpser looked up. 'Its' gaze was like a bullet into his heart. He felt his throat constrict. It was Claire. After all these years, she had returned, but it was not the bright young woman he had married who sat half-curled up on the floor.

"Find Pugh. I Oracle. Train. North. Death in the dark. Hack and slash. Mountain home. End it. Bone and fate."

Pugh listened with horror to the words tumbling from his former wife's lips. The skin of her nose was split, and, like her neck, smeared with blood. She was dressed in men's clothes, her sex hidden by the oversized garments. Her thin hands were outstretched to him, fingers opening and closing like a child begging to be picked up.

"Find Pugh. Am Oracle. Train. Death in the dark. World on its head. Bone and fate. Train, trick, track, wire. Goddess' sacrifice. Toby dog."

The words were repeated again. And again. It became a

chant. With each new repetition her eyes blinked, or tried to. Her eyelids could not close completely. The delicate flesh had been deliberately split and left to heal misshapen. Her once beautiful green eyes were now pale and cloudy. Old-woman blind. Yet she was not. Claire saw the world as it was, could be and must not be, and it had destroyed her mind.

"It's one of them," the senior conductor said, barely hiding his disgust. "You going to take charge of it, Captain? Seeing the thing has come looking for you."

It was the last thing Pugh wanted to do. This wretched remnant of humanity was no longer his wife, yet she was. "Yes, for as long as it stays on the train."

The senior conductor nodded, and indicated for his younger colleague to follow him out of the carriage.

Claire reacted to Pugh's words by trying to struggle to her feet. Her cracked lips continued to move, but no sound came from her mouth. She looked exhausted. The madness that had driven her here had pushed her beyond the limits of her body's strength.

"Can you walk, or do I have to carry you?"

Claire wobbled on her feet. She sniffed, and blew blood out of her nose. She began to turn to follow the senior conductor.

"No, this way." Pugh took hold of her arm and began to lead her through the dining carriage in the direction of the sleeping compartments. "Corporal, return to your duties and make sure all our men know about the Glimpser's presence on the train. The Goddess knows why it is here, but while it is I don't want any trouble."

"Aye sir," Jones acknowledged, saluted and began retracing his steps.

"Mason, bring the following to my quarters: some hot water, a medical kit, food and drink, but not alcohol. A pair of boy's britches and a clean shirt."

"A nit comb and some lavender and camomile oil," the sergeant added.

Pugh opened the door to his sleeping compartment and led Claire in. She stumbled to the bunk beds and sat down on the lower one. Her hands lay palm up on her thighs, the fingers curling inwards. Once fine and soft, they were now rough, cut and bleeding.

"What am I going to do with you?"

Claire did not reply. She just stood up and began to pull the small pack off her back. Pugh took the pack and laid it aside. He was tempted to look in there to check Claire at least had some money. He felt responsible. He knew he should not, not after all this time, but he did. She was – had been – his wife.

As if she was aware of his thoughts, she reached out her small hand and placed it on top of his. The warmth of her touch sent a shudder through him. Did she know what she was doing, or was it an involuntary reaction to the questions she sensed he wanted to ask?

A sharp knock on the compartment door broke the tension. Pugh opened the door.

"Will there be anything else, sir?" Mason asked.

"No."

"You will be dining with Lord Calvinward?"

Pugh sighed and poured out some hot water into the large earthenware bowl on the wash stand. "Yes."

"You want me to – " Mason's head tilted in the direction of Claire.

"Me sleep. Stay. On train, trick-track. North, click, click. Message on the wire," Claire muttered. The movement of her lips cracked the cut on the bottom one open. A thin trickle of blood began to run down her chin.

"Take it you mean a message on the telegraph from a station." Mason pulled at the left side of his moustache, mulling over her words.

"Sergeant, take it from me, you will drive yourself insane trying to make sense of its words." He had called Claire an it. Pugh pushed down the rising wave of guilt. "Sometimes it's as plain as day. Other times a Glimpser spits out what is inside its head. That gets jumbled with the questions you and others are asking it."

Mason frowned. "I haven't asked it any. Oh. You mean maybe thinking on questions." The sergeant moved to the door. "So they are as much use as a snowball in summer."

"For the most part; that's the pity of it."

The sergeant nodded, saluted his superior, and took his leave.

Rummaging in his own bag, Pugh pulled out his wash kit and took a flannel and a cake of soap and dropped them into the bowl. Claire, unbidden, struggled out of her clothes. He

17

wrinkled his nose at the smell: the garments were so filthy they could stand up by themselves. Pugh shuddered at the sight of recent bruises and cuts on her body. Then there were older scars. He forced himself not to look at the lumpish scar tissue in the centre of her breast bone. It was, along with the damage to her eyelids, the physical legacy of the torture she had undergone. He lathered the soap on the flannel and washed Claire down like a child. He washed her hair, twice, then rubbed in the lavender and camomile oil. It would have to do. Her roughly cropped hair was alive with hair lice. It would take more than one run-through with comb and oil. He coated the sores on her body in a thick ointment and covered the worst of them in pads of clean linen. Pugh helped Claire struggle into her clean clothes, patted the top bunk, and she scrambled up. He placed the plate of food by her side, and noticed with relief he did not need to either instruct or encourage her to eat.

Pugh set aside his pistol and began to remove his belt.

"Keep the pistol loaded and on the belt."

Pugh turned sharply and looked at her. His heart thudded. "All the time. Can you tell me what is going to happen in words that make sense?"

She did not answer straight away, and Pugh wondered what inside her mind had triggered the statement. He doubted he would get any answer. Pugh rolled down the window. He picked up the bowl and threw the contents out.

"Trust only her and him. Not him, and not, not ever her. Can't tell much. Not simple things. World on its head. Click, bones, train, bones. Death in the dark."

Pugh turned and set down the bowl. Deep inside, he could feel a small knot of elation spreading. Was his wife still alive inside the Glimpser, or was it the madness speaking? He grabbed her right foot in an effort to catch her attention. She looked at his hand on her foot, then at Pugh's face.

"You want to tell me names, don't you? But that madness won't let you. By the Goddess! You didn't deserve this."

"No, not mad. Take care, watch. Sorry."

The sorry was so forlorn, Pugh cursed under his breath. Had he hurt her by demanding more than was possible for her to give? No, it was his imagination. Claire was gone. This Glimpser was not her. Yet the voices in her head had driven her to him. Told him to keep his pistol loaded, and on his belt. It was all nonsense.

Pugh turned away from her. He busied himself tidying the compartment and unpacking his dress uniform for dinner. By the time he had finished, Claire was curled up asleep. Pugh eased the bedcovers from under her and gently tucked Claire in. "I should have stopped those religious zealots. Done something. You didn't deserve this. It was the grief and I didn't see. They had no right. But what proof do I have? Who would have believed ..." Pugh stopped. He was rambling like a Glimpser about a past he could not change or forget.

Pugh looked out of the window. Dark clouds had begun to invade the sky. A storm was brewing. He could perhaps go and check on the guards that had been posted. No. It would signal to his men that he did not trust the non-commissioned officers under him. He could join Calvinward and Hotspur in the private lounge. But he had not at any time sought out their company during the journey, except when his duty dictated. To do so would arouse their curiosity. He would have to inform Calvinward at some point of the presence of the Glimpser, in case the madness drove it to seek him out. Pugh tried not to think of "it" as Claire. He sighed and sat down on the lower bunk, loath to leave her alone.

In the bed above him, Claire turned over. Pugh stiffened and then relaxed. She was asleep. Perhaps he should try to get some rest as well and take advantage of having nothing to do for a few hours. He took off his boots and tunic and lay down on the bottom bunk.

Claire, or Oracle, as she had called herself, had come back into his life for whatever reasons the voices in her head had decided she should. It had, could have, nothing to do with the past between them. He moved his left arm up under his head and closed his eyes. He needed to forget about the past and deal with the now.

The rattle of the carriage echoed his thoughts. It amplified them. A brittle song that sang Pugh into a fitful sleep swamped with half-formed dreams. *Heat shimmered through snowflakes. The train plunged down a narrow pass, impossibly steep. Calvinward laughed at the dead frozen in the heat and drank their health. Emily swayed and danced on the backs of workers hung with coloured tags. Lady Constance's dark locks fell down unbound, as she spun in front of him. Green eyes became blue, then colourless. He could feel a woman straddle him and lean forward, her long hair tickling his chest and lips. It formed a veil now dark, now white-blonde, which hid a kiss from the world. His hands reached up and cupped breasts at first large and unknown, begging for him to explore them, then small, each faction of their gentle swelling known to him. Yet he longed to repeat the lesson.*

The carriage jolted and the rattle of rain against glass echoed round the compartment. Pugh was suddenly shocked awake. He shuddered and lay there staring at the bed above him. He felt spiritually naked. Stripped of everything he had created to protect himself these last seven years. He sat up and swung his legs over the side of the bunk. Damn it to bloody hell. What time was it?

***

Pugh pulled at the hem of his dress jacket before he reached out to open the door into the private lounge. He entered, bowing slightly to the ladies present. Lady Emily was dressed in a fine evening dress of cream silk, as befitted her age, her hair piled artfully on her head, laced through with silk flowers. She was making an effort to look cool and calm, but Pugh could see she was anything but. Was it the oppressive storm outside affecting her, or perhaps the current conversation?

"Again, my apologies, Lady Constance," Calvinward said. "The conductor made an error. I was at the time in the middle of conducting my own correspondence. He thought it was one of my replies, not a message for another."

Constance folded the small piece of paper in her hand and placed it into her reticule. "My telegram was nothing important, Joshua. Estate business, but it was good of you to ask the conductor for the carbon copy. Please, there is no need for any apology. These things happen."

"Evening, Avinguard. I thought a sabre was the accustomed weapon for dress uniform," Hotspur said.

"A pistol would be a more useful weapon in the confines of a railway carriage."

"Goodness," Lady Constance exclaimed. "You are taking those stupid letters seriously aren't you?" She was dressed in deep ruby red, the silk heavily embroidered. Constance was closer in age to her daughter than she had been to her late husband, and

Pugh was well aware that the deep colour accented her mature beauty. He felt a twinge of guilt at the thought.

"My superiors are, and I—"

"—am just a soldier," Lady Emily finished for him.

"Yes, Milady." He was still going along with the pretence of the joke, even if it was the furthest thing from his mind. He wished Lady Elizabeth was still with the party. She could help with Claire. No, Claire was not here. A Glimpser called Oracle was.

"And a damn good one. I am surprised they have you doing such mundane duty as escorting me across the country," Joshua said. He walked to Emily's side and offered her his arm. She slid her silk-gloved hand through and allowed herself to be led through into the dining carriage.

The soldier on duty was standing at the far end. The man saluted. Pugh returned the salute and the soldier stood at ease, yet his eyes continued to watch the diners carefully. On either side of the carriage were lines of tables with two seats either side. Two tables opposite each other had been reserved for Lord Calvinward's party. Pugh stiffened. Three seats of the eight were already occupied by a portly senior minister of the Orthodox Chapel of the Goddess, his bird-faced wife and personal secretary.

"I asked the minister we met in the hotel to join us. Your sergeant cleared it earlier with you, I believe," Calvinward said.

Mason had not done anything of the sort. The non-commissioned officer had obviously not thought the matter worth bothering Pugh with. Pugh gave a short nod in agreement and sat down next to Lady Constance across the aisle from Calvinward.

The two tables were agleam with silver and crystal. The light was soft; candles had replaced oil lamps. With the curtains tightly closed against the storm outside, the carriage was a miniature of a dining room that could be found in any fine house in the country.

When everyone was seated, the minister coughed and clasped his podgy hands together, uttering a sketchy prayer: "May the Goddess this evening grant us her blessing on what we have achieved this day in her name. May we be worthy of her continued faith in us to act with honour to our fellows. And may we enjoy this bounty before us in the full knowledge that it is through her gifts that it is ours to share." The

21

minister, it seemed, was more concerned with his forthcoming meal than ministering to his temporary flock.

During dinner the conversation flowed back and forth, but the newly proposed bill before the Forum kept bubbling to the surface.

"It is a matter of control with regards to the labour force. It is as simple as that," Joshua said.

"Control, or profit?" Constance folded her napkin and placed it on the edge of the table.

Pugh watched Lady Emily glance from her parent to Joshua. Was she concerned about what her mother was planning to say?

"Profit is important, but suppose you gave the people the right to move freely. To work for whom they choose. I can see but one thing: starvation and outright poverty for many. A bond contract works both ways. An employer by law has to look after his workforce. If that were abolished, the working class would have no protection at all."

"Damn right, sir!" Hotspur loudly expressed his agreement.

"Are you sure?" Emily ventured. She looked at Joshua.

"I am sure. Control. Bond contracts which state the nature, terms and length of the employment. The working class in their rightful place, as it should be."

"And worked to death." Constance's words were merely a whisper. To impress the minister? Pugh doubted it. The minister was avoiding eye contact with the rest of the party. Wishing himself elsewhere, most likely. But from the look on Joshua's face he, too, had heard the remark.

The conversation faltered into an awkward silence. Lady Emily began to speak. "What does everyone think of the weather, and will it, as I have heard said, affect the game this autumn?" Obviously she felt she needed to steer the evening's conversation in a different direction. Did she see herself as Lady Calvinward already, and obligated to play hostess? There had been no announcement. Surprisingly, her redirection worked. The talk of hounds, hares and the pleasures of the sporting field took the diners through the rest of the meal.

Emily looked in Pugh's direction. "Lord Calvinward mentioned your service record earlier, Captain. I gathered from this that you have seen active service. Does not the shepherding of us seem tame?"

Emily's comments had drawn the gaze of their fellow

diners onto Pugh. They all, he was sure, knew something of his record. The Coot's Pass incident had not been some back street scuffle. He dabbed the corner of his mouth with a linen napkin. "On the contrary, I would rather have quiet duties."

"I find that hard to believe," Joshua said. He raised his hand, summoning a waiter to refresh everyone's glasses.

"Why?"

"You were involved in some of our recent border disputes with Crossmire. Which, my dear Emily, were ended thanks to your late father's skill at diplomacy." Joshua gave Emily a smile, more political than friendly. "And were you not, Captain, decorated for your part in the Coot's Pass incident?"

"A decoration I would rather not have received."

"What!" Hotspur banged his hand on the table to emphasise his words. "Why, man, I would have loved to have been part of that."

"Would you have, indeed?" Pugh turned in his seat to face Hotspur. Was Hotspur that drunk, or was it all pretence?

"By the Goddess, yes. I had to make do with seeing the ambassador from Crossmire's face when he heard the news. He was somewhat perturbed. Not that that was any proof of Crossmire's involvement in events, of course." Hotspur watched Pugh's face carefully.

It was plain he was hoping Pugh would cut in. Confirm or deny the not-so-veiled references to Crossmire's part in events. Pugh returned Hotspur's gaze, trying to keep a look of polite interest on his face.

Hotspur drew in a breath and continued, perhaps taking Pugh's gaze as a challenge. "Coot's Pass. It must have been one hell of a thrill. The way you tricked those bloody tribesmen into the fort before you blew it sky high. The heroic dash down Coot's Pass in winter, successfully getting all to safety."

"Not all. We had casualties. The men and their families paid a high price. We were hunted like animals down that pass. I saw children pay for the mistakes of adults." Pugh could feel the muscles round his jaw tighten.

"Your family?" Lady Constance asked. Claire's reported mental decline after Coot's Pass was common knowledge, and the annulment of their marriage. Only a handful knew what had really happened. Pugh doubted even Hotspur knew the whole truth. Elizabeth wouldn't have handed her husband such a weapon to use against Claire's father, Sir Henry. Not that it mattered. Sir Henry had been "retired" from politics this past seven years. Pugh folded his napkin and placed it beside his plate. As far as he was concerned, the conversation was over.

"I see your point," Hotspur mumbled. His eyes had narrowed slightly in annoyance. The bastard wanted more. "But still, you are a serving soldier and aware a military man's family must face such dangers."

A cold silence fell among the diners.

"Shall we retire to the private carriage, gentlemen," Joshua said, and, to Pugh's surprise, looked embarrassed by Hotspur's goading.

Lady Constance gave a short cough. "I was hoping that we could continue our conversation, this being a somewhat informal evening."

"Tomorrow, Lady Constance. It is late and I am sure you and Emily are quite fatigued with all the talk of politics."

Lady Constance tilted her head and gave Calvinward a smile that had nothing to do with friendliness.

Pugh had been so wrapped up in his thoughts about Hotspur's probing that he had missed the fact that Calvinward had said "gentlemen." Had Calvinward just dismissed Constance and her daughter to their sleeping compartment like naughty children who had overstepped the mark?

Pugh wondered if things said at the meal had been bait to draw him out. As a decorated soldier and the heir-apparent of his family, did his opinion really matter to Calvinward? More importantly, could it be used to further his, or Hotspur's, agenda? Or did they believe that, as the former son-in-law of Sir Henry, he could have enough influence to draw him back into politics? Possible, Pugh supposed.

But he could not believe such politicking of Constance. She was not like that. He was reading too much into everything. Claire tumbling back into his life had torn open the half-healed wound on his heart and soul. Claire. He must check on her. Maybe he could excuse himself.

He stood aside at the end of the dining carriage to allow Lady Constance and Lady Emily to pass. Lady Constance's face was composed, but there was a look of annoyance lingering in her eyes.

CHAPTER FOUR

arter said, "I better get dry first. Bring my pack down to the latrine."

Mathew nodded, and left his own pack across two carriage seats in a vain effort to reserve them. Not that it would be successful. By the time Carter was changed, Mathew's pack would be on the floor and someone else's backside on the seats. There was none of the so-called niceties of society here in third class.

Carter was soaked to the skin from his encounter with the horse trough. Even his head had gone under. The water dripped off Carter's bulbous nose, hitting the edge of his neatly trimmed beard. He was trembling, but more from emotion than the cold. Anger or disappointment: the priest of the Inner Ring was hard to read. Going after the woebegone scrap of humanity that was a Glimpser had been folly. Besides, it was illegal to interfere with them. Such beings were the stuff of legends; the last recorded one had died two years ago on the coast. Mathew did not doubt that this had been a Glimpser. He had got a good look at its face. The deformity of the eyelids, and the washed-out colour of its eyes, had sent a shudder down his spine. Or maybe it had been the words it had uttered. Were the words meant for him? Had the Glimpser been warning him of Carter's zealot tendencies, or Calvinward's? Message on a wire: was that a telegraph?

"Mathew, my pack."

Mathew handed Carter his pack and stayed by the open door, allowing Carter room to change without falling over the foul-smelling porcelain pot in the corner. Carter slipped off his soaked clothes and used his undershirt to dry his arms and legs. He pulled open the neck of the pack, helping himself to shirt, underbritches and a red priest's robe made of lightweight wool as expensive as the garment was plain. Carter threaded a belt of yellow, braided rope round his middle and knotted it at his left side. He closed his pack and stepped over the wet clothes, abandoning them. Mathew bent to pick them up.

"Leave them. I have no more use for them."

Mathew could not help himself — he spluttered and began to speak. The clothes were good ones.

"No Mathew, give them to one of the men here you think is most deserving. We have more important things to deal with."

With the putting on of his red robe, Carter had donned the manner of a priest. Before, though Mathew had always been aware of Carter's status, Carter had always taken pains to act as a working-class man, as he did. Mathew had chosen to see for himself the plight of the bond contract workers. He was under no illusion that Carter was about the business of his order. However, their paths had run together for a summer, and he hoped that Carter was at least a supporter of the proposed bill before the High Forum. Why else had he helped with the petition?

Mathew bent again to pick up the clothes, but they were gone. A man stood hugging them to his chest, his head bowed in reverence. Mathew shrugged his shoulders and moved after the priest. When Mathew reached the seats he had placed his pack on, Carter was already seated in one, and the pack was on the floor. No one had taken the seats, or if they had, they had quickly moved. He noticed that people had withdrawn as much as they could from Carter. They looked anywhere but at the man in the red robe, out of respect or fear, or a combination of both. He felt a twinge of surprise that a member of the Inner Ring could still inspire either, in this day and age. Old habits died hard.

"Perhaps, the sight of so many signatures," Mathew began.

"Do you believe that?"

No. Mathew did not. He doubted a man like Calvinward would be swayed by scribbles on a piece of paper. But Calvinward was intelligent. He would see that the petition was a source of power, and that, Mathew swore, was Calvinward's Goddess. "What is the alternative?" The lines between those for and those opposed to the new bill were becoming ever more tightly drawn. The prospect of civil unrest was becoming a very real threat.

"Look, get some rest. We had little or no sleep last night." The priest looked round the crowded carriage. "I will see if I can find out anything."

"About the Glimpser. This Pugh, whoever he is. They might not be on the train, you know."

"I think both are. They have to be. Don't worry, we will get the petition to Calvinward before we reach Gateskeep."

26

Carter patted Mathew's shoulder. He stood up and began to move towards the front of the train.

Mathew watched his fellow passengers begin to settle down for their journey. Children with their heads on their mothers' laps, women leant against their mates. The buzz of conversation became muted. The sky began to darken, not from the approach of evening, but from a gathering storm boiling down from the Clawback Mountains.

Mathew wondered if he had been foolish to follow this crazy path. It had not been what his father had wanted, but even he had seen the benefit of it at first. Of late, their correspondence had become bitter. Both had slowly realised they could not change the opinion and position of the other. Mathew reached inside his waistcoat pocket and pulled out his father's last letter. His father was demanding he should come home or risk being disowned. He returned the letter to his pocket and tried to relax. The heat in the carriage increased. Mathew's eyes began to droop.

How long he slept, he did not know: three, perhaps four hours. He awoke with a crick in his neck and a dull twinge in the bottom of his stomach. An over-full bladder. He shifted in his seat, got up and made his way back to the latrine, reluctantly shutting the door behind him as he tried not to breathe in through his nose. Mathew undid his britches and stood, one arm braced on the wall, as he relieved himself.

Through the wall he could feel the vibrations of the engine: they were changing. The train was stopping. A hiss of steam brakes. The soft squeal of metal on metal. The sound of slamming doors, footsteps, and voices drifted into the carriage, accompanied by the smell of coal dust. Mathew refastened his buttons and opened the latrine door. The outer door of the carriage was open. Mathew stood in the entrance for a moment, then dropped down onto the side of the track. Perhaps some fresh air would clear his thoughts.

The train had stopped at a rough non-station, which consisted of one large water tower and a huge mound of coal. A number of men were loading coal, while the train's firemen supervised the taking on of water.

The sun was no longer visible. There would be no golden sunset this evening. Lightning ran through the dark clouds. The streaks of light were quickly followed by a rumble of thunder. A rough breeze whipped dust-eddies round the legs of the men loading the coal. It rattled a single length of metal wire, which trailed down from the telegraph wires that ran alongside the train tracks.

At the foot of the wire, the senior conductor squatted, his portable telegraph equipment at his feet. The man was busy transcribing a message for a tall figure by his side. Calvinward.

The Glimpser's words. *"Message on a wire, see, listen."*

Mathew drew in a breath. He pulled his cap out of his belt and put it on, pulling the peak low over his face. Mathew began to move towards the two men. He was not alone on the side of the track. A number of others were taking advantage of the train's stopping to stretch their legs.

"Well?" Calvinward said.

Calvinward was dressed in evening attire. His right hand was outstretched and his left rested on his hip, the image of a polished dandy. The man was not only out of place alongside the men working here, he was out of step with the mood of the country. Was it really worth the effort of presenting the petition to him?

"It takes time," the conductor replied.

"I need to send at least two more."

The conductor grunted, tore off a piece of note paper and handed it to Calvinward. He narrowed his eyes and made to place the paper in his trouser pocket, but missed. The small wad of paper dropped to the ground and was blown in Mathew's direction.

Mathew felt his heart thud. He bent quickly, scooped up the paper and pushed it into his pocket. He increased his pace and returned to the train. He looked back. The conductor had switched off his machine and was climbing up the telegraph pole to unhook the wire.

As Mathew climbed back into the carriage, the air above was split by another flash of lightning. Suddenly, the rain began. Mathew regained his seat and watched the water running down the window. The train began to move. Mathew's hand went in his pocket, fingers pinching at the crumpled message. Carefully, he pulled it out and laid it on his knee, smoothing out the creases.

"All is ready at Hitsmine. Will inform you of the results before you reach the capital."

What did it mean?

Hitsmine was a large town at the centre of the steel-making industry. Day and night the blast furnaces roared, illuminating the skyline with a hellish glow. The industry relied heavily on a bond contract workforce, and unrest with the conditions was rife. "By the Goddess!" Mathew sat up. Calvinward couldn't be foolish enough to set a light to that powder keg.

"Damnation, the weather has turned quickly."

Mathew looked up. It was Carter. Mathew had been so engrossed in his own thoughts, he hadn't seen the man return. Carter stood waiting for Mathew to shift across the wooden seat. "What do you make of this?"

Carter took the paper. His eyebrows rose nearly up into his hairline as he noted the train company's monogram on the top. "Who threw it away?"

"Calvinward."

"As to what I make of it, I assume Calvinward has got someone trying to drum up support for his position with regards to the bill."

"I was thinking more along the lines of, say, a demonstration of the 'dangers' of allowing the working class more freedom. There has been talk of workers' marches taking place in Hitsmine."

"No. We don't know he is against the bill yet."

"We don't know he is for it, either. And, of the two, I would say against. It would be a very useful weapon in his armoury. I can hear him saying, *'look at what this rabble can do. Look, we had to subdue them with police. What would they get up to if they were allowed to roam the country?'*"

"Madness. I don't believe it. It could backfire on him. Calvinward is not such a fool. It wouldn't look good on his record as a caring member of the High Forum. He always wants to look good in the eyes of the general public. He sees it as his strength, but it is also his weakness. His vanity. Lord Manling saw it too late for his own good. Calvinward had pinned him to the floor by then."

"Manling was a fool. He thought he was indestructible. As to the matter of stirring up a riot, it's what I would do if I were in his place." Mathew had seriously thought of it. If peaceful protest and petitions came to nothing, it could be the only way to make the Forum sit up and take notice.

"Yes, I see. We need to warn your people there, just in case."

"The train will next stop at the Clifton Mines Halt. We could use the telegraph there."

"We will be there, what, tomorrow morning? That gives me plenty of time to see to the matter of the Glimpser."

What was it about this Glimpser?

"You have found out something. You really want and try to speak to that crazy bunch of rags?"

"Yes, and it is not crazy, not at all. That is the whole point. This one is different. Did you not notice the purpose in its movements and utterances?"

Mathew found that thought quite chilling. "So when do we..."

"Later. We can take the petition at the same time."

It was plain to Mathew that Carter's comment about the petition was an afterthought. For a while, as they had talked, it felt like the early days when they had first met, a sharing of a mutual passion and concern for the plight of the working class. But since Carter had found out about the Glimpser, all that had changed.

***

The buzz of conversation in the carriage gave way to snores and coughs. A conductor came through the carriage. He turned the oil lamps off and placed a hooded night light at each end.

"Time, I think," Carter said, rising from his seat.

Mathew reached down for his pack, pulling out a large cloth-wrapped parcel. He followed Carter into the first-class dining carriage; his grip on the wrapped pages tightened. "How much further?"

"Just through the sleeping carriages."

They did not pass anyone in the first two sleeping carriages, but the third one was anything but empty. Through the glass pane in the door, Mathew could see a soldier. The man's shoulders were outlined by the painted flowers in the corners of the glass. Carter opened the door and they both stepped through. The soldier's hand tightened on his rifle.

"Please, be at ease. I merely wish to speak to Lord Calvinward," Carter said.

The soldier did not answer, but Mathew knew he had taken in every aspect of Carter's vestments.

"Please. We mean him no harm."

"I am sure you don't, sir brother priest, but I have my

30

orders," the soldier replied. "Corporal!" he called, not turning his head. The sound of the corporal's thick-soled army boots on the polished wooden floor was almost deafening as he approached.

"What is it, Private?"

"This brother priest wants to see Lord Calvinward, Corporal Jones."

"Yes. I have some business with him," Carter said.

Corporal Jones frowned. Mathew could see the man had his doubts. The hour was late.

"I will have to check, Brother — " Corporal Jones waited for Carter to supply his name.

"Carter."

The corporal nodded and began to walk back down the passage. The private shifted his position, standing now at right angles to Carter and Mathew. This gave Mathew a clear view down the passage. As the corporal reached half way, one of the compartment doors opened in front of him and a lady stepped out. The corporal gave a short bow and made to move past her.

"Lady Constance!" Carter shouted.

The lady turned to face Carter.

"Brother Carter, George. Is that you?" Lady Constance began to walk towards them. Carter looked at Mathew and smiled. Mathew coughed, trying to hide his surprise. Carter had not mentioned he knew Lady Constance Manling. Mathew had met Lady Constance and her daughter a number of times when he was younger. He doubted either would recognise him. He had been one among his numerous siblings paraded by his mother at the social events she had seen fit to take them to.

"Yes. Are you well, Constance?" Carter said, dropping her honorific. By doing so, he was implying they had a close friendship. Mathew could see that the implication was not lost on the corporal.

"You know Brother Carter, Lady Constance?" Corporal Jones asked.

"Oh, indeed, yes. He was a friend of my late husband's. It is good to see you again, George," Lady Constance said.

"And you, as well."

"Is there something wrong?" Lady Constance was wearing a heavy silk dressing gown, the neckline, cuffs and hem thick with lace. Her dark hair, unbound from its tight coiffure, fell

31

across the curve of her neck. Mathew mentally shook himself, the lady's beauty for a moment distracting him. He smiled; he wasn't the only one.

The corporal cleared his throat loudly, trying to focus his attention on the matter at hand rather than the flow of her ladyship's hair and the curve of her body under the silk gown. "Brother Carter has asked to speak to Lord Calvinward."

"If a member of the Inner Ring of the Goddess, especially one of Brother George Carter's standing, has made such a request, it was not done lightly. I would suggest you escort him to Lord Calvinward immediately." She paused, then added, "Perhaps tomorrow we can talk of less important matters, George. It has been a while since I have had the pleasure of your company."

"It would be my pleasure," Carter replied.

Lady Constance turned. The corporal stood to one side to allow her to pass. She moved back up the passage to her compartment, where a younger woman was waiting. Together they walked to the far end of the carriage, where the salubrious bathroom facilities of first class were situated. The click of the bathroom door closing behind the two women acted as a signal. The corporal straightened his shoulders, his decision made. He signed for Mathew and Carter to follow him.

***

"We are not dangerous," Carter said.

The way the militia captain in the carriage raised his left eyebrow informed Mathew that the man believed otherwise. The officer had stood when Mathew and Carter entered the carriage, placing himself at the right-hand side of Calvinward. The officer dismissed the corporal with a glance and a rough return of his salute, and the young soldier seemed very glad to retreat.

"And what can I do for you, Brother Carter?" Calvinward had also risen from his seat and stood, hand outstretched towards Carter.

Carter took it and shook it warmly. "There are some matters of importance I wish to discuss with you."

"Indeed. Where are my manners? A brandy, Brother Carter?"

Carter nodded.

"Hotspur, if you would be so kind." Calvinward indicated one of the empty chairs, and Carter sat. Mathew stood by his side, trying to hide his amusement that after a casual glance he had been dismissed by Calvinward as Carter's servant.

Hotspur made a show of pouring the drink, and handed it to Carter. The priest smiled in thanks and took a sip. "First things first, Lord Calvinward. I would like to pave the way for this young man to present to you a petition."

"Surely tomorrow morning would be better." Calvinward straightened in his chair and looked at Mathew.

Mathew was plainly dressed. The thick cord trousers and a cheap linen shirt, topped by a rough woollen waistcoat, made him look to be another working-class man. His bright blonde hair, clipped close to his scalp, underlined the fact, yet his hands were not rough from hours of labour. And his features did not carry the pinched look of a man struggling to make ends meet. Had Calvinward realised he was not what he seemed to be? However, he had Calvinward's attention, and would be a fool not to take advantage of it. He began to speak, lengthening his vowels in a working-class manner. "Now, Milord, by your leave. You are but two days away from the capital. You will need time to consider this."

"Will I?" Joshua's gaze moved from Mathew's face to the parcel.

Mathew stepped forward and placed the parcel on the table. He was aware that his movements were being closely watched by the militia officer. "This petition is signed by hundreds of workers in the new industries, people held by what they believe unfair bond contracts. They ask you, Milord, as a much-respected member of the High Forum, to consider their plea. Give them and their families a chance of a better life."

"Bloody foolishness," Hotspur drawled. "Damn me, Joshua, you are not going to take notice of this nonsense. Our party is not in the habit of bending to any kind of pressure," He waved his right hand in the air as if to refute everything Mathew had said. Was the man drunk? No. His eyes were far too clear and were focused on Carter. Did Hotspur think the Inner Ring was delivering the Forum Unionist party an ultimatum? The order wouldn't do so like this; they would be much more circumspect. Perhaps Hotspur was trying to bait Carter, or maybe Calvinward. It was hard to say.

"Pressure, no. But it behooves us to take notice of things, does it not?" Calvinward turned to face his fellow Forum member.

Hotspur smiled. Was he bowing to his companion's better sense? Mathew doubted it.

"My thanks, Milord," Mathew said, and found he meant it. The man was proving far more approachable than he had thought he would be.

"You are welcome, Master— " Calvinward stopped, waiting for Mathew to supply his name.

"Worth, Mathew Worth."

"Indeed." The manner in which Calvinward spoke confirmed Mathew's earlier thoughts. He had seen through Mathew's pretence. Did he think Mathew was a political agent, or had he recognised him? Mathew was the youngest son of the current leader of the ruling Stategentry party, Lord Howorth, but that put him far down the pecking order. His eldest brother was heir to their father's seat in the Forum, and was being groomed for the part. It had been expected that Mathew would stay in the militia after his three years' conscription, or enter the chapel, shunted sideways like all excess sons. It was certainly not expected for him to have any interest in a political life. Mathew began to feel more and more uncomfortable under Calvinward's scrutiny.

"Now, Lord Calvinward, to another matter," said Carter. "One in which I feel you can exert your influence, to allow me to act on behalf of one that cannot act for itself." Mathew could hear the excitement in Carter's voice.

"And that is?" Calvinward asked, politely. It sounded like Calvinward was losing interest he'd had in Carter's conversation.

"I refer to the protection of a Glimpser that is on this train. Currently, I believe, in the quarters of Captain Pugh Avinguard."

"Pardon!" Calvinward exclaimed. He turned to face the captain. "Why did you not inform me of such a creature being on board?" He sounded more aggrieved at Avinguard's lack of trust than annoyed at not being told of the creature's presence.

"Well done, Avinguard. Chain it up in the baggage car and throw the little bugger off at the next station," Hotspur said.

"No, that is — " Carter began.

"Against the law. As is any harassment. Yes, there is one in my quarters. The senior conductor and his men are aware of it, as are my men. I was going to tell you if it made an attempt to speak to you. As it is, I merely made sure it was cared for. It could be gone at the next stop. They wander, you know."

"Yes they do. Tell me, Captain, how long have you been acquainted with it?" Carter asked.

"I don't think you can have an acquaintance with a Glimpser, but to answer your question, not quite a day."

"I doubt it. Your paths have crossed before. It looks to you as a port of safety. You have *known* it quite a while." Carter drew breath and waited for an answer. None came. He sighed and continued, "These creatures do not live long. They are forgetful of the basic needs of life. It is a sad fact, but they are driven only by the voices and visions in their heads."

"To their death," Pugh said.

"Sadly, yes. Most survive barely two or three years after the gift manifests itself. Now and then, one survives longer. When one does, it is a rare creature, and of great interest to my order. We have tried to track them, but it is impossible. They are known for being unpredictable and seem to have the ability to vanish from under your very nose. As I think you might know, Captain."

"How interesting. You are saying that this Glimpser is one such?" Joshua asked, looking from the captain to Carter.

"I believe so and I wish to make preparations for its transfer to the seat of my order in Gateskeep, where it can be looked after. You could be of great help in this, my Lord Calvinward."

"Nonsense. It is what it is for the rest of its existence. Leave the creature in peace," Pugh said, his voice hard and level.

Carter looked at the captain. His eyes narrowed. "You, I assume, know more about my order than most, maybe because of your *past* with the creature, but you don't know everything. The burden the Glimpser, Oracle, as it calls itself — that, in itself, is a sign: they do not give themselves names — the burden drives them. Though, in rare cases, something else also drives them to survive; the two are opposed and start to cancel each other out, until a balance is achieved. The creature becomes again a cognizant human being. Like you and me, but with an inner switch. Something that will, in certain circumstances, plunge it back into the state of being a Glimpser. The result being, my order hopes, it will be able to explain its visions in a more lucid manner."

"By the Goddess, you mean it will be able to control what it sees." Calvinward's eyes had narrowed.

For a moment, Mathew thought the man believed everything Carter was saying. Calvinward's features hardened, and the right corner of his mouth began to twist upwards. No, he did not believe, but it was amusing him to allow the conversation to continue.

"No, but it will be able to speak far more plainly of what it sees. It needs to be protected. My order is the most suited to do so. We are the guardians of the Seer's original texts and our order predates his time. We are his true followers." Carter sounded like a gambler who had just played a winning hand, or a religious zealot who had suddenly found the physical manifestation of his belief. That was it. Carter, above everything, was at heart a true believer in the Seer's prophecies.

"This is incredible," Joshua said, looking over at Hotspur. Mathew could see he was trying not to laugh.

"It's clever nonsense," Pugh said. "You should be on the stage with such acting."

"You don't believe him, Captain?" Joshua's hand covered his mouth for a moment, to conceal his amusement. "You accuse this man of the cloth of lying. He is one of the Inner Ring of the Seer, a small, but holy, order of the Goddess."

"Exactly. The Inner Ring. A group known to play its own game in the politics of a dozen countries, even if it denies it, citing its charitable work of forgiveness and aid as its only concern."

"Easy, Avinguard. I am aware of the nature of the various political forces at work in our country and others. Congratulations, Brother Carter. I am sure your order will be proud of you, but I doubt they sanctioned this. What would be next, let me guess: you would have told me the Glimpser's ramblings, told to you in private, as you helped it with this *transition*. Worked me like a puppet on a string. What would the High Council of the Orthodox Chapel make of this meddling if they were informed? I am certain Senior Minister Carlsonmark would have much to say on the matter. Captain Avinguard has acted correctly; the creature should be left to its own devices. I thank you for the few minutes of entertainment. Good evening, gentlemen."

Dismissed. Mathew felt a wave of relief. But the petition— would Calvinward disregard it totally, now?

Calvinward looked at Mathew. "Do not worry, Master Worth. It was plain you did not know of Brother Carter's intentions. I will give the petition the attention it deserves."

36

Mathew began to speak; Hotspur's belly laugh cut him short. "He certainly will, as will I, as toilet paper."

Was Calvinward no better than the rest? Mathew began to despair of his own class. He turned towards the door, then looked back at Carter. The man's face was twisted with contempt and anger. Mathew knew he was not done with this matter. Carter got to his feet and opened his mouth to argue.

"Death in the dark, crash, smash. Stop it. Pull it. DEATH IN THE DARK!" The Glimpser, this "Oracle," bellowed from the doorway.

"Damn you!" Pugh turned towards it.

"By the Goddess," Carter cried. "I know what you mean. I will prove the nature of miracles to these fools. Let the Goddess' will be done, and may the righteous be rewarded in this world and the next!"

Carter pushed Hotspur aside, struggling to reach the outer wall of the carriage.

"What are you doing, you idiot!" Hotspur bellowed.

"Stop." Pugh's voice blended with the rasp of leather on metal, as he pulled his pistol from its holster.

"Carter, by the Goddess, no!" Mathew shouted. His heart began to race.

"Death in the dark, crash, smash. Stop it. Pull it. DEATH IN THE DARK" The Glimpser's words had turned into a chant. Its gaze locked on Carter.

"I understand. May I be worthy to stand at your side." Carter reached up and pulled the communication cord at the same time Pugh's pistol discharged. Carter's torso sagged. His body's weight dragged his hand off the cord. He crashed to the floor.

For a moment, the train continued on its journey. Then it lurched. The screech of metal vibrated up through the floor. The carriage rocked and began to tilt. Mathew, unable to brace himself, lost his footing. He fell forward. His waist hit the back of a chair. The breath was driven out of his lungs. He put his arms up to protect his face. Voices shouted, then screamed, and the world went dark.

CHAPTER FIVE

The damp chill against his back was the first thing Pugh became aware of. Then a tumbling, disjointed mass of thoughts began to form in his mind. *Train. Crash. Tumble. Air. Cold. Rain. Anger. Nothing.* Was that how it was for Claire?

Claire!

Goddess above. The train. It had crashed. He was — where? For a moment, Pugh was tempted to lie there and remain ignorant of the full horror he knew must be around him. Claire. Calvinward and the others in the carriage. Lady Constance and her daughter, Lady Emily. His men. His heart rate increased. Damn it. Snap out of it. Pugh struggled to suppress the emotions beginning to paralyse him. *You are responsible for all of them.* He drew in a ragged gasp of air and opened his eyes. Above him, the moon, Rambler, filled the sky with silver light. The rag-tag remains of storm clouds skittered round its edges, dissipating swiftly in a sharp wind. The same wind which flapped the left side of his ripped-open jacket. Slowly, Pugh realised he was lying at a forty-degree angle. He was on the grass embankment. Somehow, he had been flung clear of the carriage.

Pugh felt as if his horse had rolled on him. His left side was aching like hell. Ignore it. Push it aside. What first? Find the carriage. Find Claire. He could not do it alone; he needed help. He needed to find his men. Ascertain what had happened, and organise help for everyone. That would be expected of him. For him to do his duty. Was doing his duty putting a lump of metal in the shoulder of a priest?

"Bloody stupid fool." Had the priest, by pulling the communication cord, caused the accident, or prevented a worse one? Claire had baited the man. Consciously. Was what the priest had said true? He shook his head, trying to clear the tangle of thoughts threatening to swamp him.

He got to his feet and took a step forward. He had to focus. Cries and screams filled the chill night air: calls for help, names of loved ones. Figures scrabbled along the side of the track; their disjointed movements mimicked the horror around them. Pugh groaned as he looked up and down the remains of the train. The dark shape of the engine and its tender were still in an upright position. Its whistle screamed into the night air and the glow from its open fire box added to the moon's illumination. It would be a while before the other moon, Caresight, rose, even longer before dawn. The two carriages aft of the tender were toppled over. The first one was the train staffs' quarters. The second was Calvinward's personal carriage. Pugh began to move down the bank towards the shattered remains. The three carriages behind the smashed carriages were still on their wheels. They were the first-class sleeping compartments. After that, he was not sure. The moon glinted on the wet tops of the following carriages. They were at strange angles to each other. Some must have jumped the track. In the dark, it was hard to say. He scrambled the rest of the way down the bank and into the hell before him.

He bent down and picked up a broken window section and dragged it aside. In the moonlight he could see that half of Calvinward's private compartment was pinned under the undercarriage. If Claire or anyone else was under there, *dear Goddess*, then they were dead. He stood up, his heart again pounding with suppressed emotion.

"Captain!" It was Corporal Perkins.

A small group had begun to move with purpose towards him. Pugh turned and scrambled off the wreckage. At least some of his men were alive. "Perkins, where is Mason? What state are things in back there? Where are the men?" Pugh tried to keep his voice calm and level, but knew he had not.

Perkins pulled up in front of Pugh and saluted, his hand shaking against his forehead. In the dim light, Perkins' face contorted. Pugh forced himself not to wince at the man's expression. "Sergeant's dead."

"Blast. How many others, Perkins?"

"Only the sergeant confirmed dead, but young Thomas is missing. He was on duty in Calvinward's carriage. Down at the back, Jones said, they were just rattled about; the rest of us at the front were in the sleeping compartments. A few cuts and bruises, but nothing more."

At the mention of his name, Corporal Jones stepped out of the gloom from behind Perkins, the senior conductor joining him.

"Captain, I need the help of your men," the senior conductor said. "We need to get signal fires going up-track and down. If another train were to run into us in the dark ... " He looked up and down the remains of his train. His face was pale, and he had a streak of blood across the bridge of his nose.

"Right. Corporal Perkins, I want you grab three others. I can't really spare more, so you had better conscript some civilians and get those two fires started. There is plenty of wood about." The latter was an understatement: nothing remained of the first two carriages other than pieces the size of kindling.

"Many thanks, Captain," the senior conductor said. He took his hat from his head and wiped his brow with his right hand.

"Aye, sir. What if the civilians protest, sir?" Perkins said.

"Use your imagination, Corporal. I am going to put you in charge of aiding the conductor and his staff. They will know what needs doing and where things are. The living are your first priority. You need to find out if there are any with medical knowledge of any kind on the train." Pugh caught his breath and tried not to look over at the smashed remains of Calvinward's private carriage. "Calvinward, Hotspur, the Glimpser and two others, they were in Calvinward's carriage. And Lady Constance, and her daughter, they would have been in their sleeping compartment. All the members of the party must be accounted for." Pugh found the words dying in his throat.

Perkins nodded and moved off. Pugh looked again at the remains of the train. Already the side of the track was a sea of packed humanity.

"Bit silly getting off if you are all right, just to stand in the damp," Corporal Jones remarked.

"Fear does strange things to people," Pugh said, more to himself than the others. He cleared his throat. "You came up from the rear; how bad is it?"

"Funny, sir," Jones said, rubbing his chin, "all but one of the goods wagons are upright. So are most of third class, though a couple broke loose. Them in there I think would be in a bad way. One of second class is almost upright, like a finger, sir. A couple toppled over and smashed like these here. First-class sleeping and day carriages are undamaged, but the dining ones and the kitchen are gone. I think that is one of them on fire, sir."

"We need to get that out, or tipped over out of the way of the rest of the train." The senior conductor's eyes narrowed at the sight of the flames.

40

"I will leave it to you and Jones to get some men to see to it. I need to see if our driver is still with us and what state his engine is in. Pulling the communication cord should not have resulted in this." Pugh tried again not to look at the mess that was Calvinward's private carriage, but did not succeed.

"Nay, it shouldn't. I was on my way up to see."

Corporal Jones started bellowing at a gaggle of men standing by the other first-class carriages. Protests rose from the group and were answered by Corporal Jones, instructing them in a parade ground voice, with thrusts of his rifle underscoring the main points.

Pugh nodded to the conductor and took his leave of the man, but the conductor fell in step alongside. "Your corporal has got that in hand. I need to know what has happened. This is my train."

***

The front of the engine was rammed into what looked like part of the embankment that had slipped over the tracks. The vast machine of steel and copper had entered a good number of paces into the mass of mud and rock before it had stopped.

A man appeared on the edge of the footplate. It was the driver. His face was streaked with blood and coal dust. A body, one of the firemen by the look of it, lay at the man's feet. The dead man's fellow firemen were dragging out the hot coals from the fire, trying to lower the steam pressure. The train's whistle dropped a note, then faded, hiccupped and stopped.

"That's bloody better," the driver said. "How bad is it, Arthur?"

"A bloody mess — what the hell happened?"

"'Happened.' We bloody well stopped in a hurry, that's what happened, but could have been — Goddess knows — worse." The driver dropped down onto the track and walked to the front of his charge. He shook his head at the crazy angle of the chimney and the rivers of fast-drying mud that lathered the sides of the machine.

"It could have been worse," Pugh repeated, trying hard not to snap at the driver.

The train driver looked Pugh up and down and spoke to the conductor. "Who the bloody hell is this?"

"The captain of the militia on board," Arthur said.

"Didn't know we had any. Your lads mucking in, I

41

should sodding well hope." The driver stood back, looked at the large wheels of his engine, sighed, and shook his head. "Won't be able to see how bad things are till the morning."

"You were saying," Pugh prompted.

The driver moved closer to the engine, his hand going out to a twisted copper pipe. "Damn and shit! Still got steam. George, bleed her some more!" he bellowed. "Worse, yes. Damn bit of bloody good luck, someone pulling the cord. Not only were we braking, the conductors would have been applying the carriage brakes all the way down. If we had hit the beginning of this landslide at full speed, you would be picking us all up in pieces."

"Some are," Pugh said. The realisation of what had really happened dawned on him. *Oh Claire, you have repaid the debt you believed you owed a thousand-fold. You believed you took one life once; here you have saved how many. Goddess, please, don't let my...* "I have to get back. Calvinward and the others."

"Of course," the senior conductor replied.

Pugh turned and broke into a jog, making his way back as quickly as possible. He could see the shadowy shape of someone standing amid the wreckage of the private carriage. Claire. No, as he approached closer, he saw it was Calvinward, and the man was hitting the front of an upturned armchair.

***

The train had crashed. The thought came logically into Mathew's mind. He heard himself scream. He could not move. Surrounded. Held down on his stomach. He raised his head: it hit something soft. Mathew opened his eyes. He could see nothing, but his eyes stung. Dust, debris and fragments of the carriage were in the air around him and it was hard to breathe. *Goddess! Am I blind! No. Trapped in the dark. Alone.* Fear began to rush through him. He breathed deeply and tried to move his arms. The left one was pinned. The right he managed to move forward by bending the elbow and shuffling it forward. It came dragging a length of what felt like wood with it. Sharp needles pierced through his shirt.

Once Mathew got his arm forward, he felt around in front of him. It felt like a large armchair and smelled of dusty leather and beeswax. The chair covered his head, shoulders and down to just above his bottom. He wriggled his left arm

42

where it was stuck against the side of the chair. His fingers managed to touch the front of the seat. What of his legs? They moved freely, bending up. He tried to kneel and heave the chair off. It did not move. He tried again, straining and swearing. His heart beat faster. Mathew coughed. The air was getting fouler.

He heard a curse. Someone was thumping the side of the chair. He could feel the vibrations through the thick leather. A voice, muffled by the large piece of furniture, but Mathew managed to make out, "trapped, bogies, legs clear." Someone was there, and trying to help.

The noise of ripping leather and snapping wood bounced round the small space. He bellowed in protest at the assault on his ears. The noise stopped, then began again. He felt things falling on the backs of his thighs. The seat cushion above him started to be tugged out. It scraped down his back and jammed.

Whoever it was pulling the seat started swearing. He could hear the voice plainly now. It was Lord Calvinward. "Are you hurt?"

"I am not sure," Mathew answered, and tried to get his right hand back down by his side. The arm joints protested, but he managed. He turned his arm upwards to take hold of the cushion. His fingers slipped on the leather. He found a tear, grabbed hard and tugged. It shifted a little.

"You are stuck under a chair. Your legs look unhurt. But the chair is stuck under the undercarriage and that is shifting." It was a different voice this time. The militia captain, Avinguard.

Mathew felt the cushion shift again, as Calvinward and Avinguard pulled. Mathew added his own efforts. His fingers buried themselves in the horsehair stuffing. "It's moving!"

"Not quick enough." The urgency in Calvinward's words were emphasised by the groaning of the chair above.

"Can you wriggle backwards?" Avinguard asked.

"Maybe." He began to rock his body, pushing with his right hand. The cushion shifted again. Mathew felt the cold night air on his back. He smelt the dusty horsehair freed from the chair's stuffing. Small motes of it floated in the air, making him choke even more. Both his arms were free from the elbow down and he used them to force his body back. His chin caught on the wreckage beneath him and the skin tore. He felt the blood begin to flow, running down his neck. He was out and made to stand. His lungs expanded, drawing in a draft of damp night air.

A hand grabbed the back of his shirt. Mathew looked round. Avinguard was shouting something, but all Mathew could hear was the scream of metal and snap of wood. He stumbled through the wreckage. The metal undercarriage was coming down and crushing what was left of the carriage under its weight.

Mathew fell onto all fours. He rolled down the stone ballast and into the ditch by the side of the track. Calvinward and Avinguard were on either side of him. Mathew looked back at the remains of the carriage. The dark bulk of the bogies lay there, wheels gently turning. The moonlight glinted off the metal, sending faint beams across the nightmarish scene.

"By the Goddess, that was close." Calvinward dragged himself up the side of the waterlogged ditch. He had the air of an expensive toy that had been badly abused. He was soaked from the knees down, covered with mud and weed. His right arm hung loosely by his side.

"Your arm?" Mathew asked.

"Your chin." Calvinward walked back up the small bank and looked at the remains of the carriage.

"Not important, it can wait," Mathew said.

Avinguard had already left the ditch and was talking quickly to one of his men.

"So can this; not going to kill me, is it?"

Mathew could sense the man was shaken by events, even though he was trying to hide it. "I don't know where the others are. If they were still trapped in ..." Calvinward stopped speaking for a moment. "Goddess, what a bloody mess. Hotspur. The young soldier. Your meddling priest. I think I saw the Glimpser scuttling from the wreckage. I told Pugh so. He is concerned about it, rightly so, but I can't be sure. Then there are the ladies. I have to make sure they are safe. They were in my care."

"The rest could have been thrown free, or staggered off, dazed; we will find them all. Now let's see to your arm." Mathew bent down and picked up a length of the expensive drapes that had once covered the carriage's windows. He looked at the remains of the carriage under the bogies. If anyone else had been trapped, they were dead. Mathew felt his throat tighten.

"I said it can wait!" Joshua snapped. "I need to find the ladies. We also need to find the senior conductor, and he needs to get his hands on his telegraph machine. We need help here." Calvinward was pushing all sentiment away, trying to bury it under the veneer of being busy. Mathew could sense it. The man was drawing on his position and rank as if it were a coat, capable of protecting him from feeling. Mathew felt a twinge of empathy with the man.

"Yes, all that, but first let me tie up that arm and give it some support." He tied a knot in the fabric and offered it to Calvinward, who nodded and allowed Mathew to put his arm in a sling.

Calvinward winced. His face was pale, and he chewed his lower lip. His gaze roamed over the devastation, then came back to Mathew. "Thank you."

Mathew felt his mouth dry. Calvinward and Pugh had saved his life. Mathew cleared his throat. "And thank you. You and Captain Avinguard, you saved my life. I didn't know, I mean, what Carter said in the carriage about the Glimpser." Mathew felt he had to be honest. His own sense of honour would not allow him to be otherwise.

"No. No, of course you didn't, but the damn fool has killed the Goddess knows how many, for religious twaddle."

Mathew opened his mouth to reply, but thought better of it. Calvinward had already moved out of earshot.

***

The sun had tracked across the sky from east to west and was fading behind the mountains. The remaining first-class carriages had become a makeshift hospital, which spilled out onto the track in a ramshackle array of hastily erected canvas hovels, their floors slick with blood and vomit. One day ago the train had been the pinnacle of the modern age; now it resembled a shanty town. Aid was on its way, but for now the survivors had to fend for themselves.

"Walk on," Mathew said, and pulled on the reins of two of Calvinward's carriage horses. The horses shuffled forward then stopped, reluctant to move any further. Mathew did not blame them. The animals' hides were slick with sweat. They had mud up to their hocks and hung their heads low. "A small break then, we have more of that shattered carriage to clear." Mathew patted each on the neck. He was tempted to sit down, but dared not. He knew if he did he would be asleep in an instant.

"Oh the poor darlings," Lady Emily Manling said. She was standing on the stone ballast by the side of the train. Strands of her dark hair had come loose from the braids on either side of her head, thin black wisps teased ever thinner by the faint breeze. Her eyes were narrowed against the harsh, late-afternoon sun. Her shoulders were slumped, face pale and drawn. She stood with her hands clenched together in front of her. There had been no accusation in her voice, nor in her expression.

Mathew rubbed the neck of one of the bays. The animal snorted in response to the caress. "They are well, I assure you, Milady. We have been making them work a bit harder than they normally do. Won't do them any harm. They are well-fed and fit. Least they are alive. We didn't have to put a bullet in them like a number of the others."

"I heard the shots earlier." Tears began to roll down Emily's face. She sniffed and roughly wiped them away.

The horse nearest to Emily shuffled closer. It yanked at its bridle and whinnied softly. "I am sorry, I don't have anything for you." She rubbed the animal's forehead. The creature huffed in disappointment and shook its head. "I can't even help in there without ..." She shuddered and her face became more ashen. Mathew knew what she meant.

"Being sick. Frightened half out of your mind. You are not the only one. No one should be unmoved by this." Mathew's arm waved in the direction of the wreckage.

"But one should ..." Emily began, but there was no conviction in her voice, only pain.

The sound of a train whistle cut through the air. Mathew looked towards a column of smoke coming up behind the train wreck. People began to shout and move towards the approaching vehicle.

"Is that the special train coming to help us from Hitsmine?" Emily shaded her eyes against the sun's glare. The red engine was smaller than the black-and-copper-coloured monster that had pulled the northern express.

"Hitsmine is that way." Mathew pointed back towards the engine. Despite everything, he could not hide the small tinge of amusement in his voice.

"Oh." Emily gave a small grin in reply, and shook her head at her own lack of any sense of direction.

"That is a small local passenger train that was coming up behind us. The captain commandeered it earlier. This will be its second run. He and Calvinward intend to cram as many of the walking wounded, women, and children on it as they can. Hopefully it has brought up help this time."

"I doubt Joshua's motives for helping those less fortunate are purely unselfish," Emily said, biting her lip at her indiscretion. The waiting crowd moved closer to the approaching train. They had begun to shuffle into two lines. The soldiers were going down the rows, indicating for people to either move forward or stand aside.

"I think you are wrong, Milady. He did save my life," Mathew replied, feeling a little uncomfortable with the change in the conversation's tone. Besides, was not Lady Emily on the point of being engaged to Calvinward? At least the current newspaper gossip said so. He clicked his tongue at the horses and began to walk them towards the rear of the train.

"Yes he did, didn't he," Emily said, a note of confusion in her voice. "You said women, children and walking wounded?"

"Yes, as many as can be shoehorned in, but it is not a large train. It has two, maybe three carriages at most, and a few goods wagons. I reckon most of us will be stuck here for another day or two."

"I don't think I can," Emily sobbed.

"Yes, you can." Mathew dropped the horses' reins and stepped towards her. He reached out and began to rub her arms with his hands in a vain effort to comfort her. Emily burst into tears and Mathew held her until her sobs turned to hiccups and sniffles. She gently pushed against Mathew's arms. He released her and stood there looking down into her eyes.

"I am sorry," she said, and tried to wipe her face with her fingers.

"No, don't be." Mathew pulled the front tail of his shirt up and cleaned her face, then gave her a crooked smile. "Feel better?" He let the damp edge of his shirt drop back down and stood watching her struggle to regain control of her emotions. In that moment, she looked very brave and beautiful.

"A little."

"Emily."

"Mother." Emily sniffed loudly and turned round. Lady Constance was standing on the small metal platform at the rear of the nearest carriage.

"We need to start moving people, if you will guide this gentleman and the others." Lady Constance had one arm round the shoulders of a man. His head and shoulders were half-covered by a blanket. He seemed a little unsteady on his feet. Emily left Mathew's side and walked to the rear of the compartment. She reached up with her right hand to help the man step down.

There was something familiar about the man. Mathew frowned. He could say that about anyone here. One face had begun to blur into another, the longer he went without sleep. "I best be getting on."

"Thank you," Emily said, smiling.

Mathew returned the smile with one of his own, gave her a slight bow, and began to lead the reluctant horses towards the rear of the train. Emily, Lady Constance and a stumbling line of people kept pace with him. Mathew found he kept looking across at Emily. She was doing the same. Silly, but it seemed to lighten the plight they were in.

As they came level with the first of the goods wagons, Mathew stopped. Emily continued with her charges. Mathew stood there watching her and Lady Constance. The man wrapped in the blanket turned towards Mathew, then climbed into the train. Again, he felt he knew him. He began to wonder who, but never completed the thought. Calvinward was walking towards him, telling him to bring the horses forward.

***

Pugh lay stretched out on a pile of hay in the wagon that had carried the horses, still dressed, with a rough blanket thrown over him. He was trying to get some sleep, but had not yet succeeded. His kept going over events since the crash a day and a half ago. Calvinward was sure he had seen Claire; she had trodden on his arm in the wreckage. But there had been no sign of her since. Pugh had had the older children among the passengers search the embankments, and surrounding countryside, in a league radius for survivors. They had found a number, but no Claire, which meant she was obviously not hurt. She must have left, driven away by the voices in her head. However, she had left her pack. The pack was Claire's lifeline to a normal existence. He did not think she would have abandoned it. This alone made Pugh think that Calvinward was wrong and he had not seen her. Claire lay crushed under the bogies of the private carriage. Pugh did not want to believe it. He wanted to believe that she was walking down a road somewhere.

The rasp of a foot on the wood of the wagon floor startled Pugh out of his thoughts. His hand reached out for the pistol at his side. Stupid. There was no danger. His hand clenched shut, and he let it rest on his upper thigh.

"Captain, I am sorry to wake you," Lady Constance said.

"Milady, is there anything wrong? You yourself retired not so long ago," Pugh mumbled and sat up. He rubbed his unshaven chin and pulled a length of straw from his hair. He took the cup of tea Lady Constance was offering to him, and sipped it, then burst out coughing. The tea had been laced with something stronger than tea. He took another, longer, draft and set the container down by his side.

Lady Constance smiled, trying to hide her amusement. "Nothing wrong, but two trains running side by side have been spotted coming up to the other side of the landslide."

"Damn. They made good time." Pugh got to his feet. "We can get the rest of those that can be moved away well before the midday. The seriously injured will have to wait awhile. You will be in a hotel in Hitsmine by mid-afternoon." Pugh moved to the door. People were shouting and running forward.

"That is what I want to speak to you about. I feel it is my place to stay." Lady Constance pushed back a stray lock of hair that had fallen in front of her eyes.

"I don't think that is necessary, Milady. The train should have brought medical staff."

"Captain, we do not have neat hospital notes for those who have been hurt. I, and some of the others, need to stay to make sure things go smoothly." Constance placed her hand on Pugh's arm. "But I feel my daughter should go. Her nerves are quite strained."

"I see." Pugh did not know what else to say.

Lady Constance's hand dropped from his arm and she cleared her throat. "Please understand, I am acting as any parent would. We have family friends in Hitsmine: Sir John Thornton, who owns the Hardlash smelting works. She could go there, if I could prevail on you to allow me to send a telegram to him. Then there is the matter of the journey."

"The journey?"

49

"Yes. Our maid was killed, as you know. So I was hoping one of your men could escort her," Constance said in a rush, avoiding his gaze.

It was impossible. He needed all his men here. Emily would have to stay if Constance wouldn't allow her to travel with some of the other women, and without a male escort. Then again, perhaps he could arrange something. "I can't spare a man, Lady Constance, but I might be able to arrange another escort. Would young Mathew be suitable? He is an honourable young man. Both Lord Calvinward and I have come to trust and like him since the accident."

"Yes, if you could arrange it. I would be so grateful." Constance kissed Pugh softly on the corner of his mouth, and quickly took her leave.

Pugh's hand came up to his face and touched the warm, damp section of his face. His pulse quickened at the salute and he found himself watching Constance walk back towards the sleeping carriages.

CHAPTER SIX

he heat in the carriage increased with each mile. No ivory-tipped fans circulated the oppressive air. No fine blinds could be pulled down to deflect the midday sun. Mathew had seen the expression of surprise on Emily's face when they boarded. She had not voiced her thoughts, unlike the bird-faced minister's wife. The woman still tutted at each perceived breach of polite behaviour. The children on board were the victims of most of her censure. They were understandably fractious: hot, tired and sensing their parents' apprehension. For many, the journey's end was not going to be a joyous reunion with family, but a continued one into the unknown. They were bond contract workers, their contracts sold on the open market for a profit. Forced to move. A new life not of their choosing.

"Are we nearly there yet?" Emily asked.

Mathew mouthed the word, "no," and grinned.

Emily smiled in return. She glanced down at the folded cloak on her knees, then began to toy with a large, finely crafted brooch on the collar. She picked at one of the diamonds with her nail. She looked up at him again. Mathew coughed. He was a little embarrassed that he had caught her studying him, and looked out of the train window at the dark soot-grimed houses slowly passing by. The air of Hitsmine seeped through the cracked windowpane; it tasted of iron and coal dust. The skyline was a mass of factory chimneys belching thick, black smoke, lit from below by the glow of the numerous foundries.

The train lurched to a stop with a hiss of steam-powered brakes, and people began to get up. The doors were thrown open and voices shouted from the platform, telling people where to go.

"Why are they doing this?" Emily asked.

"They need to get people sorted. Most here don't have any money. People need somewhere to sleep, a good meal, and to be processed before they go on their way."

"What do you mean, processed?"

"Their papers checked, to see who they are and who holds their bond contract. Their permission-to-travel card

51

needs to be verified, and their masters informed of their whereabouts." Mathew picked up his bag and placed it on the bench beside him. He opened it, pulling out a letter and a small black book. He took a set of thick, folded parchments from the book and returned it to his pack. The documents and letter he tucked into his waistband.

"I just did..."

"Did what you wanted, went where you wished."

"Yes." Emily slipped her cloak on and stepped off the train onto the crowded platform. The fine quality of her garment stood out from the drab clothes of those surrounding them. For Mathew, it underlined the inequality of society: those who had, and those for whom it was impossible to possess.

"That way, Milady." Mathew pointed towards a barrier where a man in an inspector's uniform stood. Emily nodded, and began to make her way through the crowd.

"Sir," Mathew called. The inspector turned and frowned at them. "Sir," Mathew repeated. "This is Lady Emily Manling. I have been tasked by her mother, Lady Constance Manling, with escorting her to Sir John Thornton's home. I believe there should be someone here to meet us."

"You have proof?" The inspector held out his hand. Mathew put down Emily's case and pulled the letter from his belt, handing it over. The inspector read it and looked again at Mathew. "You are one Mathew Worth, from Seabreeze, clerk and second overseer for that estate."

"Yes sir." Mathew handed the man the set of parchments. The inspector leafed through them and nodded.

"You were travelling on your master's business."

"Yes."

"And that is?"

"My master's business."

"Aye, but there is no one here to meet you, as far as I know. I suggest you get a cab. It is getting late." The inspector handed the documents back and waved for one of the porters to open the barrier.

***

Mathew watched the cabby hold his cab door open. The man was only just presentable, though his horses were in good shape. The carriage had, by the look of it, once been a lord's transportation.

52

The faint outline of a crest could still be seen on the door. It was roomy and equipped with heavy blinds, so that the passengers could ride shielded from sights that might offend them.

Mathew offered his hand to Emily to assist her, then climbed in and slipped onto the thick leather seat opposite. He had to admit he had enjoyed the time he had spent in her company. Emily was a strange mixture of innocence and worldly knowledge. Exactly the sort of young woman his mother would have loved to be introduced to as a possible daughter-in-law. In fact, Mathew had relaxed so much in Emily's company, he nearly let his assumed persona slip. In one way, it was a good thing they were parting. When next they would meet, if they ever did, she would most likely be married. And he would be poured into an evening suit, escorting his sisters and mother. Would Emily acknowledge, or even recognise, him? Mathew bit his lip. The thought of not being honest with her did not sit well. Anyway, Mathew did not want to return to his old life, even for a small while. However, he had the feeling that he would not be able to present the case on behalf of the working-class people unless he did.

It was early evening; the streets of Hitsmine were full of people. The smell of the horses, unwashed humanity and factory fumes filtered into the carriage. Harsh metallic whistles from factories and foundries could be heard, signalling a change in shifts. Progress was slow, and the curses of the driver frequent. The vehicle made its way down Cross Street and into Halstock Square, on the far side of which stood Sir John's large town house. It was not a long journey, but this evening it was unending.

"What's that?" Emily sat forward and put up the window-blind. Her eyes widened in concern.

Mathew frowned and moved along the seat, slipping the sash on the other blind. The carriage had been forced to the side of the road by the pressure of the crowd. An icy chill began to creep up Mathew's spine. *Dear Goddess, it could not be.* "It's a protest march of some kind." He opened the window and leaned out, shouting up to the driver. "Turn us round, return to the station. I will pay you double." A voice in the crowd jeered at him. The cry was echoed by others and the mob surged towards the carriage.

"Can't, sir," the driver called. The vehicle lurched, driven forward by the mass of people.

"Try, man, we don't want to get caught up in this." Mathew ducked back into the carriage as someone threw a stone. It hit the side of the vehicle and rattled down onto the cobbles below the wheels. Mathew shut the window and closed the bolt across the door, quickly doing the same on the other. The carriage rocked, went forward, then stopped suddenly. Emily squealed and slipped on her seat from left to right.

"It will be all right," Mathew said, certain that it was anything but.

"Did you say protest?"

"Feelings have been running high here." *That was an understatement.* Mathew put the pack on his back and moved over to her side. The shouts outside gained in volume and pitch.

"Damn it, man! Get us out of here!" Mathew bellowed again at the driver. A horse screamed in pain and the vehicle dropped suddenly on its left forward side. The wheel had snapped. Emily and Mathew slid across the seat in a tumble of arms and legs. Voices shouted abuse. Faces loomed in the left-side windows, twisted with hate. Fists hammered the carriage and hands tore at the door.

Emily screamed and Mathew pulled her roughly to his side. The faces vanished. A bugle sounded, then — silence. Mathew and Emily scrambled to their feet close to the right-side door. There was barely enough room to get out, but the other side would plunge them into the middle of the riot.

"The militia?" Emily asked.

"Oh, Goddess, they can't!" Mathew's words were lost in the rising crescendo of horses' hooves on the cobbles. A horse and rider blocked out the light from the left-side window of the carriage. "We have to get out of here. Take your cloak off."

"My valise. My mother's letters. I was supposed to insure that they were delivered."

That damn cloak was a cleft stick. Mathew was sure the rioters would see the cloak as belonging to a member of the gentry. On the other hand, the militia could see it as a sign of looting. The thought of a sabre slashing down across Emily's beautiful face made him shudder. "We stand a better chance if you are not wearing it; leave the case — it will only hamper you." He reached for the carriage door and slipped the bolt. Emily nodded and let the garment fall from her shoulders. Mathew took her hand in his. "Stay close to me."

54

Mathew climbed up the sloping floor and jumped out, dragging Emily with him. They struggled down the outside of the carriage and fought through the seething crowd into the square. The large cobbled area, with its gurgling fountain, had become a battleground. Knots of mounted militia were trying to force the protesters from the square. Sabres rose, then slashed down, coming back up slick with blood. Emily screamed. A soldier was dragged from his horse in front of her, his head pulped with a hammer, sabre taken.

The windows of the houses round the square were smashed, doors kicked down and contents looted. Emily was crying. She clung with both hands to Mathew's arm as he forced a way towards a small alley. He glanced back at their carriage. It was partly ablaze, Emily's case torn open by looters, the contents trailed across the cobbles. The carriage crashed to the ground, crushing the bodies of those killed and wounded by the first pass of the militia.

A rioter rammed into Mathew's side. Mathew pushed him away. The man's hand tore across Mathew's chest, trying to grab hold of him. His fingers tore loose the papers in Mathew's belt. *No. Goddess, no.* Both tumbled out. Mathew grabbed for them, but caught only one, and thrust it into the neck of his shirt.

Suddenly they were in the alley and clear of the horror. "Run, Emily!" *They had a chance to get clear.* He glanced at her. She was dishevelled, her chest heaving with fear, the skirt of her expensive walking dress rent, but she was whole. They ran side by side down the alley. At the end, blocking their way, stood an unyielding line of the local constabulary, enforced by a row of mounted militia. Mathew slithered to a stop, the hobnails in his boots sparking on the street cobbles. He slipped his arm round Emily.

"That's a sensible lad," said a sergeant in the front line of police.

Mathew put his free hand up to show he had no weapon. The sergeant nodded and waved his nightstick.

"Don't say anything," Mathew whispered. They were quickly bundled through the line and into a barred wagon along with others, some of whom were badly hurt.

"But we have to explain." Emily slumped out of Mathew's arms and to the floor. She drew her legs up and curled her

55

arms round them. Her eyes, round with emotion, looked pleadingly up at Mathew.

He crouched before her, taking her face in his hands. "They won't believe you, Emily. Listen to me, trust me in this. Be silent, leave this to me. I promise you I will get us out of this, but don't say anything. They are looking for an excuse to— "

A woman screamed, as if to emphasise his words; a soldier was dragging her towards their prison. He hit her sharply across the face and threw her like a sack of grain into the wagon. Mathew knew he had to hide his own fear. He had to be strong so Emily could be. But he could guess at what was awaiting them, and it pounded at the back of his mind.

Emily began to cry, and Mathew kissed her. She tried to pull away, then returned the kiss for a moment and buried her head in his shoulder. Mathew could taste the salt of her tears on his lips. His heart thudded for a moment in response to Emily's returned kiss. The paper that had been torn from his waistband was the letter from her mother. He had no way to prove who Emily was. She had no bond contract papers or travel papers; she had never needed any.

CHAPTER SEVEN

A plume of white mist hissed from one of the steam-driven cranes that had been brought up to the crash. The whole area resembled a building site. It thronged with men, horses and machines, picking away at the remains of the northern express like a flock of crows. It was very different from when the first trains arrived two days ago. The train for Hitsmine blew its whistle, signalling its intention to depart shortly to any and all stragglers.

"That was the last of the injured on board," Constance said.

"Yes, and you will soon be with your daughter," Pugh said.

"And what will you do, sir?"

"Me. There is still the threat against Lord Calvinward. My orders were to provide protection for him until the matter is resolved."

They were waiting for Calvinward to join them. Pugh looked back down the track towards the site where the remains of Calvinward's private carriage had been. The heavy undercarriage had been removed and the debris sifted through. Only two bodies had been found. One was the young soldier on duty, the other, Hotspur. Of the priest and Claire there had been no sign. She had vanished as swiftly as she had appeared.

"You will be in the capital." Lady Constance smiled up at him, and her hand touched his arm.

Pugh placed his hand on hers and returned the smile. Their friendship was well on the way to becoming something else. He started to frame an answer to her question, but Calvinward interrupted them.

"There you both are. I have made arrangements for Hotspur's body to be returned home. We need to send word to Elizabeth when we reach Hitsmine."

"Poor Elizabeth. I know how it feels to lose a husband that is your world. And of course there are consequences for your party, Joshua, having lost its leader."

Pugh coughed, trying to hide his snort of amusement at Constance's statement, but from the glance Calvinward gave him, he had not succeeded. Clive Hotspur was certainly not Elizabeth's world. He wondered if Hotspur's death would have any effect on her at all, save for that of having to wear mourning.

"Indeed," Calvinward said, "but she will have you and

her family to support her. As to the party, they will be huddled in corners as soon as the news is out, plotting on whom they intend to support."

"You will be standing," Pugh said.

"Of course he will," Constance replied.

"It is not a position I have ever wanted, but if offered the post..." It was the standard stock answer of any politician in his position, but Pugh wondered if, for Calvinward, it was the truth. During the last few days, Pugh had seen glimpses of the man behind the politician's mask and found he rather liked the man, and had begun to consider him a friend. Calvinward was very good at the game of politics, but his end goal, Pugh had come to realise, was not that of his fellows.

"So, to Hitsmine," Pugh said.

"Yes, we will be there soon after dark. Elizabeth, I hope that young man, Mathew, is still in the city, or at least left an address at which I can contact him," Calvinward said.

"You want to question him about the priest?" Pugh asked.

No, not really. I doubt our red-robed friend's path will cross with ours again, and if it does, he will be suffering from selective memory loss. Besides, he didn't actually do anything wrong. In fact, pulling the cord could be seen as saving lives. No, I want to talk to Mathew about that petition he presented me, and what he saw during his travels collecting the signatures. It could be useful in the days to come. He is also wasting his talents and needs a focus."

"I will inquire as soon as I am able. Do you mean to take him on in a junior capacity? He is working-class, is he not?" Lady Constance said.

"Talent has nothing to do with class, Lady Constance, and I think Mathew is not quite who he seems to be. He is clever; his working class accent was nearly perfect."

"Oh, I see."

Pugh offered his hand to Constance to assist her into the train. She smiled and allowed him to help her board.

***

Before a dozen leagues were covered, the train's rocking to-and-fro had lulled Pugh to sleep. He dreamed: fractured images; faces; flames and cries. Again the plunge down the icy pass; this time Constance was at his side. Not Claire. No, it was not right. He woke with a start. The train had stopped.

58

"We are here, Pugh," Lady Constance said.

"You intend to take a cab right away to Sir John's?" Calvinward asked.

"Yes, and you?"

"I will stay with Pugh and his men here at the hotel. I need to get in touch with my people and party. Give Emily my regards, and say I will see her again soon."

"Constance, it is you?" A man's voice came from the shadows.

Pugh's fingers went to the polished handle of his pistol, and he looked round for his men. Corporals Perkins and Jones moved forward, signalling the rest to circle round the edge of the platform.

"Sir John, this is most unexpected. Lord Calvinward, Captain Avinguard, this is Sir John Thornton," Constance said, her hand going out to Sir John. "Is Emily with you?"

"Constance, gentlemen, please let us go into the Station Hotel..." Sir John did not finish what he was trying to say. A small number of men could be seen running from the main body of the station. Those in front were fairly well-dressed and had the expression of hunting dogs in sight of their quarry.

"Lord Calvinward, a moment sir, your feelings at this time," the leading man shouted.

"Damn press!" Pugh snapped, and signed for his men to form a barrier between the approaching reporters and his charges.

"Please, before you say anything, please, we must go into the hotel." Sir John caught hold of Constance's hand and almost dragged her towards the hotel.

"Sir John, where is Emily?"

"We best do as Sir John suggests," Pugh said.

Calvinward nodded in agreement, reluctantly, turned away from the assembled press and walked quickly towards the Station Hotel.

"Get them out of here and set up a guard on the hotel, Sergeant Perkins," Pugh said. Perkins grinned at his promotion, saluted and began to bellow orders.

Pugh opened the hotel door and strode after the fading figures of Calvinward, Constance and Sir John. He reached the open door to a private parlour as Sir John's wife took Constance's hand and led her to a seat in front of the glowing fire. The lamps were lit, but turned down. That, and the glow from the fire, made the room feel small.

"Please come in, Captain," Sir John said.

Pugh entered and noted that in the room, waiting for the newly arrived party, were a fresh-faced lieutenant in militia green and a pot-bellied police inspector in deep blue. They stood either side of the fireplace like bookends. Something had happened. The press were on to it, and Sir John wanted to inform Calvinward and Lady Constance first. "What has happened?"

The decanter in Sir John's hand rattled, as he poured out four large brandies and handed one each to Calvinward, Pugh and Constance, keeping the fourth for himself.

"Where is Emily?" Constance asked again, her voice beginning to shake. Lady Thornton sniffed and patted Constance's arm.

Sir John coughed. "She is dead."

Pugh gasped in disbelief.

Calvinward leant back in his seat, a look of shock on his face. The militia captain and the police inspector looked anywhere but at the bereaved mother. *What the hell had happened?* How could Sir John have been so cruel? Then again, there was no kind way to tell a parent of their child's death. Lady Constance's hands opened and the brandy glass tilted. The pale gold liquid fell and spread across the polished wood floor, glistening in the firelight. Her eyes brimmed with tears. She sat up straight, obviously struggling to hide her emotions. Why even try to hide them behind a false veneer of manners and rank? It was her child.

Calvinward rose to his feet. "What, exactly, happened?"

Pugh felt for the man. He could see in Calvinward's face the horror of someone else's plan gone out of control, turning round and destroying not only what you want to achieve, but people you know. Claire had tried to warn him, and he had ignored it. He swallowed hard and cut in before the police inspector could speak. "I can guess. There was a protest of some sort. Instead of controlling the crowd, letting them say their piece, you panicked and sent in the militia to break them up. And all hell broke loose."

"What of the young man with her? Pugh, you should have agreed to send one of your men," Calvinward said accusingly.

"The young man died, we believe, trying to protect her. From what we can ascertain, the cab carrying Lady Emily and the young man was trapped on the edge of the square. It was attacked by the rioters after the first charge."

"They saw it as belonging to the enemy," Pugh said.

"Yes, it was overturned, looted and burnt. Lady Emily's belongings were strewn across the square, and this," said the police inspector, pulling a soiled letter from his pocket, "was found later."

"It was the letter I gave Mathew," Constance said, her voice barely a whisper. "My daughter ..."

"She and the young man must have been attacked by the mob. Their bodies were found under the burnt-out carriage. From their position, the young man was protecting her either from attack, or the coach as it was thrown over," the young officer finished for the police inspector.

"Where are they?" Calvinward asked, looking towards Sir John.

"Their coffins are at my home."

"I would like to see my daughter," Constance said, standing. She struggled to keep poised and dignified.

"That wouldn't be advisable. Both were badly burned," Sir John said.

"You are certain of the identification?" Calvinward asked.

"It couldn't be any other. We found a diamond brooch on the remains of a cloak by the young woman's body. Besides, it has been two days. If they had been swept up in the arrests, they would have tried to send word to you or me," Sir John said, his voice dropping to a harsh whisper.

"I would like to retire," Lady Constance said, looking to Lady Thornton.

Sir John's wife nodded. She gently took Constance's arm. "Of course, we have had a room made ready."

***

Pugh watched Calvinward hug his broken arm to his side and look down into the spitting fire. "I want to know every detail of what happened, so I can understand what we could be facing in the next few days."

"You are not the only one," Pugh said. He helped himself to another brandy. "Milord." He offered the decanter to Calvinward.

"My thanks, but no — I want a clear head."

"Of course."

"Getting drunk will not solve anything, Pugh."

61

"No, it doesn't. You have to accept responsibility for what you have done at some point, and accept the consequences," Pugh replied, and walked back and sat in the chair Constance had vacated.

"We three were not — "

"Responsible? In a way, we were: we all agreed to send Emily here ahead of us. Lady Constance believed her daughter's nerves wouldn't stand the continued strain of being at the crash site; I agreed to find someone to escort her; you were happy to let her go. Did you know of the situation here, Milord?"

"No one could have," Sir John blustered, and tossed off the last of his brandy, his gaze darting from the young lieutenant to the police inspector. Both looked uncomfortable, the young officer in particular.

"Details?" Calvinward asked again.

"We have given them," the police inspector said.

"Have you?" Pugh said. "A riot does not just happen. A town forum should have had some idea of what was happening on its own doorstep."

"I agree," Joshua said.

The lieutenant cleared his throat. His action brought a glare from the police inspector. "Milord, my orders were overruled by the civilian authorities."

"Ouch, boy, how did you get yourself into that ball of hot fat?" Pugh gave a bitter laugh.

The young officer glanced at Pugh, looking for support. He nodded and the young man began to speak. "We had been ordered to *assist* the police when it became clear that the protest was far larger than was expected."

"So you knew it was going to happen." Calvinward had sat forward, his eyes hooded. He had one finger pressed to his lips, which were vibrating slightly. Had he expected events to boil over, or had a hand in the riot? No. The man Pugh had come to know wouldn't have. Would the politician? Had Hotspur, with the help of a third party? It was the sort of thing he was capable of. *Goddess*, if that man had had agents stirring up trouble, he had left Calvinward with a mess that could tear the Forum Unionist Party apart at the seams.

"Been building for weeks, no matter what we did: damage to machines; increased sickness; orders delayed through slowed production. All the normal ways the working-class make their displeasure known. Some of us were addressing it. I personally was negotiating a small pay rise. I could afford it, and the shift restructuring I had been working on was about to go into operation. I try to treat my workers as people. Problem is, some don't." Sir John sighed and moved to the window. He pulled one of the large drapes and peered out into the street.

"You are not expecting more trouble?" Pugh asked.

"No, the whole event has shocked the town. Things are almost shut down," the police inspector said. The sweat on his face began to gather along his brow line. Pugh was sure it had nothing to do with the heat of the room.

"Continue." Calvinward addressed the young lieutenant.

The young man nodded his head and ignored the glare of the police officer. It was plain whatever agreement they had come to previously had been abandoned. "As I said, my orders were countermanded."

"It was getting out of hand. I did as I saw fit," the police inspector blustered.

"You relayed orders to my men on the west side of the square to leave their line of containment and move forward, weapons drawn. In fact, you ordered them to clear the square with force. I wanted to – intended to – hold a perimeter. There I could filter the crowd after it had worn itself out chanting and smashing a few windows. A few heads broken, but nothing more."

"It was getting bad in there. My men couldn't control them."

"Because you have been doing the employers' dirty work for months – still are, with regards to the prisoners. Rubber stamping deportations to prison work houses for the Goddess knows how many, without proper conviction or recourse."

"Against the law, there, inspector, sending orders in the name of a militia officer. Besides the other matters," Pugh said. "You tried to get control of your men, Lieutenant?"

"Yes, but by that time they were fighting for their lives. I managed to stop the troops on the other sides going in. It could have been worse. I think all parties are reeling from it, sir."

The police inspector swallowed hard and looked at Sir John. Sir John dropped the drape and turned round to face the inspector. "I warned you, you wouldn't be able to wriggle free this time."

The police inspector mopped his brow with his sleeve. From the expression on his face, the man knew his days were numbered.

"Now, if I could have the use of someone's writing hand, I have much to do," Calvinward said.

"I thought you would; I have my secretary waiting. Also, one of Hotspur's people is here, man called Colliridge. He has been asking to see you as soon as you return."

Calvinward frowned, then slowly nodded. One of Hotspur's political agents, Pugh guessed, looking for a new employer

***

Calvinward and Sir John were discussing what should be done. Pugh looked at Calvinward. The man waved his hand in dismissal. Pugh felt his hackles rise and opened his mouth to reply, but thought better of it. Calvinward did not mean it. The man was mentally consumed with the task he believed only he could solve. He knew Calvinward could not. The country would be affected by the consequences of this riot for years and no amount of politicking could change that. He left the room, brandy glass still in hand.

"Sir!" Perkins snapped to attention, saluting his superior.

"At ease, Perkins," Pugh said, and returned the salute. He looked down the corridor towards two of his other men standing by a third, who kept to the shadows. It must be this Colliridge, the political agent of Hotspur's, waiting to see Calvinward. "Rota done, Sergeant?"

"Aye, sir."

"And which, pray, is my room?"

"Number eight, sir, first landing."

Pugh nodded.

As he turned down the long passage leading to his room, he saw Lady Thornton saying goodnight at a bedroom door. The door closed. Lady Thornton pulled her fine silk shawl up her shoulders and walked across the hall to her own room.

Pugh made his way down the passage until he was level with the room Lady Thornton had left. He raised his other hand to knock, then let it drop. He doubted Lady Constance would wish to speak to him. He had refused to detail any of his soldiers, and had suggested Mathew escort Lady Emily. He had killed the two young people, as surely as if he had put a pistol to their heads. He wanted to explain, to tell her he understood what she was going through. He raised his hand again and rapped on the door.

"Yes?"

"It's Pugh. Captain Avinguard." The door slowly opened. Pugh stepped inside, closing the door behind him. Constance was reseating herself in a large wing-backed chair. A small lamp on the table beside her cast shadows over her tear-stained face. He stood half a dozen paces in front of her, swirling the brandy round his glass.

"Is that your first, or your last?" Constance said.

"Not the first, and as to the last, not sure yet."

"What can I do for you, Pugh?"

"I have come to say..."

"That you are sorry? It wasn't your fault. You didn't kill my daughter and that young man."

"Didn't I?"

"You made a suggestion. I agreed. If you killed her, then I did too."

The memory of Claire blaming herself for the death of their child rose in Pugh's mind. "Don't—"

"Don't blame myself? I was her mother!" Constance snapped. She stood up.

"Yes, you were, but you can't take the blame for this. You did not cause it." Pugh stepped forward and placed his glass on the table.

"Forgive me, Pugh, but you can't understand."

He did understand. He had to make her believe that he did. Pugh took hold of Constance's hand and held it to his chest. "I do. You see, I had a son once. I only saw him a handful of times. Never even held him. He was born at the station up on Coot's Pass. He came too soon, but he was strong, least at the beginning. So I never thought to take much notice of him, believing we would have all the time in the world. I was too busy. Too caught up in my duty."

"The station was under attack, was it not?" Constance said, her hand turning in his.

"Yes, but how long would it have taken to hold him?"

Constance moved closer and placed her other hand on his chest. "He died in the retreat from the pass."

"Yes, he was too small. The cold— even adults succumbed."

65

"And your wife, Lady Claire, blamed you?"

"No. That's the pity of it. She never did. She said she understood why I had acted so. Understood my duty to everyone was more important. She said it was her fault: she was his mother. The guilt destroyed her, but you are aware of that." *A half-truth as always.*

"I am so sorry."

Pugh let go of Constance's hand and placed his fingers under her chin. He titled her tear-stained face up and looked deep into her eyes. "I don't want to see another beautiful, proud and clever woman I have come to care about destroy herself because of misplaced guilt."

Constance sobbed. Pugh let go of her chin and took her in his arms. Her fingers knotted in the fabric of his tunic. He could feel the warmth of her body against him. It was intoxicating. He kissed her, relishing the softness of her lips. Constance recoiled slightly, and Pugh began to stammer out an apology. *Fool. Now wasn't the time.* Constance brought a finger up, placing it against his lips. She took his hand and turned it palm upwards, kissing it gently.

"Constance, I don't think—" *Yes, he did. He wanted to, very much.*

"Please Pugh, don't think. I don't want to think any more this evening." Constance leaned forward and kissed him full on the mouth.

Her passion at first surprised him. It was her grief, he told himself; she wanted to be held, to be consoled. There was nothing wrong in holding her and returning her kiss. He would leave in a little while.

He asked, "Do you want me to leave? I think it might be for the best. Our friendship is too important to me."

She did not answer, merely took his hand and led him to her bed.

In the dark afterwards, Pugh lay still, listening to Constance's breathing. It slowed, and she slipped into sleep. He remembered the touch of her white flesh under his fingertips and the warmth of his skin against hers; the rasp of the silk sheets; her cry when her passion reached its peak. His own release was no less powerful. He, too, had cried out, but could not recall what name he had spoken. For the act was a mirror of his dream on the train, Constance's shape and form blending in his mind into another. Pugh could not separate them.

66

He lay there for a while longer, trying to reason the consequences of his actions, but could not. He had wanted this. So, it seemed, had Constance. All he could see in his mind was the reproachful look in a pair of sea-green eyes.

Pugh rose and dressed. He walked back to the side of the bed. He reached out and pulled a lock of Constance's dark hair from across her face. Constance stirred in her sleep and turned over. He let the soft length of hair drop. "I am sorry." But to whom he was saying the words, and for what reason, he was not sure.

CHAPTER EIGHT

The voices thundered in Oracle's mind. She ran into the carriage, screaming. Pugh shouted. The others in the carriage shouted. She watched their mouths move, not understanding anything save that this moment was important. The sound of Pugh's pistol firing stopped her scream. She had heard such sounds before and knew it meant death. "Death in the dark. Crash. Smash. Train. Track."

One man stumbled forwards, looking from her to Pugh, to the figure of the priest slumping to the floor. "By the Goddess!" His words became lost in the high-pitched squeal of metal.

The lamps hanging from the ceiling tilted, spraying oil. Oracle lost her footing. The world turned upside down. Another man fell over the back of one of the chairs, doing a forward roll over the seat and to the floor. The chair followed, trapping him. His legs moved, then went still.

She slid towards the far side of the carriage. She waited for the touch of Pugh's hand, but it never came. The carriage toppled and the black shape of the bogies shut out the newly risen moon. Oracle screamed in pain. Her hands went to her right side, under the rib cage, and closed round a long shard of glass imbedded in her flesh. Bile rose in her throat. She spewed out the contents of her stomach and passed out.

Oracle awoke rolled into a tight ball against the oak sideboard. It had stopped the iron undercarriage from crushing her. The dark mass overhead groaned. The wreckage began to slip. The voices in Oracle's head began, slowly at first, then louder and louder. She brought her blood-stained hands up to cover her ears. The gesture did not stop the words. *Move quickly, go. Leave this place. East, you know where. Go.*

She tried to uncurl and felt the glass fragment in her side move. A fresh warm trickle began to run down her hip. Oracle slowly got onto all fours. She sat back and screamed in pain.

Fight it. Don't black out again. Not yet.

Oracle pulled at her shirt and wrapped the tails of it round the length of glass sticking out of her side.

"I am me. I did it. You said you understood. Loved me, despite. I want to find my home in you." She was not sure if it was the voices, or the woman she had been, speaking. She stumbled up and trod on the hand of a man lying in the wreckage. He cried out. Oracle ignored him and staggered from the carriage's remains. She crossed the ditch and scrambled up the grass embankment, onto a small narrow path.

"Sails on the water, swords in the air. Hack, slash. White flesh on silk. Rough hands, not lady's hands. Broken bodies. Accept the consequences. Mountain home. Alive not dead. Guns in the air. Toby seek. One step, two steps, go there. Safe there, know me there." *Which me.* The thought rose to the front of her mind. A thought created not by the words, but by the woman she had been, or, perhaps, what she was becoming.

On through the night she stumbled. The small path reached the tree line. The beginnings of the wilder forests began closing in. Suddenly the path widened. It had joined a dirt road wide enough to take a carriage. The second moon, Caresight, rose. It hung low on the horizon; its silver beams trickled through the trees lining the road.

To the right, she could see the shadowy shape of a bridge with the dark shadows of houses on the other side. A small, sleep-wrapped village, unaware of the chaos being enacted a few leagues away. Not that way: she turned left and headed away from the settlement.

Dawn came. Puddles steamed in the track. The smell of damp pine wafted from the trees. Oracle stopped for a moment to regain her breath. She was at the gates to an estate. Oracle tried to walk down the drive. She stumbled and fell to her knees. Pain exploded in her injured side. She screamed and dropped onto her left side on the ground. The voices were begging, promising the woman she had once been all manner of things if she would move.

She shook her head. "I am sorry."

"Nay, don't say that."

She sobbed and looked up; silhouetted against the morning sun stood a man. He was dressed in a tweed hunting suit that had seen better days. Over his arm he carried an old-fashioned long musket. Oracle could smell the faint scent of spent black powder as he uncurled the shoulder strap and slipped the gun onto his back.

"Hack, slash, white flesh on silk, rough hands, not lady's hands. Fight for him. Alive not dead. End it, turn the world on its head, religion and politics. Good man. Goddess' sacrifice. Toby bite."

"Gently, shush." The man got down on one knee. He pushed away her hands from her wound, and hissed through his teeth. "What have you been up to? Let's get you up to the house and see to you."

The man carefully picked her up and began to walk down the drive. The smell of him was familiar and comforting. Images flooded her mind, fragments of a past surfacing from the madness of possible futures. The man clicked his tongue and spoke comforting words, which hovered on the edge of her barely conscious mind.

A small, wire-haired hunting dog ran towards them, barking. "Back off, Toby," the man said, sharply. The dog stopped, barked again and fell in at the man's heels. The drive widened to form a large space at the rear of the house. Part timber, part brick, the building squatted with an air of total comfort in its wooded surroundings. The man kicked hard at the main rear door.

"By the Goddess, where are you!" the man bellowed, and kicked harder, then turned away. He began walking towards the side of the house by the stables. The small dog barked and ran from the man to the door and back again.

"What is all the — Milord!"

"There you are, Mrs Turner. Hot water, bandages and my medical bag," the man ordered, and strode past the rotund woman into the hall.

"White flesh on silk. Rough hands, not lady's hands. Carrots with the venison."

"Nay. Oh, tis the child. I thought — Mandy, Thomas!"

"Did you think it was a tramp?" His lordship began to climb the stairs.

"It could have been. Get the child to a bed, and I will send Thomas for the doctor."

"No, that you will not do, for word would soon get out that it is here and who it was."

Mrs Turner frowned and stepped ahead to open the door to his lordship's room. "It! You call your own child an it? She needs a doctor. Shame on you, Milord."

"No doctor. And I do know something of medicine, you know. Hurry with my bag."

"She is not one of the estate animals."

Sir Henry ignored his housekeeper's muttering and

placed her on the bed. She reached out her hand and touched his face. He caught it and kissed it. She smiled and tried to speak, but the pain turned the words into a scream. Tendrils of agony tore through her body. Even though the voices tried to make her stay conscious, they could not.

***

"Your bag, Milord."

"Thank you, Thomas."

She had passed out. *Thank the Goddess*. He had to act, and quickly, else she would die. *Bloody well damn it*. Part of him wanted her to: little of his daughter remained in the creature.

Mrs Turner walked to the other side of the bed and heaved the pillows out from under Claire's head. She signalled for Sir Henry to lift Claire, so she could turn down the covers. It was no bloody time to be thinking of saving expensive bed coverings.

"If you are going to play doctor, you need to be able to see what you are doing and not have your patient sinking into a goose-feather quilt."

Sir Henry lifted and she removed the covers. He laid Claire onto the stark white of the bed. His heart lurched in his breast. Her face was burned brown by the sun and her hair bleached near-white. Her features were drawn and heightened by emaciation.

Thomas placed a table at Sir Henry's elbow, on which lay his black bag.

"Hot water and linen," Sir Henry reminded Mrs Turner. "And blast it, woman, it is already damn well hot in here. We don't need a fire."

"Yes, we do. We will need more hot water than we can carry from the kitchen. Mandy, where are you, girl?

Sir Henry nodded, reluctantly acknowledging that she was correct. He began to inspect the seat of Oracle's wound. He did not wish to attempt to remove the blood-soaked shirt at this point.

Sir Henry turned and opened his bag. "Here, Thomas." He reached in and took hold of a cloth-wrapped bundle of surgical instruments. "Have these boiled and brought back in the hot water. Also, I want you to go to the ditch that runs along the side of the house. I need some clown's woundwort, as much as you can find."

"Bit late in the season, Milord."

"I know, but it is best fresh. The ointment is too diluted for a wound like this. The glass is high, I think — can't be sure until we remove the shirt. Nor how deep. If in the liver, we have a chance; if it is in the gut, there will be very little hope."

Even as he said the words, Sir Henry did not want to think on that. A stomach wound was a painful, lingering way to die. He looked at the dull blue bottle of opium on the table. All that was needed was a fraction too much. A soft moan drew his gaze back to the bed. Claire was stirring. "Gently, I need you to be quiet." He took hold of the bottle of opium. The blue glass felt cold, like death. Should he do it? No. Not yet.

"Schemes, plans and consequences. Block out the sun, hurts, confuses us. Guns above. Alive not dead. We am sorry."

"Dear Goddess, never say that, never."

Thomas came back into the room and carefully placed a bunch of clown's woundwort on the table. The reddish-pink hoods of the flowers were near the end of their life, but the leaves were plentiful and plump with growth. "Let me help, Sir Henry."

"Thank you, Thomas, if you could lift." Sir Henry pointed towards Claire, whose hands were weaving above her head. Thomas gently lifted Claire by her shoulders. Sir Henry pulled her chin down to open her mouth and poured in a spoonful of the opium syrup. Mrs Turner and Mandy came into the room, the former carrying a large bucket of steaming water, the latter a pile of crisp, white linen.

"The wash bowl off the stand, Mrs Turner," Sir Henry ordered.

"Are those instruments ready?"

"Cook was sending one of her lasses with—" Mrs Turner's words were cut off by the clatter of feet down the hall. A small kitchen maid ran into the room, a pan of boiling water held at arm's length, the damp splashes on her thick, white apron testament to her hurried journey.

The girl handed the pan to Mrs Turner, who placed it on the table next to Sir Henry's bag.

"Thank you." Sir Henry took off his jacket. He slipped the cufflinks out of his shirt and rolled up the sleeves. "Mandy, this is not the place for you."

"Sir, begging your pardon, but you will need more than one pair of hands," Mandy said.

He had no time to argue. *Be it on her own head if she faints*

72

or gets the vapours. "Strip the leaves off the clown's woundwort. Wash, then place them in the mortar and bruise the leaves enough to make the juice form. Mrs Turner, I want you to be ready with wads of linen when I remove the glass. Thomas, get ready to hold it down."

"I wish you would stop calling your child an it," Mrs Turner said.

"What do you want me to call it?"

"The child has a Goddess-given name."

Yes, she did. But, if he allowed himself to say it, he doubted he would be able to do what needed to be done. *Triple damn them all to hell for doing this to my child.*

Claire tried to move, and Thomas knelt on the bed and pinned her arms down. Sir Henry cut at the shirt round the glass. The bloody fabric crackled. "A damp cloth, Mrs Turner." He took the cloth and wiped away the blood, spreading the stain. Claire's muscles tensed at his touch. She began to fight against the pressure of Thomas' hands.

"Dear Goddess," Mandy whispered.

Sir Henry took a wad of linen and wrapped it round the glass. Taking a deep breath, he took hold of it and pulled. Claire screamed. She struggled for a moment, then collapsed. Her head rolled to one side. Thomas sobbed and let go of her arms. Sir Henry's hand shook as he placed the cloth-wrapped glass on the table. He resisted the urge to throw it across the room.

Mrs Turner pushed at the lips of the wound with a lump of damp linen. A red stain sluggishly filtered down the threads of the fabric. Sir Henry motioned for her to remove the cloth. He plucked a slender length of steel from the pan and gently probed the wound. Nothing. No glass left in that he could find. The blood began to flow faster, soaking his fingers.

"The leaves, Mandy."

The girl handed the mortar over to him.

Sir Henry took a handful of the leaves and pressed them against the wound. Mrs Turner applied a thick wad of linen and held it in place. "Crush some more, Mandy."

Sir Henry rinsed his hands in the bowl. The soap froth on the surface of the water turned pink. A small spark of hope began to grow in his breast. The wound was indeed high, so with luck it should heal. The problem would be infection. He took the length of cord and threaded it through a needle. Mrs

Turner removed the linen. The leaves fell away, littering the sheet with vein imprints of red. Already the wound was a thick line of congealing blood. Sir Henry swiftly sewed the wound shut and washed it again, applying more of the leaves. "When I change the bandages in the morning, I will apply the ointment." Sir Henry bound the wound and stepped back from the bed. He ran his blood-stained hands through his thinning hair and closed his eyes. *The Goddess help me.* He had done what he could for now.

Standing with his back to the roaring fire, Sir Henry quietly watched Mrs Turner wash Claire and put a nightshirt onto her small body. Mandy ran a comb through Claire's fine, near-white locks. *It was too much.* Sir Henry gave a sob and started to say her name; he pressed his clenched fist to his mouth to stop the words.

Mrs Turner lifted a tea pot from the table, which had been repositioned near a chair on the left-hand side of the bed. Sir Henry blinked. It was a bitter, familiar scene. His late wife had lain like this, with the chair and table set the same.

"I will keep watch." Sir Henry moved toward the chair.

"Not alone," a familiar, but unexpected, voice said from the bedroom door. "It seems I have arrived none too soon."

Sir Henry turned, and there stood Lady Elizabeth Hotspur. She was stripping off a fine pair of dove-grey gloves and handing them to Mrs Turner.

The housekeeper took them. "I will make sure your room is ready, and the quarters for your maid."

"Thank you, Mrs Turner."

"Elizabeth, it's Claire." Sir Henry stepped towards Elizabeth, his arms outstretched. He had forgotten she had telegraphed she was coming. Claire's plight had driven everything else from his thoughts. But he was glad she was here. Elizabeth understood.

laire's movements woke Sir Henry. He reached for a bell on the table and rang it, bellowing, "Elizabeth, Mrs Turner, Thomas, dear Goddess, I need you!"

"Me, Oracle, both."

Claire was burning with fever. Sir Henry lifted her from the bed and carried her to a tin bath, lined with a large amount of red wool fabric. He placed her in the bath.

Elizabeth ran into the room. Her paisley shawl trailed off her right shoulder and her lace nightcap was askew. She picked up one of the buckets filled with cold water and poured it over Claire. "Thomas, refill it." She waved the empty bucket at the young man standing at the door. Elizabeth lifted another container, splashing water down her front. "Henry, more feverfew."

"Not working— I need to try something else." Sir Henry got to his feet and crossed to the table.

"You can't be feeding the child that."

"It works, according to Doctor Chambers' article." He came back to Claire's side with a small linen bag. Reaching into the bag, he pulled out a mould-encrusted apple and slice of bread. It was a risk, but he was out of options. "Thomas, a glass of water."

The young man set down the bucket and moved swiftly to obey his master.

"Dr Chambers had only tested this mould on animals and criminals, or so you said," Elizabeth retorted, brushing the wet hair away from Claire's eyes.

Sir Henry took his pocket knife and scraped the mould off into the glass of water Thomas held. "Pinch her nose." He pulled Claire's slack mouth open.

Elizabeth began to say something, but thought better of it and did as she was told.

Sir Henry poured the liquid into Claire's mouth and massaged her throat to make her swallow. *Goddess, no.* He could not feel Claire's pulse. The glass fell from his hand. He slumped down in front of the fire, all his conviction and strength gone.

Elizabeth took hold of Claire's shoulders and shook her. "Don't you dare, young lady, I will not have it. Breathe, by Goddess, breathe!" She stopped shaking Claire and hit her. Elizabeth's fist slammed down right on the lump of scar tissue

75

in the centre of Claire's breast bone. Again, she struck Claire. A whoosh of air hissed out of Claire's mouth, and the pulse in her neck fluttered. Claire began to breathe. It was ragged, but she was breathing. The enormity of what she had done struck Elizabeth. She sat back and began to sob.

***

Sounds from the bed disturbed Elizabeth's sleep. She shifted her position in the chair and rubbed her eyes. On the bed, Claire was attempting to sit up. Sir Henry moved to the bedside and placed his hand on Claire's forehead, keenly aware of Elizabeth's questioning gaze. Claire's skin was cool. Relief flooded through him: the fever had broken.

"We will bathe you and make you comfortable. Clean sheets, yes," Elizabeth said.

"Thank you. Sails on the water, time," Claire said, and bit her top lip. A look of frustration crossed her face.

Sir Henry stiffened. "Rest. Please, you are in no state to move on." He exchanged glances with Elizabeth.

"Hard to think. So much in my head." Claire sounded annoyed.

"You are safe here, no need to worry." Elizabeth patted Claire's hand.

"I am not worried, I want to thank you, tell you I love." The pitch of Claire's voice changed. Her breathing increased. "Schemes and plans. Block out the sun. It hurts, confuses us. Guns above. Alive not dead, see the sails on the water. Turn the world on its head. Stop it go away, leave me in peace for a while."

Sir Henry felt a strange excitement in the pit of his stomach. The words were a mixture of a Glimpser's disjointed ramblings and coherent speech. "I understand. I will leave you in peace soon."

"Not you, the voices. I meant I never stopped. You, mother, Pugh. My home. My home in you. My love." She coughed. "So tired." Claire began to slip into a deep sleep.

It was impossible. The words had made sense. The voice had been that of his child, her cultured, light tones unmistakable. Elizabeth reached over and squeezed his arm. Her face was alight with joy.

***

"You wish to try and sit up today?" Mrs Turner asked. "But first, let me draw the drapes."

"No, please, the light hurts." Claire pushed back the covers from her legs. "Sit, on a chair and think. Colours on the water between the sails. White flesh on silk. Damn him!" Her fist pounded on the bed.

Sir Henry set down his breakfast cup on the mantle and sighed. Not for the first time, he wished Elizabeth was still here. The afternoon after Claire's fever had broken, a telegram had arrived. Elizabeth's husband was dead. Killed in a train crash. Sir Henry knew she was torn between her duty, family, and the events unfolding here. But, in reality, Elizabeth had no alternative. She had to return to Gateskeep. He had promised to write to her every day, informing her of Claire's progress. He had also promised to think over the proposal Elizabeth had brought from Lord Calvinward. Calvinward wanted him to return to politics and take part in the upcoming High Forum debate. The young man was playing both ends against the middle with regards to the Howorth Labour and Industry Act. And the death of Elizabeth's husband had placed Calvinward in a very awkward situation. Undoubtedly, he would be the next leader of the Forum Unionist Party. That being so, if any of his fellow members got wind of his dealings with Lord Howorth, his goose would be well and truly cooked. The two men had put their heads together and worked out a strategy to get this bill of Howorth's onto the statute books. Not the done thing at all — but what about politics was?

"You annoyed with me. Dog on the stairs." Claire smiled and allowed Mrs Turner to push a pair of slippers onto her feet.

"No, child he is not. And if that whelp is trailing mud on the carpet again ..." Mrs Turner stood and wiped her hands down her apron.

"Much mud."

A sharp, questioning bark echoed from the door.

"Toby, here," Sir Henry said. The small dog barked again and padded across the room to his master.

"Bad dog," Mrs Turner said.

"Good dog, bite him hard," Claire replied, with a small laugh. "Is annoyed, schemes and plans, alive not dead."

"I am not annoyed. I am trying to understand."

77

"What is there to understand? The child is home and remembers." Mrs Turner helped Claire across the room. Half way, Claire gazed at her reflection in the large mirror on Sir Henry's dressing table. She shook off Mrs Turner's guiding hand and moved towards it. It was as if she had not seen herself before.

Sir Henry moved towards her, excitement tightening his chest. He hoped his child had fought free of the curse she had been under. But deep in his heart, he believed it was not possible. This current state was a small schism that would soon mend.

Since his child had been trapped into her present state, Sir Henry had studied all he could about the nature of Glimpsers, and myths surrounding their origins. He knew that they were made, not born. He also knew who was responsible. Three times he had managed to foil their plans for other innocents. It did not ease the loss of his daughter, but it had given him some satisfaction.

As a man who once was a skilled politician, with an interest in all the scientific arts, he believed that much was possible for humankind to do. How mere men had warped another human being in such a way, he did not understand. His small hope that he could find out, and then reverse the procedure, had long ago been dashed. As he watched her examine her features in the mirror, he did not know what to say or do. How could he help, and if he did, would it drive her back into madness?

"Me?" Claire's hand touched the mirror.

"Oh, yes," Mrs Turner said.

Sir Henry shushed her and stood behind Claire, his hands resting lightly on her shoulders.

"Me?" Claire asked again.

"Yes, that is you."

"Eyes wrong. The light hurts them, confuses, and makes the voices stronger, fight it."

"Yes, your eyes are different." *By the Goddess.* It was light: light, or the lack of it, affected his Claire's condition. The sick room had been in semi-gloom for days, a low-burning oil lamp and the fire the only illumination. "Mrs Turner, open the drapes a fraction."

"Light hurt. Sails on the water. My hands rough not a lady's hands." Claire held up her hands, spreading the fingers.

"No, not a lady's," Sir Henry replied. A trickle of dull autumn light entered the room. Claire flinched in anticipation. "Does that hurt?"

"No." Claire dropped her hands and pouted her lips, watching her reflection in the mirror.

"A bit more, Mrs Turner." The drapes rustled and the light increased. Toby barked loudly, sensing the heightened tension in the room.

Claire squinted. "Bad, good dog, bite him hard. Guns in the air, blood on the floor. Turn the world on its head. Suffer the consequences. Open the box. Stop them. Go to Gateskeep. Politics and religion. Sails on the water. Good man. Goddess' sacrifice. Cruel man, become the enemy of all. Toby dog. Alive not dead. Alive not dead!"

The last words were shouted. Claire began to struggle in Sir Henry's embrace. It was then he noticed that the light was reflecting from the mirror right into her eyes. He spun her round, and held her head against his shoulder. She sobbed and clung to him.

"Shut the drapes," Sir Henry ordered. The room was suddenly plunged into darkness. Claire's sobs lessened, and she lifted her head from his shoulder. He looked down into Claire's tear-stained face. "I am sorry."

"No, you understand. The light. It confuses. What did I say?"

"You do not remember?" Sir Henry asked, his eyes widening.

"No, Oracle spoke, not other me, two of me. Oracle sleeps more, like other me slept before. But is still there, will always be there, needs to be there. *Father help me be the me I am now.*"

"Yes, I will help." Sir Henry hugged her.

Claire returned the embrace, her fingers curling round his arms. "When did mother die?"

* * *

Sir Henry stood in his study. This was no ordinary gentleman's study, created for a gentleman for the sole purpose of impressing his peers rather than being used. It was crowded with tables on which lay his current investigations into nature and science. The pickled remains of dissected organs stood neatly labelled on racks. His latest acquisition lay on a tray, awaiting his attention. The deconstructed brass parts of a timepiece made in Crossmire had been carefully laid out. Sir Henry was determined to understand how Crossmire could produce far more accurate clocks than any other country at present. But neither the swollen gut of a fallow deer, brass cogs, nor even the scientific periodicals that had just arrived could tempt Sir Henry's thoughts from their current track.

His daughter was different. The Glimpser in her was just below the surface, and apt to break into her conversation. The glasses he had made helped. The array of various coloured ones lying in the remains of an open package on his desk would be better, more fashionable for a lady, as well as comfortable.

Regarding her ramblings, he had started to record them in a small notebook. There was a pattern, a repetition of certain words and phrases. It was plain these were important, but to whom, Sir Henry did not know. The voices and visions no longer commanded Claire to go to the persons they were meant for. Or did they — was it him? Should he try to act on them, and if he did, what effect on the world would it have? His interpretation could be wrong. Who was the good man, who the bad? And Goddess' sacrifice. The thought of that made him shudder. Not since the last days of the Kings had blood been spilt in any chapel of the Goddess. He was torn between throwing the book on the fire and seeking to understand its contents.

Sir Henry picked up the pile of mail on his desk and began to look through the assorted envelopes. One he pulled out sharply: it was a telegram. He picked up the letter knife and sliced open the envelope. His gaze caught the name of the sender: <u>Avinguard</u>. A chill went through him as he read.

"Mrs Turner! Where is my daughter?"

***

Claire stood looking out over the lower slopes of the mountains. It was part of her nature now, the voices lapping at the edges of her mind. She did not fight it, but just let the words flow; it did not happen often. She had tried to hold them back at first, but the confusion had been unbearable. Oracle wouldn't be denied if she wished to speak.

She pushed the mop of white-gold curls back from her temple. Claire realised that it was something more than the voices that had driven her here. She had been led by the same hand that had held hers in the midst of her fever. She felt a shiver run down her spine. For all its normality, there was something about the whole event that had frightened her. Things she was certain of were not what they seemed to be. Her eyes closed and she heard again the strange, puzzling, conversation.

"Child. Can you hear me? Say that you can."

"I. hurt," Claire mumbled.

"Can you hear me?" The voice was powerful. It demanded an answer.

She wanted to speak, but her mouth was dry. Her tongue ran round her cracked lips. "I hear."

"Good. Now look at me."

"No. The light." Claire was lying. It wasn't the light. She was afraid of who– no, what – she would see.

"Do as I say, child. Look at me."

Her heart pounding, Claire slowly turned her head. To her surprise, by her side was a small woman, old, her face wrinkled and lined. Her neck was thin and vanished into thick ruffle of lace which lined her green velvet gown.

"See, I am nothing to be frightened of," the woman said. The tone of the woman's voice belied her words, Claire knew instinctively.

"No?"

"Of course not. You have fought hard against what was done to you. Far harder than the others, that is why I knew you were the one. You will help me undo a horrible wrong. My words, and the power I give through the Seer, have been hoarded like a miser's gold and not used for the good of all. It must be removed from the hands of those who have become warped and twisted with their lust for power. You must show them what they have become. Remove what remains of your predecessor from them. They must face the consequences of their actions.

"You have said it time and time again: 'I am me.' Your mantra. Yes, you are Oracle, but you are also you. You are both, and you will help me set a new course for the future, as the last Seer did the past."

The woman who had held her hand and spoken had not been real. She knew it. Her father would not have allowed a stranger to nurse his daughter. Had the woman been the result of one of Oracle's visions, twisted by the fever that had been coursing through her body? No. Claire swallowed hard. Had it been the Goddess? If so, the weight of what the woman had said lay heavy on Claire's mind. She was a young woman, tied by convention and the expectations of others. As Oracle, she had had more freedom.

Toby barked; the noise broke into her thoughts of

fevered dreams and divine beings. She looked down at the dog, nosing in a pile of leaves. A squirrel shot out of the mound. It glared at the dog, then dashed across the fading patch of mountain grass. Toby gave a howl and took off in pursuit. Claire laughed at the dog's antics and drew her coat tightly round her: the wind had a bite in it that spoke of harsher weather to come.

Soon the first scatterings of snow would cover the mountains. Claire recalled her childhood here at the manor. The passion she had found in Pugh's arms, and the loss of their child. She strove to place the memories in an order that made sense to the life she had been re-given. Each day was a step forward, but was marked by the intervening years and the ignorance of what had happened to those she loved. She had tried to run away from grief, and had become trapped in another existence. The Glimpser's total innocence of the world was very appealing, but Claire knew she was here for a purpose. She had been given a second chance at life and she had to make that count.

She hoped with all of her heart that Pugh would be part of it. What had become of him? Her father had avoided her questions. Pugh had loved her, she knew it. Had he tried to find her while she had been Oracle? *Oh, Goddess.* She choked back a sob and began to cry.

She had wanted someone to understand the guilt she carried for her son's death, and had believed the Order of the Inner Ring could explain it to her. She reached a finger under first the left lens of her glasses, then the right, roughly wiping away the tears.

Suddenly Claire began to shake. *Oracle.* Claire felt the importance of the words the voices wanted to say, yet she was alone. If she spoke them now they would be lost. She wouldn't remember. She turned and began to run to the house.

Toby sensed her leaving and loped after, barking encouragement. She ran towards the door that opened from her father's study into the garden. Claire reached the door and grabbed the handle: it was locked. She banged on the glass with her hand, trying to catch her father's attention. "Father! Hurry!" She hit the glass again. It shattered. Her hand went through. Droplets of red fell among the glass splinters. She pushed the pain away, as she had done so many times as Oracle.

"Dear Goddess!" Her father spun round and looked in

82

horror at his daughter. Claire could see the fear on his face. Then he was running across the room, his feet crushing the glass shards. He fumbled with the bronze key. The door swung open. Claire rushed in, her dress sweeping up glass and blood. Her father grabbed her arms and looked at her. Claire could see he believed he was losing her again. She tried to tell him he wasn't, but Oracle was demanding to be heard.

"Father. Listen. Write." Oracle wouldn't be denied any longer. The glasses on her face were askew. She tried to fight her way out of her father's embrace. "Write. The words. Important."

Sir Henry let go of her and ran back to his desk, snatching at a scrap of paper. Turning it over, he placed a pencil to the surface as Claire began to speak. "Good dog, bite him hard. Guns in the air, blood on the steps and floor. Stop it Father. Open the box. End them. Tear them down. Go to Gateskeep, speak in the forum. Politics and religion, change them. Clatter of the machines, spinning, spinning the thread. Alive not dead!" A dull pain began in her hand. She lifted it; the blood dripping from the cuts looked unreal.

"Here. Let me see," her father said. Claire gave him a wan smile. She could see he was struggling to contain his emotions. "Thankfully, you have just a few small cuts."

"What did I say– did it make sense?"

"The remark about going to Gateskeep was again high in your conversation."

"We must go."

"Yes, and I admit, Claire, if circumstances were different, I would. However, I will send my vote by proxy. It is dangerous. If we were to go anywhere I would take you south, somewhere warm and quiet for the winter." His eyes flickered to the scrap of paper he had scribbled on.

Claire frowned. She could feel the tension building inside at her father's refusal. Claire stopped. Her heart was thudding; she could feel its increased pace against her ribcage. "You have studied the Inner Ring, haven't you, Father? Rings and fire." Sir Henry nodded. Claire drew in a deep breath. "They lose track of the Glimpsers, don't they. It as if the creatures are trying to hide from the very men who created them. Alive not dead. Would anyone believe I am one? Good dog bite hard."

"Child, they know you were changed; they would be waiting for you."

"How many know? Secrets within secrets, it is their way. If they took me by force it would expose them. We go. I know you want to protect me, but we, Oracle and I, have a job to do. Will you help me?"

"Does this job include the destruction of the Inner Ring?"

"You have worked for that for a long time, haven't you, father?"

"Yes." Sir Henry's right hand patted the breast pocket of his jacket, searching for his pipe.

"Here." Claire picked his pipe up off the desk and handed it to him. She took up the piece of paper on which her father had written. She looked at the words, seeking to find sense in them. Then, seeing the reflection of other writing on the reverse of the paper, she turned it over, expecting to see more of her ramblings.

"Claire ..."

Claire's eyes widened as she read. *"Henry: Be aware someone is asking questions about the whereabouts of and concerning a mutual acquaintance. Regards, Avinguard."*

"Pugh knows?" She felt the bile rise in her throat.

"Yes. He tried to find you. Even went absent without leave."

"H- he did?" Her legs began to give way. She had to face this. Live with it.

"Yes. We caught up with you within the first few days — the Glimpser in you."

"I understand. White flesh on silk." She could not run from this. Pugh had looked for her. He still tried to protect her father. She wished that she could, this moment, be Oracle, removed from all emotions and the agony they caused.

CHAPTER TEN

arter stood before the mirror. He was stripped to the waist, examining his right shoulder. It had been thirty days since Avinguard shot him. *The Goddess curse him.* A ragged wound extended a good two finger-widths under the line of his collar bone. Carter rolled his shoulder up and hissed in pain. Avinguard had stood in his way, and still did. He would find the creature and bring it back to his order. He would prove to his fellow priests that he was not wrong. The Glimpser had been on the cusp of becoming something more. His fellows wouldn't dismiss him so easily next time. He would stand before them with the Seer reborn at his side. A wave of excitement at the thought made his stomach knot.

"You were lucky, going to a backstreet barber-surgeon like that," Harrison said.

"I didn't have much choice, and if it had not been for Lady Constance, I wouldn't have made it from the crash site alive." Carter picked up his shirt off the back of a chair and slipped it on. No red robe tonight. His order, despite what the outside world believed, did not expect their members to forego the lifestyle of a gentleman. It did, though, expect total obedience to its canon from the moment a man took his oath.

"You were in quite a state when you reached here, wide-eyed from poppy and fever. Not a nice situation to find oneself in." Harrison walked across to Carter's side. He took hold of the chair and straddled it, resting both arms on the back.

"Admit it, Harrison, old boy. You had a purse on my snuffing it."

"I might have." Harrison laughed. "The Goddess was with you that night, my friend. Avinguard could have had your eye out if he wanted. Damn good shot by all accounts. He was trying to stop you pulling the cord. In his eyes, you were behaving like a mad man. Or rather, a man who had had his plans exposed and wanted a quick getaway."

"And if I hadn't? If I had not seen the Glimpser's purpose?" The Glimpser had looked directly at him. At that moment, Carter had felt the hand of the Goddess on his shoulder.

"Yes, damn close thing, that. Pity you lost the creature

85

after the crash. If we had managed to get hold of it, we would have been able to determine if what you said was true."

Harrison doubted him. Of all his brothers in the higher cadre, Harrison was the one Carter hoped would believe him. "It is what the higher cadre of our order has striven for, for over five hundred years."

"How can we be sure we are doing what our Goddess desires?" Harrison rose from the chair.

Carter picked up Harrison's hat, cane and gloves and handed them to him. "You doubt our order has seen the true meaning of the Seer's words. The price paid is small. Those that offer themselves do so freely, to feel the embrace of the Goddess and release from their sins and guilt." Carter coughed and placed his own hat on his head. He indicated with a wave of his hand for his friend to precede him.

Harrison closed the door and slipped his arm through Carter's as they sauntered down the cloister. "It is the meaning of true gift, I believe, that is open to more than one interpretation. How do we know that the Seer meant *his* gift?"

"Oh my, Harrison, you are playing the advocate tonight, aren't you?" Carter laughed.

"I intend to, right through dinner — but devotions first, my friend."

Carter frowned and stopped walking. Harrison smiled and continued to walk towards the sound of chanting. The voices of his fellow priests echoed down the cloister. In the lower chapel, the prayers of welcome had begun.

***

Carter bowed his head in reverence as he entered the large, circular chapel. Thankfully, he and Harrison were not the last to take their places. The large circle of thick, plaited red leather, which was suspended by five chains from the ceiling, had not yet been lowered, the service proper not begun. The leather was the symbol of his oath and order, frowned at by many in the Orthodox Chapel for emphasising the torture of the Seer during the revolt against the last king. The Seer had been bound by dampened strips of red leather, pulled tight, and as they had dried they had tightened further. The Seer had held true to his belief in the cause he and others were fighting for. He had foreseen his torture and welcomed it as it

86

bound him to the future. Standing within the lowered ring at prayers, the Inner Ring believed, symbolised their own binding to their order's vision of the future. They wore this emblem on their right index finger, a twist of red leather threaded through a matching one of silver. Carter twisted his ring on his finger, delighting at the feel of the warm metal.

The service itself was not like others. No songs sang the praise of the Goddess, no prayers were offered to her for the well-being of land or individual. No one invoked her aid to soften the hearts of men. Carter scoffed at the idea that their deity could be so swayed. Her statue did not occupy the centre of the room, as it did in an Orthodox chapel. It stood to one side, a mere onlooker. This one was neither large, nor made of brass to reflect the light of candles and thus the Goddess' blessing on the congregation. This statue was of stone, roughly carved, barely recognisable as the Goddess. It had survived from a darker time in history. Harrison had once said, in jest, perhaps it was not the Goddess, but an older, darker deity.

Carter had laughed, but tonight he found himself wondering if perhaps it was true. Nonsense. His order worshipped the Goddess, through her servant the Seer. His words, his vision of the future, with the order in control of both spiritual and secular power – no country's government could stand against them. Carter did not doubt this interpretation. It was the iron core of his belief.

The large prism which did command the centre of the room began to turn. The fading light of the day streamed in from a window set in the western curve of the wall. It struck the prism and sent coloured beams across the faces of the brothers present. The brother leading the service called out the number of the first chant, asking his fellows to raise their voices and focus their minds and harness the power of the Goddess through the light, channelling it to their collective will.

***

Carter had found it hard to keep his mind on the service. The channelling this evening left him not energised, but drained. The smell of ozone released normally clarified his thoughts; tonight he felt stifled and unsure. The same could be said of the meal: his belly was full, yet he was hungry. Harrison had so far not been cooperative. The meal had dragged on until the

87

room was almost empty. Harrison put his gold pince-nez on his nose and peered at the label of the wine bottle.

"Another?" Carter asked, out of a politeness he was not feeling.

"Thank you." Harrison watched the red wine circle round the bottom of his glass. "Devotions tonight were distracted, don't you think?"

Carter frowned. "No, I think the order is of one mind, as always. We will see the outcome of our prayers; we always do. The setting sun had strength tonight. You saw the beams from the prism."

"They were unfocused, like the minds behind the prayers. Too many agendas; too many ideas. Maybe that is as it should be. Chaos. It is happening all around us. The world is changing too fast, carried on an ever-increasing tide of progress: steam power, and the dalliance with trying to harness the power of lightning. This new law before the Forum is just the latest manifestation. Soon nothing will remain of the world we knew as boys."

"I think you need to get a new pair of glasses, my friend. It was not unfocused to me." Carter tried not to snap. The conversation was not going the way he wanted it to.

Carter met Harrison's gaze. Had he noticed the tone in his voice? Carter hoped not; he did not want to antagonise the man.

Harrison cleared his throat and spoke again. "I believe I know what you want, and it is almost as impossible as finding the creature."

"You do."

"Yes, you want to find out if any one of the captain's family, or immediate friends, approached our order in the last ten years. You know the rules concerning this. Those who perform the ceremony do not know them except as *the candidate*. It is for the order's protection. Their families might not be understanding when we give their loved ones the gift of our Goddess in the hope that our Seer will be reborn in them." Harrison smacked his lips as he tasted the wine. "It's good."

"One person would know."

"The order's Seer Confessor. But he is sworn to silence on the bones of the Seer with regards to the identity of those he confesses. Could you ask a man to break such a vow?" It was plain Harrison was waiting for an answer.

"I need to convince him of what I heard and what I saw. Something we have looked for, for so long. And that the

Glimpser was known to Avinguard. If I knew the connection, I feel sure I would be able to find the creature. It will return to Avinguard's side, or perhaps to another member of its family."

"Sit in Avinguard's pocket." Harrison laughed, then became serious. "So, what proof do you have that the creature was changing?" Carter began to speak, but Harrison held up his hand, forestalling him. "Yes, I saw a copy of your statement, but tell me in your own words."

"The creature had named itself, referred to itself as 'Oracle.'"

"It might be a name someone called it at some point, and it remembered."

"They don't remember from one moment to another."

"True."

"The way it behaved in Haywood-on-the-bow."

"Yes."

"The way it spoke directly to me in the carriage."

"Agreed, but that is not proof. Pity Avinguard didn't take notice of anything the creature said. If he had, Lady Emily could possibly be alive now. And the political situation wouldn't be so fraught. Another riot was narrowly averted last week. That makes more than a dozen in the past thirty days."

"Yes, a waste; Lady Constance blames herself. As for the riots, I feel some of those are not as spontaneous as some would have us believe." Carter tried to contain his annoyance at the change of subject.

"Someone stirring the pot: the Crossmire ambassador, for one. Perhaps. As for the mother, her self-blame and grief was soon consoled by the good Captain Avinguard." Harrison chuckled.

"Yes, a strange relationship, that; a matter of opposites attract, I suppose. I wonder if they will marry."

"She is a widow, and his marriage was annulled. Not that Lady Constance would follow the drum; Avinguard would most likely resign his commission and become a gentleman of leisure. He would have enough to keep him busy, spending Lady Constance's money."

"His marriage was …. How interesting." Carter sat forward. "I mean, I didn't know he was married."

"Oh yes, he eloped with the only daughter of Sir Henry Fitzguard. It was a very small scandal. It happened before you came here from Crossmire. It did not occupy the wagging tongues of society for long; not enough juicy facts for them to dwell on. The union ended in disaster. A child dead, and the young woman thrown back into arms of her family. Her father applied for an annulment on behalf of his daughter two years later. She had gone into complete decline. Avinguard did not contest it, and the matter was swept under the carpet, so to speak, by all parties. I doubt anyone even remembers it happening at all. You know how society is, easily distracted."

"I see." There it was: the answer to his question. He felt a knot of excitement begin to form in his stomach.

Harrison picked up the bottle of red wine and poured Carter another glass. "Yes." Carter took the glass and saluted his companion.

"Good. And the matter of trying to approach the Seer Confessor...?"

"I don't think that will be necessary."

"Good. Now, what shall we do with the rest of the evening? The theatre, or Madame Castleton's assembly rooms?"

CHAPTER ELEVEN

The cab stopped by Madame Castleton's establishment on the north of Vantage Square in the eastern half of the city. A doorman opened the door of the vehicle. Another ran forward with an umbrella to shelter the two men from the fine rain which had begun to fall.

"Welcome, gentlemen," the senior doorman said with a bow. He indicated with a wave of a gloved hand for his subordinates to help the newly arrived gentlemen off with their outer garments. Coats and hats were quickly removed, and one of the footmen showed Carter and Harrison to a table in the main room.

Carter sat down facing the dance floor. The evening was young, and with the knowledge he had wanted in his grasp, he was determined to enjoy himself.

"Well, well, will you look at that." Harrison chuckled.

"What?"

"Avinguard is here, with the beautiful Lady Constance on his arm." Harrison tilted his head in the direction of the dance floor. There, turning in each other's arms as they whirled across the floor, were the good captain, now promoted to major, and the lady.

"Hmmm ...," Carter replied.

"You are not going to quiz Avinguard about his late wife in front of his new lover, are you?" Harrison said.

Carter did not answer, merely raised his left eyebrow and reached for the port. He poured himself a small glass and offered the bottle to Harrison. Carter lifted the glass to his lips and savoured the taste. It tasted of victory. He held the small glass up and looked through the rich dark liquor. "Lady Hotspur is here with her brood and, oh yes, Calvinward."

"I think her husband's passing hardly caused her an instant of grief. It certainly did not affect her social calendar," Harrison answered, adding, "That youngest daughter of hers is very attractive, far too much to be Clive Hotspur's get."

"Possibly she is not. Lady Hotspur, being who she is, would have covered her tracks better than a mouse running in a snow storm. I doubt you could prove anything, if you spent a dozen years on it."

Harrison burst out laughing. He removed his gold pince-nez so that he could wipe his eyes with his finger.

"Will you excuse me for a moment," Carter said. Harrison smiled and took a drink of his port. Carter glanced towards the dance floor as he walked across the room. Avinguard said something to Lady Constance; she replied and flicked her fan in an annoyed manner. Avinguard spoke again and his arm slipped round her waist. The music began again. They swayed off across the floor, but Lady Constance's face was stormy.

"They make a beautiful couple, don't they, George — or rather, Brother Carter?" Lady Elizabeth Hotspur, the very person he had come looking for. "You have been very remiss, sir. You have not been in my company for more than two thirds of the year. Since Lord Manling died, to be precise."

He smiled at her, bowed and took her offered hand, kissing it. "Indeed, I am glad Lady Constance has been able to move on past her great loss in the same manner you have, dear lady. And I have been busy doing my duty to the Goddess, of late."

"You wish to join my small party?" Elizabeth said, pointing with her fan to a table set on the edge of the dance floor, at which sat a number of her offspring and Lord Calvinward.

"Sadly, dear lady, I am entertaining a fellow brother." Carter waved his hand slightly, in the direction of Harrison.

"Pity."

Carter looked again at the dance floor. "Do you think they will marry?"

"Who? Oh, Avinguard and Constance. Perhaps; both are free of entanglements."

"I thought the good captain—forgive me, major— was married."

"Was, George; it was annulled." Lady Hotspur smiled, but Carter saw there was no friendship or warmth behind the expression.

"Of course. If you would excuse me," Carter said, giving Elizabeth a short bow as he took his leave. She inclined her head in reply.

As he walked back to Harrison, he could swear Elizabeth Hotspur was standing there watching him. He did not look back to confirm his thought. The woman was clever, and he feared that the few words he had said had caught her interest more than he would have liked.

***

"I am sorry, Constance. I didn't mean it; please forget it," Pugh said. The music changed tempo. He tightened his hold on Constance's waist and they stepped together, their bodies, at least, in time. Constance had insisted they come tonight. The invitation from Calvinward had been a vague one, yet Constance behaved as if it had come on a gold-edged card. Since Hitsmine, Pugh's relationship with Constance had veered from intimate in the extreme to that of barely acknowledging each other. Tonight, despite her outward display of affection, Pugh knew Constance had not come here to be with him. His suggestion that they leave and partake of a more intimate dinner, and perhaps the theatre, had met with a stony rebuff that had left him stammering an apology.

They passed close to the edge of the dance floor and Pugh caught sight of Elizabeth deep in conversation with ... Carter. He was sure of it. The dance took them away and into the middle of other couples, making it hard for Pugh to keep sight of the man.

"Pugh?" Constance asked. She had noticed his preoccupation with something other than herself.

"Carter is here. Over there, leaving Elizabeth's side. I swear it's him." They stopped dancing. He took Constance's hand and began to lead her quickly off the dance floor.

"Elizabeth is not speaking to anyone. See, she is going back to our table. Are you sure it was him?"

"It was him. He was talking to Elizabeth, as if he knew her."

"Who knew me?" Elizabeth sat down at the table next to her youngest daughter, and her friend, Abigail Kentward. Calvinward was walking away from the table. In fact, he had gone upstairs to one of the private meeting rooms soon after they had arrived, then returned and now was leaving the room again. Was this the reason Constance had been so keen to be here? Had Elizabeth been right when she had implied that Constance was as much a shadowy player in the game of politics as she? Constance had, during their dance, openly asked Pugh who Calvinward was meeting. He did not tell her, but of course he knew: he was in charge of the security of the High Forum and its members. That, and his promotion to major, had not been something he had asked for. Dealing with the needs and objections of a few hundred High Forum members was worse than training a whole battalion of raw recruits. The young lieutenant in charge of

Calvinward's personal protection suffered Calvinward's displays of vexation at the imposition with good heart. If this meeting was the reason behind Constance's desire to be here, how had she found out about it?

"My dear Elizabeth, Pugh thought he saw the priest involved in the train crash, one Brother Carter, speaking to you," Constance said, as she sat down next to Elizabeth.

"Yes, he was. He asked me if I thought you two would marry. He seemed very interested in your married state, Pugh." Elizabeth opened her fan and looked at the fine painted silk, then closed it with a sigh.

"My what?" He was at first confused by what Elizabeth was hinting at. Clarity dawned. He felt a sudden chill. His recent harsh words with Constance and thoughts of why she had wanted to come tonight were suddenly of no importance.

"Marriage, Pugh. Yours to Constance, as your former one to Claire has been annulled some five years."

"So you spoke of Claire, to Carter." Pugh's voice was cold and brittle. Carter would already know about Claire and what they had turned her into. Or would he? How many in the order actually knew the names of those who had been subjected to the horror? Perhaps Carter was acting on his own, but for what reason? He had to warn Sir Henry.

"He asked, and I answered offhandedly," Elizabeth said carefully.

Pugh rose and clicked his fingers sharply at a passing waiter.

"Sir." The waiter bobbed his head.

"I need to send a telegram, urgently."

"I will send the bellboy to you, sir, at once." The waiter gave a short bow and hurried off.

"To whom would you want to send a telegram at this time?" Constance asked casually.

"Military business. Perhaps something he has remembered he needs to do most urgently, eh, Pugh?" Elizabeth rose from her seat, her hand going out to a passing gentleman. "My dear Montgomery, a word with you, please. Excuse me, Constance, Pugh. Now Montgomery, with regards to that bay mare of yours for sale...." The rest of Elizabeth's conversation was lost as she moved off.

Pugh did not answer. He merely nodded to the bellboy who had arrived, then took a pad and pen off the boy's silver tray and quickly wrote a message. He ripped the message off, turned it over and blotted the ink on the slip below, before slipping it in the envelope. He placed the envelope on the tray along with a large, silver coin.

The bellboy's eyes widened at the sight of the coin. "I don't think I have change, sir."

"The change is yours if you get this message away in the next hour."

"Sir." The bellboy fingered the peak of his red cap and set off at a brisk pace.

While Pugh had been dealing with the bellboy, Constance had reached over and taken the pad. She scrutinised the misshapen, blotted reflection. The addressee was partly clear: Sir Henry Fitzguard.

"Have you seen enough, madam?"

"I did ask."

"And I declined to say."

"Yes, you did, because ..." Constance left the word hanging for a moment. "And don't tell me it is not important." Constance closed her fan, giving the outward appearance that they were engaged in a normal conversation.

"I wished to inform my wife's father that he might be having an unwelcome visitor. He has no liking for the Inner Ring and its ways."

"And why, pray, would this priest, Brother Carter, visit your ex-father-in-law? Your marriage was— what— annulled. I thought you had no dealings with Sir Henry since."

"The reason why is between myself and Sir Henry."

"A friend would have trusted a friend and told them."

"A friend wouldn't have asked. Constance, where my wife and her father are concerned, it is personal."

Constance stood. "Could you arrange a cab and take me home? I think I do not feel well."

Pugh did not inquire as to her health, or express how sorry he was. He knew the sudden 'illness' was Constance's way of extracting herself from a potentially embarrassing situation.

Constance reluctantly laid the pad down and moved ahead of Pugh towards the door. Elizabeth was in her path. "Leaving so soon?"

"Yes, I feel unwell," Constance mumbled and stepped round Elizabeth.

"Home and bed is the best place for you, my dear," Elizabeth cooed and gave an understanding nod. "Your telegram sent, I hope, Pugh?" He did not answer, merely gave a short bow to Elizabeth and carried on after Constance. "Good. I am so glad; you should follow it up with a note or letter, you know — clarify the situation. Isn't that what a good officer always does?"

***

Colliridge watched Calvinward from the door of the well-appointed study. The man, still resplendent in evening dress, rose from his desk and turned up the oil lamp. Yellow light splashed across the room. It bounced off the neat piles of paper that had been prepared for Calvinward's attention. Small, coloured tabs separated various stacks. Foreign and domestic matters, Colliridge surmised. Calvinward picked up a brandy glass, walked to the sideboard and refilled it. He took a drink of his brandy and returned to stand by his desk. Only then did he address Colliridge. "I expected you earlier."

Colliridge did not reply. He merely closed the study door and walked towards the fireplace. His tight, grey militia pants were covered with dark runnels of mud. It was almost impossible to see the colour of his knee-high boots. The plain jacket he was wearing was spotted with damp and he sported three days of beard. Calvinward frowned as Colliridge unceremoniously flopped down in one of the large chairs near the fire and hooked his right leg over the arm.

"Brandy?" Calvinward waved in the direction of the decanter.

"No, but I will have one of those cigars." He had been half-inclined not to come tonight. When he had contacted Calvinward in Hitsmine concerning the various tasks Hotspur had implemented, Calvinward had dismissed him. Oh, he had paid him handsomely for his past trouble, but his intentions had been plain. He did not see the need of keeping a political agent on his payroll. Now things seemed to have changed. Was this a delicate matter of some kind that he did not wish to entrust to his own staff?

Calvinward flipped open an inlaid rosewood box, picked it up and offered it to Colliridge, who took out a cigar, held it close to his ear and rolled it gently between his thumb and middle finger. He placed it carefully in the top pocket of his jacket. Calvinward returned to his desk and sat on the corner. He was still waiting for a reply to his first question.

Colliridge grinned, "I was seeing to a client's business. So you have become friends with the noble Avinguard." One of his other employers, in fact his current main one, had informed him of the growing relationship between the two men and wanted information about it. This employer was concerned that Calvinward was attempting to have the heir to the Avinguard name become a supporter of his policies. Calvinward would not be the first. Sir Henry Fitzguard had managed to marry his daughter to Pugh, though that union had been short-lived and any plans Sir Henry had had vanished with the marriage's annulment. The Avinguards still had considerable influence among the gentry at large; surprising, as it was nearly five hundred years since their ancestor had given up the throne in favour of a hereditary ruling High Forum. Old loyalties did indeed die hard. The Avinguards seemed content with serving the country in other ways, mainly in the militia; they even left their seat in the High Forum unclaimed.

Calvinward did not answer.

"Bet he was not happy with the refusal to search folks entering the High Forum."

"No."

"Likes a tight ship, does the major."

"You know him?"

"In a round-about way,"

"I see."

"Not really. As far as he is concerned, I am dead. Or rather, the soldier I was pretending to be. I died in the retreat down Coot's Pass. Actually, I slipped away once I had the chance. I wasn't being paid to die for my country, if you get my meaning." Colliridge laughed. "So, to business, Milord."

"Yes, business. I have one matter that I feel you can find out the truth behind." Joshua leaned over and flicked open a book on the table.

"As you know, my rates are not cheap," Colliridge said slowly.

"Price is not important. I will settle all expenses, with a bonus."

Colliridge smiled slightly and inclined his head in acknowledgement of the offer. So this was a matter where Calvinward did not want to have a trail leading back to him.

"I want to know who wrote this and what they are up to. A lady's honour is at stake." He held out a letter to Colliridge.

Colliridge struggled to hide his surprise. He slipped his leg off the arm of the chair and got to his feet. As far as he knew, Calvinward, if he had liaisons with any skirt, was as careful as a chapel mouse. Not a whiff of scandal. "Been a bit indiscreet, Milord? Didn't think you would make that mistake. By the Goddess!" Colliridge exclaimed, as his eyes tracked the first few lines of the letter. "I see. If someone muddies the water." He whistled through his teeth. Lady Emily Manling. No. The letter could not be from her. No wonder Calvinward did not want any of his own people near this. He carefully read it, turned the paper over, and read it again. It was clever, and he could see why it had rattled Calvinward. If it got out that a young, innocent girl of Emily's class was rotting in a workhouse jail, abandoned by the man the general public believed was her betrothed, even if there had been no announcement, Calvinward's credibility would be in shreds.

"You understand. Good. It is impossible, of course, but if it were to get into the papers .... If they have some wench that could pass for the lady in question, it could take days, even a season, to clear up. It would draw attention from the matter of the bill." Calvinward's voice was level, yet Colliridge swore there was a slight tremor in it.

"You have the envelope? That will tell me a great deal. It would be franked, public post office or private company." Calvinward reached over to the book again and pulled out the required item. "Good, let me see. That narrows the field a bit." He shuffled both in his hands, then looked at Calvinward's outstretched hand. He smiled. Not going to let him keep them— pity.

Calvinward did not return the smile, and took the envelope and letter back. "I thought it would. Someone there is playing a dangerous game. It would fit, though; the workers rounded up after the riot in Hitsmine were quickly shipped to various jail workhouses. No trials; false papers rubber-stamped by bribed officials; the poor devils swallowed in the system. You will need this." He picked up a miniature picture. His fingers lingered on the shiny painted porcelain, then he handed it over.

"Pretty."

"She was. I want names. I want to know who is behind this."

"And…"

"And then I will decide what will be done."

"Could take me a while. What with getting there, and poking my nose without getting caught, and frankly it will not be cheap."

"Take as long as you need. Money is no object, I told you that."

***

Colliridge stood on the pavement outside the Crossmire Embassy. Dawn was breaking; pale pink tendrils of light outlined the rooftops of the city that led down to the river. The embassy was situated on the high northern ridge on the city's outskirts. It was surrounded by its own grounds: a country within a country.

He took the cigar out of his pocket and lit it, savouring the taste. Damn good. So was the deal he had just brokered with the Crossmire ambassador. The gentleman's annoyance at being woken at such a Goddess-forsaken hour had soon been replaced by delight. The ambassador was very interested in the supposed fate of Lady Emily Manling, though, like Calvinward, he was certain that it was a swindle of the highest order. The guarded look the ambassador had given him towards the end of the conversation told Colliridge that the ambassador believed the swindle could be aimed at him. And if it was, and Colliridge was involved, well, there would be no diplomatic niceties with regard to what would happen next.

The days after the riot at Hitsmine had been a morass of tangled events; it was quite possible that Lady Emily had been swept up by the police. The bodies found were badly burnt. Still, time would tell. Colliridge knew he would make a damn good profit no matter what.

he sky in the east barely held the promise of any light for the day. Mathew walked across the factory yard towards the mill. He pulled his jacket tighter in an effort to block the damp chill of late autumn. The large mill of the workhouse jail overshadowed all the other buildings. He was not alone in his journey: children, blurry-eyed, their narrow, pinched faces old and worn out before their time; men and women, stoop-backed, carrying a burden that only the dregs of their self-worth kept from crushing them.

Mathew climbed the stairs to the third floor. Large spinning machines lined either side of the long room, each with over two hundred spindles. When the machines' spinning rails had moved to their full extension, there was a gap of some four paces between the machines. Here in this off-shoot of hell, Mathew had worked for the last thirty-seven days. It was hot in the room, even now in late autumn, the floor discoloured and slick with oil fallen from the spindles, air thick with motes of raw cotton. Mathew muttered a greeting to his fellow workers and began to oil the spindles. The foreman, standing at the end of the room, turned the oil lamp up to compensate for the lack of natural light at this hour. It was a signal for work to commence.

"Right, let's be getting started, eh?" Robert, the spinner in charge of the machine Mathew worked at, walked slowly towards Mathew. He was in no hurry to begin the back-breaking work. No one was.

Working the machine along with Mathew and Robert was Sally. She worked, as did Mathew, as a big piecer, besides repairing the broken threads on the spindles. They, along with Robert, did all the general maintenance. Alongside the three adults, two small lads, Albert and Charlie, worked as scavengers. The lads crawled under the threads as the spinning machine's carriage clattered forward, drawing the thread out. They swept away the cotton fluff and fragments and kept the machinery free from obstructions. The boys also took their turn in repairing broken threads in places larger hands could not reach.

"Ready, lads?" Mathew looked at the two boys. Both nodded. Like all the children in the workhouse jail, they were small for their age, with skin pale from lack of food and sunlight. It was back-breaking and dangerous work, none more so than for the two young boys, who lay on the oil-smeared floor with the carriage trundling over their heads.

A groan from above marked the first movement of the long, metal drive shaft from which hung sets of belts attached to each machine. The groan increased to a whine as the speed built up.

Robert engaged the machine's drive and called over the rising noise, "I'm going to have a draw."

Sally nodded and took up station on her length of the machine; Mathew did the same. The spinning machine kicked into action. The narrow, sharp-rimmed wheels at either end and in the middle ran the carriage out with a rattling din.

The cream thread spun onto the spindles. Robert stopped the machine. Mathew cracked his knuckles and repaired his first thread of the day. Robert watched the foreman out of the corner of his eye. Like the others on the floor, he took his time checking the machine. Long enough to give everyone a breather, but not long enough to bring one of the guards over at a run. "Right, here we go."

As the morning progressed, Mathew tried to keep his mind on his work, but it kept straying to two things: Emily and the position they found themselves in. He despised the system that had allowed the events they had been caught up in to happen. Mathew wanted to uproot it, root and branch. One thing he was glad of was that Emily had not worked long in the mill. The governor had a new wife, a young woman who was determined to shine in the middle-class society hereabouts. She wanted – no, demanded – a decent lady's maid. Emily had, to her surprise, been selected from the row of women paraded for the young wife to choose from. Chosen, Emily later told Mathew, because she was relatively clean. Emily's job was not, in one sense, easier. She was at the beck and call of her mistress, day or night.

Mathew had expected to be free by now. Had the authorities in Hitsmine not notified the Seabreeze estate? It was standard procedure when a bond contract worker was arrested. Mathew was sure that the moment the senior overseer received the notification, he would bring it to the notice of Mathew's father. The senior overseer had been the conduit through which Mathew had kept in touch. Though of late they had disagreed, Mathew could not see his father allowing him to rot in a workhouse jail. Mathew had lain awake at night going over what he would say to his father, how he would explain events. However, as time had passed he had begun to worry. He had used what was left of the coins he had to bribe a guard, when they were still in Hitsmine jail, to take a note to Sir John Thornton. It was obvious the guard had considered it his lucky day, ripped up the note and pocketed the coins. The condemned had even been refused visits from a chapel minister, though one cleric had repeatedly tried up to the very day the inmates had been bundled into carts to be taken to the workhouse jail

At least he had managed to convince the assistant warder on their arrival that Emily was his wife. They had a policy of keeping families and couples together. It was a strange and uncomfortable situation, to be so close to her and not be able to tell her of how much he cared for her.

After one wakeful night, when sleep had been eluding both of them, Emily had confessed she had stolen some of her mistress' writing paper and had written to Calvinward. She had placed the letter among her mistress' correspondence to be taken to the post office. The punishment, if she had been caught, would have seen Emily whipped in the yard. Calvinward had the influence to do something; her mother did not. He was the only logical choice. To Mathew, it was like a slap in the face. It was he who had held her when she needed holding and kissed away her tears.

Since their internment, Mathew had scoured every fragment of newspaper that had come his way. Calvinward had played Emily's demise like an ace in his hand. As a gentleman, he was appalled; the would-be lover, angry beyond measure. The politician in Mathew understood and even admired Calvinward's use of the situation. Like Calvinward, Mathew was a man with a personal mission. He wanted to improve the lot of the working man on whose back the country's wealth was built. And the jail workhouse factories were the bottom of a vile heap. Mathew felt his chest tighten in anger at the thought. Many thrown into the jail workhouse system were arrested because their skill was needed in a certain factory. The spinner, Robert, was one. The man had been here five years, quietly fighting his own battle to survive. These factories were very profitable to run. The backers saw the locked-in workforce as a sure way to squeeze out a larger profit.

The thumping rhythm of the machine vibrated through Mathew's body. The backs of his thighs ached from standing at an angle over the machine. His fingers were numb, his eyes and throat sore from the thick atmosphere filled with cotton motes. The conditions were hardest on the children. Robert did his best to spell the boys. Charlie sat at one side, carefully chewing on a slab of dark bread. His friend and counterpart was crawling under the machine. Mathew watched Albert through the cotton threads. The youth scuttled under the fine lines of cream, his thin body pressed close to the floor. The carriage had reached its farthest limit, shuddering as the spindles spun, then it gathered itself for a swifter return. Albert was reaching across the line of the middle wheel, pulling at a lump of soft thread, when the carriage began to move back.

"Watch your'sen," Sally said, concern tightening her voice.

Mathew fumbled a repair on a thread, his stomach rolling with unease. The lad was too far under the frame. Albert was wriggling back, his outstretched hand full of fragments. His shirt cuff caught on the narrow track on which the middle wheel ran. He squealed and fought to free his arm, legs drumming on the oily wooden floor.

"Fucking hell!" Robert reached over, struggling to stop the machine. He was too late. The wheel went over Albert's wrist, the snap of the youth's bones lost in the thunder of the machine. Gouts of blood spewed across the floor. The machine rattled and hissed in protest, the middle wheel dragging the lad's severed hand in its stuttering wake.

Mathew stooped down, grabbing hold of the lad. Albert had curled in a ball, shielding the bleeding stump with his body. The shock had bleached his face white, and he fought to breathe. Mathew sat, trying to force the lad's arm out so he could examine it. Blood ran through Mathew's fingers and splashed warm and damp across his face. Sally, sobbing, attempted to bind her shawl round the boy's arm, but the blood swiftly soaked the fabric.

Charlie pulled on Mathew's right arm, trying to speak. His face was white, eyes wide, his mouth contorted. It could be him struggling and screaming in Mathew's arms.

"Hold 'im bloody well still!" Robert bellowed, pulling off

his belt. Mathew tried to tighten his hold. The youth was doing more harm than good. He wondered if Robert was going to hit him. *No, he can't.* But Robert slipped his belt round the lad's upper arm and cinched it tight. The leather bit deep, crushing the flesh.

"It's bloody well not working." Mathew felt the boy's blood soak into his trousers. *No, no, no, please for Goddess' sake, no.* Albert's struggles were getting weaker.

"Fuck!" Robert undid the belt and pulled it tighter. Albert's eyes rolled back in his head. His body flopped as if all the bones had been removed. The youth's face was grey, waxed with cold sweat.

"Oh Goddess ..." Sally sniffed and pushed harder with her shawl. The lad's blood had covered her hands.

Charlie's young face streamed with tears. He was suddenly lifted into the arms of one of the women from the machine behind Mathew and carried away from the carnage.

Mathew tried to speak, but his mouth wouldn't work. Bile filled his throat. The boy had little enough chance of life in this place; now the bastards had taken even that away.

Robert let go of the belt. He placed a finger on Albert's throat just under the ear, then pulled at his slack eyelids. "He's gone."

Mathew eased the dead boy from his arms and laid him on the blood-smeared floor. He looked up into the tear-swollen eyes of Robert.

"We did our best, don't blame your'sen." Robert turned and nodded to his opposite number on the machine behind. The man moved forward with a large blanket to cover Albert.

"Why are these machines stopped?" The voice of the foreman could be heard over the death rattle of the other machines on the floor. All had ceased their spinning.

"There's a lad dead here; show some bloody respect. Had his hand taken off by the wheel." Robert straightened up and faced the bullnecked man, toe to toe.

"Get rid of him and clean up the mess. And don't forget that piece of offal under the machine," the foreman snarled, pointing to Albert's severed hand, still clutching the small ball of threads.

Mathew felt his chest tighten in anger. *Goddess damn him for an unfeeling bloody sod.* He began to get up from the floor.

"Easy, Mathew, it's not bloody worth it." Robert pushed down on Mathew's shoulder in an attempt to stop him. But

Robert's words did not register. Mathew lashed out at the foreman, hitting him hard and knocking him into the carriage of the next machine in the line. The foreman floundered on the threads. The spinner in charge of the machine yelped, then shouted encouragement to Mathew. Mathew hit the foreman again, full on the chin, knocking him further into the web of threads. Again and again he hit the man. His field of vison narrowed. All he could see was the face of the foreman streaked with blood, lips and nose split. The bastard bloody well deserved it, and more.

"Watch it, lad!" Robert shouted, as the trample of feet could be plainly heard. The throb of machines had fallen silent, to be replaced with a ripple of angry voices.

Two of the guards on the floor, night sticks swinging, bore down on Mathew. They did not get very far: both were tripped up and punched as they fell. One managed to pull out his whistle and blow. The high-pitched noise echoed round the room. Suddenly there was chaos: threads were cut on the machines, creels full of rovings overturned and power belts torn down. The rest of the guards went down in a hail of fists and feet. Robert was still trying to pull Mathew off the foreman. Mathew fought against Robert's intervention, then abandoned his attack and looked down room. The end doors had been flung open and guards streamed in, swinging their nightsticks at anyone in their way.

"Bollocks!" Robert held up his hands and moved away from Mathew.

***

All was burning pain. Mathew struggled to breathe. He lay on the whipping frame, waiting for the next stroke to fall. Five had sliced into his flesh, and Mathew did not know if he could survive another one. It came. The cut, splayed ends of the thick birch rod dripped blood as it whistled through the air towards Mathew's sliced back. It hit, but the blow was lighter, no force behind it. Mathew straightened in his bonds. The next blow came, same as the previous one. The guard was toying with him, Mathew was sure of it, but the rest of the blows were similar. The blows were hard enough to look as if the sentence was being carried out, but light enough not to increase the damage.

The blows stopped. Mathew shuddered. What was the

105

guard up to? What price was going to be asked of him, of Emily? *Oh, by the Goddess, no.* Never. He would take twenty lashes rather than allow that.

He felt the guards untie his arms. Mathew pushed himself up from the frame and looked round, seeking Emily in the ranks of the governor's household staff. All the inmates of the workhouse had been assembled to see the punishment. He could make out her silhouette: another woman had an arm round her waist,.

The foreman, Blair, would have, as the workers said, *marked his card for this.* From now on, the guards and foremen would be watching him. One step out of line and he would be on the frame again. He had drawn attention to himself and to Emily, and it was the last thing he had wanted to do.

"To your quarters." The guard who had wielded the birch rod was at his shoulder. The clash of clogs being stamped hard on the cobbles echoed round the yard. "Seems others share our opinion of things here."

Mathew glanced sideways at the man. The guard was smiling and gave Mathew a sly wink. "Get to your quarters and I will try and get you something for that back, and no, there will be no charge. Not all of us are black-hearted buggers, nor are we all here by choice." The guard stepped back and said in a louder voice, "Get out of my sight, you bloody bastard!"

Mathew tried not to react to anything the man had said. He forced himself to walk towards the dormitory. Each step jolted his back. The cold morning air cut into the bloodied welts, increasing the pain. Once inside the doorway to the stairwell, Mathew leant his right side to the cold brick wall. The blood was running down his back. He could feel it pooling against the waistband of his britches and drying,. His shirt was ripped open up the back, the fabric hanging against his arms.

He pushed clear of the wall; grasping the handrail, he began to climb the steps. One, two, each foot raised and placed down, counted. At each of the five floors Mathew passed, he felt a perverse sense of triumph. Finally, Mathew pushed the door to the upper dormitory open. Slowly, he made his way down the bare, white-scrubbed floorboards to the small section he and Emily called home. He sat heavily on the edge of the rough bed. Mathew's sight swam; all he could think of was the pain. His head went forward into his hands, and he heard himself sob.

106

The sound of footsteps brought his head up. "Emily. Goddess, you should not be here."

Emily laid the small, white bundle in her hands down on the bed. "The butler, Harris, has given me till mid-morning."

"At what price," Mathew mumbled bitterly.

Emily gave a small smile. "He asked for me to request help with the governor's wife's dresses. He named a girl in the carding room."

Mathew sighed and nodded his head. Emily took his hand and brought it up to her face. He could feel the tears on her face. "Oh, Mathew." He could not bring himself to look at her.

"I am sorry. I have drawn attention to us, but I couldn't just stand there." He felt his voice failing in his throat. "Albert is dead."

Emily shuddered, tightened her hold on his hand for a moment, then let go. "Let's get your back cleaned up." As she spoke, Emily unwrapped her small parcel and placed two bottles carefully on the small chest that held their worldly belongings. She took a bowl and went to get some water from the washroom at the far end of the dormitory.

Mathew shrugged out of his rent shirt, wincing as the movement pulled the lacerations on his back. He reached out to the bottles. The small, green glass one, he knew, was iodine. He shuddered at the thought of that pouring over his back, but it was a necessary evil and he knew it. The other was plain rough pottery. He picked it up, pulled the cork out and sniffed it. Brandy.

"Take a drink, it will help."

"I doubt it." Mathew set the brandy bottle back down.

Emily gave a small sob and squeezed his shoulder. The touch of her fingers on his bare flesh brought another sort of pain. He loved Emily, and he knew his actions today had hurt her.

Carefully, Emily took the linen that had wrapped the two bottles, soaked it in the water and began to wash Mathew's back.

"It could have been worse."

"The guard eased up."

"Yes. I am not sure why."

"Oh Mathew, you must be careful." Emily placed the red-stained cloth into the water and picked up the bottle of iodine.

"Don't worry, he won't touch you. I would kill him first."

"Oh, Mathew." Emily leant forward and gently kissed his brow. "Ready?"

Mathew nodded. Emily poured the iodine down his back.

He gripped the edge of the bed and tried not to scream. After she had finished, he sat there, stunned and shaking. Emily picked up the brandy bottle and held it to his mouth. Mathew gulped the liquid down and felt a fire light in his gullet and stomach. He reached up with his hand and covered Emily's on the bottle for a moment, then took the bottle from her and set it down. "Oh, Emily."

"Help me rip my other apron," she said, and after taking a small key from her pocket, opened the chest.

Soon Mathew was wrapped in lengths of linen from just under his arms to his waist. The pain in his back had faded to a dull ache. He sat there holding Emily's hand, turning it over in his. "We will get out of here, I promise you."

"I know." Emily leaned against his shoulder. His arm slipped round her. Emily returned the embrace and tilted her head up. He kissed her full on the mouth. There was nothing friendly in this salute; it was raw, hard-held passion, suddenly released. Emily tried to pull away, then surrendered.

Mathew explored her lips with his, tasting the sweetness of her mouth with his tongue. He broke the kiss, stammering, "Emily, I am sorry."

"Mathew, there is no need to be. I — I think I love you."

Mathew took her gently in his arms and kissed her again, savouring every moment.

"I see someone has beaten me to it." It was the guard who had flogged Mathew. "And you are running as big a risk as your husband. It would be a pity to see skin as lovely as yours cut by a birch rod." He placed the small sack he had in his left hand on the rough blanket by Emily's side.

"I had permission from the butler, Mister Harris; you can check," Emily said sharply. She disentangled herself from Mathew's arms and stood up. "Do you know the time?"

"Getting on to midday," the guard replied.

"I best be going." Emily squeezed Mathew's hand and gave him a reassuring glance before taking her leave.

The guard half-turned and watched Emily walk down the length of the dormitory, then turned back to face Mathew. Mathew's eyes narrowed. He looked at the guard, trying to gauge what the man was up to. The guard wore the normal rough blue jacket and small, soft cap of the guards, yet his legs were encased in a pair of well-made militia grey britches, the sort a career soldier, maybe even an officer, would wear.

"Not bad looking, your missus. Sharp too, I wager." The guard pointed to the sack. "Some more iodine, linen and a few other things. My name's Colliridge, by the way."

"Why?" The question was blunt and to the point.

"Why, indeed." Colliridge rubbed his chin, "I know you."

"Do you?" Mathew stiffened.

"Coastal man."

"Yes," Mathew said slowly, his eyes watching the way Colliridge's right hand strayed to his nightstick. Was the whole thing in the yard a prelude for arranging an "accident"?

"You served in the 6th District Corps when you did your time in the militia."

Mathew had not, but his papers said he had. The details of which would have been copied onto the records held here at the workhouse jail. This man had done some sniffing around. "Yes."

"Don't you remember me, Robert Colliridge?"

"Not sure. Been two years since I was in the militia," Mathew said slowly.

"Aye, it has," Colliridge replied. His hand moved off his nightstick and across to his belt buckle. "Anyway, I remember you. You were a hot-head then, I seem to remember, banging on about workers' rights."

Mathew had been nothing of the sort. He had been a model junior officer and had kept his thoughts to himself. This man was fishing, and Mathew wondered whether he should spit out the hook. No, best swallow it and go along with this Colliridge, and try and find out why, and for whom he was working. "Aye, and look where it got me."

"And I thought staying on with the militia was an easy ticket."

"What happened to you?" Mathew made a show of reaching for the sack on the edge of the bed.

"Fell foul of a stuck-up bum creeper of an officer. He whacked me down and sent me for duty here," Colliridge said, a hint of bitterness in his voice. False, of course: the expression in the man's eyes did not change.

"A number of them in the militia need weeding out," Mathew agreed, and pulled at the neck of the sack.

"Aye, and Pugh Avinguard is one of the worst,"

Colliridge spat. The venom in Colliridge's voice was real, his face twisted with suppressed anger.

Mathew looked quickly up from the sack, struggling to mask his surprise. Was Colliridge trying to draw him out, to get him to admit he knew Avinguard? Was it possible this man was trying to see if Mathew had been on the northern express when it crashed?

"Never met him during my service," Mathew answered truthfully. Someone knew who he, or Emily, was.

"Anyway, I best be getting back. But thought I would let you know you have an old mate from the 6th District Corps on the other side, so to speak." Colliridge held out his hand.

"Thanks, I will remember." Mathew took Colliridge's hand and shook it. Colliridge let his hand fall back to his side, nodded and left.

The conversation made the incident in the mill pale by comparison. Mathew had not seen the man before today, though that was not impossible given the number of guards and inmates. Did Colliridge really believe Mathew would believe him? Yes, during your time in the militia you met hundreds of men, some you did not remember. But to have one claim he knew you from a corps you were not even part of, were a member of only on forged papers .... Mathew shook his head.

There were, Mathew could see, two possible sources for the interest. One, Colliridge had been sent by his father. Mathew dismissed that; they had been alone. Colliridge would have dropped any pretence and spoken openly. Colliridge would have known who Mathew *really* was, something Mathew had yet to admit to the woman he loved. The second was far likelier and more worrying. Mathew rose from the bed and moved stiffly towards the window. Emily's letter must have reached Calvinward. It was very possible that Colliridge was a political agent in Calvinward's service, and he had been sent here to find out the truth behind the letter.

What would Calvinward do when informed that both of them were very much alive? Mathew reached up and rubbed the dirt off one of the panes on the window. He looked out on the marshes that surrounded the mill. If things had been difficult before, now they were downright dangerous. He needed to quickly find a way out of this place for Emily and himself. Mathew could no longer wait for his father to act.

110

The dull pain in Mathew's back throbbed in time to the turning of the white sails on an old windmill. Its jagged reflection in the water was picked out by the hazy, midday autumn sun. *"Sails on the water."* The sight matched the garbled words of the Glimpser that Mathew had heard a season ago.

CHAPTER THIRTEEN

rother George Carter of the Inner Ring was watching his valise being placed onto an icy platform. He glanced around through flakes of snow. The station was merely a single platform with a small gaggle of buildings along its length. These comprised a waiting room, ticket office and station master's house, what the railway entrepreneurs called a "halt" at the end of a small branch line. There was no financial benefit in providing anything other than a simple means of getting passengers onto the train.

The rest of his fellow passengers had disembarked, and a small group of porters were unloading the two goods wagons. The train had been uncoupled and run forward onto a small turning circle. A twisted plume of smoke marked its journey. The train rolled off the turning circle and chugged down the small side track till it was forward of the junction with the main track. The harsh thud of the points being moved echoed through the flurrying snow. Slowly the train began to reverse into position, ready for its return journey.

Carter stamped his feet and waved a hand at the porter. "A cab or carriage. Is there any to hire?" He intended to present himself as a gentleman interested in renting one of Sir Henry's shooting lodges later in the season. Not an unusual request, and it would gain him entry to the estate.

The porter smiled and touched a finger to the edge of his cap. "Aye, sir, but both are out. If you want to take a seat in the waiting room, they won't be long." The porter reached for his valise and Carter made to follow the man.

A tall man dressed in a tweed coat stepped out of the waiting room, a young woman on his arm. The woman was addressing a small, wire-haired hunting dog at her heels. "Such excitement, Toby." Her voice was light, cultured, yet had a familiar ring to it. "Easy, you will wag your back end away."

"Who is that?" Carter asked, placing a restraining hand on the porter's arm.

"Oh, that's Sir Henry. He's going to the capital for the winter season—first time for a long while. Her ladyship being well an' all."

"Her ladyship?" It could not be. Had Harrison sent him

off on a wild goose chase? Carter felt his eyes begin to narrow.

"Aye, Lady Claire, been ill for a number of years, but she be well now," the porter replied in the manner of a proud uncle, and made again to pick up Carter's bag.

"I have changed my mind," Carter said.

"Pardon sir?" The porter frowned.

"Place my bag back on the train. I intend to return to the capital," he ordered.

"Very good, sir." The porter sighed. Carter fumbled in his pocket, brought out a gold coin and handed it to the porter.

"Very good, sir." The porter's voice brightened. "I will make sure you get a good seat; got a few going besides his lordship, what with the weather turning and the gentry gathering for the season."

The porter took up Carter's valise and escorted him into the first-class carriage. At the door, the porter handed Carter's valise to the conductor in charge. The conductor gave a forced smile and showed the priest to an empty seat.

"No, further down if possible. This is too close to the door." Sir Henry and his daughter had settled in seats about ten paces ahead on the left. The conductor tried to hide his annoyance and indicated for Carter to move forward. "There, if you please." Carter pointed to the seats opposite Sir Henry.

"Very good, sir." The conductor put Carter's valise on the luggage rack above the seat and moved away.

Carter unbuttoned his coat and made a show of sitting down. He inclined his head to Sir Henry, who gave a small, absent-minded smile. Carter drew a small, leather-bound book out of his pocket and opened it, pretending to be engrossed in the pages.

The train jerked. The dog, on the seat by Lady Claire, barked sharply, then placed his head on his mistress' lap. Carter could see she was dressed in the height of fashion in a fine woollen walking dress. A pillbox hat sat at a jaunty angle on a pile of blonde curls. The priest could see why a man like Avinguard had been attracted to her; even with the gold-wired, blue-tinted glasses, Claire Fitzguard was stunning. She was an ideal example of beauty in the classic style.

Carter began to doubt everything Harrison had said. This young woman might have been at one time suffering from a prolonged bout of nervous collapse, but he did not, could not, believe this woman was the creature he had seen. Carter began to fume.

Sir Henry pulled off his leather gloves and laid them carefully aside. He opened up a small writing case and began shifting through a pile of letters. He picked one up and glared at it, sighed and put the paper down.

"What is wrong, Father?" Lady Claire asked.

"We should not have got my agent to reopen the town house. These," Sir Henry said, tapping a pile of letters and cards, "are invitations to balls, dinners and events of all kinds."

"It was to be expected, Father. We couldn't have stayed at a hotel. You would be expected to entertain, if you are to be attending the Forum sitting. A hotel is. Is. damn! Calvinward on the steps. Good man. Goddess' sacrifice. Cruel man, become the enemy of all. Sails on the water. Suffer the consequences." Claire's left hand slammed the table in frustration, making Carter jump. Was this young woman Oracle? Had she become what they, his order, had worked, hoped and prayed for all these years? He no longer pretended to read his book, but looked, wide-eyed in triumph, at the young woman.

"Claire, I am concerned. You are not yet strong enough." Sir Henry reached over and took his daughter's hand in his.

"Please, I need to get back into a life. I need to be in Gateskeep. Steps to the chamber, guns in the air. Go to the High Forum as soon as we arrive. Oh bugger and damn. I wish I could say something in a sensible order for you and remember it." Claire stopped speaking and looked up at the conductor standing close to her shoulder, a notepad and pencil in his hand.

"Sir, Milady, hot toddy?"

"Not for me, thank you," Claire said.

"Of course not, milady, perhaps some hot milk with nutmeg and cinnamon." The man made a note on his pad.

"Thank you — how kind," Claire said.

The conductor gave her a short bow and continued down the carriage.

Sir Henry tapped the itinerary on top of the pile before him. "We will go to the High Forum the moment the connecting train gets us into Gateskeep. I need to register, and if it runs to time, we should be there by lunch tomorrow. We

114

have a private carriage on the express this afternoon, sleeping compartments and lounge combined. We will have to eat in the first-class dining car, though."

"Don't worry, people will have to get used to me and my slightly mad ways. Good dog, bite hard," Claire said, and returned her gaze to the scenery outside the window.

Carter continued to stare at the young woman. He mumbled his thanks to the conductor as the steaming glass of hot toddy he had ordered was placed in front of him. The drink was cold before he shook himself out of his thoughts to take a sip. He had been right; his faith had been rewarded tenfold. This was the Glimpser. Her slips into rambling could mean nothing else. Carter marvelled at her control. She had proved worthy of the burden, and it had been given to him to discover this miracle. Carter's lips began to form a prayer of thanks to the Goddess. He coughed and struggled to regain control of his emotions. He was vindicated, and the new order was so close he could taste it. Carter was impatient; he wanted the train to be at its destination now. Things had to be put in place quickly, the young woman taken by force if needs be. When would this train reach Hitsmine? He had to telegraph his order. Carter tried to keep his gaze on his book, but found he was looking again at Lady Claire.

His glances had not gone unnoticed. Not by the lady or her father, but by the dog. Each time Carter glanced sideways, his observation was met by a growl. The small dog was quivering with anger by the time the train stopped. As Carter rose to leave, the dog barked sharply, drawing the attention of both Lady Claire and her father to him.

Sir Henry glared at the animal. "My apologies, sir, he is not used to trains or strangers, but he will have to get used to both."

"No need to apologise, good sir," Carter replied, watching the conductor pull his valise from the luggage rack. "I understand."

"Do you?" Lady Claire said.

Carter felt the air in his lungs freeze. A feeling stirred in the pit of his stomach: something familiar, yet of an intensity that he had never felt before. A cold trickle of sweat began to trace down his spine. "Forgive me," Carter began.

"Never," Claire said, her voice barely above a whisper.

Carter did not answer. With a shaking hand, he merely

115

tipped his hat at a frowning Sir Henry and left the train. Once on the platform, the feeling in his stomach grew. His faith in his order, in their vision of the Goddess and her prophet the Seer, had been suddenly ripped from him. He gagged. His hand came to his mouth.

"Is there something wrong, sir?" asked the porter to whom the conductor had handed Carter's valise.

Carter tried to speak. He could not. *Slighted.* He had been looked on and found wanting. "No, I am worthy. I found you," he mumbled. He balled his right fist into his stomach and tried to draw air into his constricted lungs. The tension gave. His lungs expanded and the pain vanished. Carter pushed back his shoulders and tried to draw together the ragged ends of his faith.

"Pardon, sir?" The porter asked.

"It is nothing. The telegraph office, where is it?" Carter asked.

"It's on the left of the ticket office, sir. You need to go over the bridge, sir, towards the main entrance." The porter waved a hand in the direction of the stairs.

"Good, and the express to Gateskeep — when is that due to leave?"

"Soon, sir, it's due to go at two after noon."

Carter glanced up at the large clock hanging from the bridge. He had time; of course he had.

CHAPTER FOURTEEN

Sir Henry heard his daughter's whispered words and stared after their fellow traveller. He waved to the conductor. "Who was that gentleman?"

"I am not sure, Sir Henry. Did he annoy you? Do you wish to make a complaint?"

"Why would you say that?"

"If you forgive me saying so, Milord, he was a strange one."

"Red, hate, blood and ropes," Claire clamped her hand over her mouth, her eyes widening in annoyance.

Sir Henry stiffened at her outburst. Was it possible that the man had been a member of the Inner Ring? "You were saying he was strange."

"Yes, the moment he got to the halt, he changed his mind and came back," the conductor said.

"Did you see where he went when he got off?"

"No, though I might be able find out before your other train leaves, Milord." The conductor rubbed the thumb of his right hand against the index finger, hinting that a small fee would turn the 'might' into a distinct possibility.

"That would be very satisfactory." Sir Henry reached into his pocket and pulled out a soft leather purse. He took a coin out and offered it to the conductor. "I will leave it in your capable hands."

The conductor grinned and turned on his heel, vanishing down the length of the carriage.

"Gold, sails on the water, bubbles and rope, end beginning. Bugger it, my foot has gone to sleep."

"Language, Claire." Sir Henry led the way off the train, holding out his hand for his daughter to take as she stepped down on to the platform.

"Not the mumblings, Father?" she asked, as their servants, Thomas and Mandy, joined them.

"No. Now, which way, Thomas?"

"The second platform, Milord, over the bridge, and we have very little time to get comfortable."

Sir Henry nodded and took Claire's hand in his arm.

A plume of smoke from a train passing below billowed up over the side of the bridge, enveloping them. Stepping through the vapour was, in a way, the same as trying to understand Claire's spluttered words. Would making sense of one set of words negate the next set, or change them? What would be the consequences of acting on them? The conundrum of the snatched phrases had sparked so many thoughts about the nature of time, predestination, and the matter of free will that Sir Henry had spent many evenings writing to fellow, gentlemen scholars. He hoped, during his stay in the capital, to put the questions to them in person, as well attend a number of lectures at Clarmont's scientific institute. Each day, it seemed, brought a new innovation and discovery. Trains and steam-powered factories seemed now the norm, yet twenty years ago they did not exist. Claire's return had brought about his own. His doubts about coming to Gateskeep were now firmly behind him.

***

"Not too bad, "Sir Henry commented, looking round the well-appointed private car. "I believe there are two sets of double sleeping compartments in this carriage. I want you to share with me, Thomas, and you, Mandy, with Lady Claire."

"Keep an eye on me. Blood on the floor. Guns in the air." Claire pulled the long hat pin from her hat and handed it, along with her gloves and cloak, to Mandy, then dismissed her.

Sir Henry walked to the small table by the window overlooking the platform. On its polished surface were a number of newspapers and periodicals. He sat down in one of the overstuffed chairs by the table and picked up the Gateskeep Sun. "Emily Manling's memorial service was yesterday. Damn waste."

"Alive not dead. Sails on the water, bubbles and rope." Claire sat down opposite her father.

Sir Henry lowered the newspaper. "Claire ..." his face darkened with concern.

"I said something about Lady Emily, didn't I?"

"You remember." Sir Henry leaned forward.

"I don't think so."

"We can always go home, or south. I don't need to be in Gateskeep." Now they were nearly there, he knew it was right, but he had to let her know he would abide by her decision if Claire changed her mind.

118

"Yes you do. Howorth. Guns in the air. Besides, you are looking forward to it."

A rapping noise on the carriage's glass door turned Sir Henry's head. It was the conductor from the other train. Sir Henry stood and walked to the door.

"Milord, the question you asked," the breathless conductor said.

"Yes."

"The gentleman went to the telegraph office. I believe he purchased a ticket on this train. Second class, I am thinking. The senior conductor in charge said first was full." The conductor's fingers were again rubbing together.

"Very good, my man. I don't suppose you managed to find out anything about the telegram he sent." Sir Henry reached for his change purse and slipped one coin, another, then another out.

"Milord, it's against the law to divulge the contents of personal telegrams, even if, of the hundreds sent, I could find it. Not that I would be looking for it." The conductor's fingers stopped rubbing together and went to his trouser pocket.

"Of course, of course." Sir Henry weighed the coins in his hand and offered them to the conductor. "For your extra trouble and *any expenses* you incurred in getting this information."

"My thanks, Milord." The conductor brought his hand out of his pocket. As he took the coins, he placed a screwed-up piece of paper into Sir Henry's hand. Sir Henry closed his fist quickly and nodded to the conductor. The man returned the nod and left the carriage, stepping onto the platform as the train began to move.

"Father, did you break the law? Tap, tap, letters on the wire."

"No, not break — bent." Sir Henry returned to his seat, placing the ball of crumpled paper on the table. He patted his top pocket and pulled out his pipe. His thumb pressed the cold ashes in the bowl. Did he really want to read the message? It could be faked, of course.

"Well," Claire said.

"Here goes nothing."

"Four gold coins is not nothing."

"It is only money."

"You say that when you haven't got any."

"Was that Oracle speaking?"

119

"It was me."

He pulled the paper open and read it. He did not have to read more than the addressee: Brother Harrison, the Haven of the Inner Ring, Hostmain Street, Gateskeep.

"Red robe."

"Yes, they know you are coming."

"Good. Stop it, Father, so we can turn the world on its head. Open the box. End them. Tear them down. Speak in the Forum. Politics and religion, father, both must be reshaped. Good man. Goddess' sacrifice. Cruel man, become the enemy of all. Toby dog."

***

Sir Henry watched the end of the debate from the main doorway to the floor of the High Forum.

"Order, gentlemen, order, I say." Lord Tavengill, master of the High Forum, was hard-pressed to keep control of the debate. Members were on their feet, shouting. Many were red-faced, unable to contain their anger. Clenched sheaves of paper were brandished like swords. Arms waved. Members stood toe-to-toe with their fellows, preening like fighting cocks. The very air crackled with emotion. One man stood silent and still amid the chaos: Lord Joshua Calvinward.

"Gentlemen!" Lord Augustus Howorth, leader of the Stategentry party, bellowed. "Gentlemen! I wish to hear what Lord Calvinward has to say."

His words were taken up by fellow members of his party, and the opposition. Lord Tavengill heaved himself out of his ornately carved chair. His face was red; sweat ran down his fat cheeks. The ceremonial sword in his hand waved to and fro. "Order, gentlemen! Let Lord Calvinward continue!"

The members began to quiet down. Some sat, turning their backs on Calvinward, indicating their disgust at his perceived back-pedaling on previously-agreed points of the bill. Howorth, though, Sir Henry noticed, was glancing down at his feet. He knew what was coming; of course he did.

"Order!" Tavengill gave one final bellow.

Calvinward looked round at his fellow members and then at the documents he was holding.

"Get on with it!" A member shouted.

"Order!"

"The amendments proposed for the bill," Calvinward began.

"Woolly thinking!" Another voice shouted from behind him.

Calvinward turned to face his fellow member. "Sir, might I suggest you look at the last page. And I quote: *'To insure a slow, but complete, implementation of the bill, it is proposed that the High Forum undertake to set up a completely independent inspectorate that will oversee, at a grass-roots level, the changes that are necessary in all industries, and so safeguard the interests of both bond contract worker and employer, thus insuring that the needs of one are not forfeited for the benefit of the other.'* In other words, gentlemen, both sides have to work together."

Howls of anger and astonishment erupted. Sir Henry doubted that any of the members heard the ringing of the Forum bell, marking the end of the session. The debate had come to a ferocious end. The place was a sea of thrown ballot papers. Calvinward's proposal of an inspectorate in the act's amendments had been played with all the skill of a card shark. He had timed the moment with perfection. It had nullified all the previous days of debate, and had the far left in Howorth's Stategentry party baying with frustration. It had shocked quite a few of Calvinward's own party as well, especially those to the far right.

Joshua's progress from the room was slow. His back was slapped and hand shook. Lord Augustus Howorth was waiting by the end of the lower row of seats. From where Sir Henry was standing, he could catch their conversation.

"Calvinward, that's a bit of an about-turn, eh, what?" Howorth said. He pulled his silver watch from his waist coat pocket and flipped the engraved lid open. His words were at odds with the expression in his eyes. It confirmed everything Elizabeth had said to be true.

"On the contrary, it is a different approach to the matters facing our country. One I have wanted to bring before the Forum for a long time."

"Hogwash." Howorth snapped his watch shut. "But damn well-played hogwash, give you that."

"From a master in the dealing of such, I take that as a compliment."

"Careful sir, you will someday be so sharp you will cut yourself."

"I doubt it, sir, I doubt it." Joshua gave his opponent a small bow.

"I don't. You eating?" Augustus said, suddenly changing the subject. "Fancy a late lunch at the Dog? If, that is, we can get those soldiers that sit on our tails to allow us." Howorth winked at Calvinward, who gave a laugh and indicated for Howorth to walk with him towards the doors.

"We better check with the young men who have the woeful task of looking after us first. I don't want them falling foul of Major Avinguard."

Sir Henry smiled. He had seen enough; time for him to leave. Claire was waiting for him in the antechamber. He knew she was tired, but on no account would she admit it. Sir Henry worried that the strain of being exposed to the crowd milling in the large, marble-floored room would be too much for her.

Claire was standing in one of the many pools of light which cascaded through the high, narrow windows of the chamber. She was looking round, watching the dispersing crowd make their way to the massive stone staircase which led down to the lower-entrance lobby. Toby was at her feet, his small head pressed into the blue wool of her skirt. Thankfully, the animal was overawed by its surrounding, and not indulging in his normal pastime of causing trouble. Sir Henry reached Claire's side and took her arm.

"Fitzguard!"

Sir Henry knew the voice: Howorth. He turned and smiled at the two approaching men. He had wanted this meeting to be a little more private, but he could not avoid it. "Howorth, you old dog. A right mess you have been stirring up, you and this gentleman. You, sir, I take it, are Lord Joshua Calvinward." Sir Henry offered his hand first to Howorth, then to Calvinward.

"We know you from your picture in the paper," Claire said. "But the drawn likeness does not do you justice, sir. Bugger it. Toby heel. Bite soon. Hard to the bone." She gave Sir Henry a small smile, in an effort to impress on him she was in control. "Sorry, I know I must try and watch my language, but it splutters out."

"Do not concern yourself my dear — I am sure the gentlemen have heard worse in their time. Try not to use it in front of the other ladies," Sir Henry said.

"Straight-laced. Corsets and bustles much too tight. Out of fashion soon. Oh dear, I better be quiet, my apologies." Claire blushed.

122

Sir Henry watched the two High Forum members' reactions to Claire's words. Surprisingly, Calvinward's lips were twitching in amusement at her pronouncements. Howorth, on the other hand, had taken half a step back, as if embarrassed by her display. "Augustus, Joshua, if I may call you that?"

Calvinward nodded slightly.

"May I present my daughter, Claire, who has recovered enough in health to attempt a return into society, and to be my hostess while I am here."

"Claire?" Howorth said.

Claire tilted her head to one side and held out her gloved right hand. Howorth hesitated for a moment before he took it, kissing the air a fraction above the fabric of her glove before he released it.

"Yes, me, for all my sins, I am still alive and kicking. Slightly ragged in the mind, but sane and intent on doing my best here in Gateskeep for my father and — " Claire's gloved hand came quickly to her mouth, covering her next words. Her hand dropped to her side. "As you can see, I am sadly given to nervous outbursts of nonsense, in between the sense, or is it the other way round? You will have to excuse me, dear sirs. I have no control over it. It's the result of my illness, but quite harmless, I can assure you."

Claire extended her hand to Calvinward, who said, "Of course you are."

It was plain to Sir Henry that Calvinward was noting his daughter's good looks, as well as comparing her behaviour here with her old reputation. Or perhaps with what Pugh might have said about his ex-wife. According to Elizabeth, Calvinward and Pugh had become good friends. An odd relationship, that. Sir Henry found it hard to think of anything they had in common. Perhaps that was it.

Claire was also scrutinising Calvinward. Even though her eyes were hidden, she, or perhaps Oracle, was taking in every aspect of his features and behaviour. And Sir Henry was sure Calvinward was aware of it.

"Dog and beef. Guns in the air." Claire's right hand reached out towards Sir Henry. He took it. She was shivering.

He knew it: this was proving too much for her. For a few moments, he had begun to believe everything was as it had been, but it was not. Claire was different. Special in ways he doubted he would ever understand. "Gentlemen, if you will excuse us."

"Of course, till we meet again." Howorth bowed to Claire and again shook Sir Henry's hand and began to move off.

Calvinward held out his hand to Sir Henry and said, "I hope you and your daughter will dine with me soon."

Sir Henry looked at Claire, who gave a slight smile. "We will be delighted."

"Lady Claire." Calvinward gave more than the normal bow, turned and followed Howorth.

"Are you well, Claire?" Sir Henry asked. Claire gave a small nod and tried to smile, but the upturning of her mouth faded. She was pale, and her breathing was ragged. "We are going now." Sir Henry tucked her left hand through his arm and led her through the large, brass-studded doors to the main staircase.

A stiff, winter breeze billowed up from the open main door below. It ruffled the hem of Claire's walking dress and stirred the lace veil on her matching hat. The marble staircase was wide. The pale sun flickered through the expanse of glass roof. Interspersed along the wall on either side were deep-set niches containing works of art.

"Guns in the air! Blood on the stairs. Run! Run! Knock them to the floor Toby dog, bite to the bone. Goddess' sacrifice. Guns and blood!" The words burst from Claire's mouth. Her fingers tightened on his arm, and she tugged at the fabric of his sleeve. Her other arm pointed down the stairs towards Calvinward and Howorth.

"Claire, what on earth?"

"Guns and blood! Run! Run!" Claire increased her pace down the stairs. Sir Henry followed. Soon they were running, dodging between others that were descending. Something was going to happen — he felt it. Ahead of them, Calvinward and Howorth had stopped and begun to turn round, the clatter of feet above them having gained their attention. Claire let go of Sir Henry's arm and ran full tilt into Calvinward. "Claire, stop! What on earth!" Sir Henry bellowed, as a volley of gunshots thundered in the air above them.

Calvinward, off balance, lost his footing. His left arm went out to stop his fall. Claire caught it with her right hand and pulled him over. Down he went, sprawling on his back on the steps. Calvinward grunted in pain, began to rise, then thought better of it. He twisted round so he could see in the direction of the shots.

Sir Henry threw himself down onto the marble steps. "Get down, Howorth! Both of you stay down!"

A fierce tide of screams and cries echoed off the high ceiling. People dashed in all directions. Many fell. Some dropped, bonelessly, onto the marble steps. Sir Henry tried to see what was happening. *Guns in the air! Blood on the stairs!* The words Claire had recently uttered were coming true. He began to feel sick.

"Goddess!" Calvinward began to move.

Claire tightened her grip on his arm. "Stay down. Don't move, safe here. Move dead."

More shots rang out, close by. Fragments of stone flew up and peppered the left side of Calvinward's face. He instinctively flinched. Slowly his hand came up and gingerly touched his face. He was bleeding. "Hell and damnation."

But what of Howorth? Sir Henry shuddered. When the first shots had been fired, Howorth had been rooted to the spot. Then he had slumped to the floor. Was he badly hurt, even dead?

"Howorth, are you unharmed?" Sir Henry wriggled along the cold marble to the prone form of Howorth, praying under his breath to the Goddess that the man was all right. No. He had been shot. A trickle of blood ran from the ripped sleeve of Howorth's jacket. The sick feeling in Sir Henry's stomach began to spread.

"Damn. Blast. Bugger. Guns in the air. Up, look up, the balcony above the main door to the lobby. Go. Go. Sails on the water. Alive not dead. Toby, heel." The dog whined, struggling to obey his mistress. He hopped up one step, then down again.

Above the door into the antechamber was a large, ornately carved balcony: a place where formal declarations had been made for centuries. It was perfect to sit and pick off the members as they descended. As he looked up the staircase, Sir Henry saw it was littered with, *oh Goddess*, bodies— perhaps five or six, but he did not doubt there were many more. Carefully, he looked behind him towards the entrance to the street. He could not see all the way down, but he could see

125

people were in small groups. Some huddling together, others pressed round the statues and under the paintings displayed in the alcoves.

"Not move," Claire said, hitting Calvinward in the chest. "They tried." She pointed to a jumble of fabric and limbs a few paces away. Another shot rang out and Sir Henry ducked.

"We have to move into the niches," Calvinward said, trying to stop the anger in his voice, but not succeeding. He began to inch his body across the steps.

"My daughter is right; we can't, not yet." Sir Henry placed a restraining hand on the shoulder of Howorth, who was struggling to rise. Sir Henry glanced to his left. The young officer, who had been escorting Calvinward and Howorth, was there. He had a hand pressed to his shoulder, the blood trickling through his fingers. The officer gave a sharp nod, reinforcing Sir Henry's words. Calvinward reluctantly stopped moving.

Howorth looked towards Calvinward, then at Sir Henry. "A sniper. Who and why, for the Goddess' sake? Can't people see they are tearing the heart out of the country?"

"Using a rifle?" Calvinward moved up onto his elbows, ignoring Claire, who was telling him to keep his head down. He looked up at the balcony.

"No, you couldn't get that many shots off so quickly with a rifle. I would say a militia officer's pistol, perhaps two or three of them ready-loaded."

"How many shots fired, do you think, Sir Henry?" Calvinward looked around.

"A good dozen and a half, maybe more. Not that good a shot, though. Perhaps the distance might have something to do with that."

"He has stopped firing, least for now. Must be barricaded in there. Look." Calvinward's words drew Sir Henry's gaze back up the staircase. A number of figures in militia green crept out of the door to the lobby and down either side of the staircase, dodging from niche to niche. *About damn well time.*

"Yes. Over before it begins, turn the world on its head, have to be safe," Claire cried, pulling at Calvinward's jacket sleeve.

He looked at Sir Henry. They had no other choice. They had to take their chance. Sir Henry nodded slowly in agreement. Howorth did the same. Sir Henry took a deep breath that did nothing to settle the sickness in his stomach.

He looked first at his daughter, then Calvinward, then Howorth. He began to count.

"Toby heel, mad dash. Sails in the water, bubbles and rope. Pull it down. And turn the world on its HEAD!" Claire shouted and was on her feet, running, Toby following.

"Claire! Damn you!" Sir Henry bellowed, and started after her. Calvinward did the same. A stream of bullets snapped through the air. Sir Henry felt something tug his jacket. His heart lurched, and in that split second he waited for a bolt of pain, but it did not come. He ducked low and flung himself down. He slid on his bottom and hit hard against the stone wall. A shot buried itself in the wall above his head. His heart pounded, and struggling for breath, Sir Henry moved quickly down the wall. Here he joined his daughter and Calvinward behind a statue in one of the niches.

Where was Howorth? Sir Henry turned round and looked across a scene of devastation. *Goddess be thanked.* Lord Howorth had run the other way, taking with him the young officer. They were both safe on the other side. Others, too, had seized the moment and run for safety in the various alcoves. Near the top of the stairs, Sir Henry could see a militia officer, the fading daylight flashing on his gold epaulets. The officer looked sideways at the few men who had snaked out down the steps. He spoke quickly to one of the soldiers by his side.

"He is going to make the bastard show himself," Calvinward said.

Sir Henry agreed and found he, like Calvinward, had developed a sickly fascination with what was happening at the head of the staircase.

"Fire soon," Claire whispered.

The soldiers sprang from their positions, fanning out across the steps. Their rifles came up, aiming at the balcony. A blizzard of shots rang out, tearing at the heavy red velvet at the back of the raised platform. A number of shots rang in reply. Soldiers fell. Their comrades scattered, changing position. They began to load and fire their rifles at will. Suddenly the firing stopped and a loud, crashing noise was heard from the balcony.

127

CHAPTER FIFTEEN

Pugh stood at the top of the marble staircase and addressed the captain by his side. "Get those people back from the entrance. I want the whole place cleared of spectators, including the press. Yes, I know, Forum members are crying about their autonomy, but they will have to put up with us being in control for now. Bring the medical personnel in through the west staff door. All wounded to the members' dining room on the ground floor.

"I need a list of casualties and survivors as soon as possible. And has Master of the High Forum been found yet? As to the dead, no removal by relatives until identity has been confirmed. Place a guard on the temporary morgue if need be, Captain." This was the latest in a series of orders he had rattled off. The events of the past few hours had been a boil waiting to burst. Pugh had known it; so had others, but they had refused to see. All had indeed been turned on its head. Whether the Howorth Labour and Industry bill was placed on the statute books or not, Timeholm would never be the same. The High Forum would have to agree to his requests to search members of the public, and Forum employees, as they entered the building. Some of the more obscure entrances needed to be sealed up. The place was a five-hundred-year-old rabbit warren. Who knew how long the sniper had been up there?

"The survivors, sir?" The captain asked.

"Yes, Captain Gunmain, have them taken to the members' club and given a good brandy. Assign two junior officers to talk to them. We need a picture of how events started. And keep the damn press out of there."

Gunmain saluted Pugh and turned to relay his orders.

The hastily wrapped body of the man responsible for the carnage lay on a makeshift stretcher a few paces from Pugh. His pockets had been searched, and the neat leather bag he had with him. The four new-model pistols used each cost more than a working man could earn in a lifetime. The man's clothes were well-made and his fingernails manicured. A gentleman: if so, a very disgruntled one. There had been two letters in the bag. Pugh had them tucked inside his jacket; he had not yet read them. One was addressed to the Master of the High Forum, another to a Lady Canvish.

Pugh began to walk down the steps. The staircase was littered with hats, canes, garments of all sorts. Blood was smeared across the white marble steps and parts of the wall. It was as if some artist had decided to redecorate the staircase to represent some strange hell. Bodies were being placed on makeshift stretchers. Some moved, weakly, their hands reaching up for the comforting touch of another human being; others were still, faces covered by coats and jackets. Soldiers helped survivors down the steps, directing them with murmured words. The level of noise on the staircase was no more than a gentle hum; all were reluctant to raise their voices. He was sure that there were people he knew among the injured and dead. Some he would have spoken to earlier today.

He reached the bottom of the staircase, nodded to the guards on duty, and turned down the corridor on the left. The hush that had fallen on the staircase did not prevail here. Cries of pain and sobs mixed into hellish sound that would have any sane person putting their hands over their ears. He merely clamped his jaw tightly: he had a job to do.

Pugh followed two men carrying a stretcher into the senior members' committee room. The drapes had been hastily drawn across the windows at the far end. The long table in the middle of the room housed a number of stretchers, which had been placed widthways over the polished oak. The men placed the stretcher on the floor under the desk.

"Push it sideways. Going to have to stack'em close. Got a few more yet," one of the soldiers said.

"Need another room — reckon that bugger got a good dozen or more," his companion answered, pushing the end of the stretcher. The hand of the corpse fell off the edge and hung there. The thick, twisted gold ring on the index finger caught the light from the sputtering oil lamps set in the ceiling and drew Pugh's attention.

The soldier placed the hand on the chest of the corpse and patted it. He gave the edge of the stretcher a further push to move it closer to the far end of the table. "That'll do."

Pugh began to move among the dead. He stopped by the stretcher the men had brought in, and crouched down. He looked at the ring. Yes, he knew it. Pugh reached forward, pulling the cloth off the corpse's face. Lord Tavengill, the very man who had been the most vehement and outspoken against the proposed security measures.

"As you can see, we're short a Master of the High Forum," Lord Howorth said. His voice lacked its normal confidence and power.

Pugh looked back towards the door. The leader of the Stategentry party was standing there. He was in his shirt sleeves, the right one ripped and the arm itself roughly bandaged.

Pugh replaced the cloth on Lord Tavengill's face and stood up. "Lord Calvinward and I have volunteered to try and identify as many as we can."

"It also gives us a little privacy to continue our discussion," Lord Calvinward said from the doorway. "A decision must be reached quickly, and an announcement made. Lord Tavengill's death must not stop the house sitting tomorrow. We must go on. A day of mourning in a few days, yes, but for now all must be as normal." Calvinward walked into the room. His conversation was all business, but Calvinward, like Howorth, had not come through unscathed. The side of his face was peppered with cuts and had, by the looks of it, been dabbed with iodine. Pugh did not envy the task the two men had appointed themselves.

"Too soon, too soon," Howorth said.

"Nonsense, don't you agree Pugh? We must not show the enemy that they have scored a victory. Life, the work of the Forum, must be seen to go on." Calvinward approached the first stretcher balanced across the table. He reached out, hesitated for a moment, and gently removed the coat from the face of the victim. "*Goddess*. It's Kentward's youngest girl. She must have been here to see that brother of hers take his seat."

"We are not at war, Joshua. Kentward, you say? Damn!" Howorth's shoulders slumped.

"I am sorry to say it is a war, Milord. One that you won't win, only gain a ceasefire at some point." Pugh watched Howorth reluctantly pull back a covering from another corpse. Timeholm was in the grip of the beginnings of a revolution. What path it would take only the Goddess knew, and perhaps a ramshackle Glimpser with near white-blonde hair.

"Clive Haventrent." Howorth winced and rolled his left arm.

"You are in pain, sir. If you wish to retire, I can continue alone," Calvinward said, an expression of genuine concern on his face.

"No. I am quite up to the task, I can assure you. Though the Goddess knows what would have become of both of us if it hadn't been for Fitzguard's sharp thinking."

"Sir Henry is here?" Pugh asked, trying to keep his voice level.

"Yes, and his daughter. They knocked us both to the floor when the gunman started firing. Saved both our lives. And, Augustus, think about it. He is the ideal candidate for the position of Master. He is well known, with no current ties to either party." Calvinward continued to move along the line of dead.

"That might be so. But he made it plain he is only here for this debate."

Pugh felt himself stiffen. They both must be mistaken. Claire no longer existed; only a creature driven by rambling voices lived in her body. To even begin to think that she might be here, and be well, was folly. As for knocking the two men to the floor, yes, he could believe that of Sir Henry. Perhaps he had done the same to the woman, and they had jumped to the wrong conclusion.

"Even if he is, it would be an ideal temporary measure, don't you think so, Pugh?"

"It is not for me to say." Pugh cleared his throat. "Gentlemen, when you have finished, could you write a list of the victims for me? And is Sir Henry in with the survivors?"

"Of course, of course, and no, Sir Henry and his daughter are assisting the wounded," Howorth said.

***

Stretchers carrying the last of the wounded hurried along the corridor. A contingent of nurses in starched, white hats, escorted by a harassed lieutenant looking very much out of his depth, followed in the stretchers' wake. Three doctors brought up the rear of this strange parade.

Pugh stood aside to allow them to pass. Opposite him the door to the members' club was open. He could hear Captain Gunmain addressing the occupants and fielding questions. It sounded like Gunmain needed a bit of support. He waved a soldier by the door over. "I want you to go into the senior members' committee room. Give Lords Howorth and Calvinward my compliments, and ask on my behalf if they could assist Captain Gunmain."

131

The soldier saluted and hurried to do Pugh's bidding.

"A wise decision, Major."

Pugh looked across the corridor. Senior Chapel Minister Carlsonmark was standing there. *Hell and damnation.* This was all he needed. A chapel minister aiming to preach at him about the Goddess' will. Carlsonmark was the youngest of the seven ministers who sat in the High Forum. During the rout on the stairs, the man must have lost his tricorn hat; a mass of unruly brown curls fell across his forehead and made him look younger than his forty years.

"Thank you, Minister," Pugh replied.

"You are welcome, Major. I will not detain you. I know you have much to do, but if you need any help beating sense into the heads of my fellow High Forum members in the next few days, with regards to security, I am at your disposal."

"I... thank you again, Minister." Pugh nearly spluttered in surprise. It was certainly not what he had expected the man to say.

Carlsonmark gave a small nod and walked away, heading in the direction of the temporary morgue. Pugh noticed the man's grey robe was heavily stained with blood. It could not be his. He moved too easily and did not seem in pain. *Goddess.* How many had the minister held in their last few moments?

***

The door to the dining room was partly shut; as Pugh placed a hand on it, his nose was assaulted by a familiar odour. He had smelt it at Coot's Pass, in the aftermath of battle, and in the middle of the train wreck. It was the smell of pain and death, a sour mix of blood, iodine, human sweat and excrement. Pugh felt his stomach roll and his chest tighten. The images of the train crash and the horror of Coot's Pass were superimposed in his mind on the scene before him.

A man with his sleeves rolled up and hands stained with blood was tightening a bandage round a woman's abdomen. Her dress had been removed, and she lay with her legs partly covered by the froth of her lace petticoat. One shoe hung off the toes of her left foot. For a moment the man's features were that of the medical officer who had been stationed at Coot's Pass, then the bespectacled, harassed family practitioner who had been on the train. Pugh blinked and the man's features formed into Sir Henry's, his beard more sprinkled with grey since Pugh had last seen him, the crow's feet on the side of his face etched deeper. However, his eyes were still powerful, reflecting the mind behind them. Pugh began to smile. It was good to see Sir Henry again, even in these circumstances.

The hospital nurses began to make their way through the tables. As one they shrugged out of their blue capes and began to take over the care of patients from willing, but inexperienced, hands. Pugh began to head towards the leader of the group of doctors that had accompanied the nurses. He needed to know what the current situation was with the injured.

"Really!"

Pugh glanced sideways—the familiar tone of the voice caught his attention. He froze, unable or unwilling to believe his eyes. It was not possible. Claire stood there, brushing back a wayward strand of her hair with a blood-stained hand. Her face was stormy. How he remembered that anger. How it broke like a summer tempest: there one moment and gone the next.

"Leave this to me." The nurse addressed the woman who was the image of Claire.

"Leave it, bubbles and robe. Damn you. Keep the pressure there, don't go poking. Alive not dead. Sails on the water. The bullet is in there. The doctor knows it is, along with a good lump of his shirt. Both need to come out, don't leave any fabric in. Good dog, bite hard."

Oh Goddess. It was her. Her speech a mixture, part Glimpser, part rational. Why had not Sir Henry told him? Had he been cut out of the life of this new, reborn Claire without a thought? Of all the foolishness, coming here and exposing herself to the Inner Ring. The questions and ragged "what-ifs" swamped all Pugh's thoughts of his present duty. All he was aware of was that the woman he had loved and lost was there in the room.

"Claire, you are here?"

She turned from the nurse and faced him, her once beautiful, sea-green eyes masked by a pair of blue-tinted, gold-rimmed spectacles. "Pugh. Damn you, white flesh on silk." She turned away, dismissing him, returning her attention to the nurse.

How dare she, what did she know? Had she really been a Glimpser? Damn, he thought, don't think that. She had, she was, but not now. The woman before him was the old Claire, from the haughty tilt of her head to the regained womanly curves.

133

"I was surprised to see you. If you had let me know you were coming to the city...," Pugh said, carefully, suddenly mindful of the eyes of others on him.

"Why? The past is past, sir. Sails on the water, turn the world on its head."

"Yes, the past is past, but I would have still liked to know of your coming to Gateskeep. To ensure there was no needless embarrassment for either of us," Pugh answered, as coldly and as formally as he could. His heart was thudding.

"Make an appointment with my father after you have finished your duties, sir. I am here at his behest to act as his hostess. Damn, white flesh on silk. It will be too late. What did I say, Father?" Her last words were half-choked, all her pride and anger swept from her face.

"Claire." Pugh stepped forward, his left hand outstretched, his desire to hold her and to understand warring with his anger.

"No Toby!" Sir Henry shouted, as a streak of fur leapt from the floor. Pugh tried to snatch back his hand, but this gave the dog the target of his lower arm. Toby's jaws closed and his weight dragged Pugh's arm down. He bellowed in pain and grabbed the dog by the scruff of the neck with his other hand.

"Bite to the bone," Claire whispered, and fell to her knees sobbing and beating the floor with her hands.

"Let go, Toby, release!" Sir Henry commanded, grabbing Toby and helping Pugh force the dog's mouth open.

The agony of the bite joined with the emotional upheaval in Pugh's heart. Suddenly the dog yelped and let go. He looked from the blood-coated mouth of the dog in Sir Henry's arms down to Claire, sobbing on the floor. Her glasses had slipped down, revealing her colourless orbs. Her lips moved, but the words she was trying to say were locked inside.

"It seems that in this recent encounter between us I have again been wounded," Pugh said. Small pinpricks of blood were soaking through his wool jacket, embroidering a ridged pattern of red. Suddenly Pugh felt his legs weaken, not from the pain in his arm, but rather from the shadows he saw in his wife's Glimpser eyes.

***

134

Pugh was holding his injured arm and looking at her, his gaze asking questions his voice did not.

"Sir, your arm?" One of the doctors was by Pugh's side, a length of linen in his fist. Pugh gave a twisted smile and allowed the doctor to take hold of his arm.

"Take the dog and lock him in a room somewhere till I decide what to do with him," Sir Henry said to one of the soldiers close by, handing over the subdued animal.

Sir Henry knelt by Claire's side. She sobbed and hugged him, the words of Oracle spilling out in harsh whispers. "Damn, white flesh on silk. Alive not dead. Spinning, the spinning. It will be too late. Rage and anger. Death. Follow Toby, good dog, lead the way. Open the box, tear them down. Rule the Forum. Politics and religion, Father, change them. Don't let him use it as a weapon, watch him, Pugh."

"Claire, I must get you away from here." Sir Henry tightened his hold on his daughter.

"No. My fault I should have seen." Claire pushed herself free from her father's embrace. Oracle had faded away. She was alone with the turmoil of feelings that the sight of Pugh had brought. What had she said in her ramblings in those few moments? It had triggered hate in Pugh's eyes, she saw it. Of what she had been, or the past between them, that was not over, nor forgotten. She sniffed and wiped away the tears, leaving dark red smears across her cheeks. "Pugh?"

"A doctor is seeing to his arm. The thickness of his jacket saved him from too much damage; Toby only has a small mouth. Damn that dog, we should not have brought him."

"But the others here that need help." The chaos had taken on a strange order. Another group of medical staff, militia men this time, had arrived and were assisting. Stretchers were now being moved out of the room. The place felt suddenly empty.

"There is nothing for us to do here now; let us get that no-good dog and take our leave." Sir Henry took her hand, guiding her to the side of the room where he had thrown his coat and jacket along with Claire's. Silently, he helped Claire into her jacket and cloak. Once attired, they moved to the doorway.

"Sir Henry?" It was Calvinward. He stood in the corridor.

"Milord." Sir Henry bowed slightly as Calvinward came through the open door, followed by Howorth.

"You are leaving?" Howorth asked, and glanced in the direction of Pugh.

Claire gulped. "My dog bit Major Avinguard." She had mumbled the words, "good dog bite deep," for days, not understanding, till that moment Toby leapt at Pugh, whom the dog was going to bite. She felt the burden of what she was settle heavy on her shoulders. Hate me, Pugh. Better than loving me. I must live with this. I must. Again the thought that life as Oracle was better surfaced: no feelings or knowing what damage your words and actions did to others. No seeing the pain in the eyes.

"Nor any joy." The old woman's voice echoed deep in her mind, offering her comfort. "There is happiness, too, love and laughter. Lose one, you lose all."

"By the Goddess. What did he do?" Calvinward said, quite startled, and looked at Pugh. It was obvious he was finding it hard to believe that Pugh could act churlishly to a lady.

"Nothing, merely spoke to me. The dog perhaps sensed something, sails on the water. Over, lost and gone, waste." Claire cleared her throat and looked at the disapproving face of Lord Howorth. Her eyes closed for a moment. "I nearly destroyed an honourable man with my behaviour. Our marriage was annulled after I was taken ill. His career has since flourished. We have both moved on. I am not what I was, and he is still the honourable man." As she finished speaking, Claire's gaze strayed to Pugh. He had removed his jacket and rolled up his shirt. His lower arm had been bandaged.

Howorth followed her gaze with his own and coughed. "Forgive me, Lady Claire, I have misjudged you. You have as much courage and honour as he." Howorth gave her a bow. Claire felt her father's hand on her shoulder.

"I see," Calvinward said. "Understandable, and brave of you, my dear. About the dog?"

"I may consider having him shot," Sir Henry said, sharply. "He attacked a man. Come, Claire, we are in the way."

"Sir Henry, we must talk. The three of us, Avinguard and others. Tonight, at my home," Calvinward said.

"I don't think ...," Sir Henry began.

Claire could feel Oracle suddenly awake inside her. "Rule the Forum and accept politics and religion." The words blurted from her mouth. Her eyes widened. Suddenly a wave

136

of sickness grasped her stomach. This speaking and not remembering, yet being aware of speaking, was it worse than not being aware of anything?

CHAPTER SIXTEEN

The hour was late. Sir Henry looked down the long table in the centre of the formal dining room in Calvinward's town house. Gathered round it were some of the most important men in the country: High Forum members; senior ministers of the Orthodox Chapel; police and militia. General Sir Albert Fitzmarshall coughed. He folded the letter in his hands, once, twice, and held it to one of the candles in the centre of the table. The paper flared, sending an additional layer of light across the assembled faces. Sir Albert crushed the flaming paper into the dregs of his wine. The paper hissed and spat, sending a column of dark smoke towards the ceiling. "That is my answer, Major Avinguard. Your resignation is not accepted."

"Hear, hear," Calvinward said, his words echoed by the other diners, including Sir Henry.

Sir Henry watched Pugh shift in his seat. Was he intending to force the issue? If so, Sir Henry had other ideas. He needed Pugh to stay in his current position. Sir Henry pushed away the plate in front of him. He, too, had a piece of paper. He unfolded it and looked at it again. "As I am now acting Master of the High Forum, I concur with the general. You are needed where you are, Avinguard. As for today's horrific event," he said, brandishing the letter at his fellow diners, "it was the act of a lone gunman."

Senior Chapel Minister Carlsonmark coughed to gain everyone's attention. "Sir Henry, are you totally sure it was the act of one man? I know that I speak for the Orthodox Chapel as a whole when I say that we hope no stone will be unturned in discovering the truth behind today's events." His fellow senior minister, Hornwick, nodded in agreement.

"Everything points to it, but Chief Inspector Veinman," Sir Henry said, nodding in the direction of the man, "will of course continue to investigate the matter."

"Indeed we will," said Veinman, "but all indications do point to this being the act of one individual. Sadly, gentlemen, this can be the hardest to predict."

General Sir Albert nodded in agreement. "The Forum must allow Avinguard to implement changes to security. We also need an increased police presence. The militia will, if needs be, provide support, but I would prefer this to be done on a situation-by-situation basis. I do not want to see the High Forum declaring martial law in my lifetime."

"Well said, sir." Calvinward rapped the table with his fingers and watched the effect of the general's words on his fellows.

Sir Henry was sure he saw relief on Calvinward's face, but it was hard to judge. Calvinward was an expert player in the game. It would be foolish to believe everything the man said or did as gospel. The scale of the unfolding events that had followed the riot in Hitsmine had confounded many. He had to wryly admit he, also, had underestimated public feeling regarding the proposed bill.

"It is agreed, then, that the Forum sits tomorrow," Howorth said, reaching for his wine glass. Sir Henry noticed that Howorth was pale: his arm, or perhaps it was the fact that the gunman had been one Sir Canvish, a firm advocate of the bill. Canvish had removed his support when the bill had not gone far enough for his tastes. His letter shocked all at the table. Canvish had written that Howorth had abused the trust of the working class and knew the bill would never be passed. Canvish had been an outspoken fool, but none here had believed him to be a fanatic to such a degree.

"Yes. We will begin with a few moments of silence in respect. Then the Forum will confirm me as Master. And my first job will be to announce that it is business as usual. I will suggest a national day of mourning at some future date. I defer to you, Minister Hornwick, in this." Sir Henry looked at the senior of the two chapel ministers.

The man did not answer, but looked at his fellow, Minister Carlsonmark, who again answered for the chapel. "Of course, Sir Henry, but it must be a day driven by respect for the dead and injured. Not one to be used for political posturing by either side."

"In that, we are in agreement," Sir Henry said.

A slight cough from behind drew Calvinward's attention from his fellow diners. It was his butler. The man leaned close and said, "a gentleman you were expecting has arrived. I have shown him to your study, sir."

Joshua frowned. "Gentlemen, will you excuse me for a little while? Please continue; I will rejoin you shortly."

"Nothing wrong?" Sir Henry asked. He glanced down the table towards Pugh, who began to stand.

"Nothing, I assure you. I shall not be long — please continue," Calvinward said, and made his way to the door. He glanced back at the table as he left the room. Pugh was still standing, watching him leave.

***

Calvinward's departure from the room acted as a trigger, with most of the dinner guests quickly begging to be excused. Sir Henry became the ad hoc host, wishing them goodnight and saying he would convey their thanks to Calvinward. Soon there were but four gentlemen remaining round the table: Sir Henry, Lord Howorth, General Sir Albert and Pugh.

Calvinward's butler brought out another bottle of port, along with a box of cigars, and placed them on the table. Sir Henry got up, moved down the table and sat next to Pugh. Lord Howorth did the same, picking up the bottle of port as he did so.

"So, you are going to lock us in each day?" Lord Howorth asked Pugh.

"Seems that way."

"Might actually get some business done, eh," General Sir Albert said, laughing.

"We might at that," Lord Howorth said.

"Sir Henry," Calvinward said from the doorway.

Sir Henry turned in his seat. "Lord Calvinward."

"I would have wished for our first meeting to less fraught. Don't you agree, Howorth?" Calvinward shut the doors to the dining room behind him and walked to the table. He took a seat next to Howorth.

"Indeed. To business," Howorth said, leaning forward.

"And that is?" Sir Henry looked round the small group.

"Will you support us?" Calvinward asked.

"In getting this bill on the statute books? This morning I would have said yes, but now I am Master of the High Forum and I have to be ..."

"Impartial, exactly, sir!" General Sir Albert said.

"I don't understand," Pugh said.

"It's what we need. Goddess knows, I wouldn't have had it this way, but with Lord Tavengill gone we have more than a good chance. He was sticking his fat fingers in everywhere. It was one of the reasons I asked Elizabeth to speak to you, Sir Henry. We had enough to impeach him if we had to, but there was no one here we could trust to replace him. We needed someone who would give the act a fair hearing."

"But with you being semi-retired...," Howorth added.

"A hell of a risk, gentlemen," Pugh said, shaking his head.

These two men had been prepared to take down the Master of the High Forum. Had either of them arranged the shooting? Impossible. They were the main targets, were they not? Sir Henry felt a chill at the back of his neck. "Today ..."

"No." Calvinward's answer was brutally sharp. "I would personally sacrifice anything to get this bill through, but orchestrating something like today, never. What good would it do except force my fellow members to become deeper entrenched? If I achieve nothing else in my life than this, I would die a happy man. I know I shocked Howorth when I approached him."

"Why?" Sir Henry asked. He was curious. He could see that Pugh was, as well.

"I have seen what a man bent on personal glory can do. Manling was behind much of the ill affecting our country over the last thirty years. Look at our soured relationship with Crossmire, for one. I would rather be remembered for doing something that helped our people rather than used them."

Was that it, was Calvinward a woolly-headed idealist? Sir Henry did not believe it for a second. No. Calvinward was a politician who actually believed it was his duty to serve the country and its people. He was as rare as a snowball at midsummer. He reminded Sir Henry of himself in his younger days, before he became cynical of the whole political system. It was the reason why Howorth had thrown in his lot with Calvinward, and why Pugh liked him. Calvinward, for all his studied veneer, was like a rising sun full of promise. Sir Henry suddenly felt sick in the pit of his stomach. The words Claire had uttered: *Goddess' sacrifice.* Not possible. He had had too much port; it was affecting his train of thought. But the feeling lingered, making the bile rise in his throat.

***

A thick plume of smoke rose from the funnel of the gun ship. Unlike its predecessors, it did not have to rely on an incoming

141

tide to navigate the river Holm so far upstream. Colliridge wondered if any of its sister ships would be joining it. It had taken up station downstream of Highspire Bridge. Both the Forum building on the opposite shore and the Inner Ring's headquarters behind him were in range of its guns. Protecting whom from whom?

"An eventful day," the man standing next to Colliridge said, pulling up his coat collar against the evening chill.

"Indeed." Even he had been surprised by events. But the random acts of an individual could not be predicted.

"Polarised opinions more, do you think?"

"Maybe."

"And maybe not. It could have the opposite effect."

"That would be welcomed by some." Colliridge did not like these open air rendezvous. Yes, he understood the ambassador's reasons for them. Two gentlemen, wrapped against the evening air, out for a stroll.

"It would depend on various factors. But an aye or nay majority in the vote will cause unrest nevertheless."

"And unrest is very desirable?"

The ambassador did not answer. He turned and began to walk along the bank away from the Chapel of the Inner Ring. Colliridge joined him. The chapel sat on the eastern bank of the river Holm, the High Forum building on the western side. The dark bulk of what remained of Timeholm's past seat of power lay before them, its spires illuminated by the moon, Caresight. The Highspire Bridge had linked the two halves of the castle. Each spire was the gatehouse of its half. If the section of the castle on the west of the river had fallen to the enemy, the section on the east would have been able to cut itself off. Great gates had been situated in the centre of the spires, but the gates were long gone. Horse-drawn traffic clattered daily across the bridge, watched by the entwined figures carved into the stone on both spires.

They walked a good dozen paces before the ambassador spoke again. "So the lady is indeed alive."

"Yes."

"And what I outlined earlier. Can you pull it off?"

"Of course, but where Lady Constance is concerned, are you sure she will blame him?" Colliridge had his doubts. The lady in question was intelligent; it wouldn't be easy to fool her. Calvinward, on the other hand, had already made up his mind.

"Don't underestimate a lioness protecting her cub. Besides, Calvinward's coolness to her of late has bruised the lady's ego somewhat. Her husband's death has left her shut out. Power is addictive. And the lady has a taste for it. She will bite."

"What of the young man?"

"You said he was a bit of a rebel, with what he believes is a just cause. He could be useful; besides, the Lady Emily might be very reluctant to leave without him. He can be disposed of later, if necessary."

***

Colliridge stood by the fire, holding out one hand to the sullen blaze in an effort to warm his fingers. He turned as Calvinward closed the door.

Calvinward walked quickly to his desk. He pulled the small, silver key from his waistcoat pocket and opened the centre drawer. He did not speak, merely pulled out a leather-bound folder and a large, calfskin money pouch.

"Is that my final payment? I was hoping for a box of those cigars." A small jest, which brought no smile to Calvinward's face.

"You can help yourself."

Colliridge pulled out the small portrait of Emily from the pocket of his long coat. He looked at it, then up at Calvinward, before handing it over.

Calvinward took the small plate of painted porcelain and placed it in his waist coat pocket. "So?"

"So?" Colliridge repeated, and reached over, flipping the cigar box open. He pulled a leather bag from his other coat pocket and began to place the cigars into it. Carefully, he began to answer Calvinward's question. Or rather, give the answer he had been paid handsomely for. The ambassador was a client who appreciated his skills. In addition, Colliridge could extract a little payback for all the months of work Calvinward had ruined with his dismissal. "I traced the letter to a workhouse jail on the edge of the Cornstone Marshes. There is one hell of a big cotton mill in that jail."

"Indeed."

"Yes, but badly managed. Easy to slip in."

"You were able to find who wrote this." Calvinward's right index finger tapped on the leather folder before him.

"Yes and no." Colliridge stopped, closed the bag and

143

replaced it in his coat pocket. "I found out who it most likely would have been. A young woman with a passing resemblance to Lady Emily, and a man who was her brother. But you needn't worry, Milord." He leant forward, placing his hands on the desk. "An outbreak of typhus put an end to the matter."

"You mean they are dead." Calvinward's eyes widened.

"Yes."

Calvinward slid the money pouch across the desk. "I will not say it was good doing business with you."

"No. Are you sure you don't want to keep me on a retainer?" There was not a cat in hell's chance of it. Nor would he take any more *work* from Calvinward, but to not ask would rouse his suspicions. Colliridge buttoned up his long coat and held out his hand. Calvinward did not take it, merely waved towards the door. Colliridge nodded and walked to the door; as he opened it, he could not resist looking back. Calvinward had moved from behind his desk and was standing by the fire. The letter and envelope were in his hand. He tore it in half and threw it into the flames.

***

Colliridge stepped out into the cold night air. He was not the only one leaving. A number of Calvinward's guests were waiting for their carriages to be summoned from the lines on the opposite side of the road. Colliridge pulled up his collar and walked with purpose away from the house. Events had gone better than he could ever have hoped for. The letter was gone. No proof of any sort to back up either side's actions.

He crossed the street, nodding to a policeman on his beat. Colliridge was on his way to a large house on Highmarsh Square, the home of the widow and helpmate of a former employer. They had made a remarkable pair. Lord and Lady Manling had been more ruthless than any Colliridge had met before or after. Even the ambassador for Crossmire, for all his skulduggery, had not yet proved to be their match.

As he reached the stone steps to the house of the beautiful widow, he began to frame in his mind the words he was going to say. The lady was expecting him: he had sent word earlier. Colliridge reached up and rattled the brass door knocker. The door opened.

"Lady Constance is expecting me."

"Of course, sir, if you will follow me," the butler answered.

Colliridge was shown into the late Lord Manling's library. Sitting by the fire, with the evening edition of the Gateskeep Sun open on the small table beside her, was Lady Constance. The lady was as beautiful as he remembered. In fact, more so: Constance had developed a maturity since her husband's death, which suited her. Avinguard was a bloody lucky dog. He had always been lucky. By rights, the man should be nothing but bleached bones up in Coot's Pass, and the whole garrison with him. It was what had been planned by the lady before him, and her husband. Who would believe the lovely woman before him had a mind sharper than most of the seated members of the High Forum? Manling had been going to use the garrison's loss as a springboard for annexing the hill tribes. But then-Lieutenant Avinguard had taken command when the major in charge had been wounded and his captain killed, and things had turned out very differently. Avinguard had gotten Colliridge nearly killed, half-frozen and trapped in that place. He could not forgive or forget it. Colliridge took risks, yes, but only if he had the upper hand and his own skin was not involved. He shook off the memories and bowed to the lady before him.

"Sir, the hour is late. Has one of your other employers been monopolising you?" Constance said.

"I have no other employer at present." Colliridge took the seat opposite Constance. He leant forward, hands on his knees.

"I find that hard to believe."

"It is true. I have not yet found a gentleman or lady who is the equal of you or your late husband."

"You mean one worthy of your talents." Constance gave a small laugh and picked up the newspaper, carefully folding it so one article was prominent. She laid it on her knee, as if reluctant to let it go.

"That as well."

"I thought you would have beaten a fast road to the door of Lord Calvinward." The fingers of her right hand traced over the words on the paper, then abandoned them to rest on the arm of her chair.

"He is not worth the effort." Colliridge sat back in his chair and crossed his legs.

Constance's right eyebrow arched upwards in barely concealed surprise.

"As the last task I set you was completed several days ago, what brings you to my door at this time of the night?"

"Your daughter."

"My daughter is dead," Lady Constance said flatly, her face hardening. Her body tensed. The paper on her knees shuddered and gently slipped to the floor.

"So you believe; so does everyone. I do not." Colliridge leaned forward and picked up the paper, glancing at the displayed article. The words in darker type caught his eyes. It detailed Sir Henry's, and Lady Claire Fitzguard's, involvement in the events of this afternoon. That explained Lady Constance's distraction. Did she know who was behind the event? Sir Canvish had been one of her late husband's devotees.

Lady Claire: that was a surprise. Marriage annulled or not, Pugh Avinguard was still carrying a torch for the chit. Avinguard might still avail himself of Lady Constance's charms, but any influence, or use as a source of information to her, would be negated in many respects. Colliridge filed the information away and returned to the matter at hand. The newspaper he placed on the arm of his chair.

"You do not." The scorn in Lady Constance's voice was plain.

"Hear me out, Milady," Colliridge began.

"Very well," Constance said, but her eyes still remained narrowed. Colliridge was not sure if she yet believed him, but she was interested enough to listen.

"Yes, the facts were convincing: the bodies badly burnt and an incompetent police inspector intent on covering his *reputation*. But Lady Emily and her escort escaped the carriage, only to be thrown into jail." Colliridge stopped, partly to allow Lady Constance to assimilate the information and partly to have her refute it.

"Nonsense. If they had been, they would have tried to contact me, Calvinward or Avinguard," Constance said, the pitch of her voice rising.

Colliridge shook his head. "Do you think they would have been believed? Goddess, the authorities in Hitsmine were trying to sweep everything under the carpet, pretend it hadn't happened."

"No." Lady Constance's rebuttal had no force of conviction behind it. Colliridge knew the lady to have a sharp intelligence; she need only be primed. She was quite capable of drawing her own conclusions.

146

"Yes — imprisoned, and your daughter without any form of identification."

"Dear Goddess, if that is true...."

"You can be thankful that the young man she was with was fairly clever and somewhat besotted with her."

"Mathew?"

"Yes, the young man placed her name on his documents as his wife." Colliridge stopped for a moment and watched a stunned look mix in with the emotions warring for control of Lady Constance's features. "In name only — a good ploy to keep them together so he could look after her."

He watched her organise her thoughts, mentally forming questions to ask. Questions he already had suitable answers for. He had worked for this lady and her husband for a long time. They had orchestrated so much, including the events of Coot's Pass, the original hanging out of the fort as bait. Colliridge wondered how the woman reconciled her actions at that time with her relationship with the man who had been in the centre of that whirlwind. Or did she dismiss it as totally inconsequential?

"How did you come by this information, if it is indeed true?" Her hands unclasped and she stood, turning towards the fire.

"Quite by chance, I can assure you. I was at a workhouse on some business. I saw Lady Emily. I remembered her from when she was a child running down the passage to this very study. I didn't at first believe it so. I did some checking, and I believe it is her."

"I see. Have you told any others?"

"You mean Lord Calvinward? I know the press have been saying that they were engaged. If there was such an arrangement, would he want her back under these circumstances? He would not want soiled goods."

"My daughter is not that. And no, there was no formal announcement of any kind."

"No, I thought not. And the young man is honourable and fairly intelligent. I can assure you there is no stain on Emily's honour. He has a single-mindedness that reminds me of your late husband." Lord Manling had never believed he could be wrong or out-manoeuvred and that had been his undoing; everyone could be, at some point. This young man was the same. Colliridge had seen it. He had also become

147

convinced that Mathew was obviously not who he said he was. This called for a little investigation before he returned. He doubted a working-class man would have such a highly developed opinion of self-worth.

Constance looked down into the flames. "How much would it cost to get my daughter and this young man out of that place?"

CHAPTER SEVENTEEN

athew had thought the spinning room was hell enough. The grave digging was proving to be its bottommost tier. Old men and women and newborn children did not survive long here. It was the norm. The onset of winter, like that of summer, killed the weakest. Now it was different: the faces hidden under the hastily sewn linen bags were young men and women. There was a sickness spreading, and from what he had heard it was not only the inmates dying. The face of the doctor, going about his duties in the poor imitation of an infirmary, wore a haggard and frightened look.

He shuffled along, his arms full of the linen-wrapped feet of one of the latest victims. His fellow ditch digger, Burt, carried the head. The rattle of their leg irons marked their passage. "This is the twelfth. You think we will get it in the ground before sunset? That next set of holes is not half-finished and that bastard Blair has us bringing another cart load out."

"Perhaps he is being paid a bonus per body," Mathew said, and leaned to the right to get the corpse out of the narrow door.

"I can bloody well believe that," Burt replied. He heaved the head and chest of the corpse onto its predecessor in the back of the small wagon. The thin horse in the shafts waffled as it felt the wagon shudder. It turned its head to look at the men.

"Get a move on," the guard on the wagon seat snapped.

"We got one more." Mathew pushed the feet of the corpse further on. "Sorry." Stupid to say that. Speaking to the dead would not ease the sickening fear that one day, soon, it would be Emily he would be lifting into the wagon.

The graveyard had been filled many times over the years, the first graves at an eight-foot depth, some of these latest ones at barely three. Bones and half-rotten flesh turned up in more than one pit. Mathew followed Burt back into the infirmary. The harassed doctor was talking in harsh, hushed tones to the governor. The two men stood in the doorway of the doctor's small office. Mathew tilted his head, straining to hear.

"Moving her could be dangerous," the doctor said. "There is no guarantee of a cure for her, even if she were in the hands of the lauded Dr Chambers of Gateskeep himself. The illness will run its course."

"You mean my wife will die the same as these." The governor snarled. "I won't have it."

"If you had done what I asked and allowed me to implement a mass steaming and boiling of clothes, not to mention the disinfection of the dormitories, this would not have happened." The doctor snarled back, running his thin hand through his unkempt locks.

"That would have cost time and money and besides, there is no proof that it is caused by fleas."

"No proof. I know that where there is no louse-infested population, there is no typhus." The last word was barely audible, but Mathew latched onto it.

Mathew stumbled in his chains. *Typhus. Oh, Goddess.* None of them stood a chance. The disease would leave the workhouse a charnel house. Emily said her head hurt this morning, and the governor's wife was stricken. Mathew felt the sickness in his stomach increase.

"'Ere mate." Burt nudged him to keep moving. Mathew reached for the next corpse, then stopped. He laughed at the irony of his actions. What good would it do, not touching this one — how many had he carried, over the past few days? He took a good, firm hold of the feet and on Burt's nod, lifted. The ill-sewn seam opened on the corpse's left side and a thin, pale arm tumbled out, covered in tell-tale red eruptions. The corpse joined the rest on the wagon.

"Move on!" The horse's head jerked up at the guard's command and it began to strain against its harness. Slowly the wagon's wheels creaked forward. Mathew and Burt fell in behind. Their small caravan ambled past the governor's house, and Mathew looked up at the windows. "Please, let it be a headache."

The wagon stopped by the gate, waiting for a rider to enter. A tall man came through, astride a well-bred animal. He was wrapped for riding in winter, in a thick, dark woollen coat. A wide-brimmed hat was pulled down low over his eyes. The animal came level with Mathew, and he noticed that the man's boots were old, but good quality. Mathew frowned and looked up, trying to see the face of the rider, but he could not. The animal went past. The wagon again began to move.

"Wait, hold that damn wagon!" Someone bellowed over

the clatter of hooves. Mathew glanced back. The man was backing his horse up, turning it round. "Hold it, I say!"

"Bugger it," the guard muttered, but stopped the wagon's progress. Mathew moved to the side of the vehicle, seeking shelter from the bitter wind. The man on the horse continued to shout at the assistant governor standing by the gate. Strange, Mathew thought, that man rarely left the books in his snug, warm office. "That's the man, my bond contract servant, one Mathew Worth. I want him and his wife, Emily, ready to travel."

Mathew stiffened, his eyes darting from the rider to the assistant governor. *Damnation. Who the hell was this?* The horse was now alongside him, the man leaning down from the saddle. Mathew's eyes widened in surprise. It was the guard, Colliridge, the whiskers he had previously sported gone, his accent pure Gateskeep gentry.

"Good Goddess!" The horse pressed Mathew closer to the wagon, cutting him off from any escape. His heart began to hammer in his chest as his surprise began to turn to fear.

"I think not, Sir Mathew," Colliridge said, behind his hand. "Now get what you want to take from this bloody, forsaken hole, but make sure it looks like a good pack. Then we get the Lady Emily and we are off."

Mathew did not move. *It was a sodding trick.* He looked Colliridge in the face and gave him a sharp nod of rejection.

"Don't trust me? Bloody well don't blame you. No time to explain: take the note out of my boot." Colliridge made the horse sidle even closer. Mathew could feel the warmth of the animal. His nostrils were filled with the sweat-damp smell of it. It had been ridden hard. Against his better judgement, he looked down to the man's boot in the stirrup. A gleam of white paper was sticking out. "Hurry. They will notice things are not right soon."

Mathew bit his lip and took the paper.

"Go, man. I want to be out of this pigsty. Don't you?" Colliridge straightened up and moved his horse away.

Mathew bobbed his head, touching his fingers to his temple, mumbling. "Yes, sir, 'course, sir." He broke into a stumbling run, the chains between his legs clashing on the cobbles. The cold air bit at his lungs. Mathew reached the doorway to the dormitories and was stopped dead by the bulk of the foreman, Blair.

"I have been looking for you. You should be out digging

in the dirt like the dog you are. I am taking you off the graves, and you is coming out on the fens with me." The words were followed by Blair's balled fist. Mathew tried to dodge, but the blow caught the top of his shoulder, knocking him off balance. The chain between his feet tangled and Mathew went down. Blair's foot came out, catching Mathew in the side.

The cobbles under him began to vibrate. The sharp neigh of a horse sounded above as the animal leapt over him. Mathew twisted to one side and had the view of Colliridge smashing the butt of a fine, old-fashioned officer's pistol into Blair's face. Blair howled, cowering against the wall of the building. Mathew could plainly hear the soft sound of a trigger being pulled back.

"So, Mathew, do you think a bastard like this deserves to be shot?" Colliridge's words were smooth, emotionless.

Mathew was, for a moment, horrified. Then he gave a crooked smile. Yes, a man like Blair was a leech on his fellows. He fed off their fear of him. He was a bully and would be the cause of the death of more boys like young Albert. "Yes."

The pistol discharged. The single shot entered Blair's right eye, exploding out of the rear of his head. He hit the wall and slid down, a wet trail of blood and brains tumbling after.

Cries and screams filled the yard. "Go," Colliridge snapped. "I will deal with the excuse for a man that is the governor. Go quickly."

Mathew threw himself through the door and up the stairs. It was happening so quickly. A trap, very possible, but if Colliridge got them outside alive, Mathew would take his chances. Just being on the outside of this place was all he needed.

He heard the crackle of the paper in his jacket. Mathew reached in and pulled it out. It had one line scrawled on it, and a signature.

"*Trust him.*

Constance Manling."

Could it be possible that Colliridge was working for Emily's mother? Had Lady Constance not believed her daughter dead? Not possible: the newspapers that Mathew had managed to get hold of had been full of the description of "Emily's funeral" and her remembrance service.

Mathew shook his head in disbelief; it did not matter. He knew in reality he had no other choice. It could already be too late; typhus was all around. He stood and opened the chest and pulled out his pack. They needed nothing but his book and — Mathew picked up the cloth-wrapped bundle of his and Emily's papers. Yes, those as well. No trace of them would be left except two names in the ill-kept records of the workhouse.

Mathew retraced his steps as quickly as he could. He hobbled into the cold air of the yard, merely glancing at the two men removing the body of Blair. Emily was standing at the head of Colliridge's horse. He tried to catch her attention, but she was looking up at the man in the saddle. She only turned on hearing the clatter of his chains.

On her cheeks were two bright spots of colour. She stepped forward, hugging Mathew. He could feel her heart thudding against him. "Emily, what is it?"

She placed a finger against his lips. He kissed it. His concern for her, for both of them, deepened.

She leant forward and whispered, "I know this man. He worked for my father."

Mathew tried to speak. He was stunned. There was much here that he did not know. Questions burned in his throat. He swallowed hard; they would have to wait. Mathew still did not trust Colliridge. It was quite possible that the man had worked for Emily's father. It did not mean he still worked for her mother. Both of them could end up floating in the fens, face down, before nightfall.

"Get those leg irons off my property," Colliridge shouted.

***

Sir Henry cracked his knuckles and wished the sound was that of a number of High Forum members' heads banging together. He had been tempted all morning to use the pommel of the sword of state to knock some sense into them. With a sigh, he shrugged out of the formal over-gown and threw it over the chair.

The office was still littered with boxes containing his predecessor's belongings. It had only been four days since the shooting. Sir Henry's aide, Michael, the youngest son of Lady Hotspur, had promised to have them cleared by this evening.

Sir Henry felt in his pocket for his pipe and tobacco pouch. He filled the pipe, lit it, and began to mull over what had been said during the morning session.

A knock on the door was followed by the creak of its hinges as it opened. Sir Henry turned: it was Michael.

The young man cleared his throat. "Major Avinguard to see you, sir."

Sir Henry nodded. He could guess what this was about. Pugh had been trying to see him privately since the shooting. "Let the major in."

Pugh entered, all stiff-backed military, his face dark with emotion.

Sir Henry cleared his throat, "I didn't contact you, because Claire didn't request it."

"I see."

"I am sorry, but once she realised it had been seven years...." Sir Henry puffed at his pipe, watching the curling smoke rise.

"She was not aware of the passage of time?" Pugh walked across the room and stood before the fire, then turned his back to it and clasped his hands behind him.

"I believe not. For her the events of seven years ago are as yesterday. It is hard for her."

"It has been hard for us all. I beg your pardon, Sir Henry, but Claire's being here is utter folly. As for myself, I would like to be part of her world again if she will allow."

"Claire is safe. She is never alone. Day or night, someone is always close. I thank you on Claire's behalf for your concern. I am sorry that you had to find out in the manner you did. I had intended to call on you, but events overtook us. As to being part of her new life, that is for her to decide. And you have moved on, have you not?"

"Things happened. But you realise, don't you, that she has crossed Calvinward's path. It will not be long before he puts two and two together."

"The train, yes — but Calvinward saw her for only a few moments, didn't he? Do you still love her?"

"I don't know; it is complicated. I want to be part of her life: I want to protect her; look after her; make sure she is safe. As to Calvinward — you will not fool him for long. It could cost you his trust."

It was obvious to Sir Henry that Pugh still loved Claire, as she did him. Both were intent on doing the honourable thing of letting the other be free. For a moment Sir Henry wondered if he should say something. Best they work this out themselves, or not. "I don't intend to lose it. We have a chance here, Pugh, to change Timeholm for the better. Say, ten years with Calvinward at the helm and we won't know this nation. Howorth and I agree that we have a great senior statesman in the making."

"You are saying Calvinward is that good a man." Pugh began to chuckle.

Sir Henry laughed, but the laughter left a hollow feeling inside. Claire's words, *good man*, were stuck at the front of his mind. "No. He has as many faults as you or I, but I feel he will be good for this country in ways we cannot yet grasp."

"You might be right, and as to Claire ..."

"What will happen, will happen." Sir Henry did not understand much of what Claire muttered, but some things were plain. He had allowed himself to act that day in the High Forum, driven by the thought that he was doing good. Claire's mumbled words had agreed with him. However, certain other words, up till then only rarely spoken, had now come to the fore. Should he act again, or hope matters would work out for the best? One could be as bad as the other, and the consequences could be horrific. One thing he had decided was to not have the dog Toby put down. The dog still featured far too much in Claire's strange conversation.

"No need to announce me, Michael," Lady Elizabeth Hotspur said from the doorway. Sir Henry knocked his pipe out on the side of the fire before stepping forward to greet her.

"Oh, Pugh, am I interrupting important affairs?" Elizabeth held out her hand to him. He took it carefully, as if he were handling a snake: not a bad assumption with regard to Elizabeth. Sir Henry knew she had developed a fondness for Pugh over the years, though Pugh obviously still doubted it.

"No, Elizabeth, I am leaving. Perhaps we can continue this discussion another time, Sir Henry." Pugh released her hand, bowed to Sir Henry and left the room.

Elizabeth half-turned and watched him go.

"Do I have to kiss your hand?" Sir Henry said, placing his pipe on the mantelpiece.

"No, you dear man." Elizabeth laughed, stepping forward to embrace him. She placed a soft kiss on his cheek and stood back, examining his face. "You look tired — are you eating properly?"

Sir Henry did not answer.

"I see, well: Claire and I have been busy this morning, spending your money at various establishments. She has a suitable dress for the opera and Calvinward's supper dance in the theatre's yellow room after. She has also bought a carriage-load of books. She is at home under Mandy and Thomas' care, resting and reading."

"About tonight: I am not sure it is a good idea. I do not want Claire to become the centre of everyone's attention."

"That's what she shall be if she does not attend tonight. People will gossip. It is known she is here in the city, and — by your own admission — here to be your hostess. She will be safe, besides: in her own words, 'Dance in the yellow room.'" Elizabeth opened her reticule and pulled out Sir Henry's notebook. "See, I have recorded what the dear girl has said today." She handed the book to Sir Henry.

"And have you had time to read any of the ones I have underlined?"

"Yes, and you are right. You must not act until the situations the words resemble begin to unfold. To act before could undo the final result."

"Which is?"

"Turn the world on its head, politics and religion."

"No matter the cost?"

"Who is to say the cost in human terms would not be worse if we didn't act? The Goddess disposes as she thinks fit: I think it is her darker side we are seeing; she will act coldly and ruthlessly, destroying even life to serve her ends."

CHAPTER EIGHTEEN

Colliridge sat in the coach as it sped across the city. He was delighted at the turn of events. These last few days, he believed, had opened up a profitable future doing the thing he loved above all: putting the ideas and plans of others into action. And the young man opposite, Colliridge was sure, was going to be part of those plans. He was Sir Mathew Howorth, the third son of a stick-in-the-mud liberal member of the High Forum. Mathew, though clever, was even more fanatical about his cause than Colliridge had first believed. Mathew believed the worst of his own class; he saw them as greedy and self-serving. Whereas the working-class were noble, downtrodden beings that needed to be uplifted. Colliridge had strongly hinted that Calvinward had indeed received Emily's letter and sent him to investigate. He had not quite painted Calvinward as a moustache-twirling villain, but Mathew, wounded as he was from his experiences, had needed little encouragement to see the man as a career politician of little scruples.

"There," Mathew said, finishing the second of two notes. He handed them to Colliridge. "The thicker one is for my father. I have tried to give him the basic facts."

"You will need to see him in person – quite quickly, if not tonight." The carriage pulled to a jolting stop outside the theatre. The sound of the coachman's shouting was followed by the rattle of footsteps and the opening of the door. Colliridge slid from the seat and stepped out into the chill night air; Mathew followed.

The disdainful gaze of the doorman tracked over the new arrivals. Colliridge gave a small laugh. "A gentleman does not always arrive dressed to the nines."

"Indeed." The doorman looked to the two soldiers on guard duty.

"I see the good Major Avinguard has this place buttoned up. Most excellent." Colliridge watched the two soldiers exchange a glance. "We have no intention of entering beyond the foyer, gentlemen."

"What!" Mathew exclaimed, scuffing the ice-layered pavement with his wooden clogs.

"No, we will wait, while these good gentlemen see the

notes are delivered. I expect we will be greeting the major soon, along with the other people." Colliridge opened his long coat slightly, making sure his well-tailored militia grey trousers, officer's trousers, were on show. He had often posed as an officer in the militia intelligence corps. In fact his whole dress was typical: half-uniform, half-civilian; Colliridge knew it was not lost on the two soldiers on duty.

The one on the left coughed and said, "You on duty, sir?"

"Always, soldier, always. We need these notes delivered."

The two guards again exchanged looks, and the one who had spoken nodded and gave Colliridge a salute. "Have the notes taken up, and allow them into the foyer — but no further, mind you."

"Good man," Colliridge handed the notes to the doorman. "I take it the main staircase has a guard top and bottom."

"All are guarded, sir," the soldier replied, placing two fingers to the edge of his cap.

"Good show, good show." Colliridge stepped into the dimly lit entrance hall.

"Clever," Mathew said.

"It is a matter of knowing which rope to pull, Sir Mathew." He reached into his pocket and pulled out one of the cigars he had taken from Calvinward's. He placed it in his mouth, savouring the taste of the tobacco. He did not light it, merely rolled it from one side of his mouth to the other.

"It is nearly over," Mathew said.

"On the contrary, this is the beginning. You have your story straight in your head, haven't you? Make sure you tell the same to all. Don't be tempted to divulge more details to one than another. People are going to chatter about this. Many believed that Emily was on the brink of becoming engaged to Calvinward. Don't give them more fuel is my advice, and don't take it onto the floor of the Forum. Argue the bill, not your adventures."

"Why, my experiences could sway many ..."

"Very possible, Sir Mathew, but the bill is on the brink of being voted on. To lengthen the final debate could result in the bill's being set back till the next session. It would be giving opponents of the bill a golden ticket. How many bills have vanished without trace when the High Forum re-sits? I council you, listen to Lady Constance; she will help you."

"I had not thought of that."

Colliridge was going to add that if Mathew refrained from speaking at all, he would perhaps gain a sympathetic vote, but he did not get to say it. Lady Constance arrived at the foot of the stairs, her face flushed, pulse beating in the hollow of her neck. Very attractive. Colliridge gave her a short bow.

"Mathew?" the lady stammered, coming forward. "Emily?"

Mathew smiled. "At your home."

"Dear Goddess," Constance whispered, as if she was afraid to believe it. "Is she ...?"

"She is not well, though her illness is not as bad as we first feared. Sir Mathew sent for the renowned Dr Chambers before we left," Colliridge said.

Constance began to tremble and Mathew slipped an arm round her. "Come."

"Yes. I ... Sir Mathew?" Constance repeated.

Colliridge could not help but smile. Even concerned as she was for her daughter, Lady Constance was taking stock of this new information.

"All will be explained," Colliridge said, and made towards the door of the theatre. He opened it to allow Mathew and Constance to pass through. As he was about to close the door, he felt someone behind him. He looked back. There in the shadows at the foot of the stairs a woman stood, the feathers in her elaborate hairstyle casting an eerie shadow. Before he could speak, the woman turned and ran up the stairs. Colliridge frowned. How much had she heard? He could do nothing about it. *Bollocks.* He quickly made his way to the carriage. The vehicle started off before he was settled in his seat.

"Emily – alive, not dead?" Constance asked.

"Goddess! The Glimpser – it said that." Mathew sat back in the carriage, a stunned look on his face.

"You ran into one of those on your travels?" Colliridge asked. His interest increased.

"Yes, a small bedraggled thing, with white-blonde hair," Mathew said. "I think it was trying to warn me."

"It might be well to mull over any other of its words you remember, if you get time." Colliridge had, where possible, collected the creatures' sayings.

"You believe in them?" Mathew asked.

159

"Only a fool would dismiss any source of information. Speaking of which, you might not get much time before you have to defend yourself, Sir Mathew," Colliridge said.

"How so?"

The coach stopped and the door was thrown open by the waiting footman.

"Our departure was watched." Colliridge aided Lady Constance to step down from the carriage. The door to her home was open, the light pouring out.

"By whom?" Mathew asked.

"I am not sure. Lady Constance, whom were you with when the note arrived?" Constance was already at the bottom of the stairs, her housekeeper at her elbow.

"Lady Elizabeth Hotspur."

"I suspect Lord Calvinward and Sir Henry will be here before the next hour is passed. You need to look to your story, sir. Remember, you have an ace in the hole with Lady Emily," Colliridge said, looking from one to another.

"My daughter is not a pawn in some game, sir!" Lady Constance snapped. Even though she said these words, Colliridge knew that Lady Constance would allow the girl to be just that, even moving her further onto the board herself.

"Indeed not, Milady, but we must look to the protection of her name. Both Calvinward and especially Sir Henry will be open to that."

Constance nodded and turned, moving quickly upstairs.

Colliridge looked at Mathew and gave a bow.

"You are leaving?"

"I think it is for the best, Sir Mathew."

***

Calvinward's after-show party in the large yellow room of the theatre was in full swing. Pugh was making his way back to a room on the second floor when he spotted Lady Hotspur and Lord Howorth speaking by the door. The man looked harassed and not a little angry. Plainly, his exasperation with Elizabeth had led him to drag his hand through his greying yellow hair more than once. Pugh felt for him: having Elizabeth pin you to the floor on some matter was not an enjoyable event. Howorth broke away from Elizabeth and hurried down the corridor, barely acknowledging Pugh.

Elizabeth stood there watching the man go. Her gaze flickered to Pugh, and her expression softened into one of relief.

"There you are. I have no need to set out looking for you. We need to find Sir Henry, and, Goddess, Calvinward." Elizabeth's fan slapped against the open palm of her left hand again and again, indicating annoyance or anger — Pugh could not decide which.

"Something wrong, Elizabeth?"

"To quote Claire, alive not dead. Turn the world on its head." Elizabeth strode through the milling members of the gentry. "Henry!"

Pugh stopped for a moment, then double-stepped to catch up with Elizabeth.

"Such haste, Elizabeth. I was wondering if you would take a turn with me, seeing Calvinward has retained part of the orchestra for our continued entertainment." Sir Henry was watching his daughter dance.

Pugh followed Sir Henry's gaze with his own, and his thoughts went back to their conversation earlier that day. It was complicated. Each time he tried to fight his way through the morass of his thoughts, he became bogged down in the memories, both good and bad. Sir Henry had said that for Claire the events of seven years ago were as if they were yesterday. In a strange way, they were for him as well.

"Now is not the time for dancing," Elizabeth admonished, her fan increasing its tempo on her hand. "Come, we must find somewhere privy to talk."

"I am spurned, Pugh, did you hear?" Sir Henry joked.

Pugh made to move off and find Constance, but the look in Lady Hotspur's eyes forestalled him. He found himself following. "I think Elizabeth has something important to say. Perhaps to explain some of her recent behaviour."

"I act as I see fit," Elizabeth snapped, showing her irritation.

"What has rattled your cage so badly, Elizabeth?" Sir Henry took her arm and drew her towards the wall, away from the main hubbub of the room. Pugh followed, though he glanced round seeking Constance to reassure her that he was still here. He had been her escort tonight, and after that night at Castleton's he felt he needed to be a little more attentive.

"Rattled me. That, Henry, is an understatement. Pugh, tell me the name of the youth who supposedly died with Emily Manling."

161

Pugh was taken aback by the question and stammered. "Mathew."

"Howorth?" Elizabeth asked, her expression hardening.

"No, Worth. An assistant overseer at Seabreeze."

"Elizabeth, what is this all about?" Sir Henry said.

"I believe I have seen him."

"Who?" Pugh and Sir Henry asked together.

"The young man who was with Lady Emily. And I think you will find his name is Howorth, not Worth. It has been a few years since I have seen him. And of course it would be Seabreeze — it's one of Howorth's smaller estates. An ideal contact address."

"Elizabeth, enough of this nonsense." Pugh struggled not to shout. Claire, her face flushed with dancing, was coming towards them on the arm of Calvinward.

"I will say more, damn you, Pugh." Elizabeth's voice quivered with anger. "A letter arrived for Constance. She left to meet someone. I followed. In the foyer, she met with two men. One was a Howorth, I swear it. You can't mistake that corn-yellow hair colouring. Besides this one had inherited Augustus' aquiline nose. A younger son, I think: they have a large brood. Constance addressed him as Mathew, and she asked where Emily was."

"Pardon?" Joshua's voice broke into Elizabeth's flow of words. The man had stiffened, his face had grown cold. His hand on Claire's arm had tightened. Pugh felt for him. Though he knew there was no formal engagement between Calvinward and Emily, he was aware that Calvinward did care for the girl, having known her since she was a child. Perhaps he might have made an offer for her hand at some point, but that became moot when Emily was presumed dead.

"I think you heard, Joshua. I understand your concern, but please let Elizabeth continue," Sir Henry said, and looked at each face in turn, his gaze finally lingering on his daughter's.

Pugh tried not to stare at her. Claire's face was stormy, her brow furrowed.

"Mathew said 'at home.' They left with the other man, a cock-sure dandy if ever there was one. To top it all, when I was rushing back here to inform you, Howorth was beating a hasty exit. I asked him why. He replied he had important family matters to deal with."

No one spoke; the moment stretched. Claire broke the silence, her voice shaky. "Alive not dead. Scandal and deceit. Consequences for all. Beat him, pay the price of victory. We go to Lady Constance's home."

"Forgive me, child. But it is best you go nowhere," Elizabeth said, and stepped forward, her arms reaching out to Claire. Claire leant into the older woman's embrace.

"Alive not dead, horror and sickness. Vengeance and hate. I must go."

"No, dear lady, you will stay with Lady Elizabeth. We must get to the bottom of this. Lady Constance could be in the hands of a liar and a fraud," Calvinward said coldly. "Gentleman, will you two come with me to Lady Constance's home?" Calvinward's features were set as stone, his voice controlled, but with an undertone of anger.

Sir Henry nodded and called to a waiter to bring a cab quickly. He looked at Elizabeth.

"I will see her safe home and wait till you get back."

"No," Claire said.

"Is this you, asking?" Pugh said sharply through Sir Henry's spluttering.

Claire chewed her lip and looked defiantly at him over the top of her glasses. "Yes."

"The answer is no: it is not your business. It is Lord Calvinward's, and to some extent mine. Sir Henry, please do not feel you have to come with us."

"As I said, I would be glad of Sir Henry's company," Calvinward said, as the waiter ran up to say there was a cab waiting at the door.

Sir Henry and Calvinward bowed and took their leave, quickly vanishing down the stairs. Pugh then took his own leave, giving a faint smile to both women. Elizabeth again surprised him by reaching out and squeezing his arm.

"If I had said it wasn't me?" Claire called after him.

"Then I would have demanded you come," Pugh called back, and ran down the stairs.

athew enquired. "How is she?" as Lady Constance re-entered the main parlour.

"Dr Chambers is still not sure as to her condition. She has a fever, but it is not typhus," Constance said.

"So it is not as bad as you feared. Take heart, dear lady." Lord Howorth was standing with his back towards the fireplace. He lifted the coattails of his jacket to allow the warmth of the fire to reach his backside. A familiar posture, one that should have made Mathew at ease, but tonight it was doing anything but. "I am not saying I don't believe you about events. But one thing is plain: you can't confront Calvinward in public about this letter. You have not one shred of proof, except your word and that of Lady Emily."

"Like hell I won't. He knew — I swear it. Colliridge had the information that Emily and I were in that place. I thank the Goddess the man came to Lady Constance with it. I believe Calvinward was prepared to abandon Lady Emily to her fate for the political gain her death had brought him." Mathew rose from his chair. He did not mention the telegram; now was not the time. He drew a hand through his unruly hair and paced across the room. As he turned, he saw the expression in Lady Constance's eyes and regretted his words. "I am sorry."

"No. Please. Emily is safe. But I agree with your father — you need irrefutable proof. It would be your word against his." Her voice hardened with anger.

"Mine and Lady Emily's," Mathew added.

"Yes, Lady Emily: think on it," said Lord Howorth. "Do you wish her to speak out publicly about these events? It's not the sort of thing you put a young, delicate lady through. This is going to be bad for her, once it comes out — swept up in a riot, locked in a workhouse jail all this time and forced to live as the wife of a man she was not formally married to." Lord Howorth listed the items like a shopping bill. "That, thankfully, you can remedy as soon as possible, if Lady Emily feels as you say. I am sure Lady Constance agrees with me there."

"Mathew," Lady Constance said, her hand going to her mouth.

"Lady Constance, Emily is my wife by her choice, if not by law as yet. Her honour is mine. I will do what I can to protect it.

But I will make sure Calvinward knows we know about the letter." He looked towards his father. Lord Howorth said nothing. Mathew went to speak again, but was interrupted by the butler announcing the arrival of three gentlemen.

"Send them in, if you please," Constance said, rising from her chair to greet them.

"Constance, is it true?" Pugh said, coming to her side.

Mathew watched Constance nod and give a small sob.

Pugh aided her to sit and looked across at Mathew. "Well?"

"My son will explain everything, Lord Calvinward," Howorth began. "Sir Henry, good to see you. This event has shaken me somewhat. Your advice would be welcome." Howorth waved his hand at Sir Henry, indicating for him to take a seat.

Sir Henry refused with a shake of his head. "You mean I have experience dealing with scandal."

"My father didn't mean...," Mathew spoke to Sir Henry, but kept his eyes on Calvinward. His face was a blank mask, impossible to even glimpse the thoughts going on behind his eyes.

"Yes, he did. He is not mealy-mouthed when it comes to facing the truth. I am not going to beat about the bush on this matter; it could cause as much trouble for the High Forum as a bomb on the floor of the house." Sir Henry's answer was brisk and to the point.

"My thoughts exactly, gentlemen," Calvinward said. "I suggest that what is said and decided here tonight concerning you, sir, and Lady Emily, stay between us. Pray tell us of the events. So we might have a picture of what we will be dealing with."

Mathew nodded and began to speak. He kept, like Colliridge had advised, to the basic facts, but knew the listeners would not be satisfied. He told of the riot, their arrest and placement in the workhouse jail, a vague account of how they were rescued by someone recognising them, and most importantly, in his mind, the matter of the letter.

"Knowing a little of the aftermath in Hitsmine after the riot, I can see how it could have been difficult to get word of your arrest out. You did try, didn't you? And afterwards, when you were in the workhouse jail?" Sir Henry asked.

"Yes, I tried. I bribed a guard in Hitsmine, to no avail. The prisoners were even refused the services of a minister of the Orthodox Chapel. If one had attended, I could have persuaded him to carry a message. As Emily worked as lady's maid to the governor's wife, she risked being whipped to smuggle a letter in with those of the household."

"Lady's maid. Whipped." The horror in Lady Constance's voice made Mathew wince. He had added to her anguish.

"A letter. Lady Constance — " Pugh began. Constance shook her head in denial.

"To Lord Calvinward," Mathew said.

"Joshua, did you receive such a letter?" Augustus Howorth looked right at Calvinward.

"Augustus. If I had received this letter, do you not think I would have investigated? The consequences of not doing so would not bear thinking about." He looked first at Mathew, then Lady Constance, his eyes slightly narrowing. "If it proved true, I would have acted. What purpose would it have served me to allow the daughter of my late mentor to languish in a workhouse jail? *Goddess above.* I don't doubt your version of the events, Sir Mathew, but I do not have this letter you speak of in my possession."

"I see," Mathew said, making no attempt to hide the sarcasm in his voice.

"Sir Mathew, there is no need," Sir Henry said. "A letter can easily go astray. If Lord Calvinward said he didn't receive it, that is enough for me. We need to deal with the matter of what is to be publicly said regarding Lady Emily, and yourself. The actual events will not serve; they leave too much for others to play with."

"Isn't there a need for clarity about the letter? I honestly feel Lord Calvinward might have decided to do nothing on receipt of it. Wash his hands of Lady Emily to avoid any scandal attaching to his coattails. And as to events, surely the truth is best," Mathew said.

"You are not thinking clearly, Sir Mathew; perhaps it is the aftermath of your ordeal. Can you not see that for my part the scandal would have been nonexistent — in fact, the very opposite would be true? If I had known of her incarceration, I could have played the knight errant to the rescue. And so-called real facts, my dear Sir Mathew, are a dangerous thing to bandy about." Calvinward looked right at Mathew.

"The scandal begins and ends at your door, sir," Constance said sharply. "My daughter has been in hell and is

166

now ill, sir, and I hold you responsible. You received this letter, I swear it, and did nothing about it. You merely wished to remove a perceived threat to your image."

Calvinward glanced at Lady Constance, his brow furrowed deeper in puzzlement. The frown vanished. To Mathew it looked as if Calvinward had placed the last piece in a puzzle. Calvinward cleared his throat. "Lady Constance, forgive me saying this, but you are over-wrought by these terrible events. I am not responsible for what has befallen your daughter and Sir Mathew. However, allow me to illustrate how these events could be interpreted by someone skilled enough to twist them to their own advantage.

"Sir Mathew. You are one of Lord Howorth's sons and were working as a political agent for him, or perhaps against him for nefarious others. Posing as working-class and dogging my tail, correct. You used the train crash and my rescuing you to gain my confidence. You spirited Lady Emily, believed by many to be my future wife, away under the cover of a riot. You had myself, her mother and the world believe she was dead. At the height of the most important debate ever to take place in our High Forum, you produce her — to what end?"

"Damn it, Joshua, you are playing it a little fast and loose here. There is no need to be so harsh with the boy," Lord Howorth protested.

"Indeed," Sir Henry added. "I know this is upsetting, but..."

"But ...," Calvinward repeated, "Gentlemen, you know as well as I how this type of game is played. How cruel wagging tongues can be without any axe to grind. Give them a political motive, they can be lethal. I do not doubt, Sir Mathew, events unfolded as you said, and I do not doubt that Lady Emily wrote a letter to me. But it did not arrive, if it ever made it out of the workhouse jail."

Mathew was stunned. He opened his mouth to speak, the anger pounding in his temples. "That is not how things were. I cannot see anyone twisting facts this way. The truth must be told."

"You can't? Enlighten us — how would you lay these facts before the public?" Sir Henry said.

"Item: yes, I am Lord Howorth's son, the third in fact. I was not working for my father as a political agent, but merely gathering information concerning the conditions of the working-class countrywide. I became involved with the

167

petition. Our paths, Lord Calvinward, crossed when I agreed to deliver it to you. I didn't take advantage of you or your friendship during the train crash. I was, and am, grateful for you rescuing me. Captain Avinguard, and Lady Constance, asked me to escort Emily to Hitsmine." Mathew stopped, glancing again at the others in the room, trying to gauge their thoughts and possible reactions.

"But you were travelling under false worker's bond contract papers, using the very law your father seeks to pull down to hide your identity," Sir Henry interrupted. "Forgive me, it is a common enough practice for those working as you did, on a political mission. But the press, especially currently, in the aftermath of the shooting, would take this up as a prime example of the abuse of influence and power, and use it to blot out all other facts. It would be spice for their sauce."

"It wasn't like that," Mathew replied, taken a little off guard by the point of view.

"No?" Pugh asked.

"No. I did what I could to protect Lady Emily. When we arrived at the workhouse jail, as I said before, I put her name down as my wife."

"I understand your desire was to protect Lady Emily by your action; all here do, and your situation gave you little choice — but, as the others have said, the truth is not going to serve. This fact alone will result in hundreds of vile comments at Lady Emily's expense. We need another version of events. One question, Mathew — all these months, you never had a chance of getting free?" Pugh said.

"You would have fought your way out, Captain?" Mathew's retort came swiftly, then he regretted it; he did not wish to alienate Avinguard.

"No, I would have thought, then fought by whatever means I had to protect the woman I loved. And it is Major now. You fumbled it, Mathew. In many respects you placed yourself in the situation you ended up in. You were facing a few thick-headed jailors; you could have used your knowledge of the law and society to run rings round them. But you only saw the injustice and shackles of your circumstances."

What did these men here know of the plight of the working class? He knew — he had the scars on his back to prove it. They were arrogant in their beliefs and blind to the plight of others, despite saying they understood. Pugh was shaking his head. Sir Henry was rubbing his fingers through the tip of his beard, his gaze on Calvinward. Mathew's father had moved from the fire and poured Lady Constance a glass of fortified cordial, but refused to look at his son.

Events had not turned out as Mathew had expected. He had believed Calvinward would hotly deny everything, tainting himself. But he hadn't. Joshua stood there, one hand behind his back, the other, the arm he had broken in the train crash, held slightly bent at his side.

"Lord Calvinward, have you anything else to say?" Constance said, the glass in her hand shaking. Lord Howorth patted her shoulder, his face a mask of concern.

"Yes. I am sorry I allowed the press to speculate that Lady Emily and I were engaged, but that was as far as my sins went. She honoured me with her friendship during the last year, and I valued it."

Mathew snorted at this.

"Yes, honoured," Calvinward repeated. "If I wanted to make political capital of her death, I would have done more than attend her funeral."

Constance looked at Calvinward. Mathew tried to read the emotions on her face. She was distraught and concerned for her daughter, angry at Calvinward, but also, Mathew sensed, at Pugh. There was also the shadow of something else, something he could not quite put his finger on, and it puzzled him.

"As I was saying," Calvinward resumed, "Lady Emily's supposed death, along with the death of others in the aftermath of Hitsmine, has had a profound effect on the nation. The amendments I have proposed to the bill in the High Forum will produce a slower pace of change than the original bill, I grant you, but a fairer and more permanent one. Surely you can see the sense in this, Sir Mathew. Support the bill and your father instead of confronting me about events I had no hand in."

"You speak of politics at this time?" Constance snapped.

"My dear Lady, that, it seems, is exactly what is already happening here. For what reason, I cannot understand or say." For the first time, emotion touched Calvinward's voice, and the tone of it surprised Mathew: a mix of indignation, anger and condemnation. At whom it was directed, Mathew could not be quite sure; it could not be Lady Constance, whose concern was only for her daughter.

For a moment, Mathew believed it was real, then dismissed it as mere misdirection on Calvinward's part. "I see."

Calvinward shook his head in exasperation. "Let us finish this. Lady Emily is alive, and I, for one, intend to try and protect her honour, not drag it through the mud. We must agree on a story and hold fast to it."

"Yes, agreed!" Lord Howorth cut in, nodding at Mathew. Mathew clamped his lips shut.

"What shall it be," Sir Henry said slowly, looking first at Mathew, then at Calvinward.

"You have a suggestion, sir? I would willingly hear it," Calvinward said, and moved for the first time since he had entered the room. He walked past Mathew to the fire and held his right hand out to the fading blaze. Mathew noticed that it trembled. Calvinward clenched it into a ball, allowing it after a few moments to fall open, now completely steady. Mathew grudgingly admired the man's control.

"Say that, as far as everyone was concerned, Lady Emily was dead. She had, unknown to all, been swept up in the riot and committed against her will to a workhouse jail. By chance, Sir Mathew, here, on visiting the establishment on a fact-finding mission for his father, managed, after some difficulty, to get her released. During this time, a bond of affection developed between them. And on their return, Lord Calvinward agreed to Lady Emily's request to be free from any supposed ties between them."

"Very simple, sir," Mathew said.

"Simple is best, young man. It leaves nothing for the press or gossips to get hold of. Stick to it and weather the storm. Believe me, both Major Avinguard and I know. We have had seven years of it, and have reshaped our lives because of it."

"Mathew," Lord Howorth said, looking at his son. Mathew nodded and opened his mouth to speak, but was forestalled by Calvinward.

"Then this matter is closed, for my part. Lady Constance, I am very glad that Lady Emily is alive. Please give her my regards. I wish a goodnight to you, Lady Constance, Lord Howorth and you, Sir Mathew. Sir Henry, Avinguard, shall we?"

Sir Henry nodded and said his own farewells. As the

man's eyes fell on him, Mathew wondered about the relationship between Sir Henry and Calvinward, and more importantly his father.

"If you don't mind, I will stay awhile — if Lady Constance agrees," Pugh said, reaching for her hand.

Pugh, if you don't mind, I would prefer that you leave," Constance said.

"Of course," Pugh said, a shadow falling across his features. He bowed to Constance and followed Sir Henry and Calvinward.

"That demon of a man. You see, Mathew, he is everything he is purported to be. How could he say those things? Forgive me — my nerves. I must go to my daughter." She moved towards the door.

"Of course," Lord Howorth said, and gave her a short bow. Mathew did the same, and watched Constance leave.

"Mathew," his father said.

Mathew turned to face his father. "You don't believe me, do you?"

"As I said, you have no proof of this letter being delivered. Calvinward did not deny that the letter had been written. He just said he had not received it. You will argue yourself black and blue, to no avail." Augustus moved back to the fireplace and again took up station in front of it.

"And you believe him over me."

"I didn't say that, Mathew. This is not a matter of doubting you or Lady Emily. What I do know is that if Calvinward had received the letter, he would have made enquiries. To not do so would be very foolish, and Calvinward is anything but that."

"He is corrupt, in the pay of those who have the most to lose if the bill becomes law."

"He is a politician, my son, as am I. He does what he believes is right for our country." Lord Howorth drew in a deep breath. It sounded as if he was making a difficult decision, but could see no other alternative. "I have worked for years to get an act of this kind passed in the High Forum. This is the first time there has ever been any hope of success. Perhaps if I were to arrange a private meeting between Lord Calvinward and yourself, somewhere. Let the three of us talk things over ...." He looked towards the door through which Lady Constance had left.

Mathew was tempted. No: Lady Constance — and, more

especially, Colliridge — had warned him before his father had arrived that things were not as they seemed between his father and Lord Calvinward. That there were whispers that his father had sold out the bill, with regard to the amendments. He found it hard to believe, but, after tonight, perhaps correct.

"No, I think not, Father."

Lord Howorth sighed heavily, and his shoulders slumped.

"But there is one thing you can do for me, Father," Mathew said.

"Yes, Mathew."

"You must grant me permission to act as your speaker towards the end of the debate. Let me pose a series of questions in your name on the final day," Mathew pressed, trying to make his father understand.

"The debate is nearly finished; the amendments are proposed and seconded. To go over old ground during the last days of debate could do more harm than good. Do you want the bill to run out of time and be referred to the next sitting? It would sign its death warrant. We need to convince members who are still unsure how they will vote in a few hours, not confuse them." Lord Howorth frowned at his son and shook his head. Mathew realised that whatever relationship he had with his father had been damaged further.

***

Sir Henry leant back in the cab. Events were moving in a direction he did not like one bit. Augustus's son had obviously been a starry-eyed reformer, who had, during his time in the workhouse, come face-to-face with the dark underbelly of Timeholm society. Something had happened in the workhouse that had set Mathew on a path that none of them, when they had entered Constance's home, had foreseen. Mulish would be a kind word for it, but it could develop into something else. If someone reinforced this trait in the boy, he could become a wayward clockwork toy, wound up and let loose under the feet of passers-by. It was worrying. Sir Mathew had been convinced that Calvinward had received the letter. Had it been intercepted? Sir Mathew had also been very vague about his and Lady Emily's rescue, and neither he nor Calvinward had pressed Sir Mathew on that matter; perhaps they should have. "Joshua?"

"Sir Henry," Calvinward replied, being formal. He was sitting opposite Sir Henry and Pugh. He sighed. "Pugh, Sir Henry, what if I said I had — "

"You received the letter, didn't you?" Sir Henry said. It all fit: the way Calvinward had spoken about the letter, what he would have done if he had received it.

"Dear Goddess, Joshua! You did make enquiries, didn't you?" Pugh sat forward, disbelief colouring his features. "Why didn't you admit it?"

"Of course I did — I am hurt that you would think I would not, Pugh. As for admitting it, what good would it have done? I sent a man, whom I believed would get to the heart of the matter, and he led me to believe that it was a forgery, that Emily and Mathew were dead. Now it seems he sold the correct information to the highest bidder."

"Lady Constance, or others?" Sir Henry asked.

"Who is to say, but I believe there were other ears listening to our conversation this evening that we were not aware of."

"But you should have spoken out, defended yourself — as it is ..." Pugh's disbelief was beginning to turn to anger. Sir Henry could tell from the tone of his voice.

"My reputation is no blacker in the eyes of those present than it was before."

"What of Augustus?" Sir Henry asked. "If he finds out now, it could damage all you are working for."

"That was one of reasons I didn't speak out. It took me a long time to convince Augustus I was genuine about my support. Our alliance is more fragile than you know. He is a good man, and this would shake his belief in my conviction. Once the vote is over, I will tell him myself — if, that is, he fails to win his son over. If he does, then I will tell them both before the vote and step back and allow Augustus to take the lead once the act is passed."

"You sound very sure that the bill will be passed." Pugh said, the anger in his face draining away.

"I have to be. Though, as to the other matter that has arisen this evening, that remains to be seen."

"What other matter?" Pugh asked.

"The possibility that Sir Mathew might, despite everything, make waves for Calvinward and his father over the bill," Sir Henry said.

173

"That is if Augustus cannot persuade the boy to meet with me," Calvinward said.

"That could be very dangerous, and destroy all you both have worked for. If he still decides to oppose you after you have tried to explain, it would be like — "

"Putting a gun to our heads, Sir Henry, yes it would. But I am betting on Sir Mathew's intelligence and curiosity. Obviously his treatment, and the treatment of others he witnessed in that workhouse jail, has hardened his opinion of the two-faced nature of his own class and politicians." Calvinward tweaked the blind on the cab window and looked outside. A bitter cold mist had begun to rise from the river. It surrounded the street lights, making them flicker and fade as they passed by.

"It will be an uphill task to convince him. Others will even now be pouring their version of the current political situation into his head. They could seek to turn him into a tool to cause as much disruption as possible, then abandon him to his fate. It would be a pity for the boy. He is, like you said, Joshua, intelligent, and it would damage any hope he has of a future career in politics. It would also cause a great deal of personal anguish for Augustus."

"Constance?" Pugh asked.

Sir Henry shifted in his seat. "That is the question, isn't it? It could be, or it could be various individuals working through a third party, with one aim — to muddy the bloody waters and stop the bill. Many of the gentry see the bill as an attack on our Goddess-given place in the world. And Crossmire's emperor would be delighted to see our country so consumed with internal affairs that we take our eye off them. And you know, Joshua, it is possible that Sir Mathew will be speaking in the High Forum very soon — either on your side, if you can convince him, or against you."

"Bollocks!" Calvinward let go of the blind and sat up straight.

"I beg your pardon, sir," Sir Henry said, trying hard not to laugh — but it was no laughing matter.

"I am at a loss," Pugh said.

"I am being dim-witted tonight, aren't I? You are right, Henry. There was no direct male heir to the Manling seat in the High Forum. As Lady Emily is his only child, the seat and vote will be her husband's to claim. If the Lady Dowager Manling agrees."

"Yes, I think she will." Sadness tinged Pugh's words. Apparently, he had begun to realise that Constance was not the beautiful, unworldly widow she liked the world at large to believe.

"Constance will agree. She has an almost aesthetic interest in the game for its sake alone. Move a pawn here and see what transpires." Sir Henry felt a chill that had nothing to do with the frost beginning to form on the streets of Gateskeep.

CHAPTER TWENTY

Pugh stood by one of the tall, narrow windows in the ballroom of Sir Henry's house. The room had been designed to give the occupants access to the three-tiered terrace gardens. Pugh narrowed his eyes and looked at the men outside. They had begun a general search of the small boathouse set in the river wall.

None of the guests would be arriving by the river, which gave him only one official exit and entrance point. *Thank the Goddess.* The security had to be flawless. The ball was taking place after the voting on the Howorth Labour and Industry Act. No matter which way the vote went, emotions would be running at an all-time high. Today was a cusp in the country's history, and one he felt would affect them all. He did not want a repeat of the High Forum shooting.

"Copper coin for them, bubbles and rope." Claire's comment brought Pugh out of his reverie, and he turned to face her. "Religion and politics. Turn the world on its head. You have come in person to escort Father to the Forum today."

"Yes." He wanted to say more, but remembered they were not alone. Servants were placing arrangements of blooms, which ranged from the palest yellow to flame red, on small pillars round the room. They were also hanging gauzy, ivory-coloured drapes edged in gold against the walls. The two large, glass chandeliers had been lowered to the floor and were being polished and fitted with long, slender candles.

Claire's gaze followed his round the room and came back to his face, as his came back to hers. "Elizabeth was telling me that one summer she arrived to help Mother with the final preparations for a ball, and the chandelier nearest the east wall had fallen, after the candles had been lit and it was being hoisted into place. Mother was standing there swearing like a bloody trooper."

"Claire," Pugh said.

"I didn't say something, did I?"

Pugh noticed her eyes widen, behind the coloured lenses. "No, you don't say much these days, just the odd word or three."

"Perhaps Oracle has got bored."

"Perhaps. I intend to keep you safe." The words came out in a rush: it wasn't what he intended to say, but he was glad he had.

"I know," Claire replied. Her gloved hand came out and gently touched his right cheek, where it remained for a moment, then dropped to her side.

"Who was that speaking?"

"Both of us," Claire said, turning away and heading for the door to the wide formal staircase. Pugh glanced one more time out of the window before he followed, catching up with her on the stairs.

As he fell into step with her, Claire began to speak. "Elizabeth and I visited Lady Emily Howorth yesterday after chapel, along with Senior Minister Carlsonmark. Religion and politics."

"You did? Is she is better, and receiving visitors?" Pugh said, wondering where the conversation was leading.

"Yes. I think during her time in the workhouse jail, she grew up."

"I see."

"Do you? Her new husband and her mother don't. Regret and pain. More the pity. Lady Emily is very frustrated at being kept wrapped in cotton wool. She wanted to come tonight, but her husband has decreed otherwise, saying she is still unwell. Nonsense — she is well enough," Claire said. On reaching the bottom of the stairs, she smiled at the footman waiting with her short cloak.

"Oh," Pugh said. He gave a nod to both Sir Henry and Elizabeth, who were waiting for them.

"Minister Carlsonmark said she has not even been allowed to attend chapel," Elizabeth said. "That is why he went with us. I don't think Lady Constance was very happy about his being there; he is too progressive for her taste. Poor girl is going to rue the day she fell for that boy." Elizabeth banged her neat walking cane on the tiled floor. "And as for young Mathew, Augustus has tried to knock some sense into his head, but so far made no progress. He has found it most distressing that the boy is avoiding him. He feels sure that if Mathew knew of the history and reasoning behind the amendments, he would see the sense of them."

Sir Henry nodded in agreement. "Calvinward has written to him twice, asking for a meeting, and both letters have been returned unopened. I, myself, approached him in the Timms coffee house; he did me the courtesy of at least pretending to listen to me, but I don't think it made any impact. He was with a number of High Forum members who had been firm allies of the late Lord Manling, and their disdain for my arguments was very plain to see."

"I find it quite baffling that he has so steadfastly refused to meet Calvinward," Elizabeth said.

"I am surprised to hear you admit anything baffles you, Elizabeth," Sir Henry quipped.

"I am frequently, but I never generally admit it," Elizabeth retorted.

"You think the vote will go Calvinward's way?" Pugh asked. The butler held out his coat for him. He slipped the garment on, but did not button it up; he wanted free access to the gun on his belt.

"The Forum would be fools to not vote for the amendments," Elizabeth said.

"They have been fools before, more than once," Sir Henry replied. He placed his hat on his head and signaled for the front door to be opened.

"Correct as usual, Henry, but it would ill serve the people who will benefit the most from this act. Change must come, but slowly. Some are working to have the power to hire and fire as they will, and damn working-class rights. And not all have a seat in the Forum, I can tell you.

"People like Sir Mathew Howorth are a Goddess-send to them. He sees only the noble cause and not the bitter aftermath that could result. Calvinward, on the other hand, has clearly seen what might — no, will — happen if safeguards are not in place." Elizabeth emphasised her small speech with jabs of her cane as she braved the blast of cold air rushing into the hall. Sir Henry sidestepped Elizabeth's final blow and held out his hand to help her mount into the waiting carriage. She nodded her thanks. Claire followed her into the carriage, then Sir Henry. Pugh looked back and forward, checking the small, mounted guard. He glanced up to the soldier on the box with the driver. He nodded to the two men and entered the carriage.

As the carriage swayed forward, Pugh thought on Elizabeth's words. She seemed sure the bill would pass. Was this to do with her knowledge of her late husband's influence and his dealings with the Forum? The thought was dismissed as soon as it formed. Pugh doubted Elizabeth had shared anything willingly with her unlamented husband. No, it was because Sir Henry supported it. Not that the man had said so: in fact, he had said nothing on the matter. It was his past beliefs. Sir Henry wanted it law, so it would form a base that could be built on.

Sir Henry played the long waiting game. That was how he had survived these last seven years: he had waited. Pugh had not; he had tried to move on. Or at least he had believed that, until that moment when a small, unkempt Glimpser had tumbled back into his life. But Claire had never been out of his life, or mind, since he had first met her.

The carriage turned in to Forum Square. The carved marble façade of the High Forum building showed for a moment through the carriage window as the vehicle made its way down the opposite side of the square. The view changed to that of the river bank, with its cobbled park walk studded with trees. Framing the tops of the trees was Highspire Bridge, with the Haven of the Inner Ring on the far bank. The mounted escort closed in around the carriage. Pugh leaned out of the window. They were in a queue of carriages waiting to drop off their passengers.

"My apologies, Sir Henry, the checks are taking some time," Pugh said.

"To save us time, you best take Elizabeth's cane," Claire said with a small laugh.

"What, deprive an old woman of her cane?" Elizabeth huffed.

"You are not old, and they are illegal, if I remember correctly," Sir Henry said, chuckling and wagging his finger at the lady opposite him.

Pugh's eyes narrowed. He looked closer at the cane: it could not be. Yes, and a beautifully made one at that. "A sword cane." He felt quite a bit of pleasure at finally being able to make Elizabeth feel discomfited.

"I need it," she said, her voice barely audible. "I need it to protect Claire if needs be."

"I see," Pugh replied. Her answer was not the one he had expected.

"She, too, promised," Claire said. Claire had begun to shake, her hands writhing on her lap.

"Claire, are you all right?" Sir Henry asked, leaning forward.

"We must turn round," Pugh said, as he realised what was happening. The stress of the day was having an effect, even before it had really begun. She had to go home.

"No, Pugh. No. You said at the theatre, if it was Oracle speaking, you would have let me go to Lady Constance's. Try or die, ware the wheel of progress, too fast too fast. Gateskeep burned and tumbled. War within. Toby seek, river and ice. Blood on the petticoat, staining the floor. Immortality. Good man. Goddess' sacrifice. Politics and religion, it must be done. Find out or else she will turn the horror into more. Keep my promise, end it. Smash it. Hold us safe for the future."

Pugh was run through by the words. He reached out, taking Claire's hands in his. "I will hold you safe. Claire must return to the house." He looked round the faces in the carriage. All were saying no: Claire's most of all.

***

Sir Henry's hand strayed to the hilt of the ceremonial sword strapped to his side, his fingers tapping on the ornate pommel. He was aware of the weight of the formal robes across his shoulders. He had entered this hall as a Forum member, an appointed minister, ambassador and recently as Master of the Forum, yet today his mouth was dry with apprehension.

Was it Claire's words, written in that rough notebook? He shook his head in denial. This day would turn the world as he knew it on its head, no matter which way the vote went. He did not need Claire's ramblings to tell him that. It was the hints of what might happen next that frightened him. Those words were rare, only uttered twice before today, the hints of a civil war and Gateskeep in flames. Would the passing of the bill be enough to change that event?

The harsh blare of trumpets announced the Forum was seated. Sir Henry squared his shoulders and watched the doors before him swing open. He took a deep breath and stepped forward. Soldiers, ramrod straight, stood against the oak-clad panelling round the edge of the room. Pugh stood to one side of the two High Forum clerks at their desks, his hand on the grip of his pistol, the holster unclipped.

When he reached the Master's chair, Sir Henry turned and bowed to the assembled members. They stood and returned his bow. Sir Henry unsheathed the ceremonial sword and sat in the ornately carved, high-backed chair, resting the blade across his knees. He looked first round the faces of the High Forum members before him, then up to the right, to the overcrowded public gallery. He could make out the pale face of his daughter where she sat with Elizabeth, and to their far right was Lady Constance Manling. His gaze dropped to the ornate silver timepiece on the wall to his left. It was the third hour before midday.

He looked towards the seats that held the seven senior members of the Orthodox Chapel. They looked out of place in their full, grey gowns edged with the colours of the rainbow, among the array of men in morning coats. Sir Henry expected Minister Hornwick, the eldest and most senior, to rise and call the High Forum to prayer. But no, Minister Carlsonmark stood instead. "I call on the Goddess to watch over us and guide our decisions, this day of all days. For the choices we make here and now will shape the future of our country. This Forum was founded on the belief that no one individual can decide the fate of many. No more is that idea being tested than it is today. Goddess, hear our cry and may our decision be right and true for the people given into our care. Goddess be praised in all ways."

"Goddess be praised in all ways." The Forum echoed as one.

It was time to begin. Between now and noon, final questions would be asked — normally a formality, but in the right hands it could be used to bring down a bill. Both supporters and detractors of the bill would want to say their piece.

"Sir clerks, are you ready to do your duty before the Goddess and this Forum?" The sound of his voice stilled the lingering whispers and the shuffling of bottoms on leather-covered seats. Both clerks stood and bowed to Sir Henry. "Final questions, gentlemen, with regards to the Howorth Labour and Industry Act, proposed by Lord Augustus Howorth, amendments proposed by Lord Joshua Calvinward. Before I throw questions open to the floor, I will ask two, as is my right as Master."

A ripple of ayes greeted his words. Sir Henry looked at Calvinward. The man was sitting on the front bench on the right of the house, his legs outstretched and crossed at the ankles, his back against the red leather back of the long bench. Sir Henry looked across the floor at Augustus Howorth. The man was sitting ramrod straight with his knees together, the papers in his hands resting there. He was looking at the tiered benches opposite, at his son. Mathew Howorth was sitting two rows behind Calvinward, in the former seat of Constance's husband: just as Calvinward had predicted. How much of what was going to happen could be laid at Lady Constance's door? Was she behind Mathew's refusal to meet with his father and Calvinward? It was quite possible. The air could have been cleared, the matter of the letter put to bed. What other things had she, and the former supporters of her late husband, whispered in the boy's ear? Sir Henry's mouth became dryer and his stomach began to churn, no longer from apprehension, but surprisingly from fear. "My first question is to you, Lord Howorth. Have you any objection, sir, in whole or in part, to the amendments proposed by Lord Calvinward?"

Lord Howorth stood, bowed in Sir Henry's direction and placed his right hand round the lapel of his morning coat. He cleared his throat. "I have none whatsoever. In fact, these amendments put teeth to the act, while protecting our people during this time of transition. And I openly state my support for them." Lord Howorth sat down amid a wave of excited mutterings which rose in tempo; some members began to applaud.

Sir Henry looked from the seated Sir Augustus to his son Mathew. The young man's face was a mask of suppressed anger. So that was the lay of the land, was it? He felt for Augustus.

"Order, gentlemen, order," Sir Henry called. "My second question is to Lord Calvinward. Do you, sir, have any objection, in whole or in part, to the act to which your amendments will be attached?"

Calvinward uncrossed his legs, got slowly to his feet and bowed to Sir Henry. He looked round the High Forum, then up at the public gallery. "None whatsoever, and I will defend this act with my very blood and bone: I swear to the Goddess, and may she aid me in this." The Forum erupted at Calvinward's calling on the Goddess to witness his oath. Sir Henry was hard-pressed for a while to bring the members back to order. Part of him thought it was all over, that the rest of the time before the vote would be filled with a few mumbled questions. In fact, it began so, most questions fielded well by Lords Howorth and Calvinward.

Sir Mathew Howorth rose and bowed to Sir Henry. "I would like to pose a series of questions, Master of the Forum, if I may." The young man stood, holding a small sheaf of papers in his hands. He was well-dressed, the creases of his britches razor sharp, and not a speck of lint on his morning coat. He looked the very image of an up-and-coming member of the Forum. Sir Henry found his gaze drawn to Mathew's eyes; they were hard, unflinching. The boy had obviously charted his course and was determined to follow it, more's the pity. Elizabeth was right – he could not see further than his own nose.

"And you are, sir?" Sir Henry asked, for the benefit of the Forum members. "I do not recognise you as a member of this Forum. For which family do you speak?" He waved one of the clerks forward.

"Master, I am Sir Mathew Howorth, and I am taking the seat of the Manling family, through my marriage to Lady Emily Manling." Mathew gave a document to the member in front of him, who, in turn, passed it down to the clerk.

The thin-necked clerk peered at the paper for a moment and then nodded to Sir Henry.

"Very good, Sir Mathew, whom do you wish to address?"

Mathew tilted his head in acknowledgement and began. "My first question is for Lord Howorth. Why did you accept these unnecessary amendments to the bill?"

Lord Howorth rose from his seat and bowed to his son. The papers in his hand were clutched in a tight roll which tapped his thigh, keeping tempo with the ebb and flow of his words.

"I honestly believe the amendments are necessary." A wave of agreement met his reply, a number of gentlemen applauding by slapping the leather on the backs of the seats.

"So you abandoned the work of years, concerning the plight of the working class," Mathew said, looking not on his father, but at Lord Calvinward. Baiting the hook, Sir Henry thought, and leaned forward in his seat.

"No, I never abandoned it. This is not the first time I have tried to convince the Forum of the need for change. I was called a fool. A blinkered idealist. The previous bills were killed like unwanted children, by men frightened of change, who clung to their power like misers. Now, for the first time in our history, we have a chance of changing the lives of thousands of our fellow countrymen.

"The act in its original form was but a spring board. We have, in this Forum, debated it for weeks. The amendments

183

came out of this debate. Each man has had his say, each word scrutinised until a consensus has been reached to vote on the matter today. It can't be delayed. It must become law. I will not see another act still-born that could free our fellows. Yes, with the amendments in place it will be a slower and more gradual change from one stage to another, but it will safeguard the rights of all concerned." With this, Lord Howorth bowed to his son and sat down, indicating he had finished and was not prepared to be questioned further.

"I see, you have changed your mind or been persuaded that it would be of more benefit to you, personally, not to push for a clean bill." A rumble of mutterings and calls of "nonsense," interspersed with a few claps, greeted Mathew's final words.

"Take care, sir," said Sir Henry.

"I didn't attack my father's honour, merely voiced an opinion."

A ripple of laughter followed.

"You are treading a thin line, Sir Mathew. You are new to the Forum; remember, honour is easily bruised and insults here in the house have led to bloodshed on the streets."

"Indeed I will." Mathew gave Sir Henry a short bow amid another ripple of laughter.

Mathew's father had bowed out, trying to salvage something from what threatened to become a messy affair. If Mathew turned to attack Calvinward, he would have more of a scrap on his hands.

"The second member you wish to question?"

"Lord Calvinward."

Calvinward stood, turned to face Mathew and bowed.

"The amendments — will they not shackle the working class even further, burdening them with producing evidence of their bad working conditions and their grievances against a corrupt system?" Mathew spoke not at Joshua, but to the Forum at large, his gestures more suited to speaking from a public platform.

"On the contrary: we must insure that every aspect of the current system is inspected from root to tip of branch, before we act. Cut away the bad timber, but leave the good, solid heartwood. And the eyes of those who will enforce this new law will be sharp, I promise." Calvinward kept his attention politely on Mathew, as if they were speaking in the corner of some private club. Sir Henry nodded his head in approval; it was well done, a display of manners and respect that did not go unnoticed by the other members.

"Eyes can be easily blinded."

A few ayes followed Mathew's quick remark.

"True. So it is our intention to put to work those who know firsthand the exploitation that goes on." Calvinward spread his hands to emphasise his words.

"Meaning the employers." The supposed clarification was a mere point off sarcastic in its tone.

"You obviously didn't read the amendments clearly, sir. The inspectors will be drawn mainly from the working class: men who have fought to acquire an education against the odds, and whose personal honour is unquestioned." Calvinward smiled and opened his hand to a fellow member sitting alongside him, who placed a ragged copy of the amendments in his hand. "I am sure Sir Clarence will let you borrow his copy, so you may read the section for yourself."

"I see, and no, I already have more than enough copies." Mathew cleared his throat, for the first time pressed back on the defensive.

"Do you see?" The reply came swiftly and surely.

"I see people locked more firmly in their state: one from which we are honour bound to raise them." The retort followed as sharply.

"I would rather they rise under their own efforts, honour intact. We must move towards a state that encourages the individual to do his best, but also protects him."

"You mean you would pick and choose: take only the best and leave the rest as fodder for an evil system."

"Did you not hear what I said, Sir Mathew? Encourage and protect. These factories you so hate are creating our country anew; we must adapt or perish as a people, as a nation. Yes, parts of the system must be changed. The workhouse jail system, for instance, which will be the first to come under the umbrella of this act. At the moment, such places stand outside even bond contracts, the workforce subjected to horrors beyond imagining."

"You can't know."

"I do know, sir. I have read report after report submitted with the bill, many undertaken in secret for your father, the

185

men compiling them often in fear for their lives. And might I add that I am looking forward to comparing the one you undertook with those I have already studied." Joshua again smiled at Mathew. Sir Henry noticed the cynical twist of the man's lips. Was he taunting Mathew with his knowledge of events? If so, he was sailing close to the wind, and Sir Henry was not sure if he approved. If Calvinward decided to humiliate the young man, it could miscarry.

"You will be surprised, sir," Mathew retorted, "but you still have not completely answered my question."

"I will answer your question with another one, sir. If we abolish the bond contracts overnight, what will happen to the working class?"

"They will be free." Mathew's statement was followed by howls, jeers and calls of "well said."

"Order, gentlemen!" Sir Henry called.

"Free to watch their children starve," Calvinward retorted.

"Nonsense!"

"No. If the bond contracts no longer existed, then employers would be free to dismiss whomever they choose. So in an instant you would have a family with no roof over their heads and no food in their bellies." Calvinward's tone was lecturing. His manner brought more than one chuckle of amusement from his fellow members.

"An employer would not cut his throat in this manner," Mathew said, his face showing total conviction in what he said.

The boy was so convinced of the greed of his own class, of their unwillingness to switch from a sure bet to a risk. Experience told Sir Henry the opposite: the factory owners had gotten where they were by undertaking such hazardous ventures.

"He wouldn't be cutting his throat. No bond contracts, and without even an inadequate law to safeguard individuals' rights, an employer would be free to pick and choose. Face the truth of the real world, sir. It is messy and complex. As much as we would wish for something to happen, making it happen without hurting those we are trying to protect is a great deal harder." For the first time, Calvinward looked away from Mathew. He made a show of shaking his head.

"You are creating a nightmare scenario to suit your purpose, sir," Mathew snapped.

"It is the lure of profit, sir, which shapes the scenario I have drawn. At the moment an employer has obligations under the bond contract system. He has to provide for his employees. Even if his business fails, he has to look to their wellbeing until their contracts are handed over. We must not remove one law until we have something in place that addresses the needs of both sides." A huge shout of approval and ayes rose, echoing round the high beams of the vaulted ceiling.

"That does not excuse the evil that is being done, sir. The people need to be free." Mathew pushed on with his argument, his voice rising over the clamour that Sir Henry was trying to calm.

"I beg you, in the name of the Goddess, Sir Mathew, open your eyes. Meet with your father and myself, as we have asked, talk over the bill, and work with us. And like Major Avinguard said a few nights ago: think, then fight, using what knowledge you have of the law and society to *change it*, not sweep all away without thinking of the future." As Calvinward finished speaking, a round of applause and the stamping of feet began. He acknowledged the spontaneous reaction to his words and made to sit.

"Is that how you explain to yourself your actions with regards to Hitsmine?" Mathew's voice drowned out the shuffling of bodies and the murmur of voices that had followed.

Calvinward stiffened and turned sharply, his face showing emotion for the first time. Then it was gone. There was the man Sir Henry had begun to know, with all his faults and fears, beneath the veneer of the politician. Was Hitsmine the same to Calvinward as the events of seven years ago were for him? As Coot's Pass was for Pugh? That one moment when you see the result of another's actions, and the horror it brings in its wake.

"You are referring to Lady Emily's ordeal: that, I believe, is not a matter for this Forum, but a private one, as well you know," Calvinward said coldly, followed by a loud aye from his supporters.

"Indeed, Sir Mathew — those events have no place in this discussion, and I am surprised you are bringing them up," Sir Henry cut in, the sword in his hand coming up and pointing at the young man, then dropping down.

"I was not referring to those events. I was, however, referring to another leading up to the riots — or rather, to the manipulation of certain persons."

187

"The riots were the result of miscommunication: a group of workers, trapped by their situation, with no recourse. There, in that one riot alone, you have the justification for the amended act."

"And that was your plan all the time: to create a situation that would be the proof for your amendments to the act," Mathew retorted. He looked round the room, watching the effect of his words on the men there.

"I am no Glimpser, sir; I have not the gift. It is easy, with hindsight, to see connections where there are none." Calvinward let a trace of sadness enter his voice.

"So, you deny any part in setting up the riot through the actions of a third party?"

"You mean I used a cloak and dagger political agent. Please, Sir Mathew, do they exist outside the fictional series printed on the inside back page of the Gateskeep Sun?"

"So this copy of a telegram from an agent in Hitsmine, in reply to your orders, is nothing." Sir Mathew opened his right hand and removed the scrap of thin paper from among the other pages.

"How did you acquire that, Sir Mathew? Telegraph messages are protected under the law." Sir Henry stepped forward, waving to one of the clerks to take the message.

"It was thrown away by Lord Calvinward when he was dictating a series of telegrams at an early evening halt of the northern express."

"If I threw it away, it couldn't have been very important," Calvinward quipped, and responded to the following outburst of laughter with a small bow.

"Enough, sir, this is not a time for jests. As Master of the Forum, my task is to judge the contents and order whatever action needs to be taken, as it is being presented as evidence of misdoings on the part of a Forum member."

Mathew recoiled slightly at Sir Henry's words. He was reluctant to hand the paper over to the clerk, who had moved to his side.

"Sir Mathew, you have brought a serious charge against a fellow member: that of inciting a riot in which citizens of our country died. You claim you have proof. It is a very serious matter, and one that must be placed before myself, as the embodiment of the law governing the behaviour of Forum members. And if the one charged is found guilty, the severest of sentences must, by the law, be carried out before sunset." As he spoke, the sword in his hand came up straight and level, the silvered point hovering in Calvinward's direction.

"That is – " Sir Mathew began.

"Not what you sought. You wanted this matter to usher in a formal legal investigation. Sadly, by accusing Lord Calvinward here on the floor of the High Forum, you have prevented my allowing that more civilised alternative." The boy had misjudged: he thought he knew all the laws governing this Forum. He had thought he could delay the vote by plunging Calvinward into an investigation that would most likely turn up nothing. Curse the boy, he had put Calvinward's head on the block. Sir Henry tried to dismiss the sick feeling rising in his stomach. If the evidence was as damning as Mathew believed, he would have no other choice. Why had Mathew not mentioned this the other night?

"I see." Mathew handed over the message to the clerk, who scurried down from the third row and handed the paper to Sir Henry. He took the small scrap of paper, similar to the one he had received on his journey to Gateskeep. Had his action been so very different from Mathew's? On the outside, no, but the reasons were different; he tried to rationalise, but failed. He had committed a crime: driven by the desire to protect his daughter, but a crime nevertheless.

Sir Henry opened the message and read it. His eyes widened, relief overwhelming him. *"All is ready at Hitsmine. Will inform you of the results before you reach the capital."* Thankfully, it could mean anything: it was not proof at all. Sir Henry sighed. "Hindsight, as Lord Calvinward previously said, is a wonderful thing, Sir Mathew. You came to the conclusion after the events at Hitsmine, least I hope so. Else it would hint at yourself having prior knowledge."

"I was, at that time, observing events. The unrest was plain to see," Mathew said.

Sir Henry glanced round the room. A number of members were nodding their heads in agreement. The youth had struck a chord with some of the more radical members who had supported the act in its original form and would believe anything of Calvinward.

"So you reasoned a man who wanted to make political gain would stir things up even more to prove his point."

"You do not believe me?" Mathew's voice was hard, trembling with emotion.

"I think you are, most likely, mistaken. The telegram could have a dozen meanings. Lord Calvinward, I ask you to cast your mind back."

"I will try. I was not the only one using the telegraph. A number of messages were received for Sir Clive Hotspur, and other travellers ...," Calvinward began.

He brought the arm he had broken round from his back and gently rubbed it. Calvinward looked up at the public gallery. Who was he looking at? Not Claire or Elizabeth. *Goddess*, it was Lady Constance. Was the telegram something to do with her scheming, and it had snared Calvinward by mistake? What would he do, out the lady here in the Forum? No, that would look very bad and have the place in uproar. However, Calvinward would, at some point, want an answer from the woman as to her possible involvement.

Calvinward continued, "I sent a number of messages through Hitsmine, to be passed on to my office and my estate overseer. I tied up the conductor and his machine for a while. The one I threw away might have been a reply to one of those. It could have been the one concerning the new gates being made for the estate drive. I wanted a certain design, and the foundry in Hitsmine was being a little difficult."

"It is a lie!" Mathew bellowed. "He cannot prove that."

"Be quiet, sir!" Sir Henry shouted in reply. "Can you, Lord Calvinward?"

"I can produce the order and excessive bill." With this, Calvinward turned, bowed to both Sir Henry and Sir Mathew, flipped up the tails of his morning coat and sat. The Forum erupted into bedlam. Hands clapped, men hooted and cheered. Calvinward again looked towards the public gallery. Sir Henry looked as well. Constance had gone very pale.

"Order, order. The bell! The bell!" Sir Henry shouted to the clerks. The two men reached for the rope hanging in front of them and pulled together. The large, single bell hung in the rafters began to sway, slowly, then faster. Its silver tones crashed over the heads of the gentlemen below and, reluctantly, voices silenced.

"I have not finished," Mathew began, the frustration in his voice plain for all to hear.

190

"Lord Calvinward has sat down, sir — the questioning is over. As to the serious matter you placed before me, I find no evidence in this missive to support your claim; it is too vague. I suggest we let the matter drop, for all concerned." He watched carefully as Mathew swallowed his defeat, bowed to Sir Henry and sat back down. Sir Henry nodded, glancing up at the clock. "It is well past midday: the voting shall begin."

***

"Lord Calvinward," Sir Henry said. Calvinward raised his head and opened his eyes. The High Forum was all but empty. A few members lingered by the door; the rest had voted and left. The result was to be announced after a luncheon break. "Are you going to vote, sir? I need to close the box."

"Close it," Calvinward said, and stood, brushing at an imagined crease in his trousers.

"You are that sure — a single vote ...?" Sir Henry began.

"If it would take a single vote to get this act and its amendments passed, then it is not worth passing," Calvinward said quietly, well aware that his words had been overheard by the few remaining members and would fly round the rest well before the Forum re-sat after lunch.

"You are sure?" Sir Henry stepped down from his chair and walked the few paces to the clerks' desks.

"Yes." Calvinward walked towards the door, glancing back when he had reached the exit, to watch the removal of the box.

"Seal it and remove it to the small committee room. Those five members who picked the black ball of abstention yesterday are waiting to do the count."

Avinguard nodded and motioned four soldiers forward to act as escort for the box.

"Pugh, if you don't mind?"

He stopped and turned, a frown on his face. "Sir Henry?"

Sir Henry walked to Pugh's side and spoke, his voice barely a whisper. "I might be mistaken, but I got the impression that the telegram had nothing to do with Calvinward, but he knew about it. It was the way he was looking at someone in the public gallery."

"I am not sure. I was not privy to everything, but, *Goddess*,

191

I think there was mention of a lost telegram. I seem to remember Calvinward apologising to Lady Constance, and acquiring a copy of some message for her that had been lost."

CHAPTER TWENTY-ONE

The lawn in the centre of the cloisters was thick with ice. Colliridge noticed that there were three — no, four — sets of footprints across the white expanse, all smeared, the footprint owners hurrying. Novices, late for breakfast. They certainly wouldn't be late for early morning prayers: for a novice of the Inner Ring, devotion to the rituals of the order came above even that to the Goddess. The sun had risen above the low roof of the main chapel. Thin beams of light cut across the stone floor of the cloister and illuminated the plaques on the inner wall.

Behind each finely chiselled name lay the moulding remains of the country's great — and often not so good — considered worthy of being buried in the chapel. As per the ambassador's message, Colliridge had arrived at the memorial to the late Lord Reginald Hawcross after the end of prayers. He had even lit a candle to the long-forgotten gentleman, in case there were any other early morning visitors to the cloister. That was nearly half an hour ago. He stamped his feet, blew on his hands and walked a few paces to the right. As he turned back, he noticed he was no longer alone in the cloister. Standing at the west end were two figures: one a priest, and by the richness of his robe and gold-corded belt, he was a member of the higher cadre; the other was a woman, tall, and even though she was wearing a heavy, hooded cloak, Colliridge knew who. It was her carriage and the way she bent her head to receive the priest's blessing: Lady Constance Manling. The blessing given, the two walked towards him.

"Good morning, Milady, sir priest," Colliridge said. Constance did not answer, merely inclined her head in acknowledgement of Colliridge's greeting.

"You are Colliridge?" The priest asked.

"Yes."

"You come highly recommended by this lady."

"I am grateful for her ladyship's confidence in my skills."

"We — I — have a job that needs the utmost discretion."

"I am always at milady's service," Colliridge said, enjoying the priest's discomfort at being ignored. So, ambassador, the Inner Ring and Lady Constance: a most unholy trinity. The enemy of my enemy is my friend, as the old saying goes.

The boathouse was old, the flimsy wooden structure built on the stronger foundations of a previous building. Colliridge lay on the warped decking of the small landing, peering over the side. The river was in full winter flow. Drunkenly, it rolled its way to the sea, hindered by debris and layers of ice. In the shelter of the boathouse, the ice had not crept in. It hung like a torn, ragged veil across the entrance.

"Well?" Carter asked.

"The river is too high – look at the steps." Colliridge gestured towards the wooden ladder that led down off the small jetty. The dark shadow of more rungs lay under the surface of the inky water.

"That is obvious, Colliridge. Harrison said that the grate was tucked right under the landing, with a set of stone steps below. He brought the boat right in."

Colliridge had not swallowed the story Lady Constance had told him earlier. It was all nonsense, this act of charity on the order's behalf: their desire to take the Lady Claire into safe custody, because her father was ignoring the signs she was becoming mentally unstable again. The woman had always been unstable, as far as he was concerned. She had been a self-centred, high-strung bitch up in Coot's Pass, and he doubted that had changed over the past seven years. She had encouraged Avinguard in his harebrained plan, got him shot at, half-starved and frozen on the retreat from the pass. He should have been miles away, warm and safe. It had been Avinguard's fault: he had changed the guard roster. Her father had sat in the mountains, since Coot's Pass, like a spider. The man had, on more than one occasion, thwarted the political plans of the order. The Inner Ring were about to up the stakes, and Lady Constance and the ambassador were, for the moment, willing to help.

Colliridge had begun to suspect that Lady Constance, for all her indicating otherwise, was against the act becoming law. That would have been a path her late husband would have taken. The late Lord Manling believed that the gentry had the Goddess-given right to rule. The Inner Ring certainly weren't fond of it, for all their talk of helping the poorer class. And anything that upset the status quo was on the ambassador's agenda. Where did that leave

Sir Mathew Howorth? The innocent dupe. He wouldn't be for long. Colliridge knew Lady Constance would find some way to embroil the young man so deeply within her plans that he could not remove himself, not without facing the destruction of his budding political career, or worse. Poor sod. Oh, this was proving to be intriguing as well as extremely profitable, though he currently did not fancy the idea of wading in ice-cold water through a half-flooded tunnel. If, that is, they found it still unblocked.

"During summer, this is winter." Colliridge got to his feet; he needed a lantern. He dusted his trousers and glanced around the boathouse.

Carter began to speak, his words incoherent. Bloody priest, what was up with him?

"Hands up, you pair." The words were accompanied by the sound of a rifle's bolt being drawn back and locked forward. Colliridge slowly turned his head. In the doorway stood a soldier, the shadow of another behind him. The man had the butt of his rifle to his shoulder and was signalling with a wave of the barrel for Colliridge to comply.

Colliridge forced a smile on his face. "Well done, soldier: I will report your sharp eyes to Major Avinguard, if you will let me." One of Colliridge's hands dropped towards the inner pocket of his coat.

"Hands up, I said," the soldier repeated.

"I was merely getting my documents; I work for army intelligence. And this gentleman is a member of the Inner Ring — he is assisting me. Show the good soldier your ring of office, George?"

Carter glared at him and roughly pulled off his left glove, revealing the large ring of twisted, red leather entwined with a twin of silver, wedged tightly on the second knuckle of his index finger. The soldier's rifle wavered at the sight of it. He stepped two paces into the boathouse, his companion following. "Let's see those papers — slowly, mind you."

Colliridge smiled, more at the expression of surprise on Carter's face than at his own cleverness. His papers were genuine. They had been acquired during his work for the late Lord Manling. Colliridge withdrew the leather wallet from his pocket and handed it to the soldier's companion. The man looked through the document. "Pardon us, Captain." He gave Colliridge a salute.

"Understandable, gentlemen, but now you are here, you might be able to help us," Colliridge said, returning the soldier's salute.

"What?" Carter spluttered.

"Can you see a lantern?" Colliridge said, again enjoying the priest's discomfort.

"One over here, I think, sir," the second soldier called.

"Good, any oil in it?" Colliridge asked. The soldier rattled the lantern. It made a soft sloshing sound. "Oh, brilliant, bring it here. We had a tip-off that someone might have stashed some weapons and explosives in a large drain runoff under the landing. But, damn me, I couldn't find it, let alone the supposed guns."

"Want some help, sir?" the first soldier said.

"Thanks," Colliridge replied, over Carter's attempt to deny the request. "But it means going down the steps and maybe into the water by the wall."

"That's all right, sir, done worse," the second soldier said, ignoring the glare of his fellow.

The two soldiers laid down their rifles and descended the steps. The leader carefully felt around with his feet when he was thigh-high in the water.

"Feels like a ledge running round the wall. Harvey, hold that lantern high."

His companion obliged.

Colliridge lay down again on the cold wooden boards and peered under the decking, watching the man's progress.

"There, looks like a large grate — the water about a quarter of the way up," Harvey called, waving the lantern deeper into the gloom. He joined his fellow soldier on the slick ledge.

"Can you open the grate?" Colliridge asked.

"Aye," the first soldier grunted, and began tugging and pushing at the grate. "Goes inward — give us the lantern, Harvey. Goddess, it stinks in here. Hold on, a set of steps leading up a bit. They are out of the water."

"Is this wise?" Carter whispered.

Colliridge leant closer to the priest and whispered back. "According to your information, there is a drain coming in from the left. Ahead looks like a dead end where the passage narrows so much you are hard-pressed to squeeze through sideways."

196

Carter called, "Any sign of anything, an oilcloth-wrapped bundle?"

"Nothing, sir; the passage narrows so much that a man could hardly get through it, let alone put anything in there. Looks like a dead end, sir," the first soldier called.

"Get yourselves out of there. I owe you a few pints for this," Colliridge said with a laugh. Just then the sound of a cannon firing echoed from downriver.

"Damn, the vote is in," Carter said.

"We best be moving," Colliridge said. He pulled out his purse and slipped the first soldier a couple of coins.

The man grinned and took the coins, then frowned. "How did you get in here, sir?"

"Through the house, of course," Colliridge bluffed, winking at the soldier. "And we will be going out that way. Come on, Brother George. No peace for the wicked." With this, he strode out of the door the soldiers had come in. As he walked, he made a mental note of the positions of the braziers the soldiers were setting up: none on the river wall itself, as he thought. Avinguard was banking that the men on the terraces would stop any intruders — but it wouldn't prevent the ones under their feet.

***

The sound of the signal gun still reverberated in Mathew's mind. He refused to think on it as a death knell. Yes, the act and its amendments had been passed, but nearly half the Forum had not agreed, and the ripples from the result were already being felt. He walked slowly down the wide staircase. Every other step, he and Constance were stopped by one member or another. Cards were exchanged, words of support or offers of help given. Others obviously felt the same way.

"You believed all was lost," Constance said.

Mathew returned the bow of a well-wisher and turned his attention to Constance. "Yes. I believed I had misjudged the whole thing, thrown away our only proof of what Calvinward truly is."

"Deny it he may, but the mud will stick. He is disliked by many. They will believe you, as I believe you."

"Of course you are right, but we must not let up the

pressure as the act moves into committee. We have time to prepare codicils. We could tie it up for years." Mathew tried to smile and offered his arm to Constance.

"No, you must leave the act to go through unmolested. To attempt to meddle with it in committee will look like sour grapes. Spend the time between now and the next session in cementing friendships and alliances. Then begin work on a new act, to nullify this one. It is all a matter of move and counter-move: knowing what your opponent will do in a given situation, and even manufacturing that situation, is key."

For a moment Mathew felt uneasy. Had not Calvinward's creating of certain circumstances resulted in Lady Emily and him being thrown into a workhouse jail? Then again, it was what a good politician did to ensure the policies he espoused became law. He must put aside all doubts and do the same from now on.

Further down the street and to one side stood Sir Henry and his party, including Calvinward, waiting for their carriages. "It was almost as if they knew what I was going to say."

Before Constance could answer, the carriage arrived. The footman jumped down, lowered the step and opened the door for them. Constance moved quickly into the dark interior of the carriage. She thanked the footman as he placed a thick rug round her knees. "Yes, uncanny and very clever, but I doubt it went unnoticed."

"The young woman — she is Sir Henry's daughter, Avinguard's ex-wife?" Mathew asked.

"Yes."

"Strange — I know I have never met her, but there was something so familiar about her. I think it is the tilt of her head and those eyes hidden behind those glasses. The glasses themselves are unusual, are they not?"

"Yes, they are to correct some eye condition, so I am told," Constance replied.

Both of them lapsed into silence. The carriage clattered to a stop outside Constance's town house in Highmarsh Square. Constance stepped onto the icy pavement. A few flakes of snow skittered by, dappling her walking dress with white specks. She shook the fabric and moved up the granite steps to her home. Mathew began to follow, then stopped. To the right of the steps, one hand on the curved railings that ran outside the house, stood a man. It was the Inner Ring priest, George Carter. He was well-dressed, and held his hat and cane clutched before him.

"Good day, Mathew, Lady Constance."

Mathew's mouth dropped open in shock. He blinked in total disbelief at seeing Carter alive. For a moment Mathew was again in that hot carriage on the northern express, listening to Carter's madcap words concerning the Glimpser. Words that had led to Carter's seemingly insane action of pulling the communication cord, only the action proved not to be: the train had been slowing when it hit the mudslide. How many lives had Carter saved that day? Mathew had believed the man dead, crushed beneath the bogies of Calvinward's private carriage.

"My dear George, I hope everything went well today," Lady Constance said.

"Yes, it did. Mathew, I know my appearance here is a shock to you, but with Lady Constance's help, I have been looking into certain events. What I have found out concerns today's events and how I believe they have been manipulated."

"Please, join us — tea, or perhaps something stronger — the day is a bitter one, is it not?" Lady Constance's words were formal, but Mathew knew that the meaning behind them was not. He looked from Constance to Carter, gave a short nod and followed Constance into the house.

Mathew stood in the hall, watching Carter. Constance's footmen and butler divested them all of their winter coats, gloves and hats. The layer of fresh snow on the shoulders of their garments had quickly melted, filling the air with the smell of damp cloth. It reminded Mathew of the mill.

"Lady Emily?" Mathew asked the butler. He found himself hoping she was asleep, so that he did not yet have to go up and speak to her. She would want to know what had happened, and he, of course, would want to tell her, but Carter's arrival brought the whole day into a different perspective.

"She is resting, sir," the butler answered.

"Then I won't disturb her."

The three of them made their way into Constance's private parlour. The thick, red drapes had already been drawn. The light from the oil lamps mingled with that of the roaring fire, giving the room a warm, homey feel. A picture of Constance's late husband stared down from above the mantelpiece.

Mathew indicated for Carter to sit in a chair to the right. He gave a small smile to Constance, who had sat down on the left of the fire. He, himself, took a seat directly opposite the mass of shimmering flames.

"So," Carter began, "your daughter is recovering."

"Yes," Constance replied.

"I am glad. You didn't believe her dead, Mathew. Quite an adventure you had finding her. And my felicitations on your union." Carter was making small talk, that was plain. Did he not know that he, Mathew, had been presumed dead? Of course he did.

The door opened, and the butler brought in a tray of tea and placed it on the table by Constance's side. She dismissed him with a smile and busied herself with pouring the tea. She passed a cup to Carter, who muttered his thanks. He set it down on the small table by his elbow and shuffled in his seat.

Mathew waited until the door closed behind the butler. He was unsure of how to begin.

He did not have to. "First, to answer your unasked question, Mathew, I did think I was dead when that carriage tipped over. I was carrying a lump of lead in my shoulder, bleeding and — "

"But you quickly left the scene once you realised you were not dead," Constance said.

The smile on her face, and the answering one on Carter's, told Mathew she was indulging in a small jest at Carter's expense.

"I tried to follow the Glimpser, but it lost me within a few feet. I knew then, if Avinguard found me, I would actually be as good as dead."

"Why?" Mathew asked. Pugh might have thrown Carter in a sleeping compartment and turned the key, but he would not have killed the man in cold blood. Avinguard had shot because he thought he was protecting those he was charged to. Even Pugh's words of the other night had been prompted by his adherence to his own hidebound militia code.

"Because of the Glimpser. I realised that Avinguard was trying to protect it. He saw me as a threat."

"Were you? Are you?" Mathew asked.

Constance gave an audible hiss. Mathew looked at the woman. Her forehead was creased in a frown. Was there something about the conversation that was not going the way she wanted it to?

"No. I was, and still am, trying to get it into the protection of my order. I want it safe, not as a tool of others. But as I was saying — I knew I had to look to myself and inform my order. I didn't wish to abandon you, Mathew; however, I had to serve my order first. With Constance's help, I managed to get onto one of the first trains from the crash site. By the time I reached Gateskeep, I was at death's door."

So Lady Constance had helped Carter. Did Emily know of this? She had never mentioned it. "I see."

"That, I suppose, explains your actions, but as regards the glimpser ...," Lady Constance said.

"I don't know if Mathew has told you what I said about the creature on the train," Carter said.

"Some, but please," Lady Constance said, but the look on her face belied her words: Constance knew far more than she was letting on.

"I said, the burden of what they are drives them, sadly, to their death, but in rare cases something else drives them to survive. The creature starts to become again a cognizant human being. Like you and me, but with an inner switch that will, in certain circumstances, plunge it back into its state of being a Glimpser. This is a delicate balance. A Glimpser in this state needs to be protected; my order is the most suited to do so. One of the most important signs my order look for is the one where the creature gives itself a name."

"Oracle," Mathew said slowly. It suddenly dawned on him: Carter had actually been telling the truth, that day in the train carriage. Mathew's heart began to race with the implications of what Carter was saying. A Glimpser that was almost human and able to relate to others. It was a wonder and a tool of such danger and magnitude, it was hard to comprehend.

"Yes, and they seek out people from their past, ones they can trust. It sought out Pugh, and he did try to protect it. I see that now. But the one that it sought out is, sad to say, using it, or allowing another to use it. Only on my return to Gateskeep was I able to find out the former identity of the Glimpser and trace its path after the train crash."

Constance spoke, in part denying what Carter had said. "But I thought they were born so, and they didn't know any other life."

201

"No, the gift always comes upon an adult who, up to that time, seems normal. It begins with a serious mental illness, which causes many to be locked up by their family." There was a look in Carter's eyes that told Mathew this was not quite the truth. Something else perhaps triggered the Glimpser in a normal person, something the order would rather not say outright. Understandable – if you knew a loved one held within the propensity to be a Glimpser, the horror of living with that would be unbearable.

"Mental illness – oh, by the Goddess, you don't mean it's her? Lady Claire?" Constance cried.

"Yes, Lady Claire. The glasses she wears not only hide the outward sign of her gift, but, I warrant, protect her eyes. A Glimpser is sensitive to light, as was the blessed Seer." Carter looked at Constance and smiled.

"I felt I knew her." Mathew gulped. A cold shiver crept down his spine. He moved towards the fire and took a large log from the basket by the side, placing it on the weakening flames. *Dear Goddess.* Lady Claire was with her father, and that made her subject to Calvinward's influence. Mathew looked towards Constance. The twist of her fine mouth told him she thought the same. Carter's next words confirmed his mounting fears about the creature that was Lady Claire.

"It is sad that her own father is using her." Carter shook his head.

"But Pugh, he knows?" Constance whispered.

"He has tried to protect her out of duty, but has found himself blocked by others. I believe the good major wants her to be free to follow her own path."

Mathew dusted his hands and walked to Constance's side. He took her hand and held it. He was at sea, storm-tossed by what he had heard. He did not quite share Carter's belief in Pugh's actions.

"Her speech is often a strange mix, I see it – but she knows who she is," Constance said, returning the pressure of Mathew's hand.

"The spirit of the Seer is awake in her, but she is vulnerable. She needs to be protected."

"Calvinward." Mathew finished for Carter. Everything that had happened made bitter sense. "They knew, by the Goddess, they bloody well knew! They have been piecing together the future and using it to their own ends." Mathew's grip tightened on Lady Constance's hand. He felt her wince and released it, mouthing his apologies. She shook her head in understanding, and placed her hand on his arm in a gesture of comfort. He was thankful for it; it helped anchor him. A man alone, he could fight and be sure he could win. But against a man guided by a poor woman whose only use to him was that of a looking glass to the future? It made Mathew's stomach churn. He looked towards Carter. That was why the priest was here; he wanted their help.

"Yes, and they are denying the poor young woman both safety and the chance to continue her growth into what she should be."

"You must make everything public," Mathew said. If the order did this, it would condemn both Calvinward and Sir Henry not only to a workhouse jail, but perhaps even a gibbet. The law was strict with regard to Glimpsers: they were considered special in the eyes of the Goddess.

"Who would believe us, Mathew? My order has striven to prove this for five hundred years – to prove a Glimpser could one day be the chalice that would hold the returning soul of the Seer. Even the Orthodox Chapel, especially the council of senior ministers, does not approve. We are barely tolerated by them these days. If we had this young woman safe in our keeping ...."

"Talk to her," Constance suggested.

"One of my order would not get within ten paces. We have a plan to get her into our keeping, but need some help."

"You mean kidnap," Mathew said.

"Yes, but if the Seer in her asks for release, we will do so, and allow her to go where she wills – which is not the case at present, I assure you. She is watched all the time by her father's staff, even soldiers placed round her home." Carter clasped his hands together on his lap.

"You want our help," Lady Constance said.

"Yes, when Lady Claire first became aware of the madness descending on her seven years ago, she contacted one of our order. He met her secretly a number of times and helped her leave her father's house by a tunnel that runs from the house to the old boathouse – an escape tunnel built in a far more dangerous time. I can easily get into the house that way, and I believe tomorrow night, the night of the ball, to be the best time. The house will be full of people. If you could help us arrange for Lady Claire to be in the library at a certain time, we can take her to safety."

"I see. And what if we refuse and try to warn Sir Henry of what you intend to do?" Mathew said, playing the advocate, testing Carter. He would help, but not if it placed Constance or Emily at risk.

"Do you not believe me?" Taken aback by what looked like a refusal, Carter rose to his feet, anger inundating his voice. "Look at the events since the Glimpser came onto that train; think on what it said, trying to warn us all of coming events, of its own change — and we failed it. If you so much as approach Sir Henry on this, he will destroy you."

Mathew smiled. "What do you want us to do?

CHAPTER TWENTY-TWO

ir Henry moved forward to shake the hand of another member of the High Forum. "Most that are coming are here. Any late arrivals can be announced by a footman as they enter the ballroom. One of us can greet them there," Claire smiled, letting her gaze roam from the wide open door to the street, to the curving length of the staircase which led up to the second floor.

Not everyone who had been on the invitation list was here. That was to be expected. A number of members, their families in tow, left Gateskeep the moment the High Forum closed its autumn-winter session. For others, refusing to attend an event was part of their political act. Attending made the same sort of statement: to attend this ball, like any other upper-class event on the calendar, was to announce an opinion.

"Lady Constance, Sir Mathew, so glad you could come," Sir Henry said. Claire half-turned towards her father. His voice had tightened slightly, and his back had stiffened: signs of disapproval not obvious to others. To Claire, who had weathered the storm of her father's temper on more than one occasion, they were unmistakable.

Lady Constance, resplendent in a gown of deep mauve with silver lace trimming on the low-cut neck, walked gracefully across the polished floor towards Sir Henry. Her dark hair showed no sign of grey. It was curled and twisted onto her head, framing her beauty.   Claire smiled and offered her hand to Sir Mathew. "Indeed — I, too, am glad you both could come."

Mathew took it and raised it to his lips, the outward display of respect for her rank. The upward glance of his eyes told Claire something else: he was interested in her, and not romantically, of that she was sure. Mathew looked at her in the way a man looked at a hand of playing cards. Mathew let go of her hand and turned to greet her father. Claire braced herself for Oracle's awakening, but it did not come. She frowned.

"Is anything wrong?" Constance asked, leaning forward to gently embrace Claire in a false display of affection.

"No, nothing." Claire returned the embrace, kissing the air either side of the woman's cheeks. She could smell

Constance's rich perfume, and see for a moment the pulse in the vein in Constance's neck. The rise and fall of the flesh thudded like a drum into her senses. Again she waited for Oracle's response. The Glimpser stirred within her, sighed and fell silent. It was as if an old and dear friend had cut her.

Constance had stepped back and was already walking towards the curved staircase on the arm of Sir Mathew. "I warrant they will be gone before one hour has passed," Sir Henry said.

"Oh, I thought Constance likes to shine at events." The hall suddenly seemed empty of everyone but themselves and their servants.

"They both will shine well for a while, mixing with their supporters and showing there are no hard feelings."

"No hard feelings," Claire spluttered, and flicked open her silver lace fan.

Sir Henry took his daughter's arm and led her towards the staircase. "On the outside, that is. It is all politics, my dear."

"Damn politics." Claire took hold of the skirt of her dress to lift it slightly and began to walk up the stairs. She was dressed in the new fashion: the waistline of her gown lay under her bosom, the flow of red fabric falling from there to her feet. The front of the silk was split open to reveal an ivory underskirt, embroidered with glass beads which shimmered in the multitude of candles lighting the grand staircase.

"I would not go that far," Joshua said from above them on the stairs.

"No?" Claire asked.

"No. It is, in my opinion, a better means of settling matters than hitting each other over the head." Calvinward held out his hand. "The dancing has already begun, and I wanted the first dance, yet you were not there. I thought Pugh had beaten me to it."

Claire laughed at his tones of mock sorrow. She slipped her hand from her father's arm and held it out to Joshua. "I was about my duty as hostess."

"I forgive you, but now can the hostess of this delightful event spare me a few moments?" Calvinward took her hand and escorted her up the last remaining steps into the ballroom.

Claire smiled at him and looked round the glittering scene. The room was a mass of swirling, coloured silks and satins. Couples of all ages were waltzing to the strains of the small orchestra. The buzz of conversation underpinned the tones of the violins. Round the edge of the room, in the shadows of the draped fabric, people discussed the events of the last few days in the High Forum. They gossiped about the latest scandal, commented on business trends and the ever-faster pace of industry. Claire knew these conversations continued in the two large saloons on this floor, one set with card tables, the other with a light buffet supper for the guests.

"Shall we?" Joshua said.

"Of course." Her small fan tapped against his arm as they began to dance through the maze of couples. For a moment, the events of the last few days faded from Claire's mind. She felt exhilarated, at home in her surroundings.

As they neared the row of high, narrow windows, Claire caught a glimpse of the soldiers discreetly positioned on this side of the room. Pugh was there, in conversation with a young lieutenant, their figures half hidden by the large window drapes. The sight brought the present rushing back, and she felt Oracle stir inside her, but the creature did not speak.

"Not very talkative tonight, Claire — you are as bad as Pugh," Calvinward said.

"I can't believe you find my outbursts of nonsense so interesting, sir, and Pugh is Pugh. He has always taken his duty seriously," Claire teased.

The dance came to an end, and Calvinward led her to one side of the dance floor. He signalled a waiter carrying a tray of sparkling wine. "Actually, I do. Often your comments cut to the heart of matters instead of going round the house and garden to get there. Pugh is the same." The waiter came to his side. Calvinward took two glasses from the tray and handed one to her. "It makes a nice change to have friends who don't think they have to flatter you to make you like them. I like Pugh very much, and I like you."

"I know you like Pugh. But as for me, maybe it's because you like my father's support."

"There! You see, sharp and to the heart. I think, dear lady, I would have liked you despite the fact your father is who he is," Calvinward gallantly said, giving her a small bow.

"If I was prone to, I think I would swoon at such a compliment."

"My dear Claire, if I may call you that, I think the only time you would swoon would be if you were ill, and you would protest it very much. You have a strength I admire."

"You honour me, sir," she said, not quite sure if that was the right reply. As she spoke, she felt her heart flip. She did like Calvinward. He was good company, clever and ambitious, yet — her eyes strayed across the room. Pugh was speaking to Elizabeth, who was making her way across the room. Elizabeth continued walking into the card room, and he stopped by the door.

"No, it is you who honour me, with your friendship — and as a friend, I want to tell you something for your own good, but this is not the place to talk of such things. If I may, tomorrow ..." Calvinward's words brought her sharply back to the conversation.

"Oh, you have my interest, sir," she absentmindedly answered.

"I do hope so." Calvinward took the hand he still held and raised it to his lips. He released it and stood looking down at her, a soft smile on his lips.

Claire began to splutter, wondering what Calvinward was hinting at. There had never been anything remotely romantic in their friendship. She opened her mouth to ask him, but was interrupted by a footman before she could speak. He had come to her side, holding a silver tray on which lay a small, folded billet.

"With Lady Hotspur's compliments, Milady," the footman said. He lowered the tray for Claire to take the note. Claire smiled at Calvinward. She placed her glass on the tray and took hold of the folded paper. A frown creased her brow as she read.

Meet me in the library soonest. E.

Something important must have happened. "I am summoned away." She refolded the bill and placed it back on the silver tray. As she did so, Oracle began to stir. Claire felt a wave of relief. She had felt abandoned and lost without the presence in her mind. It was both frightening and confusing to realise that. Her hand strayed up to her glasses, and her index finger pushed the bridge hard against the top of her nose.

"Another dance when you return?" Calvinward asked.

"Yes, prance dance across the ice, Toby seek," Claire blurted, and clasped a hand across her mouth. She began to feel the familiar shaking of her body and moved quickly towards the staircase.

"Dance, not skate, but perhaps tomorrow. I have promised Pugh I would teach him, and the ice is nearly thick enough," Calvinward called after her. Claire turned her head, noticing that he had picked up the missive off the silver tray and was reading it. She stopped and began to turn, then twisted completely round: Oracle did not want to go back.

The Glimpser was forcing its control not only on her thoughts and words, but on her body. She clattered down the staircase and turned in to the shadowy passage that led to the library.

"Blood on silk, religion and politics. Alive not dead. Victory and death. Keep my promise, end it, free him Pugh, smash it. Good man. Goddess' sacrifice. Suffer the consequences. Hold us safe for the future. Try or die, ware the wheel of progress, too fast too fast. Gateskeep burned and tumbled. War within. Toby seek, river and ice. Blood on the petticoat, staining the floor, across the book. The music, dancing. Immortality."

Claire knew she had said something. The words hammered in her mind with vicious force. A whirlwind of brittle images filled her mind. The voices, hard and pitiless, were in complete control. Her hand took hold of the round, brass handle of the main door to the library. It slipped in her grasp. She placed her left hand over her right one and gripped as firmly as she could, twisting the knob.

The library was chill. The dull glow of the abandoned fire lay in the hearth; a layer of white ashes had fallen onto the marble slab set before it. The faint light from the lamps in the corridor spilled through the open door. It threw her shadow across the first row of books attached to the wall on her right. The light spun spider-thin threads across the spines of the volumes, probing deep into the gloom and finally illuminating the open door to the underground tunnel leading to the boathouse.

"Elizabeth, are you here?" Claire forced the name out through Oracle's hard grasp on her mind and voice.

"No, she is not," a male voice said from the doorway behind her. The door shut, taking with it the light. Claire took a breath to scream, but Oracle stopped her and took control, lashing out backward with a well-aimed kick. The man swore and grabbed at Oracle's arms from behind.

"Damned. Wrong. Bubbles and rope. Blood on petticoat staining the floor. Goddess' sacrifice. No escape, face the judgement. Now begins!" Oracle screamed. She brought her foot forward, aiming for another figure that had appeared out of the tunnel doorway. She missed and toppled backwards. The man holding her arms tightened his grip. She writhed, her body twisting as she fought her captor. Her spectacles fell to the floor, the red glass in them shattering. One of the table lamps blazed into life, revealing the outline of the other man. Oracle's head turned, her Glimpser eyes drawn to the light. She felt the hand of the old woman close on hers in reassurance.

"*It begins.*" The woman's words were followed by Oracle's scream. It lacked strength and soon faded away, the sound absorbed by the books lining the walls.

"Hold her tight, Mathew." It was Carter. He moved away from the lamp, shaking the contents of a small vial onto a wad of cloth. Oracle had been waiting for him to appear: the voices in her head had told her. Her gaze locked on him. He was dressed in ill-fitting garments, soaked by river water from the waist down, his hands wrapped in rags. Her own harsh breathing matched Mathew's behind her. Mathew tightened his hold on her as the cloth in Carter's hand closed over her mouth and nose. An acrid smell and taste flooded down into her lungs. She felt her throat constrict, and began to choke. Then all was blackness.

***

Colliridge stood against the wall near the door to the card room. He was wearing the dress uniform of a captain in the militia, the small knot of oak leaves on his shoulders proclaiming him part of the intelligence corps. He was enjoying himself, watching events unfold. Constance had insisted he be here in case things went wrong; she was a very wise woman. And it seemed things might be going to. He knew that her reasoning for having Mathew involved was to entrap him in a mesh he could not escape from without implicating himself. However, Colliridge had his doubts that, when push came to shove, Mathew would go through with everything. Still, at the moment, it looked like Mathew wasn't going to be the fly in the ointment.

Calvinward stood watching Lady Claire leave the ballroom: the chit had swallowed the bait. Lady Constance had managed to imitate Lady Hotspur's florid handwriting to perfection. The footman bowed and made to move away. Calvinward clicked his fingers. The footman frowned and hesitated. In that moment of indecision, Calvinward took the note off the silver tray and opened it. Good, it did not seem to have raised any suspicion — but it was a danger. Calvinward knew who Lady Claire was supposed to be meeting in the library. Calvinward refolded the slip of paper and placed it back on the tray. He looked round the room, then began to walk towards the card room. If Constance had not persuaded Lady Hotspur to abandon her game and join her outside on the terrace for a breath of fresh air, then things would be going to hell fairly quickly.

Colliridge followed Calvinward into the card room.

"Yes, Constance, I will be with you in a moment." Elizabeth laughed and ran her fingers over her pile of coins on the table. Constance was standing behind Elizabeth's chair, a look of annoyance on her face. "I want to acquire Humphrey's diamond cravat pin."

Bollocks. The woman was still here. Colliridge moved sideways towards the far door, which led from the card room into the main hallway. He needed to get to the library fast. Calvinward would obviously go speak to Lady Hotspur, and it would give him time — but he did not; he turned and walked back into the ballroom.

Constance had noticed Calvinward and moved from her place behind Elizabeth. She was closer to the other door, and was hurrying as fast as she could without drawing attention. Colliridge increased his pace. He hoped that Calvinward had gone to find Pugh Avinguard, or one of the other officers, before he went down to the library. He had reached the door when a voice hailed him.

"You, sir, you're one of Avinguard's lot, aren't you?"

Colliridge ignored the man and continued.

"I said, you there!" The man shouted.

Bloody buffoon was drawing attention to him. Colliridge stopped and turned, fixing a smile on his face. "Milord."

The man was drunk. His face flushed. "That's better. Want to talk to your superior about him not letting folks take a turn in the garden." The young woman on his arm giggled.

"It's a matter of safety, Milord. The guests are only being allowed on the terrace. You are an important member of the High Forum, Milord," Colliridge said.

"Yes, I am, aren't I — can't be running any risks. Maybe we should stay here." He patted the woman's hand, ignoring the pout on her face.

"If you will excuse me, Milord," Colliridge said.

His lordship waved his hand in dismissal, and Colliridge hurried from the card room. Of Constance, there was no sign. He half-ran down the stairs, threading his way through the scant flow of late arrivals until he reached the door of the library. It was locked. He rattled the handle. A crash and a muffled shout came from the other side. *Shit.* Where was Constance?

Colliridge looked up and down the corridor. A small pool of light was coming from the next door along. He turned and ran the few steps to it. It was Sir Henry's study. As he entered, a small, wire-haired terrier barked at him. "Quiet!" Colliridge snapped. The dog stopped and stood with his head cocked on one side, watching him, then bolted out of the door into the corridor.

On the far wall was another door. It was one of those doors that had been fashionable a hundred years before: a door on one side, and on the other it looked like part of the library wall, complete with the spines of fake books in neat shelves; it was open. Suddenly he heard the sound of a fist hitting flesh. So much for a perfect bloody plan. The fools had totally blown it. Obviously, Calvinward had caught Mathew and Carter in the act of abducting Lady Claire. But where was Constance — had she come down here? *To hell with it.* Colliridge began to turn round and retrace his steps, his sense of self-preservation telling him it would be stupid to stay. A shapely shadow moved across the open doorway. Constance. *Bollocks.* Colliridge turned back and entered the library. Constance stood by the library fireplace, watching two men fighting. Bouncing on the balls of his feet, Calvinward rained blow after blow on Mathew. He grunted in pain and brought up his hands to defend himself from the next blow. The young fool had some skill, learned no doubt in the workhouse, but he was no match for Calvinward. The man had trained with the best at his gentlemen's club. Mathew staggered back against a small table, sending it toppling sideways. His arms pinwheeled in an effort to keep him upright. Calvinward launched another undercut, and as Mathew fell, Calvinward punched him in the gut and he crashed to the floor.

212

Carter and Lady Claire had disappeared, and the door to the tunnel was partly closed. The priest had made good his escape. Calvinward was stepping over his vanquished foe and moving towards the passage door when Constance staggered and reached out a hand to steady herself. Her fingers brushed against the base of a small, bronze statue of the Goddess, standing near the edge of the mantelpiece. Her fingers tightened on it. She lifted it and stepped towards Calvinward.

Colliridge shouted, "No, Milady!"

But he was too late. She swung the bronze statue at Calvinward's head. Blood sprayed across the room. The statue and Calvinward hit the ground together. *Fuck.*

"Dear Goddess! Lady Constance, are you all right?" Mathew said as he struggled to regain his breath.

Constance frowned at the question, and looked towards Mathew. He was dragging himself up off the floor, his eyes flickering from her to the crumpled form of Calvinward.

"This has all gone to hell and bloody back, and no mistake," Colliridge said harshly. He pushed the book-effect door closed and fumbled along the line of books, slipping the metal door lock shut. He moved to the main door of the library and checked that was locked as well. He had to act, and quickly, else they all would be for the gibbet.

"I – " Constance began.

Colliridge knelt by the side of Calvinward and pressed his fingers under his chin, looking for a pulse. It was a mere flutter.

"Is he –?" Mathew stood there, struggling to get his breath. The disbelief on his face turned to shock. His hand came to his mouth and he swallowed hard.

"Half his brains are bashed out; I think that would mean a yes," Colliridge said sardonically, and got to his feet. Calvinward still breathed, but Colliridge doubted he would for much longer.

"I had to," Constance said, her voice trembling. Her breath was coming in short, sharp gasps. She began to raise her hand to her face, and stopped, her gaze riveted on her elbow-length white glove. It had gone dark, splattered with Calvinward's blood shimmering from black to crimson in the dull, splintered light from the single lamp.

"Of course you had to, my dear, brave Constance. You saved me, saved us all," Mathew said, drawing in a harsh breath. He came to her side and took her other, trembling, hand in his own.

213

"Bollocks, he has made a mess of you, Sir Mathew. We need to act quickly now and get you both away." Colliridge came to join them before the embers of the fire.

"Impossible," Mathew said. "I can't leave in this condition. I would be spotted, unless I go down the tunnel after Carter. But I will not leave Constance, and she can't leave that way — her absence would be noticed." Mathew winced as he spoke. He was leaning to the left, his breath still coming in harsh gasps. The boy must have a couple of cracked ribs. Bruises were already beginning to discolour his face.

"Very noble, sir, brave indeed, but you are going to do exactly what you said," Colliridge said. The thought of how much money he had hoped to make in the near future was fast fading away. He would be lucky to come out of this with his skin in one piece. For a moment, he was tempted to leave them to it.

"I killed him," Constance whispered, disbelief colouring her words. "I had to. I must leave. Think Constance, listen and think."

By the bloody Goddess, she was a fine woman. Despite the horror, she was trying to think of a way out. What the hell. They could get out of here, all of them. "Yes, leave, both of you. First, Mathew, quickly — your watch, cravat pin and purse. Rip your coat and waistcoat. Follow Carter: help him get the young woman to wherever. Then make your way on foot back to Lady Constance's house, first calling in at a police station to report an attack on you."

"What ...," Mathew began, stunned by the idea.

"You were attacked on your way home from the ball." Colliridge struggled to keep his voice level. Had he to think of everything?

"I think I understand," Mathew said, slowly.

"Good, say you decided to leave early to check on your wife's health and were walking, leaving the carriage for Constance. You were attacked by thieves. The police station must be one close to Constance's home."

Mathew reluctantly nodded. He pulled out his watch and handed it, with the other items, over to Colliridge. "I take it these will turn up in the hands of some thief later."

"Yes, Sir Mathew. Do you trust me?" Colliridge asked.

Mathew drew in a breath, winced in pain, and said, "I don't

have much choice, but if it is my neck it is also yours." Mathew looked at Constance. "But still, to leave Lady Constance..."

"In my care," Colliridge said. "Go, Sir Mathew, as I said. Trust. Besides, if anything happens to Lady Constance, I assume you will be after my hide and I will end up like Lord Calvinward." Colliridge moved the lamp off the table onto the mantelpiece behind Constance.

"You can be assured of that." Colliridge heard conviction return to Mathew's voice. *About bloody time.* Mathew walked to the tunnel, looked one more time at Constance and pulled the door closed behind him. So the young whelp had found his spine again. Good.

Lady Constance's breathing increased its pace. "I had to do it. He knew. The telegram. I saw the look on his face at the High Forum. He had worked it out: my involvement through you in Hitsmine; my endeavours to wreck this bill. He would have destroyed me, Emily, all of us. I told my husband not to mentor him. That Calvinward was an idealist, welded to one idea. They are the worst kind of politician. But my darling didn't understand." Lady Constance stopped abruptly and asked, "What are we going to do?"

It all made sense. What a remarkable woman she was. Colliridge stood there, observing her in the light from the lamp. Her cheeks were flushed, making her even more attractive. "We are going to walk arm-in-arm out of here. Summon your carriage from the rows in the square and go to your home. Once there, you will order your household to prepare to leave for your country estate tomorrow."

"Dear Goddess, I can't," Constance exclaimed.

"You can, Milady, you can. Let's get rid of your gloves first."

Constance pulled them off; the bloody silk came away reluctantly from her skin. She handed them to Colliridge, who promptly threw them on the remains of the fire. The silk fabric sizzled, discolouring as it began to burn. The odour of burning hair rose from the crumbling fabric in the grate.

Constance looked down at her hand and arm; they were smeared with blood. "A piece of your petticoat, Milady, and thank the Goddess that the servants haven't had time to remove this today." Colliridge moved to the table alongside the large chair by the fire. On it was a glass decanter, half full of water.

He held out his hand for the requested fabric. Constance

bent and pulled up her dress. She fumbled at the fine cotton, ripping a length free. Constance handed him the cloth, her fingers touching his. She raised her gaze to his face. He winked at her, pulled out the stopper from the decanter, and tipped some of the contents onto the cloth. He turned to her and took her hand, cleaning the blood from it and from her arm.

"Now, let's check the rest of you." Colliridge took the lamp off the mantelpiece and ran the light up and down Lady Constance's figure. Her eyes narrowed as the light rippled across her face. "Some here." He dabbed at her cheek. "And here." He dabbed at the swell of her left breast. He felt her shiver under his touch. "Damn!" Colliridge put the lamp down.

"What is it?" Constance asked.

"You have blood on the lace of your neckline. When we leave, keep your fan open and over here; there are a few other spots, but against the dark colour of your dress they could be taken for a splash of wine," Colliridge said, waving his fingers across her left breast.

Constance nodded. "But ..." She looked down to the floor. "Lady Claire's glasses."

"I know. It will have them hunting all over the city for the chit."

Uncertainty widened Constance's eyes. Colliridge squeezed her hand in an effort to reassure her. She drew in a deep breath and nodded. He slipped her hand through his arm, opened the main door to the library, and guided her down the corridor.

"Do you know if Calvinward told anyone where he was going?" Colliridge said, softly. He summoned a footman from the main front door. "Lady Constance's cloak, and inform her coachman she is ready to leave." The footman bowed and hurried away to do Colliridge's bidding.

"I don't know — no, wait, he spoke to one of the young officers on the stairs, asking for Pugh," Constance stammered. Colliridge took her cloak from the returning footman and slipped it round her shoulders. He squeezed her hand gently again, endeavouring to bolster her courage.

"Obviously Avinguard didn't take it as an urgent request. Lucky for us," he said, and led her out into the night to await her carriage.

"Good evening, sir," said one of the soldiers on duty outside.

216

"Good evening, Private, you've drawn the cold duty again," Colliridge said, smiling at the man.

"Nearly over," the soldier replied, and glanced at Lady Constance. "Take it you are not on duty tonight, sir."

"Always on duty, Private," Colliridge replied.

CHAPTER TWENTY-THREE

Pugh stood for a while, looking out of a round window at the end of the long corridor, gazing out at a dull, winter night sky. The events of the past few days had underscored his belief that his current position was not for him. He had again made a request for a transfer, but had not yet received an answer from his superiors. Until he did, he was still in charge of High Forum security, and he best get back to it. He retraced his steps down the curving staircase. Captain Gunmain was standing in the open main doorway. "All well?"

"So far. Save for the coachmen arguing in the rows as to who parks where." Gunmain laughed. Pugh looked out over the frost-rimed cobbles: the square was full of carriages waiting for their owners; men huddled round braziers; horses stood in harness, clothed in blankets. Their breath rose, a steaming mist which mingled with the freezing one that was dropping on the city.

"Got a heavy one coming down," Pugh said. The street lights dimmed as the mist began to wrap round them. Here at the door, he could feel the chill of the winter night probing with icy fingers. A damp sheen bloomed on the toes of his highly polished black boots.

"Aye, Major, and it most likely will hang a few days, getting thicker and sour tasting. Ideal for foul deeds and murder, or so the fictions on the back page of the Gateskeep Sun would have us believe."

"I have seen them happen on a sunny morning."

"So have I." Gunmain looked at his superior. "Is it true you're wanting to leave us?"

"I don't have the knack for this type of soldiering," Pugh answered honestly, his hand going to the hilt of his dress sword. He should have worn his pistol, but he could not defy tradition tonight.

"If you don't mind me saying so, sir, you take it a bit too personal, which I doubt you do when in the field."

"You might be right, Gunmain — what about you?" Pugh looked at the younger man, trying to gauge his thoughts.

"I find it all a challenge. I enjoy the complex nature of it, and pitting my wits against an enemy that changes like the weather." Gunmain's eyes sparkled.

"If the general agrees to my request and reassigns me, I will put your name forward to replace me."

"Why, thank you, sir, but he most likely will slip a more experienced officer in." Gunmain laughed and absently kicked at the whitewashed step beneath his feet.

"There are no more experienced officers at this than us and those under our command," Pugh answered, nodding to Gunmain. He turned away and made his way back up the steps. As Pugh reached the top, he heard a woman squeal and a man by the door curse. The music finished, and he plainly heard the sharp bark of a dog. *Toby.* The bloody dog was supposed to be in Sir Henry's study.

"Sir, I was looking for you," a young officer called after Pugh.

"I can see why — catch the damn nuisance, and watch his teeth," Pugh said. The dog began to weave in and out of the dancers, waiting for the next set to begin. Toby scrabbled at ladies' dresses, pulling his small body up and peering at the face of each woman. Some were shocked, others amused. It was as if the dog was looking for someone. Each time, disappointed, he barked louder.

"But, sir," the lieutenant said.

People laughed, commenting on the antics of the creature and his growing military pursuit. Toby dashed between a man's legs and into the card room. Pugh ran after.

"Toby, of all things. Down, you bad dog!" Elizabeth's voice rose above the commotion. "And no, you can't play this hand." Toby had managed to get onto her lap, his head between her hand of cards and her ample bosom. Toby was barking and shaking. Elizabeth dropped her cards and grabbed the dog's head in her hands. Toby quietened. "Now, master fur ball, how did you get out of the study?"

"Sir!" shouted the young officer who had tried to catch Pugh's attention earlier. "Lord Calvinward went to the library. He said to find you and tell you to join him as soon as possible." At these words, Toby began to bark again. The dog jumped off Elizabeth's lap and ran across the card table. The portly gentleman sitting opposite Elizabeth spluttered and dropped his cards on the floor. The dog looked back at Elizabeth before jumping off, and made for the door, where he stood barking for all he was worth. Elizabeth rose from her seat and swept across the room towards the dog.

"I see," Pugh said. "Did he say it was important?"

"Yes."

The hairs on the back of Pugh's neck started to rise. "Find Sir Henry and have him and Captain Gunmain join us in the library." The lieutenant saluted and hurried off, forcing his way through the gathering throng of interested guests.

"No, the study. If Toby is loose, Lord Calvinward must have used the door from the study into the library," Lady Hotspur said. She came to a stop by the dog and raised her hand in a gesture of command. Toby quietened and reluctantly sat, but his head kept twisting towards the exit.

"Why would he use that entrance?" Pugh asked. "Was the main library door locked?"

"Indeed. Locking doors, in my opinion, is very inconvenient for the servants, and the main library door can only be locked from the inside. Claire ... Dear Goddess!" She picked up her skirts and began to run into the ballroom. Toby hopped round her, barking encouragement. Pugh hurried after. Where was Claire? With Calvinward? Safe in the ballroom, or elsewhere in the house? Was this summons of Calvinward's concerning another matter, a more mundane one? If so, a dozen or more people bursting in on him would no doubt cause him much amusement.

Gunmain came bounding up the staircase, two steps at a time. "Trouble, sir?"

"I don't know, but keep people back from the corridor to the library, and question the men on duty in the hall. I want to know who was around in that area over the past hour."

"That will be hard. There's been a great deal of coming and going." Gunmain nodded to the lieutenant by his side. The young man raced off again, shouting to one of his counterparts hovering at the top of the staircase.

Pugh followed in the wake of the rustling silk of Elizabeth's gown. Gunmain left his side, and Pugh could hear him giving orders to the sergeant on duty in the main entrance hall. Elizabeth came to a stop by the door of the library. There was a small spill of light flickering under the door. Toby had trotted to the door of the study. The dog sneezed, glanced in and returned to Elizabeth's side.

"A lamp lit," Pugh said.

"Obviously," Elizabeth retorted sarcastically. Pugh

ignored her comment. He reached out his hand, grabbed the knob and turned. The door opened slightly.

"Not locked," Elizabeth whispered. Toby barked in agreement and pressed his nose through the small gap.

"Obviously." Pugh could not resist. Elizabeth shot him a foul look. He gave a shrug and pushed the door open. It swung back on its hinges and began to close again, but what Pugh saw on the floor had him slamming it back and striding in.

A body lay twisted on the floor, with one arm extended upward and one leg crossed over the other. Blood pooled by the head. Pugh stopped by the side of the body, already convinced who it was. He knelt and reached out to push the mass of blood-soaked hair from the side of the face.

The light suddenly grew brighter. Pugh looked toward the fire. Elizabeth was placing the cowl back on an oil lamp seated on the mantelpiece. She took another spill from the brass holder by the fire and placed it in the embers. The small twist of paper flared and Elizabeth straightened, placing the flame to another oil lamp. The light exposed the horrific scene to his eyes. On the polished wooden floor lay a toppled reading table. A small, bronze statue rested on its side by the legs of the table. Books were scattered, thrown askew by their fall. One was open, the pages splattered with a dark trail of blood. It was obvious there had been quite a struggle.

"Dear Goddess, what in hell!" Captain Gunmain said from the doorway. "I will get the place sealed and send for a doctor, and police."

Pugh looked round at his subordinate officer. "The murderer could be long gone, but someone in that horde upstairs might have seen something or someone. That is the police's domain. They have more skill in questioning people than our men, but we can begin the process." Pugh turned his attention back to the body on the floor.

The level of light increased again. Elizabeth stood over him, holding an oil lamp. "It's Calvinward, isn't it? Is he ... dead ..." Her voice failed. Was she crying?

"As good as," Pugh said. He took hold of Calvinward and turned him over. He lifted the battered head gently onto his lap, feeling the man's blood begin to soak through the fabric of his trousers. "What a sodding, bloody waste!"

***

221

Carter grunted as he laid Claire down on the floor of the tunnel. The faint light from the oil lamp played on dank strands of slime which hung from the roughly carved walls and ceiling. The damp clawed with chill fingers at the stale air. It mixed with the stink of the river, making Carter gag. He had no desire to be in here again, any longer than he had to. Here the tunnel narrowed. It had been hard enough for him to squeeze through earlier, totally impossible for him now to pass through carrying the young woman. He laid her arms out and turned her onto her side. He would have to drag her through the small gap. "Forgive me." Part of him felt ashamed at what he had done, but he could see no other course to safeguard the reborn Seer. Had she not stopped struggling when she had seen him, and allowed him administer the chloroform? It justified the act in his eyes.

Carter bent to take hold of her arms, and felt his destiny settle on his shoulders. It had been he who had found her. He would stand at the right hand of the reborn Seer and partake of the riches, glory and power that would again flood into his order. The scrape of another's footfalls echoed down the tunnel. He dropped the young woman's arms and straightened, pulling a dagger from his waist band. It had been at Colliridge's insistence that they had not brought any firearms. He saw the reasoning behind it, but at this moment he wished he had a gun.

Carter stiffened. A shape flickered in the far reaches of the light of the single oil lamp. For a moment, half a face was lit cleanly by the light, before falling into shadow again.

"Mathew?" Carter stammered and lowered his knife.

Mathew grunted a greeting. He coughed, spat onto the already mired floor and wiped at his mouth. Even in the semigloom, Carter knew Mathew was wiping away blood. His clothes were disarranged, the shoulder of his left sleeve torn down.

"Are you hurt – what of Calvinward?" The knife in the priest's hand came up again and he stared into the darkness behind Mathew.

"Dead," Mathew replied, his voice a mere whisper.

Carter blinked in disbelief. "You killed him?" He tucked the knife back in his belt.

"He is dead. That is all that matters. No need to fear; his death won't be traced to us."

"It was Colliridge?" Carter asked.

"It's not important. Colliridge is covering our tracks and leaving by another way." Mathew shrugged his shoulders, refusing to say more.

The young fool. Colliridge was by nature a survivor. If Mathew had killed Calvinward, Colliridge could already be spilling the whole tale to Avinguard and Sir Henry.

"I understand your concern, but there is no need for it. Trust me." Mathew glanced back nervously. The oil lamp behind him dimmed. "We must move and get you started upstream on the ice, but then I must leave you."

"But ...?" Surely the Goddess was not abandoning him.

"Now is not the time for questions. Isn't it enough that we have helped you? Have we not delivered the Glimpser into your hands, at great cost to ourselves? We must see to our own protection." Something in the tone of his voice hinted that the 'we' was more than Mathew, himself and Colliridge. What had happened in the library after he had fled down the tunnel?

"I understand," Carter said, and suddenly the pieces fit into place. The Goddess had worked this to protect those who served her Seer. "My order is in debt to you and Lady Constance." He again began to drag the young woman toward the narrow section.

"You can best repay it by insuring that none know of our involvement." Mathew bent down and picked up the young woman's feet. "Go ahead, ease her gently through. I do not wish any more harm to come from this night."

Carter crouched down, pressed his body against the cold, slime-coated wall and inched his way through. His right hand held Claire's wrist and with Mathew's help, he pulled her body through the gap and down the slight incline to the drain opening. Here hung another lamp. Mathew helped Carter lift the young woman to his shoulder and took the lamp off the hook. Gritting his teeth against the cold bite of the water for a second time, Carter waded in and carefully felt his way along the slippery stone out into the boat house. Mathew extinguished the lamp and abandoned it before following Carter.

No moonlight filtered in between the warped boards of the boathouse door to the river. As Carter felt his way onto the ladder, the woman slipped on his shoulder. He grunted in fear that he would lose his hold, but Mathew stopped her slipping further. Carter gave a rough nod of thanks. He could feel the gentle rise and fall of her body as she breathed. Her hands swung against the backs of his thighs, her fingertips dangling in the ice-cold water.

Gathering himself, he heaved himself up the first rung. The river reluctantly released its grip on him. Ripples of water smacked at the layer of ice that began this side of the doors. Sweat had begun to pool in the bottom of his back by the time Carter laid the young woman on the decking. It soon chilled, increasing the cold in his limbs. He was again soaked from the thighs down.

Mathew followed him and looked about. "Where to?"

"Those boards to the left side of the end of the deck are loose. We slip out through them. There is a rag-picker's sledge there on the ice. Why do you think I am dressed like this?"

"You will have to manage it by yourself." Mathew moved forward along the decking. He crouched down by the boards, his fingers feeling for the edges of the wood.

"I don't have much choice in the matter. The ice is thick upstream, along the bank. Besides, it will be better: rag-pickers are not known for working in pairs." Carter gently turned Claire over. She lay there, the red overskirt of her dress bunched up round her hips. The ivory underskirt wrapped the lower half of her body in a pale haze.

Mathew moved the loose plank to one side. He peered out into the night and gave a grunt of satisfaction. A curl of thick mist entered through the gap, seeping over the decking. Carter signed for Mathew to help him carry the young woman. He did so, taking hold of her legs. As they both lifted, the under-gown of her dress caught on the rough boards. Carter swore under his breath and heaved. The dress ripped; the tearing of silk was followed by the soft clatter of glass beads breaking loose from their rows and peppering the wood.

For a moment, Carter considered going back and cleaning away the evidence of their passage, then dismissed the thought. It did not matter. By the time anyone searched the boathouse, dawn would be here and the Seer would again be in the world. He tightened his hold under her arms and followed Mathew out onto the mist-enveloped, frozen river. Carter could feel the warmth of her body. It was the heat of a

224

fire — warm, welcoming and yet ready to burn him to the bone. *Slighted.* "Nonsense," Carter muttered, trying to shake free of the feeling.

Carefully, with Mathew's aid, he placed the young woman on the rag-picker's sledge.

He walked to the front of the sledge and slipped the towing rope over his shoulder and round his waist. Mathew took hold of it, and together they pulled. The sledge resisted their efforts for a moment, then jerked forward, skittering across the ice. "I thought you were parting company with me."

They walked for fifty paces before Mathew answered the question. Carter found it amusing how Mathew still over-thought everything. Sadly, that made him only half the politician of the man who had died tonight. Not that it mattered: once the Seer was back among the faithful, the days of the High Forum would be numbered. Only those true to the Seer would rule Timeholm and the rest of the world. It was the order's destiny.

"I will, soon. I will leave the river by the park before the High Forum buildings and double back. I will make it seem as if I am coming from the direction of Sir Henry's home, towards Lady Constance's house on Highmarsh Square."

"How will you explain your wet clothes?" Carter asked.

Mathew did not answer; he just let go of the rope. They had come level with the park. The faint outline of trees hugged the embankment. Carter did not stop; he merely leaned forward, straining to keep the sledge moving forward. Mathew scrambled up the embankment. The sounds of his footsteps on the snow-coated gravel soon vanished.

The mist thickened. Carter passed the High Forum building. The glow of the street lights surrounding it began to fade. His breath steamed before his eyes, adding to the heavy vapour that clung to him. The sledge stopped suddenly, jerking him back on the rope. He wrapped his hands tighter round the rope and pulled hard. The sledge lifted as its right runner rose over the obstruction sticking through the ice. It squealed in protest and tipped to the left, its load shifting. Lady Claire's leg fell free, the heel of her elegant evening shoe brushing the ice. Carter tugged again, and the sledge dropped back. It ran towards him, the tautness in the rope swiftly turning to slack.

Carter's heart thudded as the sledge gently nudged level with him. He glanced around. Had someone heard and was even now creeping up on him? In his mind's eye, he could see the bulk of the Highspire Bridge. On a clear, moonlit night, the two spires at either end lanced the night sky, spearing the stars. It was the base of the western spire he was making for, not the eastern side across the river, on which the main chapel of his order stood.

A lantern appeared out of the mist, gently swinging. The arm of a man came into view below the light. Carter's hand slid to the knife in his belt.

"Carter?" It was Harrison.

"Yes."

"Brothers, quickly."

Carter was suddenly surrounded by figures, his charge quickly taken away. He looked at Harrison. The man nodded, raised his lamp and blew it out.

It had begun.

CHAPTER TWENTY-FOUR

The large house had fallen quiet, encased by the thickening mist and tossed into another, more violent, world.

"Must I repeat myself, sir?" The police inspector's tone was beginning to show his growing annoyance at Sir Henry's evasiveness.

"No, you have made yourself perfectly clear, sir." Sir Henry reached for his pipe with unsteady hands. His thoughts were not on the questions the police inspector kept repeating; they were on his daughter. It never should have happened: the fault was his, no one else's. He had seen the same reflected in the eyes of Pugh and Elizabeth, but they were wrong. He had again lost his daughter to the same dangerous fools.

Then there was Calvinward. The country was losing a man who could have helped to shepherd it through these troubled times. That, too, lay at his door. It was plain to Sir Henry that Calvinward had stumbled on the Inner Ring's abduction of his daughter, and they had cruelly silenced him. That, somehow, Calvinward clung to life was moot. Sir Henry knew, as they all did, that it was just a matter of time: the man's injuries were horrendous. How they had lured his daughter here to the library had yet to be discovered. As to her removal, Sir Henry knew exactly, and that was wholly and completely his fault. A mistake, a mere matter of forgetting, that would haunt him for the rest of his life.

"I hope so. I intend to find your daughter, Sir Henry. She is, sadly, the main suspect in this, unless you can convince me otherwise."

Sir Henry stiffened, and his fingers tightened round the stem of his pipe. He tried to force himself to relax, but failed. The inspector was no fool. "I think you are mistaken, sir."

"I know you are finding this hard to accept, Sir Henry, but she is the only one of those resident in this house who is unaccounted for. And you cannot inform me of her whereabouts. We have found, besides other items, her smashed glasses in the library." The inspector began to pace before Sir Henry's desk. "Was there a developing relationship between your daughter and Lord Calvinward, perhaps a lover's quarrel that got a little out of control? Your daughter has suffered from mental disturbance in the past."

"So you think she totally lost her senses over some trivial matter and stove Calvinward's head in," Sir Henry muttered, and sat back in his chair. "A great number of the guests had left before the event. Any one of them could be responsible. As to my daughter's glasses being there, she has more than one pair. She could have left that pair in the library earlier."

"All that is possible, I grant you, Sir Henry. My men have the guest list and are working through it. We have also questioned the men on the doors and surrounding the house. No one left suspiciously or splattered with blood. I also have had a report of one guest being robbed on his way home. Is that a totally unrelated event?" The inspector stopped and turned to face Sir Henry. Again, the man was fishing for answers. They all would have to tread carefully. "Finally there is the matter that I find most unusual for a man of your understanding: you and Major Avinguard disturbed the scene of the crime. You moved the body, sir, before the police arrived."

"Body? Calvinward was alive! The Goddess knows how. And still is," Elizabeth said from the door to the study. "Really, this is going beyond a joke, inspector. You are standing here waffling on when my goddess-daughter could be in the hands of a madman intent on subjecting her to unnameable horrors. Have you considered that prospect, besides accusing her of the deed? That she witnessed it and was removed? She could be lying somewhere in the same condition as Calvinward, or worse!"

"I have, my dear lady, but I believe I first must – "

"Believe what you like, sir. Find Claire alive and whole and we will get to the bottom of this." Elizabeth stepped further into the room. Her words were enforced by the growling of Toby, who stood at her feet. The worried glance the inspector gave the dog showed the mistake the man was making: Elizabeth was far more dangerous than Toby on a normal encounter; at the moment, she was close to lethal.

"I intend to. But you remember my words, Sir Henry."

"No interfering with your investigation. I assure you, I won't cloud your avenue of detection. Believe me, inspector, no one would be more pleased than I if you found my daughter safe and well." Sir Henry rose and bowed to the inspector.

By his expression, the inspector was not taken in.

Whatever actions he took, Sir Henry knew he would have to be careful. He stood there listening to the click of the man's boot heels fading as he walked down the passage. Sir Henry realised he was holding his breath.

"Swear," Elizabeth said.

"I have gone beyond the need of swearing," Sir Henry said, looking at Elizabeth. She wore a thick, old-fashioned shawl round her shoulders, the rough wool at odds with the grey silk of her evening dress. There were dark stains on the fabric, and the hem was coated with what looked like mud. The fine, cream ostrich feathers in her hair had gathered cobwebs, and she had a smudge of something on her nose. Her left hand was clenched shut and held under her bosom in a guarding gesture. "Dear Goddess!"

"That wasn't swearing?" Elizabeth asked.

"No. Yes. I think that man is blind. He didn't comment on the state of you."

"He noticed, I can assure you. He is not the bumbling fool you hoped he would be, is he?" Sir Henry nodded in agreement. Elizabeth sighed and continued. "We both saw the way he examined everything in the library in great detail, including Calvinward, and the questioning look on his face when he found the remains of Claire's glasses. As to my state, one of his men did comment on it, as I came back into the house. I said I tripped in the gardens while walking the dog: in a way, true. You should have boarded that damn tunnel up. How many of your staff, past and present, have stumbled on it over the years and used it to sneak back and forth? If one of them sold the information to the Inner Ring, I will have their eyes and ears."

"I forgot. I didn't think. Besides, I never thought I would live here again; it didn't seem important." Sir Henry sat heavily, the strength draining from his body. He threw his pipe onto the desk. It skittered across the papers strewn there and came to rest against the notebook that contained Claire's predictions.

"Don't you dare," Elizabeth said, her voice thickening with emotion. "I won't have you wallowing in self-recrimination. If we all do that, then Claire is lost. I won't allow you or Pugh to indulge your male ego in such a manner, I swear." Toby barked in agreement and padded with muddy paws across to the fire. The dog shook himself, turned round in a circle and lay down with a grunt.

"How far did you get?" he asked, and looked up at her.

"From this end to where it narrows. There was an oil lamp. I came back and went to the boathouse. The arrogance of them. There were puddles of frozen water on the decking. And this." Elizabeth reached out with her left hand. Sir Henry rose from his seat and held out his own. Elizabeth placed her closed hand over his open palm and allowed the contents to drop.

Sir Henry flinched at the touch of the warm glass beads that tumbled onto his palm. Slowly they rolled off his hand and pinged softly as they hit the top of the desk. They were followed by a scrap of cream silk. "Claire's?"

"Yes, Claire's. Perhaps she put up a fight there?"

"Perhaps, but you forget the cloth on the floor, soaked in chloroform. I am glad we kept it from the inspector. If he had seen it, we would not be standing here, but would be on our way to the station. I don't think Claire was in any state to fight. There were also the marks on Calvinward's hands. He landed a good many blows on someone, before he was attacked. If he stumbled on them subjecting Claire to ..." Sir Henry's voice trailed off for a moment. He coughed to clear his throat of the emotions that were beginning to choke him. "We know that no one sporting injuries to the face or body left the building. Calvinward would have left quite a few marks on his assailant. They must have left by the tunnel."

The instrument and manner of Calvinward's impending death haunted him: a statue of the Goddess; his head broken open. In the manner of a tradition long put aside, a blood offering to the Goddess on the floor of her chapel. *Goddess' sacrifice.* Was Calvinward's coming death the price the Goddess asked to halt the upheaval threatening the country? He could not believe it. Sir Henry came round the table to Elizabeth's side.

"But why the half-burned rag in the fire? The inspector took great note of the contents of the grate. He had a man place everything on a tray. And there was more than a rag in those ashes — I smelt burning hair. That is the odour silk gives off when burnt. It looks as if someone had tried to clean up some blood. Blood on a petticoat. Across the floor. The book." Elizabeth reached for the book that contained Claire's predictions. Her hand hovered above the cover, then came back to her side.

"A woman, dear Goddess!" Sir Henry felt his eyes widen at the thought. Of course, it made sense. If Claire had been lured to the library, it must have been by someone she would not even suspect. Had Calvinward followed by chance, or because he suspected something was amiss? They would never know.

"You find that hard to believe, Henry? We are quite capable of killing, you know." Elizabeth reached up her hand to his face. She was not wearing her gloves. Henry felt the warmth of her touch. "The blood splattered, it must have. If she was wearing gloves, they would have burnt them. Her dress — if dark, any splatter could be taken for wine splashes. Would anyone on the doors have noticed a lady leaving without gloves? I doubt it."

"You have a shrewd mind, Elizabeth." Sir Henry felt a rush of affection for the woman by his side. He took her hand off his cheek and gently pressed it to his lips.

"Flatterer. Pugh has been a long time." Elizabeth rubbed his lips with her index finger, then gently pulled her hand away. Henry let go.

"It will take a while to get together a number of men he can trust. Besides, what we plan on doing will not be easy. He needs to have men he can tell part of the truth to." Sir Henry wondered how Pugh would go about convincing a goodly number of soldiers that it was necessary to attack the chapel of the Inner Ring. While the order was considered old-fashioned, they were still priests of the Goddess.

"Henry, are you sure she will be there?" Elizabeth's hand again went out to the notebook. This time she picked it up and opened it. Sir Henry heard the creak of the leather on the book's spine as it opened.

"Where else, but the chapel of the Inner Ring?"

"Let Toby lead the way. Claire said that so many times. She was trying to tell us that this would happen. Yes, I know we decided not to try and act on the words, but should we not look for clues to where she is?"

"Clues. I thought you were convinced she was in the Inner Ring's chapel." It was Pugh. He came in as he spoke, still wearing his thick militia coat. It was covered with a layer of damp, which sparkled in the lamp light. Toby stirred and glanced in Pugh's direction, then dropped his head back onto his paws.

"Yes, we do think that," Elizabeth answered, and half-turned.

Pugh threw his coat over the chair by the fire. "Very well, but that makes things doubly difficult. Do you know what lies behind those walls? I don't, except for the cloisters open to the public. As for men willing to assist me, it will take time."

"You haven't been able to get anyone, have you," Elizabeth began. "But we need to move soon. The thought of Claire in the hands of those, those ..."

"I know — you don't have to remind me. But, as I said, it will take time. I have sounded out a few officers and men I know. They have agreed to help and will sound out a few more. Maybe by tomorrow evening, I might have a small force able to do the job."

"That long? It could be too late. Foolish to blather on about trust — order a squad of men in."

"Oh yes, and have half of them turn their guns on me for defiling a holy place; besides, are you really sure she is there? It is too obvious." Pugh snarled back at Elizabeth, his own frustration answering hers.

"Of course she is. Where else could she be ..." Elizabeth began.

Toby started to bark — not at Pugh, but Elizabeth.

"Quiet, both of you — correction, three of you," Henry said, and scooped up the small dog as his teeth were about to close on the skirt of Elizabeth's dress.

"Traitor," she snapped at the dog, which yelped in surprise at being hoisted high.

"Toby, quiet and sit, and you two, listen to me. Pugh, with luck, you might have a few days to formulate a plan of attack if we can find out where she is being held." Sir Henry put the dog down and moved to the door that led into the library. He pushed it open and stepped into the scene of the crime. One thing out of all the events surrounding his daughter's kidnapping had been, if not a balm and comfort, a small glimmer of hope. It had been partly smothered by his self-perceived guilt. But he clung to it and needed to use it, to help others, his daughter and himself. The weather.

It was nearly dawn, though he doubted they would see much of any light today. The night mist had thickened to a fog and was beginning to taste foul. It would soon be smog,

Sir Henry was sure, and until midday, unless a breeze rose to blow it away. And he knew, from his years of study, some of the rituals surrounding the innocent and their conversion into Glimpsers. The act, according to some scholars, needed to be done at dawn with the sky bright and clear.

"*So that they shall know the power and true gift of the Goddess, as if gazing into the brightness of the morning sun, and thus walk back into the world wiped clean.*" As he said the words, Henry walked across the ill-lit room to a row of books.

"That sounds like a prayer," Elizabeth said.

"It is part of one used by the inner cadre of the order. It is taken from one of the more obscure sayings of the Seer. The cadre of the Inner Ring have taken it as their creed. I have come to believe, after all my years studying the order, that it lies at the heart of turning a normal person into a Glimpser. Clues to where she might be, other than the chapel, could be in any of these; I have collected all I can on the subject. Though I didn't bring all when we came to Gateskeep, I hope I brought enough to help." Sir Henry removed a number of books from the shelf and passed them to Pugh, who had come to stand by his side.

"And this will give us a few days, the preparations needed for this ritual?" Pugh's lips curled in distaste.

"No, the weather — the full text is as follows." Sir Henry opened the last volume he had pulled off the shelf and read: "*The true gift of the Goddess is in my very bones. When I leave this flesh, it will still be here for those who come seeking it. Those who come to your door, guilt- and grief-ridden, give them a fragment of me blessed by your prayers so that they shall know the power and true gift of the Goddess, as if gazing into the brightness of the morning sun, and thus walk back into the world wiped clean.*"

"Dear Goddess. The demons. The true gift of the Goddess, indeed. Curse, more like," Elizabeth spat, and stood back from the door to allow Pugh and Sir Henry to re-enter the study. "As for bright mornings, if the fog is thick — the fog!"

"So long as it holds," Pugh said, relief colouring his voice.

"Yes," Sir Henry confirmed, yet his heart could not share their hope.

"It will give us time to find her if she is not in the chapel. Of course, Toby! Toby shows the way." Elizabeth opened one of the books and began to look through the pages.

"You think I should ask the dog to seek Claire? Even a good hunting dog needs a scent, and I doubt Claire walked anywhere."

"She could have been dragged across the ice," Elizabeth quickly retorted.

"I beg your pardon," Pugh answered.

"You heard me, Pugh. Take the dog for a walk while Henry and I indulge in a little light reading." She waved Pugh away and turned her attention to the open book.

***

It was well past dawn, and the river mist had gained another layer: the thick smoke from the coal fires of houses and the burgeoning industries on the city's fringes. It had become overnight a smog, and had lost its pale white colour. Tinged with yellow and smelling acrid, it clung to the buildings round which it swarmed. It probed at cracks in windows and doors, seeking to find new spaces to fill. It snatched at the lungs of man and animal alike, as they made their way down the streets and alleys.

Pugh coughed and held a handkerchief to his mouth. Here on the frozen river, the smog was thicker. And cold, so cold — the ice under his feet had claws that tore through the soles of his boots. At least he was doing something, even if that something was watching a small dog weave in and out of the mist.

On his return to the house, Pugh had been tempted to seek an outlet for the growing pit of bitter pain and self-recrimination in a bottle of Sir Henry's best fifty-year-old brandy. He had not, not yet. Instead he flung himself into doing anything that had the illusion of helping to find the only woman he loved. He stuffed the handkerchief into his pocket and pulled his coat tighter. Pugh stamped his feet. The ice moved, giving a fraction, then settling. It was not as thick as he had originally thought. He glanced down, expecting to see a maze of cracks running in all directions. Calvinward had suggested he teach him to skate if the ice was thick enough today; now, he never would. Pugh had not liked Calvinward when they had first met; however, since the train crash, a strange friendship had begun to develop. Pugh sensed that slowly Calvinward was allowing the veneer of the career

234

politician to drop, and in time he would have known the real man. That chance had been taken away: it was a loss he could not yet put into words. As for Claire, this time he was not going to give up and move on: he would find her if it took the rest of his life.

The sharp sound of Toby's barking brought Pugh's thoughts back to the here and now. The dog had come back out of the mist and stood at point, his whole body quivering. "Away, seek," Pugh said, and the dog started to trot forward. He followed, glancing round, trying to see where they were. He guessed some three hundred paces or more from the house. His foot caught on something and he stumbled. He stopped and knelt down. Toby circled back, barking, telling Pugh to hurry up. His gloved fingers rubbed at the small log frozen in the ice, with part of its length exposed. The wood had been cut by a runner. A sledge — of course, it made sense. A rag picker's, perhaps; no one would think to question the sight of one on the frozen river.

His fingers ran along the trail of the runner in the ice. "Is this what you are following?" he asked the dog. Toby barked again, sounding even more annoyed at the delay. "I am coming, coming." Pugh got to his feet and hurried after.

Pugh could hear the muffled noise of horses' hooves and the odd shout. They must be close to the Highspire Bridge. Yes, out of the thick smog the rough shape of the base of the western spire began to form. Slowly, the outline began to solidify. The thick stone with its carvings was a few hands' width from Pugh. He glanced up. The bridge, which he knew must be above his head, was lost in the yellow-tinted veil. The sounds of the morning traffic passing across it rumbled above. "Where to, Toby?"

The dog did not answer, but kept his nose to the ground and wandered across the ice. Then he turned and made for some steps attached to the stone. They rose to a door, the bottom of which was set level with Pugh's eyes. Toby began to climb the steps, panting. "Stand!" Toby stopped. "To me," Pugh said quietly, and reached into his pocket, pulling out a length of leather. Toby glanced back at Pugh, a growl rumbling through his clenched teeth. "Yes, I know, but there is nothing you can do for the moment." The dog gave a soft bark and came down the steps to Pugh's side. Pugh clipped the strap onto the dog's collar. A sense of elation began to grow. The dog could be wrong, yet the animal was shaking with an excitement which was beginning to be contagious.

It made a strange sort of sense. The Seer had, according to legend, lived in the castle for the last part of his life. Had his quarters been in this spire? It was the sort of thing the cadre would weave into their cursed ritual.

Avinguard walked to the river bank and clambered up onto the path. As he did so, he tried to look over the spire. Impossible: the smog obscured his view. Not that looking at the place would tell him much, save for the position of any windows and doors. Careful, do not make things too obvious. If the cadre is in the spire, they could have men on lookout. They were arrogant sons of bitches, but not altogether stupid. Pugh heart began to hammer under his ribcage.

There was the entrance close to the river, under the bridge. Was there one on the bridge, or higher? Pugh casually strolled onto the bridge, keeping close to the stone of the wall that led to the spire. Carriages and wagons loomed out of the thick mist, ghosts passing in a rumble of wheels. The horses assumed the appearance of monsters, their breath steaming from their nostrils. Toby whined and butted Pugh's calf with his nose. "I agree, bloody unnerving." Pugh coughed again and made a mental note of the door set in the spire's side on the bridge. Part of him wanted to kick down the door and rush in. He clenched his fist, fighting back the emotion. "We have come far enough. Time for home, Toby."

As he walked, he began to think. Was Claire really in there? They had no proof. She still could be anywhere. No don't think of that; have faith in the words of Oracle. The ones in the notebook. *"Toby seek, river and ice."* But there was no mention of the bridge or the spire. Then again, there had been no mention of Calvinward's attack. Goddess, why not? He had to try and stay focused. He had said before that to try and decipher Claire's words as Oracle was impossible. It only led to heartbreak, disappointment and confusion — but it was all they had to go on.

He and Toby made their way into the park. He tried to steady his breathing. A plan to assault the tower needed to be formulated. Two outside doors, that he knew of. How many windows, floors, rooms, stairs? Which door led to which?

236

Pugh's lips tightened in frustration. They needed plans. Sir Henry, in his position as Master of the High Forum, might be able to get blueprints, though it could be that the layout been altered since the plans had been made. The spires were not occupied, though Pugh knew that they could be used as militia positions if need be. Pugh felt his anger increase. This bridge and its spires sat at the heart of the city, so close to the High Forum that he was supposed to protect, and he knew nothing of what was inside the bloody stone towers.

racle swung her legs down off the woollen cloth-covered bench she had lain on, and sat on the edge. Her shoulder sockets had begun to ache; she tried to move her arms to ease the pain. Oracle's movement caught the eyes of one of the men guarding her. He walked towards her. As he did, his face became clearer. Did she know him? She felt Claire stir in the depths of her thoughts. Yes. Claire did. His name began to form on the tip of Oracle's tongue, but the words said it was unimportant so she did not say it.

"You are uncomfortable?" Harrison asked.

"Yes. No. Irrelevant. Words. Time now," Oracle answered, licking her dry lips. She was not frightened. No visions of danger and flight flickered behind her eyes. She was where she needed to be. To speak the words that needed to be said: "Turn the world on its head. End it. Bone and fate. Death in the dark. Reflections of us. Consequences faced. Open the box, stop them. Politics and religion both must be transformed."

Claire spoke faintly in the back of her mind, now controlled by Oracle. Not fighting for control of her body, just struggling to understand.

"How should politics and religion be changed?" Oracle allowed Claire's mental question to issue from her mouth. Harsh, barely above a whisper, but it was important they be heard as well as her answer.

"Both should be, so that the individual can be allowed to grow or wither by their own choice. To take and give back in equal measure. To rise and fall and to be aware of all the Goddess' gifts." Oracle answered aloud.

"But how?" Oracle allowed Claire to snatch back the use of her voice, part of her aware of the priest who was watching and listening: it was vital he should do so.

"You can change the nature of both. People must contemplate their place in the universe. Take responsibility for their actions to others, or suffer the consequences. Only then can my gifts become manifest." Oracle's reply was echoed by the voice of the old woman who stood in the shadows.

"So I am not Claire, not Oracle, just me," Claire said, and her identity began again to sink beneath that of Oracle.

This was Oracle's time; it was she who needed to be here. She cocked her head on one side and watched Harrison draw back from her. His face was blanched white with emotion, hands clasped so tightly, his knuckles bulged through the skin.

***

The afternoon was turning into evening. The smog still lay heavy on the city, and the fear for Claire in Pugh's heart had solidified.

The sound of Sir Henry's voice drifted in from the corridor outside the library. "My thanks, Minister Carlsonmark, for the books."

"I will not ask the reasons behind your request for such heavy reading, Sir Henry, but I hope they contain what you are looking for. I shall pray to the Goddess to keep your daughter safe and return her unharmed. She is a very special young lady, but you are, I am sure, well aware of that." Carlsonmark nodded to Sir Henry and took his leave.

Pugh stepped towards the door. "How much does he know?"

"About Claire, the Inner Ring and what we are planning to do, impossible to say. He did not seem that surprised when asked for information. Worth the risk." Elizabeth was seated at one of the desks in the library, already looking at one of the books Carlsonmark had brought.

"You asked him outright?"

"Not in so many words, Pugh, but like Elizabeth said, he did not seem surprised. After the Prince's revolt and the dissolution of the monarchy, the various religious sects of the time slowly merged into one all-encompassing faith. The Inner Ring was the only one that kept itself apart. Its political agenda and obsession with the sayings of the great Seer has always made it contentious in the eyes of its Orthodox Chapel."

"Yes, we know all that, Henry," Elizabeth cut in. "Tell Pugh Claire liked the minister."

"She did? I didn't know she knew him."

"Unlike you, she and I go to chapel. It's surprising who you meet at chapel, Pugh. Senior chapel ministers, for one. Now, both of you — books."

***

The tables in the library were littered with tomes, some centuries old, yellowed pages covered with the stylised lettering of a bygone era. Slips of paper covered with Sir Henry's writing marked the places at which they were open. In the one Sir Henry was studying, the twin spires of Highspire Bridge featured in an illustration. The drawing also had small, cut-out sectional pictures showing the details of the carvings round the two circular windows on the eastern side. These aligned with both the morning sun when it rose over the city and another window in the western spire. Sir Henry snapped the book shut. He turned it over in his hands and placed it on the blueprint of the western spire.

"You believe she will be in what was a small chapel near the base of the spire." Elizabeth fussed with the drapes, drawing them and shutting off the room from the smog-wrapped night.

"It makes sense. It is the site of one of the former royal chapels," Sir Henry said.

"So we go in from the river and the bridge." Pugh rubbed his unshaved chin. His fingers came away prickling, the sensation reminding him of the tiredness he fought to hold at bay. He was standing by the fireplace. The warmth of the blaze had long ago banished the chill, but it did not touch the cold pit that contained his emotions.

"Yes, but if we are wrong ...," Sir Henry said, and pulled a chair closer to the table and sat.

"We try again, elsewhere." Elizabeth came to Sir Henry's side, placing a hand on his shoulder.

Sir Henry's hand came up and closed over hers. "Us, not you."

"It won't be even that, if you two don't get some rest."

"That will not be necessary," Pugh said, moving towards the table. He consciously avoided the place where Calvinward had lain the evening before.

"If you don't, you will not be fit for duty. The men who are going to help you are resting, are they not, awaiting the lifting of the smog?"

"Yes, but — " Sir Henry let go of Elizabeth's hand and placed both of his on the blueprint in front of him. His fingers tapped on the outline of the old chapel.

"But nothing — you and Pugh go rest. Thomas will wake you both if the smog as much as moves a fraction off the ground. I have had one of the guest rooms made up for you, Pugh, third on the left on the second floor."

Sir Henry made to argue, then nodded and rose from his seat. Pugh's lips tightened. It made sense to try, though he doubted he would sleep. Together, the men walked up the main staircase. They did not speak to each other, both closed in by their own thoughts.

Pugh took his leave of Sir Henry by the door of the room that had been assigned to him. As his fingers closed on the handle, a cough drew his attention to the young man standing in the corridor. "Yes?"

"I took the liberty of setting out a shaving kit and placing some water in the small kettle on the fire, thinking you might wish to wash and shave before you retire, sir," the young man said with a bow.

"I see, thank you ..." Pugh let the words trail off, waiting for the young man to fill in his name.

"Thomas, sir, and might I say good luck in your venture, Major."

"Thank you, Thomas," Pugh replied, entering the room.

Pugh availed himself of the hot water. By shaving and slowly getting ready for bed, he had hoped to delay the inevitable. He removed the warming pan and slipped between the sheets, his skin registering the slight warmth lingering on the fabric. It felt as if another body had just left the bed. He lay there, going over what had happened since the ball, trying to plan what he intended to say to the men who had agreed to risk their careers and lives by helping him.

In mid-sentence, his eyes closed. He was on the ice of the river, but the heat burned him, blazing down from the train that rushed overhead. Calvinward smiled at him, then his head exploded and his features reformed into Sir Henry's. Mathew was laughing with Constance over Claire's body, but as his view changed it wasn't Claire, but Emily. Coot's Pass melded into the train, then into the Highspire Bridge, which was lined with the heads of the dead. Pugh tried to explain why they were dead, but he could not. His head was there on the wall of the bridge.

He tossed, fighting against the covers. A pair of hands touched his brow, rough, not a lady's hands, yet small. They ran down his neck and onto his chest, stopping over his heart, cupping it, burning his flesh. Pugh moved his own hands up to sweep them away, but as he touched the hands they had changed shape. A small baby lay there, its soft breath tickling his chest. Pugh's arms came up and closed round the ghost haunting his sleep. The child sighed and settled into Pugh's dream embrace. Pugh felt a wave of love flood through him, banishing all the other nightmares lurking in the shadows. Holding this ghost in a way he had never held the real child, his son, Pugh fell into a deep sleep, all his questions, fear and turmoil set aside for this small space of time.

***

Carter stood at a window in the western spire of the bridge, watching the orb of the sun on the horizon slowly become visible. A wind had risen, coming in from the Greentip Sea. It swept along the length of the frozen river, dissipating the smog. He was wearing his robe of office. His right hand was deep in the pocket in the side of the robe, fingers curling round a pistol. The metal of the barrel had warmed under the pressure of his fingers.

The Seer would forgive him, Carter was sure. He did not share the others' certainty that the coming ceremony would not be interrupted. He knew at first-hand what Major Pugh Avinguard was capable of. It was a fear that nagged at him, taking form in the gnawing pain in his right shoulder. Carter doubted that the wound would ever heal completely. A reminder, both physically and mentally, of the event that had begun this and served as a warning of the danger from others.

The rest of his brothers believed that if an attack was made it would be on the main chapel. Sir Henry had studied the Inner Ring for seven years: Harrison had confirmed it. Lady Hotspur had threatened them; the manner she had used spoke of knowledge beyond the norm. Yes, he would go armed into the chapel. He would not put his trust in the guards.

Carter slowly turned. Harrison was standing in the doorway of the sparsely furnished room. No fire blazed in the small grate. The air still carried the smell of long abandonment. The whole spire had a feeling of being out of step with the city, lost and content in the memories of its own past, the men in temporary residence unwanted.

"The sun is nearing the point." Harrison looked past Carter and out of the window in the direction of the sister spire. "It is time to begin."

"You sound unsure; speaking with the Seer has unnerved you. Do not worry, it will pass. You will see the glory soon enough." Carter smiled at his friend's emotions, then found the smile fading. *Slighted.*

"She has made others unsure, as you call it. A few of our brothers, now they have actually been in her presence, have voiced the suspicion it is something else behind the young woman's eyes. They begin to doubt this course of action."

"There is no such thing as demons – you know that, Harrison." Carter laughed and crossed to Harrison's side.

"True. However, there is the darker side of the Goddess. The vengeful mother. We are on a cusp here, within a hairsbreadth of confirming the faith and actions of five hundred years of our brotherhood. What if we have made a mistake? If that is true, we can expect no mercy, for the Goddess will tear down part of her creation to save the whole."

Carter was appalled. His hand came out to touch his friend's arm.

"No. If this goes well, then at the end of the day, you and I will laugh at this moment. If not, you will feel the weight of my curse for bringing us to this pass."

"You cannot mean that; you must have faith."

Harrison stood aside from the door to allow Carter to pass. Carter began to walk down the narrow, curving, stone steps to the small chapel. The dark, dank way was lit by coarse, spluttering candles. Harrison's footsteps echoed behind him; he could hear the man's harsh breathing. "You have never been chosen to be among the hand that bears the ring before, have you? I have stood among the twenty-six, five times in my position of Seer Confessor. This woman was my first. I heard her confession and listened to her desire to be cut off from the memory and the responsibility of what she had done. She could no longer live with it. I saw her relief, then fear, as the power we harnessed through our prayer was channelled into her. I felt that power wash over me. It is still in her, and now we, with this coming act, will again impress the same power into her. I ask myself, what are we attempting to create? Is it our will that drives us, or another's, bent on a path we cannot see?"

Carter could not believe what he was hearing. The man had taken the thoughts of an advocate to the extreme. Harrison was testing his faith: that was it. Carter began to pray. *"The true gift of the Goddess is in my very bones. When I leave this flesh, it will still be here for those who come seeking it. Those who come to your door, guilt- and grief-ridden, give them a fragment of me blessed by your prayers so that they shall know the power and true gift of the Goddess, as if gazing into the brightness of the morning sun, and thus walk back into the world wiped clean."*

He heard Harrison sigh behind him and join in the prayer. Their two voices blended, joining with the voices of those already in the chapel.

***

"Major, forgive me."

Pugh grunted. A hand shook him. He snapped awake, his eyes opening. Thomas was standing over him. An oil lamp blazed on the washstand, and the drapes were still closed.

"The smog?" Pugh asked.

"It is showing signs of lifting."

"How long till dawn?" Pugh threw back the covers, pushed himself up off the bed, and strode towards his clothes.

"Nearly two hours. And Captain Gunmain has arrived downstairs with another officer. They have joined the others in the library."

Pugh stopped, balancing on his left leg, the right halfway down his trouser leg. Gunmain? "Tell him, and the rest, I will be down in a moment."

"I will, sir. Breakfast is on the table, sir."

***

Pugh hurried down the passage to the library. Standing before the door was Lady Elizabeth. Pugh began to ask her to stand aside, but the tears brimming on her lashes forestalled him. He knew why she was here.

"Calvinward? Does Sir Henry know?" Pugh asked, knowing already what the answer was.

"Yes, to both questions. A few minutes ago. Senior Minister Carlsonmark and I were with him." Elizabeth sniffed.

"Make the bastards pay, Pugh." She stood aside for him to enter the library.

***

On entering, Pugh was met by a wall of bodies in militia green. "Damn, it looks like someone has opened a tin of militia allsorts in here." The men turned as one, standing to attention and saluting. A number smiled at his attempt at a joke. Gunmain approached Pugh, his hand outstretched. Pugh took it. "I didn't want you involved in this."

"You didn't trust me?" Gunmain said, his left eyebrow rising in query.

"I didn't want you being dragged down with me, if things go wrong. The job you are doing is far too important, and – "

"I thank you, sir, for the consideration. However, if the Inner Ring were responsible for the attack on Lord Calvinward and the abduction of Lady Claire for whatever nefarious reasons, it is time someone put a stop to their politicking. And that, I feel, falls under the remit of the force I have been second-in-command of for the last season." Gunmain's words were seconded by a round of ayes. The strongest came from Lieutenant Carlmanson, who had been in charge of the detail assigned to Calvinward.

Pugh gave a rough smile and pressed Gunmain's hand harder, then let it go. He could not ask for a more capable man to join them, and felt humbled. "Gentlemen." He looked round the group. In addition to Gunmain and Carlmanson, there were two more of the young officers assigned to protection duty.

There was also Captain Fitzbennett and a Lieutenant Handmartin, with whom Pugh had served previously. They were presently attached to the city militia regiment. Then there were a pair of sergeants who were leaning against one of the bookcases: Perkins and Jones. In fact, most of the men who had been with him on the train had appeared, as if by magic.

"So, sir, what's the plan?" Perkins said.

"The plan is to get my daughter out of there," Sir Henry said from the door into the study.

"A simple thing, but not easily done." Pugh walked to Sir Henry's side. He knew the words he was about to say could mean the death of some of them. They knew it, too. It was a responsibility he had carried before, for the abstract vision of duty to his country and the very real one of comradeship to his fellow militia men. He now took it on for love. Was it that simple a root to this cause? Such fanciful thoughts did not have a place here; he needed to focus. Yet the vision of Claire as he had last seen her, the tilt of her head and the curve of her smile, was so deeply etched, he doubted he would ever forget it.

"Instruct us, sir," Gunmain said, a wry smile on his face.

"The western spire of Highspire Bridge has seven floors. But the three above the bridge level, I don't think we need to be concerned with," Pugh began.

"Why?" Carlmanson asked, rubbing his chin.

"Because we have come to firmly believe that Lady Claire is being held close to the old chapel, which is second from the bottom. That is one floor above the door at river level." Pugh tapped the blueprint; the paper crackled under his touch and moved slightly. Pugh spread his hand out to stop it and found he was covering the section that detailed the chapel. He lifted his hand quickly. Even touching that place on a map was too much to bear.

"So you are planning to send men in from the bridge level and river level. Fight their way in. That will put Lady Claire in danger." Gunmain grimaced and looked at Pugh.

"Yes, it will. Though I truly believe that her death would be preferable to what I believe the Inner Ring has planned for her," Sir Henry said coldly.

"You can imagine, gentlemen, it is going to be difficult not only to gain access, but to fight our way up and down the narrow staircase. At least the group going in from the river level only have one floor to clear. Fitzbennett, Handmartin, I am giving you that easy task." Fitzbennett twisted the ends of his large moustache and nudged Handmartin in the ribs. "Choose the men you need. The task is simple: get in and clear the first floor, make your way to the second and get in that chapel. Hopefully, by the time the rest of us get there you will have the job done and be kicking your heels. I intend to lead the party going in from the bridge level.

"If we go in before you, it will draw any guards and priests upwards to defend the two floors above the chapel. Sir Henry believes that the chapel itself will contain only the inner circle of the cadre. In that, he means some twenty-seven, the number of bones in a human hand. It is quite plain, though, that a large number of the rest of the cadre that are present here in Gateskeep will be somewhere in the tower. So we will be facing up to a hundred, perhaps more."

Pugh stopped for a moment as the number registered with the men. As an attacking force, all knew their casualties would be more. They also had fewer men by half. Pugh hoped the fact that his men were all seasoned career militia would weigh in their favour. "Some of you have done this sort of fighting before. It's not nice, and demands a high price. Let's try and make those we are up against pay most of it." A murmur of approval greeted his words. "Gentlemen, take a good look at the blueprints, and if any of you have second thoughts, then please, gentlemen, walk away. I consider it enough personal honour that you have even come."

A shuffling of feet and an increase in the murmuring of voices filled the room after Pugh stopped speaking. None left. Gunmain made his way to the table, looked at the blueprints and said something behind his hand to Carlmanson. The lieutenant grinned and left the room. Pugh frowned. Had Carlmanson changed his mind? Had Gunmain? He looked at Sir Henry, who shrugged his shoulders. Pugh returned his attention to the other men. He began to answer a question from Fitzbennett, when the door opened again and Carlmanson walked in carrying a wooden box with the symbol of the militia ordnance corps burned into its side.

"When I got wind of this, I thought we needed a little edge," Gunmain said, and signed for the men in the room to make way for Carlmanson. He placed the box on the table. Gunmain stepped forward and undid the locks. He rooted through the straw packing and brought out a black ball about the size of a large orange, with a length of fuse sticking out the top.

"Grenades. How many?" Pugh asked, as Gunmain handed him the metal ball. It felt cold. The surface was dimpled. The black paint used to prevent rust from forming during storage had been roughly applied. He gave it to Sir Henry, who turned the ball in his hands, inspecting it from every angle before reluctantly returning it to Captain Gunmain.

"Only six: that's three to a group — one to throw as a greeting card, and two to keep as backup. Hopefully one through each door will be enough to take any fight out of them."

247

Pugh nodded. A ripple of agreement ran round the men present in the room. How could he repay this man? He made to speak, but Gunmain was deep in conversation with Fitzbennett. Pugh stood back, letting them work out the details, the very things they would be risking their lives on.

CHAPTER TWENTY-SIX.

arter felt a flush of almost sexual excitement roll in the pit of his stomach. He had never been in this chapel before. In some aspects, it was the same as any reserved for the use of the higher cadre. The room was hot despite the season; thick tapestries and the seven incense braziers made the air stifling. Sweat began to trickle down Carter's face. He was among the last to enter the symbol of his oath and order. The large circle of thick, plaited red leather, suspended by five chains from the ceiling, had already been lowered. No statue of the Goddess stood in this circle, just the prism and an altar: a remnant from an earlier, darker time, ornately carved with visions of the Goddess' creations and tilted so that the upper part was beneath the prism.

The men's voices became quieter, the prayer no more than a whispered lovers' cant. The priests pressed close to the altar. On the table Lady Claire Fitzguard, Oracle, the Seer reborn, lay bound. Water gushed out of myriad holes in the stone, soaking her cotton shift. It ran through the maze of carvings and tumbled over the edges of the altar. There it pooled, before it bubbled and frothed its way down into the floor and back into the river. Her head was between two raised, carved sections of stone. A metal frame lay across her face, a macabre pair of glasses which held the delicate skin of her eyelids open.

At the base of the altar was an old, iron-bound chest. Inlaid in coloured enamelling on its warped lid was the symbol of the Goddess, an upturned "V" with a rippled line running through the bottom and top. Earth, air and water. All in the world was made by these three, and in the three the Goddess lit the fire of life. Carter had known of the chest's existence, but never before had he seen it. It contained what was left of the prophet's mortal remains — his cracked and broken bones. The feeling of excitement in the pit of his stomach deepened. He had never dreamed he would one day be standing here. Harrison moved from Carter's side and went towards the plinth. His hand touched the arm of the Glimpser and he bent over, saying something. She spoke in reply. Her words did not reach beyond the man she had spoken to.

Harrison stepped back. He bowed his head to the young woman and made his way to the outer edge of the group round the altar. Carter frowned, but soon forgot about Harrison and his strange behaviour. A shout came from the room above. Suddenly a beam of light hit the prism and the room was plunged into a swirling maze of colours, the full focus of which was directed into the eyes of the young woman. She screamed, but her cry was soon lost in the renewed chanting of the prayer. Carter's throat locked with emotion. He swallowed hard and joined in the chant.

"The true gift of the Goddess is in my very bones. When I leave this flesh, it will still be here for those who come seeking it. Those who come to your door guilt- and grief-ridden, give them a fragment of me blessed by your prayers. So that they shall know the power and true gift of the Goddess, as if gazing into the brightness of the morning sun, and thus walk back into the world wiped clean."

Carter felt the air in the room grow heavy with the power of the words. Every syllable uttered was drawing on the faith of the men who said them. That faith drew on the belief of all who held the Goddess close to their heart. The hearts were made of earth, air and water and sparked into being by the fire of life. The power grew: it was raw and untamed. His skin grew hot. He wept from the exposure to the heat. He was lifted high, exulted, smashed down and crushed underfoot. A tumult of emotion coursed through his veins, rendering him down to the sum of his parts. He was fractured and rebuilt.

He was everything and nothing. The true gift of the Goddess was flowing through him to give to the one on the altar. His mouth was full of blood. Each time he said the prayer, the words cut his throat. Part of his mind began to panic, fearing he would drown in his own fluids. But the feeling was washed away by the roaring tide of vindication. He was right: the Seer was reborn, and his hand had been the first lifted in this act of restoration.

Through the tears streaming from his eyes, he watched two of his fellow priests move forward. One climbed onto a small plinth by the side of the altar, wielding a curved knife. The priest slit the neckline of the woman's shift, exposing her upper chest. He flung his arms up, waiting for something. The other brother fumbled with the lock on the old chest. The top flew back, the old wood ridge slamming against the floor. The man reached inside and drew something out, his hand going up in a gesture of victory.

The chant began to fade. Carter continued to speak the words, but he could not hear them. He shook his head, hoping it would restore the echo of his own voice in the bones of his jaw. The spiritual power was channelled by the pure effort of the will of the priests.

Yes, it is now. The future we shall shape begins. It could not be otherwise. The priest with the knife again raised it high over the exposed chest of the young woman. The other priest stepped forward, his hand outstretched.

***

It was like before. "Not fear this time," Oracle whispered, trying hard to still the vortex of possible futures beginning to form inside her. Each voice wanted her to see their path more clearly. The world was about to turn on its head, for good or ill. A hand touched Oracle's arm. The voices turned their attention to the man's question.

"Will the order survive this, will I?"

"Survive. No. Time. Responsibility. Choice. Reap the consequences of actions." With the words said, the man and the reason why she had spoken faded from her mind.

A fan of coloured light came from above and Oracle screamed in welcome. She took the colours into herself, her colourless eyes shifting from one shade of the rainbow to another. The colours in her eyes deepened. Oracle absorbed the raw power. She drank it in. Each rainbow shade began to form a thin strand, as fine as glass drawn out and twisted by the glassblower's art. They began to knot together, forming two windows, one behind each of Oracle's eyes, through which a deity watched and hoped.

Oracle flinched at the chill of the knife as it touched her skin. Some voices shouted at her to resist, others to welcome it. One, in the harsh voice of the old woman, implored Oracle not to struggle against the pressure of the steel. To allow the holder of the knife to cut deep into her flesh alongside the piece of Seer's bone that was already under her skin. It would all be over soon. Oracle shuddered, then lay still. Blood began to flow, staining the front of her thin cotton shift.

251

The voices began to argue, seeking to drown each other out. Then they stopped, and the old woman said, *"I have a dark face."*

The spire rocked on its foundations. The reflecting mirrors above the prism shattered. The spiralling beams began to fade like a rainbow at the end of a summer storm. Glass fragments rained down through the opening in the ceiling, causing the men pressed close to the altar to scatter.

All except one.

Harrison.

He fought his way through the press of men until he was by the side of the altar. "It's finished — give it to me," he said to priest wielding the knife. The priest began to object. Another explosion. A large crack ran across the ceiling, flowing from east to west. It split into a hundred veins. One circled the brass bolt holding the chain attaching the prism. "The knife!" Harrison held out his hand. Reluctantly, the priest gave him the blood-coated blade.

Oracle watched Harrison stand over her, the stained knife in his hand. "Turn the world on its head. Politics and religion. Goddess' sacrifice. Good man. Progress and chaos."

"Yes, I understand — we were so wrong." Harrison cut the ropes binding Oracle. He threw the knife aside and began to open the screws on the left side of the frame over Oracle's face. His fingers slipped on the wet metal. Harrison grunted and pulled down his sleeve, using the thick fabric to give him grip on the screws. The metal still resisted, then suddenly loosened. He pulled the first long screw out and threw it to the floor; the second quickly followed. He pushed the frame up and to the side and carefully eased Oracle's head out from between the stone blocks. She began to struggle to sit up. Harrison took her arm and helped her.

"What are you doing?" The priest holding the fragment of the seer's bone made to grab Harrison's arm. Harrison lashed out with his fist, hitting the man in the ribs. The bone dropped from the priest's hand. He screamed and toppled backwards, falling over the old chest. It tipped sideways, emptying its contents onto the floor. The priest, his arms spread-eagled, continued to fall. His right arm hit the leg of one of the incense braziers. It rocked forward, spilling its smouldering coals over the fragments of bone littering the floor. A fine haze of smoke began to rise.

252

"End it," Oracle said. Her eyes were the colour of mourning and remembrance: indigo.

A look of confusion began to form on Harrison's face, then faded. He drew in a breath and began to stamp on the scattered bones, smashing them into dust. Oracle slid off the altar and stood by his side. Blood continued to seep from the wound in her chest. It was not important. The final destruction of the bones was. She looked at Harrison. He had seen the truth and taken responsibility. The old woman behind Oracle's window eyes began to weep. "Death in the dark!" Oracle said, and another explosion rocked the building. The bolt holding the prism's chain came away from the ceiling. The lump of finely shaped glass fell onto the altar and split into seven pieces.

***

Carter struggled to keep his footing. The sound of gunfire echoed from the floor above. The floor heaved again. Lime plaster fell from the ceiling, filling the air with the stale dust of ages. Some of the embers from the toppled brazier had caught on the tapestries. They began to smoke. Priests rushed over and began to rip the heavy fabric from the wall, trying to put the flames out.

"We are under attack!" The cry was followed by more gunfire.

"Protect yourselves. Protect the new Seer."

The leather ring surrounding the men swayed and began to move towards the ceiling, allowing the men access to the rest of the room. They spread out, seeking something to defend themselves with. Some, Carter noticed with satisfaction, had, like he, come armed.

"Stop. We must continue!" Carter shouted.

"Fool, are you so blind? It all is over," Harrison cried. He stood in a whirling mist of ash, his robe streaked with grey and bone fragments.

"No, we fight our way out. Take the Seer and — " Carter broke off when he realised what Harrison had done. He had freed the Glimpser from the altar. The box containing the remains of the great Seer was tipped over on its side; a few fragments of bone were scattered, undamaged, on the open lid, but the rest had been trampled under Harrison's feet. *The bastard. Goddess curse him.* "What have you done?"

253

"I have acknowledged I was wrong, that our order was wrong, and I have taken responsibility, knowing the consequences. It is over, Carter. Politics and religion. Both must grow and change, so the human spirit can." Harrison began to advance towards Carter.

"Betrayer!" Carter screamed, and pulled the gun out of his pocket. He stretched out his arm, pointing the weapon at Harrison, who stopped five feet in front of him.

"Chaos. Progress. Turn the world on its head. New Beginning. End of this," Oracle said, her voice deeper and richer than Carter remembered.

He looked at the Glimpser: her eyes had turned blue. The colour of forgiveness and protection. His finger tightened on the trigger. "No. It is only a setback. Everything will be as it should be."

"Yes. Over now." The Glimpser's eyes shimmered and turned yellow, the colour of wisdom that came with age, which unconditionally offered him the strength of the Goddess to ease his burden.

"Carter, please." Harrison took another step, his hand outstretched to take Carter's gun. The sound of gunfire was outside the door. Another explosion rocked the room. A blast of air pushed Carter from behind. Voices shouted.

"Militia!"

"Put down your weapons."

"Militia!"

"It's over!"

"It's not over." Carter squeezed the trigger. The gun leapt back in his hand. Harrison fell, blood spouting from his chest. The Glimpser's eyes changed colour again. Red: the colour of the dark face of the Goddess. Violence and war. The feeling he had first felt on the platform at Hitsmine began again to form in the pit of his stomach. *Slighted.* No, he was not. His arm dropped to his side, the gun tapping against his thigh.

"Secure the room, Fitzbennett."

"Aye, sir."

Carter turned at the sound of the new voices. Men in militia green were entering the room. Rifles at their shoulders, they herded his fellow priests to the right, against the wall.

"Search them well. I don't want any more casualties on either side."

Avinguard. It was that loathsome bastard, Avinguard. *Slighted.* His chest began to tighten. No. I am right. My order will rule as it did before. The Seer will be reborn. *Slighted.* Carter's arm came up again. He pulled the trigger, swiftly — once, twice, three times. The vicious sound reverberated off the stone walls. Avinguard fell.

He looked back at the Glimpser. Yes, we will win through. The woman's head had dropped forward, her gaze on the ground. Her head came slowly up until her gaze was level with his, her eyes two burning red pits. *Slighted.* He could not breathe. Pain began. It ripped into his back, shoulder and head. Then the agony was gone, but the twin pools of red had become one and he was falling into it.

***

Pugh watched the men who were making the attempt to enter the spire from the river level peel off. They vanished into the gloom-raddled park. Dawn was creeping over the horizon. The smog was fading reluctantly; it still hugged the ground, valiantly resisting the rising wind. There was little traffic. Perhaps most people had thought that the smog would linger another day and they were in no hurry to expose themselves again to the foul, yellow mist. It was a Goddess-given gift. Once the attack began, it would draw police, other militia and the general public like jam did wasps.

"How soon do we get at it?" Sir Henry said, falling into step with Pugh. Avinguard winced; this was the moment he had been dreading. Sir Henry was dressed in his tweed hunting jacket, a rifle slung on his back and his old militia sabre on his hip.

"You will be doing nothing, Sir Henry. I intend to leave you and four men on the bridge to guard our rear and help our wounded. I can think of no better man to aid our two young medics," Pugh said, far more sharply than he intended.

"I would remind you, sir, that it is my daughter in there."

"And I would remind you, Sir Henry, it has been years since you did more than take a pot shot at a game bird. Besides, you will hamper my men. They will naturally try and protect you." Pugh began to walk up the slight incline to the bridge. Nothing more was said between them for ten paces.

"I understand," Sir Henry replied, his voice barely in control.

"I am sorry ..." Pugh's voice trailed off. They had reached the edge of the bridge. Sir Henry nodded and fell back, the rest of the men weaving round him. Gunmain gestured, pointing at a number of soldiers. These men slowed their pace and gathered at the end of the bridge. Two young men carrying large backpacks bearing the white circular symbol of a medic spoke to Sir Henry.

Pugh gave one more backward glance, then dismissed him from his mind. He needed to mentally work on the plan and how it would, like all battle plans, break apart once they had contact with the enemy. It was his job to put the pieces back together again and succeed. He put his shoulders back and gave a nod to the men. They stopped, beginning to check over their rifles and fix bayonets. The officers clicked open the barrels of their pistols, as if counting the rounds. All executed in a calmness none felt.

The men were gathered close to the wall of the bridge, some ten paces from the door into the spire. Two narrow windows, once used as arrow slits and now glazed, were shoulder height either side of the door. This was a small guard room which led to a larger one, down one side of which ran the staircase. According to the blueprints, all the floors were on a similar layout save for the chapel one that was the other way round, the smaller room being the one in which the staircase ran down. There were notes on the blueprint saying that each staircase was to have its inner wall removed, opening it up to the rooms it passed through. This would allow for the easy movement of men, guns and ammunition if the spires were to be manned. Pugh somehow doubted it had been done.

"Ready when you are, sir," Gunmain said. Pugh nodded. Sergeant Perkins crouched down, half-crawled to the door and tried to turn the handle: locked, as expected. He moved back and signalled to two men carrying what looked like a small cannon barrel tied round with ropes. They hurried forward. The rest of the men scattered across the roadway of the bridge. They trained their weapons on the door and narrow windows of the spire. The two men took a firm grip of the handholds in the rope and began to swing the solid metal tube against the door. The sound of the first strike vibrated across the bridge, disturbing the water fowl on the ice below. The birds rose, circling over the expanse of the bridge, and headed downstream.

The second strike hit. Pugh unclipped his pistol and slipped it from his holster, holding it ready in his hand. The door was already showing the marks of the assault. The third strike hit and the door bounced on its hinges, giving way in the centre. The hiss of a fuse being lit drew Pugh's gaze sideways. Lieutenant Carlmanson stood there, balancing one of the grenades in the palm of his hand. A shower of sparks peppered his uniform. He winked at Pugh. "Damn, another tailor's bill coming up."

Pugh signed for Carlmanson to be ready to pull the fuse out. He had to give the men inside at least a chance to surrender. "Militia! Lay down your weapons and come out. Militia!

The sharp sound of a gunshot and the splintering of the glass in the right-hand side window answered Pugh's call. He swallowed hard and waved the men with the ram forward again. The fourth strike of the ram smashed the door inwards. The men holding the ram threw it down and sprang to one side. Carlmanson sprinted forward and threw his explosive into the shadow-filled room. The other window blew out, and what was left of the door shattered. Sergeant Perkins yelled. He waved his rifle and ran into the billowing smoke, the rest of the men quickly on his heels. Pugh followed.

The room was shattered: walls splattered with blood and the remains of the men who had been unfortunate enough to be in there. The calls of the injured followed in the echo of the explosion. It joined the shouts of the other occupants of the spire. Pugh breathed a sigh of relief. They had gained entry without any loss, but he did not think that would remain the status quo for long. If only the men in here had opened up and surrendered. Cries and bellowed orders could be heard coming from the next room: Carlmanson and a number of the men had already gone through. The sound of gunshots hammered through the air. The lieutenant ordered three men upwards to the floor above to ensure there was none of the enemy there.

"Easy, that," Gunmain said.

"Let's hope it stays that way," Pugh answered, ducking into the stairwell.

"Aye," Gunmain replied. He nodded to the three men standing on the staircase leading up. They had their backs to the outer wall, eyes on the curving steps before them, their

257

rifles cocked and aimed. The spire gave a shudder, and Pugh knew the other raiding party had gained entry. He gave a sharp nod of satisfaction, and continued his descent.

Pugh ran down the stone steps and came to an abrupt stop. The men who had gone before him were packed tightly in the narrow space. Some crouched down. The blueprints had been half right: part of the wall had been removed. From five steps in front of him, it began in a jagged line at the ceiling, falling away to about knee height. The first few of his men into the stairwell were pinned flat. Some had thrown themselves down behind the remains of the wall, their bodies flinching as shots rang overhead; others lay still, blood splattered on the wall behind them. The thick tallow candles set in the sconces above them spat, the light flickering hellishly across the carnage that had begun.

"Militia! Lay down your weapons!" Carlmanson shouted.

Bullets pinged above their heads, gouging out chips of rock and old mortar. Pugh's men returned fire, trying to keep down the heads of the men firing from behind a large, upturned oak table. Pugh tapped Gunmain's shoulder. "The grenades?" He had no other choice.

"I have one and Carlmanson the other," Gunmain said, slapping the pouch on his belt. Pugh nodded and eased himself past the captain, pressing close to the outer wall.

"Carlmanson." The lieutenant glanced round from where he was crouched. Pugh pantomimed a throw.

Carlmanson nodded and slipped his pistol back in his holster. He took out a small tinder box.

"No need, sir," Sergeant Perkins whispered, handing him the butt of a well-chewed cigar.

Carlmanson grinned and placed the cigar in his own mouth. Carlmanson lit the tar-covered rope and handed Perkins his cigar back. The lieutenant stood, the rest of the men bringing their rifles up to give him covering fire. The thud of bullets hitting the wall around Carlmanson filled the air as the grenade left his hand. Carlmanson doubled up, as if he had been punched in the chest. He fell backwards against the wall and slid down, dislodging a trail of cobwebs. Any cry he made was lost in the roar of the explosion.

Pugh felt the pressure on his ear drums increase. He raised his arm to shelter himself from the rain of debris.

Sergeant Perkins, cursing, drove the men down the stairs and into the chaos. Their rush herded the enemy out of the room and into the larger one. Pugh followed Gunmain down the steps, stopping for a moment by Carlmanson. The young lieutenant's face was pale. A trickle of dirty wax was falling from the candle set above, smearing across his brow. His breathing hitched and his eyes fluttered.

"Hold on, Carlmanson. The medics are hard on our heels." Pugh laid a hand on the young man's shoulder. It was empty comfort. He knew the man would not last that long. Carlmanson's lips began to twitch into a smile. His face muscles went lax, his eyes rolled. There was nothing else Pugh could do. He stood up, stepped over the body and ran into the next room.

The men were already into the staircase, but this time their progress was being hampered far more. Shots rang overhead, cutting round the corner. One of the soldiers at the front screamed and toppled forward. Perkins bellowed for them to move back, allow the enemy to come up to them round the corner.

Pugh reached Gunmain's side close to the wall by the entry to the final staircase down to the chapel.

Gunmain turned to him and swore. "Damn staircase is narrower. We could be here for damn days picking each other off one by one."

"Give me the last of the grenades," Pugh said, shoving his pistol back in its holster. His turn to take the risk. He could not ask another man to do it again. It was not what he wanted. Why did not they surrender? Was their faith so strong? Or was it fear — fear of their order, or the so-called Seer reborn they wanted to bring into the world.

"Sir," Gunmain said, his eyes narrowing. He reluctantly nodded and reached into the pouch slung on his belt. Pugh took the grenade, weighing it in his hand. It felt cold, so innocuous, but so deadly. His chest began to tighten. He took a deep breath, pushing away the rising unease. If he died, then he did so knowing he was fighting for the one thing that truly mattered.

He crouched down and placed the device on the floor. He pulled out his pen knife and cut the fuse. "Bit short, that," Gunmain commented, and glanced from Pugh to the men hunched round the door to the stairs.

"Don't want the sods to have time to pick the bugger up

259

and throw it back. We have bitten them twice; I doubt we will get a third one without moving the finishing line a bit." Pugh stood up, cradling the device close to his chest. He inched his way down the stairs through the press of bodies.

He could feel the warmth of their rapid breath on his face, see the slight tremor in their limbs, as the rush of combat ebbed and flowed. He tried not to look them in the eyes, because he knew what was in them; it was in his own: a heady mix of anger, battle lust and fear. His grip on the grenade tightened. A tattoo of bullets cut into the stone above his head.

"Cigar's gone out, sir," Perkins said, and handed Pugh a tuff of smoking tinder.

Pugh took it, blowing softly on it. "Get back up." Pugh held the tinder to the short fuse. He cradled the bomb for a moment, then threw it. He turned quickly. A bellow from below told him someone had recognised the device. One, two steps. Hands pressed either side against the stone. Making his way back up to join his men. The breath fighting to get in and out of his lungs. The blast hit him. Pugh was thrown forward, off his feet. His arms and hands went up to protect his face. The steps slammed into his thighs and stomach, driving the air out of his lungs. The heat of the explosion snapped at his exposed back. He felt the thud of debris hit him. The whole tower rocked. Men screamed above and below him, but their cries were lost in the roar of another explosion, beginning a repeat performance of noise and destruction.

Another device in the same area. His hands went to his ears, trying to block it out: a crushing wave of sound. But on it came, thundering through the flesh of his fingers. His head reeled and he wanted to vomit.

"Major?" A hand shook him. It was Perkins.

"I am unharmed."

Perkins nodded and pulled on Pugh's arm. Together they stumbled down the staircase, picking their way through torn and bleeding bodies. The red of the men's robes was splattered with a deeper red. Pugh's feet slipped on the gore, and he stumbled into the smaller room that led into the chapel. Here, order was being imposed on chaos. Fitzbennett's group had already burst through into the chapel. Cries and shouts came from within, and the odd shot. Against the far wall of the small room, and against the head of the stairs to the floor below, men in red robes were being lined up. Pugh could sense their anger and humiliation. They would have to be careful; these men had finally given up to a superior force, but were they beaten? Pugh ran to the door. Fitzbennett was shouting orders. The gun shots sputtered and stopped, replaced with the thud of fists and rifle butts on flesh. The man turned, as if sensing Pugh's presence. "You sent a grenade down the stairs, as we sent one across the room towards the door. It took all the bloody fight out of them. Least for now."

Pugh nodded. "Secure the room, Fitzbennett."

"Aye, sir."

"Search them well. I don't want any more casualties on either side." Pugh looked for Claire in the chaos: he could not see her. Was she here? Had all this been for nothing? One of his men pointed towards the altar: empty. Pugh caught sight of a wisp of white behind a red-robed priest. He shouted. His heart thudded with relief; it had to be her. He waved his hand. Men moved forward, forcing a passage through the last of the prisoners.

The pain suddenly hit Pugh in his right thigh, a mere heartbeat after he saw the pistol in Carter's hand discharge. He went down, his right leg rigid, locked in a spasm of burning pain from the hip down. His left knee hit the stone floor. At the same time, the second bullet tore into the top of his right shoulder. The force of the blow flung him back. He felt something brush his right cheek. His face exploded in pain and he fell backward. He rolled to his left. Blood ran down his chin, soaking his leg and chest. He screamed, but could not hear his own voice. Twisting round, he forced himself up into a sitting position. He scrabbled to get his left knee under him. Not like this. *Claire, I love you. I must tell you. Must end this. I promised I would protect you.*

His slack hold on his pistol tightened. Sight blurred, Pugh tried to see his target. His breathing hitched. Each lungful burned. He blinked: his sight cleared. Carter was there. He was standing as if alone in the room, head turned towards Claire. Pugh's finger tightened on the trigger. A series of shots pounded out of the gun. The recoil knocked Pugh off his trembling knee; he crashed sideways. Carter toppled over, screaming. Pugh's head hit the floor. Darkness began to close in around the edges of his vision.

"She is alive, I swear to you, my friend. Medic! Where the bloody hell are you!" Gunmain bellowed.

261

Pugh senses began to fade.

"Major, hell and bloody damnation, don't you dare!"

CHAPTER TWENTY-SEVEN

His heels were drumming, hard on wood. He screamed and tried to open his eyes. A body pressed him down onto the planks; he could feel the grain against his back. Slick. Damp. He tossed his head from side to side. Hands tightened on his arms.

"Damn you, Major, are you trying to undo the work I have done this last hour?"

"Claire. I need to see. She is dead." Pugh tried to form the words over and over, unaware if his voice was working.

"Alive, not dead, and if you let me get back to my work, so shall you be. Nurse — the damn chloroform, now." The doctor's features swam into Pugh's blurred vision, a mere fingertip from his own face. A piece of gauze caught on Pugh's cracked lips. He tried to fight, turned his head and strained against the hands that held him down. He needed to see Claire.

"By the Goddess, didn't you hear me? Alive, not dead."

The words suddenly tumbled into Pugh's pain-besieged consciousness: "*Alive not dead*," the words said so many times. His body stopped fighting the hands and surrendered to the embrace of the chloroform.

***

"Men are terrible patients," Elizabeth huffed, turning the bedsheet down. Her finger flicked at a speck on the crisp linen. "You can lower your arm now."

Sir Henry watched as Pugh gave the woman a lopsided grin. His good looks were marred forever. Not that Pugh had been a vain man, but Sir Henry knew he would find it difficult; any man would.

His right cheek was puckered inwards and pulled his upper lip slightly to the side. The wound was still raw: Doctor Chambers had removed the stitches and dressing only this morning. Most of Pugh's right ear was gone; Chambers had had to remove the shreds of it.

The wounds, though they looked worse, were minor — as was, thankfully, the wound to Pugh's shoulder. The bullet had not hit Pugh's collarbone; after dragging a length of fabric into the wound, it had exited out of the back of the muscle. Messy. Time consuming to repair and check for fragments of material. This wound, like the one on Pugh's face, was such that the greatest danger to Pugh was wound fever.

It had been the wound to Pugh's thigh that had caused the greatest concern. The bullet had slammed its way in, taking with it a large amount of Pugh's britches. It had come to a halt perilously close to the main artery. The young medic who had tended Pugh on the floor of the chapel had cursed the others for moving him. A mere jolt could have sent the bullet that small fraction further, and Pugh most likely would have bled to death before anyone could have applied a leather belt to the leg. Chambers had worked on the leg first, and had dealt with Pugh's return to semi-consciousness during his sewing up of Pugh's face with his normal brusque manner.

It had been seven days since the events in the spire. Pugh was still far from well. He had so far shaken off any fever, and was asking questions. Elizabeth had caustically remarked earlier that the only way they would keep him quiet would be to keep him asleep with opium.

"Well?" Pugh was demanding an answer to the question. One he had asked before Doctor Chambers arrived to check his patients here at Sir Henry's home.

"Claire has been with you. She has been sitting by your bed and holding your hand. She is alive. We would not lie to you," Sir Henry said, moving closer to the bed. He watched the frown form on Pugh's brow. "She was hurt and needs to rest. It is just that the last few days, you have been sleeping and have been quite groggy from opium."

"There were times when I was not asleep or too groggy," Pugh snapped, his voice lacking any strength. "Do you take me for a fool, Sir Henry? If she wishes to avoid me, I understand." Pugh turned his head away.

Sir Henry narrowed his lips. Elizabeth was looking at him and nodding. The faint winter sun spilled through the window and caught on the piled-up curls of her hair; she looked like a goddess, herself. Henry did not know what he would have done these last few days, without Elizabeth by his side. When her offspring had decamped to spend the rest of the winter on the family estate, she had stayed behind. She had announced that the children, all young adults, found her presence got in the way during their hunting and at-home parties. Elizabeth believed she would be of use here, until Henry got bored of her. Sir Henry doubted he would ever get bored of Elizabeth.

"You haven't answered me," Pugh said again, trying to raise himself up in the bed.

"Claire has been waiting till you were stronger; I think that time has come. Doctor Chambers is with her now. I will go ask her to come to you when he has finished." Sir Henry turned towards the door, not waiting for Pugh's answer. He noticed Elizabeth's smile of approval and sighed. This was going to be hard for Pugh. It was still for him, and would be for the rest of his life. Sir Henry had run the gamut of emotions since Doctor Chambers told him of Claire's condition. Only she was unmoved by it.

When he reached Claire's room, the door stood partly ajar; he pushed it open. The drapes were closed, and a fire screen obscured the glow of the fire. Claire sat in a large armchair, her hands lightly resting on the arms. Doctor Chambers stood in front of her, a small, lit candle in his hands. Sir Henry watched Doctor Chambers move the candle close to Claire's right eye.

"Can you see the light?" Doctor Chambers asked.

"I know where it is; I feel it," Claire softly answered.

"You mean the heat from it. The smell of the burning wax." Doctor Chambers peered through a lens at Claire's eye.

"That, as well."

"As well as?" Doctor Chambers moved the candle in front of her left eye.

"I can smell it and sense the heat as well as feel it. It is difficult to explain. I feel where things and people are. Like my father in the doorway: I feel him in shades of colour. It is silly, I know."

"You perhaps heard his footsteps and breathing, recognised them as belonging to your father." Doctor Chambers straightened up and blew out the candle. He half-turned and acknowledged Sir Henry.

"Perhaps, but how do I know Toby is trying to squeeze behind the fire screen in front of the fire?"

The dog barked at the mention of his name. Both Sir Henry and Doctor Chambers glanced in the direction of the fireplace. Claire gave a soft laugh. The dog padded over and circled by her feet, then lay down with a grunt of self-importance.

"You might have heard him: his coat rubbing against the wood; his claws on the floor. It is quite possible that your other senses are working harder. Your mind is combining the input of those senses to form a mental picture of what is around you, and you are interpreting it as a feeling and colours." Doctor Chambers took Claire's hand and squeezed it. Claire's other hand left the arm of the chair, and with unerring sureness, she placed it on top of Doctor Chambers' own. For a few moments their hands remained locked, and Sir Henry could see that the doctor was struggling to control his emotions.

Claire's hands dropped from Doctor Chambers' and fell into her lap. "So, in your medical opinion, I am blind with no chance of regaining my normal sight. Even though I don't feel blind."

Sir Henry felt his heart lurch at the word "blind." Claire had survived. In fact, she appeared to be free of her Glimpser self. There had been no signs of Oracle since she had been rescued. Her memories of her time as a Glimpser were hazy, and of her abduction in the library, she remembered very little.

"Your pupils have closed completely; your eyes no longer react to light in the expected sense. You seem to have a solid iris of bright green in both eyes. I am not sure what has caused this — our knowledge of the eyes is woefully small. The only thing I am sure of is that your eyes no longer react as they should to light. I am sorry, dear lady." Doctor Chambers carefully packed his lens away and shut his bag.

"Thank you, Doctor Chambers. It is not so bad for me. That is, I don't feel any different; I feel the world around me. I know it sounds silly. Perhaps it is just my other senses, as you say, but I am aware of everything in this room as much as if I could see it. But I know it will hurt those I love, be hard for them to accept and understand. As was my previous mental state."

"Concerning one of those people, he will not take no for an answer," Sir Henry said, walking over to his daughter's side. He still found the colour of her eyes a little unnerving. The green was the Goddess' colour that represented new life, growth and change. Was Claire still in some way a conduit to forces beyond his understanding?

"Dear Goddess. Doctor Chambers ...?"

"Lady Claire, Major Avinguard's health is still a matter for concern, but the anxiety caused by not knowing your

266

condition could at this point be the source of complications. His mind will work on other reasons why you avoid his company. I have often found that a patient's mental state has profound effect on their body's illness. I see no harm in telling him now. I will call tomorrow, to see you both." He bowed to Claire and Sir Henry, then made his way to the door.

"Claire," Sir Henry began, and gently touched her soft, near-white curls.

"No words, Father; I don't feel them in my mind at all. I am sure Oracle is in me somewhere, deep down inside. Asleep, perhaps, for now. So much is a jumble. It seems but yesterday I married Pugh, not seven years ago. It is like a dream and Oracle a creature of that dream, not me at all."

"And you remember nothing of the abduction, what happened?" Sir Henry asked again, hoping that she might remember something.

"Nothing, Father. I do not remember the ball at all. So much is missing."

"I see. Are you ready?" Sir Henry said, laying his hand on his daughter's arm. Claire got to her feet. Her head tilted towards him, and she smiled. Toby barked, and they both laughed. Sir Henry tucked her arm in his and gently led her to Pugh's room.

"Place the chair on the right side of the bed, Thomas, that's it." Elizabeth watched the young man manoeuvre the chair into position.

"Anything else, Milady?" Thomas asked.

"No, thank you, Thomas."

Thomas bowed to Lady Elizabeth and walked towards the door, standing aside to allow Sir Henry and Claire to enter.

Pugh's head turned in Claire's direction. He smiled and said softly. "You look beautiful."

"Do I," Claire replied. Sir Henry agreed with Pugh's statement. The fine cream silk dressing gown clung to her small figure and frothed in a mass of lace round her feet. Sir Henry guided his daughter to the chair by Pugh's side.

"Yes. Your chest?" Pugh asked.

"It is healing well. It wasn't a bullet: they cut me," Claire said, laying her hand on the bed covers close to Pugh's.

"Are you completely free?" Pugh's question echoed Sir Henry's.

"I don't know," Claire sighed, her fingers plucking at the fabric under them. Pugh looked down at her fingers, then up at her face. Claire was not looking at him, yet Sir Henry knew her whole attention was on Pugh.

"Your eyes." Pugh's voice broke. His hand took hers, crushing it.

"Doctor Chambers says I am blind."

Pugh cleared his throat. "Elizabeth, Sir Henry, if you don't mind."

"Of course," Sir Henry said.

"You must not overtire yourselves. You have plenty of time," Elizabeth said, reluctantly leaving the room.

Sir Henry walked to the door and stood there. He heard Pugh say in a rush, "Do we have time, Claire?"

Claire shook her head. "I don't know. I hope so — I do, Pugh."

Sir Henry smiled at his daughter's words and quietly shut the door.

"Sir Henry, Senior Minister Carlsonmark and Lord Howorth are waiting for you in your study."

"Thank you, Thomas."

"Henry, they can't, can they?" Elizabeth lightly touched his arm.

"Things are moving fast, Elizabeth. The longer I leave it, the worse it could become." Sir Henry took hold of her hand and squeezed it.

"It is not fair."

"Life often isn't, Elizabeth. Sir Henry looked towards Pugh's door. "But we have things to be very grateful for."

***

"My apologies for keeping you waiting, gentlemen," Sir Henry said, on entering his study.

"Henry." Augustus Howorth rose from his seat and reached out his hand.

"Augustus." Sir Henry took the man's hand and shook it warmly.

"Senior Minister." Sir Henry offered his hand to Carlsonmark. The cleric was standing by the window, his face half-illuminated by the late afternoon sun.

"Sir Henry." Carlsonmark took a firm hold and held it. Sir

Henry realised that Carlsonmark was examining his face. "So, you have come to a decision?" He released Sir Henry's hand.

"Yes, when the High Forum re-sits at the end of the week, I will resign."

"You can't. Not after everything," Augustus spluttered.

"That's why I must. How many members are baying for my blood?" Sir Henry walked to his desk and picked up his pipe.

"A fair few. Some are even calling for your arrest," Carlsonmark said. "That police inspector wants you for everything from obstruction of justice to treason. The soldiers involved have vanished, all save Captain Gunmain, who continues at his post. It is almost as if he is daring them to court-martial him."

"But they do not know all the facts." Augustus began to pace in front of the fire, hands behind his back.

"Facts don't come into this, Augustus. By resigning, Sir Henry is making sure your bill will not be tainted. What better way to honour Calvinward's legacy?"

"Yes, yes," Howorth said, but his tone of voice told Sir Henry he did not like it one bit. "Calvinward, of course. His funeral — do you know when it will be?"

"The day after the Forum reassembles. It will give his heir time to arrive. And, under the circumstances, it will be a private one."

"Heir? Didn't know he had one," Augustus said.

"A second cousin, twice removed. The young man never expected to inherit."

"Augustus, there is another matter; you must distance yourself from Sir Henry and his family." Carlsonmark did not meet Sir Howorth's gaze, but looked towards Sir Henry.

"Like hell I will."

"You must. The damage that it will cause if you do not can't be overestimated," Sir Henry said.

"I don't like it one bit. It does not feel right," Augustus grumbled.

"It is not a matter of feeling right. It must be done to keep you free from any taint," Sir Henry implored. Augustus was a good man, an honourable one, and not inclined to abandon others just for self-preservation. *Good man?*

"You have to see the sense in this," Carlsonmark said.

"Yes I do; Oh, very well. If you ever need anything, Henry," Augustus said, and held out his hand again.

"Thank you." Sir Henry shook the man's hand. He watched Augustus say his farewells to Carlsonmark and leave. It was for the best; he had to distance himself from everything and everyone who had dealings with the bill. If what he and Elizabeth suspected was correct, and Mathew was involved, along with Lady Constance, with Calvinward's murder, they had to protect Howorth and the bill at all costs. The decision to not pursue the matter, at least for now, was the hardest thing he had ever done. But it had to be done. The repercussions that would follow would put those currently threatening Augustus in the shade.

Sir Henry patted the pocket of his waistcoat, pulled out his tobacco pouch and began to fill his pipe. He was well aware that Carlsonmark was watching —no, studying — him.

"Sir Henry, you have not asked me about the remnants of the Inner Ring," Carlsonmark said, walking back to the window. He looked out on the snow-covered street, his face in profile.

"Those taken at the tower were given over into *your* hands, I believe. As for the rest ...." Sir Henry shrugged his shoulders and continued to fill his pipe.

"The authorities didn't know quite what to do with them, and thought it best they be placed in the care of their brothers in faith for now," Carlsonmark said, his voice flat.

Sir Henry looked up from his pipe and looked at the minister. For a moment, there was a strange reflection in Carlsonmark's eyes. A hint of red. No: it was just the reflection of the setting sun.

"Sir Henry," Carlsonmark said, "may I continue to visit?"

"Is that wise?"

"The High Forum members are not interested in the actions and whereabouts of a token figure like me in their midst."

Sir Henry's eyes widened. "They don't think that."

"Come, Sir Henry. Appointing my fellow ministers and I to the forum is seen as paying lip service to tradition. We are not expected to have any interest in politics."

"And have you?" Sir Henry asked.

"We have an interest in everything, as does the Goddess. Actions and consequences — they can turn the world on its head."

The End.

270

Lightning Source UK Ltd.
Milton Keynes UK
UKOW02f1339070515

251065UK00001B/18/P